THE CALLING

Alison Bruce

Constable & Robinson Ltd
55–56 Russell Square
London WC1B 4HP
www.constablerobinson.com

First published in the UK by Constable,
an imprint of Constable & Robinson Ltd., 2011

Published in this paperback edition by Robinson,
an imprint of Constable & Robinson Ltd., 2012

This is a work of fiction. Names, characters, places and incidents are either the product of the author's imagination or are used fictitiously, and any resemblance to actual persons, living or dead, or to actual events or locales is entirely coincidental

A copy of the British Library Cataloguing in Publication
Data is available from the British Library

ISBN 978-1-78033-383-0

Typeset by TW Typesetting, Plymouth, Devon

Printed and bound in the UK

3 5 7 9 10 8 6 4 2

Alison Bruce is a scriptwriter and author of two non-fiction c[illegible] books. She was born in Surrey but moved to Cambridge i[illegible]8. This is the third DC Goodhew novel – *Cambridge* *[illegible]* and *The Siren* are also published by Constable & R[illegible]nson. Her new novel, *The Silence*, is out now in h[illegible]back. She is married with two small children.

P[illegible] for Alison Bruce:

[illegible] are pulled relentlessly in as Bruce racks up the tension. [illegible]cing and insidious, this is a great novel.' R. J. Ellory

'A[illegible]xciting debut from a very promising new talent.' Paul [illegible]ton

[illegible]t-paced, gritty tale guaranteed to have you hooked from [illegible]ning to end.' *Cambridgeshire Pride*

[illegible]Gary Goodhew could just develop into a worthy s[illegible]sor to those venerables of the police procedural now dra[illegible]ng their pensions.' *Tribune*

Also by Alison Bruce

Cambridge Blue
The Siren

To my husband and best friend, Jacen.

To my cherished family, Natalie, Lana and Dean.

And to Lily, the little girl I'll always miss.

PROLOGUE

MONDAY, 24 AUGUST 2009

My counsellor says I should keep a journal of my dreams.
What does she know?
I need far more help than she can give me.

Blood bubbled through the scored skin, swelling and dripping. Swelling and dripping. Slipping into a languid crawl before diluting across the damp enamel, and finally plunging into the water. Each droplet billowed and unfurled in delicate ribbons before vanishing, dispersing in the bath where she lay. She watched her wrists bleed. *Strange how peaceful it is*, she thought, and sank deeper beneath the silky bubbles.

The drifting steam swirled above her, entwining the scents of jasmine foam and rose soap. She slid her head below the water, her hair floating around her shoulders, shining in the wetness. She no longer felt like hacking it off. Glad that she hadn't.

She closed her eyes, content to hear the muffled music from the radio in the hall, and the muted rain against the window. Thoughts drifted in and out.

She looked down along the plane of her outstretched body. *Imagine being beautiful. Imagine being the centre of the world.* She wished she were someone else.

She sighed and closed her eyes again.

He groped for the handle of the back door, located it and held it tight to stop it rattling.

He peeked into the house. No sign of her; if she was there at all, she hadn't heard him.

He turned it slowly, holding it tight to keep it quiet. It was unlocked, providing an open invite for anyone.

No surprise there, though.

He stepped inside and paused, listening. Music trickled down to him.

He flicked the light switch and the fluorescent tube jolted into life, reflecting a bright strip of light from the stainless-steel draining board and glinting from the chrome-edged cupboards.

The surfaces lay bare, apart from the bunch of keys and a screwed-up, tear-sodden tissue marooned together on top of the low fridge.

He walked the length of the hall. He stopped at the foot of the stairs.

She stirred just enough to twist the hot tap with her foot. The fresh water rippled into the old, and warmed her.

She shut off the tap again and dozed.

Floating, floating.

And, floating away, she saw someone else with fair hair and blue eyes. Tired, scared, bewildered blue eyes. Who was it? She couldn't see. A girl? A boy?

Someone in the woods with fair hair, fair skin and blue eyes.

She saw more: a pretty girl with a dirty face, tied against a tree.

Like me, but pretty, she thought.

He heard the running water and drew a deep breath, as if to smell her.

He grabbed the handrail, propelling himself towards the bathroom. Step by step. Quick and quiet.

He tilted his head close to the door, resting his temple against the frame.

Was she alone?

He waited and listened. No voices, but that didn't mean anything.

He stroked the satin paint along the doorframe. No whispers or giggles. Perhaps she really was alone.

Alone with her precious fucking radio.

He grabbed the handle and tried to open the door. Locked.

* * *

Her eyes flashed open at the first crack. The wood ripped apart and the door splintered open.

Her hands shot under the water, hiding her damaged wrists. Dark, clotted blood trails streaked in their wake.

He lunged forward, shouting words she couldn't understand.

'Don't hurt me,' she gasped, as she cowered naked and defenceless in the tepid bath.

'What the fuck is going on in your head?'

She couldn't reply. She stared at him, wide-eyed and shaking, and began to cry.

Between her sobs she caught the words, 'Mad bitch'.

'Answer me,' he roared.

She shook her head, unable to speak.

She wanted him to stop shouting. To stop hating her.

She began screaming.

The flat of his hand hit her full across the left cheek and the skin reddened into hot, stinging blotches. Her hysteria subsided.

'I-can't-stand-you-any-more.' He spoke each syllable with cold deliberation. 'You're like a leech, clinging and sucking me dry. Just being near you revolts me.'

Somehow his words mesmerized her. He hated her; she could see it clearly in those narrowed eyes and the way his mouth twisted as he spat out the words.

'Why do you bang on and on until I lose my temper? Until you make me snap? And now look at you.' He gestured as if waving her away in disgust.

He turned and reached out beyond the broken door, grabbing the radio from the hall table. He shook it at her. 'If you were so fucking suicidal, you wouldn't be lying there listening to this.'

Her brain reacted slowly. She only realized how the radio was attached to a cable, the cable to a plug, the plug to an electric socket, as he tossed the whole lot towards the water.

And then it tumbled in the air.

In slow motion, according to her addled mind.

And then she woke.

CHAPTER 1

SATURDAY, 26 MARCH 2011

Margaret Whiting wanted to cry: anger and frustration had bitten into her, and it clawed at the back of her neck. She wanted the tears to come, she'd wanted to sob out loud and hear her own voice, without having it shouted down by her husband or her son.

She'd stood in her kitchen, sorting washing and tossing each item on to the correct colour pile with an angry flick of her wrist. She separated her clothes from theirs, thinking *theirs* weren't fit to share the same wash. She knew she couldn't cry, so she had shouted, and Mike had then said she was hysterical and was the cause of all the upset in the family.

Oh, yes, she'd thought, *our gloriously happy family!* Her son was a liar and her husband a hypocrite, and yet she was supposed to be happy.

Just this morning had been the start of it.

The day had begun the same as always, a four-hour shift at Histon Road service station watching the very same people fill the same cars with petrol, or buy their cigarettes and bread and milk – that had been the start of it. Each time the till had rolled open, Margaret had looked down at the twenty-pound notes and the Queen had looked back. And each time Margaret had felt the Queen was looking a little more smug. Everyone had money except her, it seemed.

The clock on the cigarette counter had been nudging five past eleven as Lindsay arrived. Late again. 'Morning, Margaret. How are you?'

'Fine. How are the kids?' Margaret had replied, because that was the routine.

'Fine.'

And so it had gone on. 'Another day the same as every other bloody day,' she'd eventually complained. 'Do you know what, Lindsay? Every single day of my bloody life is spent worrying about pennies and watching everyone else spend money like there's no tomorrow. I could never spend what they spend on fuel without feeling bad about it.' Margaret had felt a surge of bravado even as she said it. If only she could talk like this to her husband Mike.

'Lindsay, do you ever feel nosey?' she'd asked.

'Oh, yes.' The other woman had grinned. 'All the time!'

'What, with Craig?'

'Oh, *suspicious* you mean?' Lindsay had shrugged. 'Not really. Just the odd minute of winding myself up, but that's about all. You're not worried, are you? About Mike, I mean.'

Margaret had lowered her voice to a conspiratorial whisper, determined now to spice up her day. 'Well . . .' She'd paused, and added to the drama with a wary glance around the empty shop. 'The other day I was putting his socks away and I suddenly had the urge to check his pockets.' Margaret had lowered her voice further. 'I didn't do that, of course, but then I even thought about checking the numbers he'd called recently on his mobile phone.'

'And?'

'Well, nothing.'

'What, you mean you didn't find anything or you didn't check?'

'Of course I didn't check.'

Lindsay had shaken her head. 'That's not suspicion. That's boredom.'

'Oh, I thought it was intuition.'

'Intuition, my arse. You're obviously spending too much time putting his socks straight, but don't let your imagination get the better of you. My mum says the devil makes work for idle brain cells. You need to spend some money on yourself. Be reckless, Mags, and buy a whole new outfit for your mum's party. That'll make him sit up and think.'

'Damn.' Margaret had winced, then. 'I should've cancelled the hairdressers.'

'Oh, no, it's not off, is it? I'm here all afternoon just so you can go.'

'No, no, it's fine.' Margaret had frowned. 'I mean it's not really a waste, but there's so much to do for dinner tonight, I need the afternoon to prepare.'

'I thought you said you'd done it all – and frozen it?'

Margaret had nodded, realizing she wasn't good at lies, even little white ones. 'There's still some more to do but, to be honest, Mike and I had a row about money. And it's true, we do need to be a bit careful.'

Lindsay had bent to pick up a Penguin wrapper, straightened it out and dropped it into the bin before she spoke. 'Mags, it's not my business but it is just a tint you're getting, not major cosmetic surgery, and it's cost you less than most people spend on fags in a week. On top of that, you've been looking forward to your mum's birthday for ages, and you've done all the hard work for it, too. Don't you think you deserve to treat yourself?'

She'd later gone to her hairdresser's appointment in a surge of rebellion, only to be told that her girl, Nicky, had rung in sick. 'I'm sorry, Mrs Whiting. I'm sorry, Mrs Whiting,' she'd mimicked their whining excuses to herself, surprisingly disappointed at missing an appointment that she'd planned to cancel anyway.

So she'd instead splashed the twenty-five pounds on a discounted polycotton blouse that she didn't like much. She then decided not to tell Mike because as far as he was concerned, she would have missed her haircut and he deserved to think that she'd ended up with in return was more housework.

Housework instead of a haircut?

Margaret had seethed with resentment all the way home on the bus. Mike himself would never catch a bus. She felt her anger surge again, reflecting that there had been a distinct pecking order since their girls had left home. Mike being number one, Steve as the heir apparent, and then Margaret herself coming last.

She always came last.

The bus stopped two hundred yards from her house and, as she walked towards the empty driveway, she started on a mental list of jobs to do before Mike's return from work. Ironing, she decided; check the food for the dinner party, load the washing machine and change the sheets.

Steve's motorbike stood beside the garage, which meant he hadn't spent the day out job-hunting. *I'll get my hair done as soon as he gets a job*, she promised herself.

She knew school leavers now had to wait for the right opening. Mike and Steve had explained that often enough. Almost as many times as she'd stood in front of the mirror and practised saying 'Steve, I'd like you to help with some housework'.

Margaret let herself in through the back door and stepped directly into the kitchen. 'Hello,' she called as she held the jug kettle under the tap, filling it for some tea.

There was no reply, though she could hear the television. He'd probably heard her, but that's the way it was with him sometimes.

'Kids!' she tutted and opened the hatch to speak.

Shock choked her at the sight, and she tried to draw a breath, willing herself to unsee it. She recoiled, folding closed the hatch doors and sealing herself away from the scene. She kept retreating, out of the back door, then away from the house.

She ducked into the bus shelter and perched on one of its plastic seats. She shivered and tried to tell herself that she'd made a mistake.

But she'd seen him, Steve her son, lying flaked out on the settee, dead to the world, with his outstretched hand resting on top of an empty bottle of Thunderbird, which stood on the carpet beside him.

She looked back towards her house and her top lip began to twitch as disgust dug deeper. 'In our own home!'

Steve had fallen asleep watching a video. He often watched videos. But now she knew what.

Pornography.

Blue movies.

Steve hadn't even stirred, and for a few seconds Margaret had watched.

The screen was filled with a woman's face, her head tilted back, gleaming with sweat, as her tongue ran slowly along the line of her upper teeth, moistening her cherry-red lips. The camera then slid down her body, following her fingers as they traced her skin down to her breasts. Her nipples, pinched erect by small gold clamps connected by a chunkier chain, were already being massaged. As the camera panned back, a second naked girl guzzled greedily between the splayed legs of the first . . .

That's when Margaret's reflexes had sent her cannoning out of the kitchen.

She now realized that her breath was coming in short bursts, and forced herself to slow her inhalations. After a few moments the hot flush of embarrassment also faded from her cheeks.

Mike would deal with it. He was a good man who hated vice and sloth and wasted money. She turned to watch the far end of the road, where it joined the main street and where she would spot him coming home. Every minute seemed like an hour, and she began to worry that Steve would awaken and hide the video before Mike caught him.

But Steve was oblivious of most things, certainly to the passing of time, and so he didn't hear his dad come home. It was only when his father's weight beside him made the settee groan that Steve knew he wasn't alone.

Then he remembered the video.

In the second between checking the screen and his father's face, he snatched for an excuse – something his father would understand.

But in an instant he knew his father *did* understand. More than that, he seemed to be looking at Steve with a kind of respect. Steve tentatively tried a laddish smirk. Afterwards he realized that he had the Thunderbird to thank for such bravado, but still felt more of a man anyway.

'I'm getting to be a bit of a film buff actually, Dad.' He laughed and knew his voice sounded tight with nervousness.

He needn't have worried, because his dad was suddenly a teenager again. 'I'm a film buff too, son. Don't you worry, nothing wrong with it at all.' He then winked, and held the Thunderbird bottle up to the light, hoping for some leftovers. 'Better in the flesh, of course, especially with the ones your age.'

'Don't worry, Dad. I have done it before.'

'Yeah, but don't tell your mother!' And they both laughed then as though it was a long-standing joke instead of a newly shared confidence.

Margaret witnessed all of this from her position behind the hatch. With a restraint that seemed to make her move in slow motion, she pushed the hatch doors further open.

'Tea anyone?' Her voice shook slightly as she spoke. And that's the picture that became frozen in her memory: Mike and Steve looking at her stunned in front of a video of two stunning blondes in patent leather boots, mauling one another on a leather couch.

Margaret finally finished with the laundry pile just as her rage reached its peak. She was alone in the house, so no one heard her. 'Why today?' she yelled. She had looked forward to today: her mother's birthday; a family gathering; a social event shared with Mike.

'Bastards,' she screamed, 'how could you?' She threw the lid of the Aladdin's basket at the wall, then kicked the basket itself on to its side. 'Bastards!' she screamed again and again, until at last the tears came and burnt hot trails down her cheeks. She collapsed on to the washing piles, sobbing and cursing herself.

Count your blessings, Margaret, she reproached herself. Her mother still loved her – and Michelle and Kaye would never let her down like this. Why had she bothered to have three kids when the two girls would have been enough? She'd have been better with those two: they didn't humiliate her like this. She drew a shuddering breath, aware she wanted to ring them, pour out her pain to them. She clambered to her feet.

They probably weren't at home, anyway, and she'd be seeing them later, at her mother's.

She re-boiled the kettle, and eventually did what she always did: she acted as though nothing had happened.

The sheets were clean and Michelle Whiting had even ironed them. She'd changed the bed to fresh linen especially for this. She could feel the smoothness of stretched brushed cotton under her hands and knees.

It was weird doing it this way, as she couldn't see Carl's face; they couldn't even kiss. His hands gripped her hips and he kept digging his fingers into her flesh, so she could feel little bruises forming against her bones. Her hair dangled over her eyes, so the ends of it swayed just above the pillow. She wondered whether she should have a trim soon, since they looked a bit straggly.

'Don't sag,' he grunted. But her arms were aching from supporting her own weight and Carl's, too, as he leant heavily upon her.

'Sorry,' she mumbled and arched her back, pushing herself up against him. Her mind kept wandering. *This is meant to be a turn-on*, she reminded herself. But it just wasn't as sexy as she'd thought it would be. Tedious was the word that sprang to mind. The first time they'd tried it this way had been on the carpet, and the grazes on her knees had only just healed. At least this wasn't quite so uncomfortable.

'This is so good,' she gasped.

'Mmmm.'

'I've never known it so good, Carl. Have you?'

'No, no,' he panted. 'I can't get enough.'

Michelle smiled, knowing Carl was totally devoted to her, and if keeping him happy meant some of this discomfort, well, that was fine. She loved having his total attention.

His fingers suddenly released her hips and he leant forward, pushing himself more deeply into her. The palm of his left hand slapped against the wall as he used it to support his weight.

His thrusting became urgent and the fingers of his right hand grasped her long hair, twisting it tightly close to the scalp. His knuckles ground against the top of her head and her neck ached as it was twisted at an awkward angle.

But she didn't complain, instead waiting for the moment when they collapsed in a heap and would cuddle up. She hoped it wouldn't take long now.

Carl wasn't thinking about Michelle's discomfort.

He wasn't even thinking about Michelle at all.

He'd started out with one of his usual fantasies: how he wasn't a lowly van driver but a powerful tycoon, and that she was his secretary paid to do whatever he chose.

But everything felt different today, and those thoughts weren't enough to stem his frustration. So this time he had turned her over and hauled her up on to her hands and knees. Because he didn't want to see her face. He didn't want to be reminded that she was Kaye's sister.

Kaye, the elder and more serious sister. The more *everything* in his opinion.

Kaye, the one he really wanted.

But, before he could stop it, she was there in his head. She pulled off her T-shirt and shimmered in front of him, pale and inviting. She drew him towards her but, even in his fantasy, he knew that she'd never let him touch her.

Because of his association with Michelle? Or because he wasn't good enough? Or both?

The word *bitch* filled his head and, as he tugged at Michelle's hair and became more frenzied, it pounded like a chant in rhythm with his body. *Bitch, bitch, bitch.*

For Carl, climax and satisfaction were not the same. Suddenly he didn't want to touch either of the sisters.

So Michelle now waited for a token of affection that Carl didn't feel like giving. He didn't even kiss her, just pulled his sweatshirt and jeans back on and said he wanted a coffee.

Michelle straightened her bed as the kettle boiled. He hadn't even noticed the fresh sheets.

Andy Burrows sat inside his old Ford Escort, watching the rain slide down the car's windows.

He'd genuinely planned to attend his mother's birthday dinner tonight, right up to the moment when he'd parked outside the house and spotted them all through the partially open curtains.

They would have assumed that looked inviting: a family dining happily together, with one space left for him. But to him it reeked of pity.

He could see his mother at the head of the table, wearing a mauve cardigan. She was probably propped up with a cushion and wearing slightly lopsided lipstick that was the wrong shade. It didn't matter to him. His mother hadn't had a favourite child though, all through their childhood, Margaret had succeeded where he had failed – and she had never been disappointed.

His mother's present lay wrapped up on the passenger seat, with her birthday card attached. He'd bought her a book on houseplants. Stupid really, since she only had two Busy Lizzies and a spider plant. Margaret would know straight away that it had come from the discount bookshop, but then she could afford something better. Margaret had it all: a nice house, a good family, a steady job. All the trappings of security that he'd never had, and which he guessed he never would. He was younger than her, and had always lagged behind.

Don't be so hard on yourself, he'd told himself at twenty, but now, at forty-six, he had spent too many years believing himself inept to even think of having ambitions. Ambitions and achievements had been the inheritance of his sister.

He could see Margaret herself fussing around the table, waiting on her family, keeping everything under control, Mike and Steve lapping up her attention. And Michelle and Carl, who were probably going to make her a grandmother one day soon. And Kaye.

She wasn't there.

He watched the window for a few more minutes. No one looked out at him. Perhaps no one missed either of them?

But they'd miss Kaye, wouldn't they, for she was special, *kind*. He wanted to be kind too, but it always backfired.

Today had been typical, since he'd meant to help. But he felt he was cursed with a kind of reverse-Midas touch. Everything he touched turned to shit.

He'd be caught out, of course, as he always was. Until then, what? Pretend nothing was wrong or simply avoid them all?

He decided to go home. He didn't belong in there.

CHAPTER 2

SUNDAY, 27 MARCH 2011

Gary Goodhew had seen dead bodies. And plenty of them.

Early on, there were a few that had made his stomach tighten and threatened him with queasiness.

There had been moments when he'd wished the clock could have stopped for the extra second needed for that cyclist to clear the path of the lorry, or that child to reach the pavement . . . Goodhew had a particular hatred of dealing with victims of road accidents; and thus normality ripped apart, often without warning. Sometimes the futility of those deaths felt close to overwhelming.

He'd been the first to arrive after several calls when ordinary people had collapsed in the street. He'd heard words from the lips of the dying, messages that had been too quiet to distinguish, and felt guilty when he couldn't pass them on.

And then there were the murder victims. Sometimes maimed or posthumously humiliated, sometimes with shock or betrayal frozen on to their face.

He could remember two instances when he'd looked away; and two more when he'd cried.

Just a single body remained nameless, and none of the others affected him in the way that that one did.

It always visited in the night, and avoiding it was the main thing that kept him awake at night. But most other dreams gave him space to think since he realized he was sleeping and could direct them, rewind and replay them at will. His grandmother had used the term 'lucid dreams', but that was all he knew.

They reminded him of beachcombing: picking up thoughts and ideas, discarding the flotsam and hanging on to the interesting finds; turning them over and deciding where to take them next. He guessed most unwanted dreams were forgotten; the others he could walk through, investigate, explore and resolve. Colours and conversation and even images were conveyed second-hand, like hearsay, but always within his control.

All the dreams he could ever recall were that way – except one.

This had been the rarer kind, the first visit, for months, of dead eyes and waxy skin. He'd tried to stay in the dream, to step back and pan the scene but had woken instead, to stare into the dark. It was 2 a.m. He didn't bother to check, it just felt like 2 a.m.

He had slept soundly until then: for six months, give or take. Long enough to think that he'd left it behind, or exorcized it or out-grown it. He wasn't sure if there was a term for being twenty-six years old and conquering a recurring nightmare, but if one existed it was irrelevant now.

And so were the possible reasons – big and small – that he'd acknowledged for breaking this pattern. He'd been developing the ability to take an emotional step back from cases, and he reckoned he'd balanced that with an emotional step forward in everything outside work.

Life/work balance: so much for amateur psychology.

He had felt that a lot had happened during those six months, but the reappearance of that dream told him that nothing much had changed at all.

He lay still, listening to the faint sounds of sparse traffic coasting through the empty streets. In his imagination, he passed through the early hours of a Sunday morning in the centre of Cambridge, with scattered groups making their various haphazard trails towards home, the drunkest being herded on by the police, while a few continued on foot; the rest dispersing via cars and taxis. He concentrated on the warmth and life and the real world outside his own imagination, until he felt awake enough to consider his dream in a less emotive way.

It was a single, unmoving image. Not graphic or violent or threatening even, just simple and repetitive but disturbing enough to throw Goodhew from the deepest sleep and kick him into a cycle of insomnia and exhaustion.

He saw a close-up of half a face tilted to one side, so that the right eye was in full view and the left was partly in shadow. The eyes were fixed beyond him, and he knew the skin would be cold to touch. It was impossible to see more: a shot so closely cropped that even the forehead and lips weren't visible. But, in his nightmare, it wasn't a photo. The face was real, and just inches from his own, and no matter how many times he tried to reach out – or move – that was all there ever was.

This dream had first come to him on the day he applied to join the police force, and most recently occurred on the final day of his last murder case. In fact it had been with him during each of the small number of murder investigations he'd ever tackled.

Not for the first time, he wondered whether it could be some kind of omen and he noted, as his eyes had jolted open, that the feeling accompanying it hung uneasily between fear and helplessness. Neither of these were emotions that he ever considered sharing, and now, tired though he felt, he stayed awake until the room paled to grey. Then, with his day-off beckoning and normality slipping back in through the gap in the curtains, he allowed himself another hour of sleep.

It was his phone that woke him. He grappled around on the floor beside his bed and simultaneously checked the time and the caller ID. He was surprised to see it was already 10.10.

The display read 'DI Marks'.

He rose on to one elbow and tried to sound fully awake. 'Morning, sir.'

There was no preamble. 'Gary, how soon can you get here?'

'Straight away.' It wasn't possible to see out of his window from where he now lay, but he still turned his head in the direction of nearby Parkside police station. 'What's happened?'

'Missing person.' Marks paused. 'I'm up to my ears and short of staff today . . . I want you to speak to her mother.'

CHAPTER 3

SUNDAY, 27 MARCH 2011

A wave of nausea shuddered through Margaret Whiting, making her sweat and tremble, and pressing hard against her lungs. 'Keep calm,' the police officer had told her on the phone, but each time her breathing steadied, another wave of sickness hit her. And, like breakers crashing on a pebble beach, dragging stones in the undercurrent, it clawed across the pit of her stomach.

She leant on the windowsill and strained to see any traffic coming down Arbury Road. She watched for cars slowing down and indicating. She knew they wouldn't be that quick, but there was nothing else she could do than wait.

She removed her glasses and pressed her cheekbone tight against the cold pane. Her breath created a small round pool of condensation, so she scribbled through it with her index finger and watched the dribbles begin to spoil the symmetry. Two daughters and a son had its own symmetry, so why had she complained, she wondered. A heavy rock of guilt weighed down on her. She hadn't meant it, but she'd *thought* it, and years of inbuilt superstition told her that this was enough.

Today she didn't want to cry, at all. She felt far too numb for tears.

Another car swung into the road, so she lifted her head above the misty patch of glass to watch. It drove on by, but then it was still too soon – only minutes since she'd phoned them.

She felt a trickle of sweat meander from her armpit and head towards her elbow. She massaged the blouse sleeve against it, mopping it, and would have then left it except for the stain which formed darkly on the grey rayon.

'Damn!' she whispered and, after one more glance at the empty road, she tore herself away from the window to change.

She tossed the blouse on to the bed and fumbled in the wardrobe for another. She felt clumsy and listless. She pulled at the clothes hanging there, dithering, until she glanced again out the bedroom window. A black saloon hesitated three doors away, then it spurted forward as if its driver were checking house numbers. She pulled the nearest blouse from its hanger.

The man parked just across the street, and she watched him as she dashed to button up her replacement top. He looked too young. They'd sent a junior.

Her fingers continued fidgeting with the buttons until, frustrated, she shoved the lower part of her shirt into her waistband and scuttled back downstairs, anxious to open the door as soon as he knocked, to show him how important this was.

She managed to reach the door before he'd even closed the front gate. She stood with it slightly ajar until he was close enough.

'Mrs Whiting?' he enquired.

She nodded and beckoned him inside before he could introduce himself.

'I'm DC Goodhew, Cambridge CID.'

She nodded again and led him to the sitting room, where she perched on the edge of a low armchair. *DC*, she thought to herself. That means *Detective Constable*. A total beginner, then.

He removed his jacket, before choosing the settee.

'I've been briefed on your conversation with our control room, Mrs Whiting, so I know the basics. And you've still heard nothing from Kaye?'

She shook her head. 'She should have been there with us last night. She wouldn't have missed it.'

'This was the party you mentioned?'

'Yes, my mother's eightieth. It was planned for weeks. Kaye rang me from work on Friday, when I was out, but she left a message to say she'd see me the next night.' Margaret wrapped her hands across her stomach and shivered.

'And you haven't seen her at all since?' he asked.

'No, I last saw her on Tuesday. She stopped by on her way home,' she replied.

'And did she seem OK?'

'Fine.'

'And how did she sound on the phone?' Goodhew had been watching her carefully since she'd opened the door to him. She seemed dazed and vague, and now sat in an odd kind of question-mark position, rocking back and forth with an almost imperceptible motion.

'Yes, fine.' A pink blotch coloured the bridge of her nose where her glasses had rested earlier. Her eyes were pink too, but not focusing. Her cheeks had faded to the colour of dusty concrete.

He needed to form a mental picture of Kaye, and Margaret Whiting's tight-lipped answers clearly weren't about to provide it.

'Mrs Whiting, this is going to take a little while. So, if it's OK with you, maybe we could make some tea while we talk about it.' He stood up and encouraged her towards the kitchen. 'It won't slow us up, I promise.'

She walked ahead of him, along the hall.

'Was the party held here?'

'No, at my mum's. She lives in Redkin Road, just off the other end of Arbury Road.' Margaret filled the kettle and continued talking as she assembled the mugs and milk and sugar. 'The party was a surprise for my mum; she's a bit difficult at times, so we thought she'd only fuss if we let her know in advance. We all see her at least once a week during the day, so it seemed like a good idea for us to get together for the evening. Do you have milk?'

Goodhew nodded. 'No sugar, though, thanks.'

'Well, I turned up with Mike and Steve first – that's my husband and son. We brought all the food with us, and everyone else was expected around seven-thirty.' She leant back against the worktop. 'There were supposed to be eight of us – including my mum.' She counted them on her fingers. 'Me, Mum, Mike, Steve, my two daughters – Kaye and Michelle – and my brother Andy, and Michelle's boyfriend Carl. But neither Andy nor Kaye ever arrived.'

'And no one had heard from Kaye?'

‘No, but Michelle and Carl were late too, so at first we thought they were all coming together. Michelle burst in all excited, and made up to the nines, of course.’ Margaret’s face brightened a little as she spoke of her younger daughter. ‘She’s such a bubbly thing, it always seems like a carnival’s rolled in when she turns up. Just as well . . .’ She turned aside as the kettle clicked off, and poured the boiling water on to the tea bags in two cups. ‘Just as well, because that Carl’s a real misery and he just slouched by the door, and then Michelle says, “Guess what?”’ Margaret stopped abruptly and pursed her lips as she concentrated on squeezing the tea bag.

Goodhew waited for her to continue but, after a few moments, a tear dripped on to the Formica. He reached across and took his cup of tea from her. ‘Are you all right, Mrs Whiting?’

‘My mum whispered, “Bet Michelle’s pregnant,” but I knew she wouldn’t be.’ Margaret wiped her face quickly and turned back to Goodhew.

‘And she wasn’t. She’d just booked a holiday, that’s all. You see, I knew it wouldn’t be anything bad, because she’d never let me down. And neither would Kaye, so that’s why I know something dreadful has happened.’

Margaret Whiting hesitated then, as though she was waiting for him to reassure her. He knew he should say something, but he’d recognized her expression: the phrase *halfway between fear and helplessness* slipped into his thoughts.

It felt like an omen.

CHAPTER 4

SUNDAY, 27 MARCH 2011

Cambridge has many open areas interspersed among its city-centre streets, with names like Jesus Green and Midsummer Common. They are mostly clean and safe, criss-crossed with paths used by students and mums pushing buggies.

Parkside police station faces on to one of these: a large rectangular green space known as Parker's Piece. From time to time, Goodhew wondered who the original Parker had been but he had never bothered to find out.

Luckily for Goodhew, Parkside Pool lay only yards away from the station, just across the corner of Parker's Piece. He liked to swim one hundred lengths at least four times each week. Not just for the exercise but because he liked the solitude.

The water was cool, and he concentrated on the smell of chlorine and the rhythm of his own breathing until the shouting and screaming of other people sounded distant. For the first eighty-four lengths they were just voices mingling with each other; echoing, booming and rebounding above his head.

Length eighty-five, his concentration broke a little. A teenage girl with wavy red hair and a Celtic tattoo squealed as she fell into the water. Her boyfriend laughed, yelled and leapt after her.

Goodhew swam on, everything else sweeping past him. He stared at the tiled bottom of the pool as he powered through his ninety-fifth length. He always kept himself to the two lanes roped off for serious swimmers, and he always swam front-crawl.

Ninety-six. He thought of Margaret Whiting and her hands trembling as she grappled with the sodden tea bags.

Ninety-seven. He thought of Kaye Whiting, pale and pretty in the photo perched on Margaret's mantelpiece. Watching him wherever he sat or stood.

Ninety-eight. Michelle, sharper featured, with a strident blonde perm and a mean-spirited boyfriend.

Ninety-nine. Kaye's uncle Andy, a devoted son who nevertheless had offered no excuse for missing his mother's birthday.

One hundred. No one knew if a crime had actually been committed, or whether Kaye would even be found.

Gary completed the final length, finishing in the shallow end, and leant back against the side of the pool. He allowed his legs to float in front of him and stretched his arms out along the side.

The pool wasn't so busy now, and he shared the shallow end with several families accompanying learner children in yellow floats and armbands. A group of four teenagers had since joined the tattooed redhead and her boyfriend, and their horseplay kept the deep end busy while the training lanes were now empty. Things were all winding down at the end of the day.

A brunette emerged from the changing rooms, her towel swinging around her ankles from one slender hand. She walked over to the railings fronting the spectator seats, smiling coyly at a couple of dads watching their offspring from the front row. She draped the towel near their knees. Practising a slinky movement she'd seen on catwalks, she swung her hips as she turned towards the water.

She was absolutely sure every man within range was watching.

Shit, thought Gary, as she slipped into the pool beside him and braced herself against the chill of the water by pressing her fingers around his arm.

She inhaled sharply. 'Oh, it's cold in here.'

'It's nice enough once you're in,' he muttered. 'Why are you here?'

She massaged his arm as she ran her fingers up it to give his biceps a squeeze. She fixed her gaze on him and smiled playfully. 'Nice bod, Gary.'

'Why are you here? I bet that's the first time that swimsuit's ever been in the water.'

'Nice, isn't it? Suits me, don't you think?'

'Whatever, Shelly.'

'Oh, come on, either it does or it doesn't? Tell me if you ever think I would look better without it, Gary.' She pouted and smiled. 'Won't you?'

'I'm not here to flirt with you.'

'Oh, very serious, Gary,' she erupted with a spontaneous laugh. 'Have I offended you?'

'No.'

'Oh, good. You see, I wouldn't want to commit an offence, Officer. That means you'd have to put me in handcuffs, and then . . .'

Here we go again. 'Look, Shelly, what do you want?'

'Whoa, Gary!' She raised her hands as if in surrender. 'If you've had a bad day, don't take it out on me.' She began treading backwards into deeper water. 'Tell you what, though, if I were a man and you were a woman, I'd say you were frigid.'

She gave up then, and he watched her in silence as the water lapped over her nipples, making her swimsuit slightly transparent.

'Oh, I remember now – Bryn's here. He's sitting in the bar in the Kelsey Kerridge,' she called out, just as she rolled on to her front and headed up the pool with a slow breaststroke.

The Kelsey Kerridge sports centre stood next-door to the pool complex, and Gary found his friend at a table overlooking the badminton courts. Bryn sat in a low armchair, with a bottle of Becks in one hand and his mobile phone in the other. The only sign of activity was speed texting by Bryn's right thumb, and he didn't look up or speak until he'd hit the *send* button. 'You saw Shell, then?'

Goodhew shook his head. 'I look pale enough, don't I? Your sister's a bloody nightmare.'

Bryn reached down beside his chair and produced a second bottle of lager.

Goodhew took a couple of swigs. 'Cheers.'

'She knows you're not interested, but she does like a challenge.' Bryn waved the phone. 'Just like her big brother . . .'

Goodhew dropped into the chair opposite. 'The woman with the clapped-out Volvo?'

'Valerie? Not clapped out, just high mileage.' Bryn paused. 'I mean the car. She left it at the garage yesterday – wants me to hang on to it there until I can sell it. I said it wouldn't go overnight, and she said that was OK. Apparently she's happy to keep popping in.' Bryn then raised his eyebrows sagely. '*Popping in* suits me fine. Not much incentive for me to find a buyer, except she wants it gone within a couple of weeks. I told her I had a mate who might be interested, though.'

'Not me, I hope?'

'You don't have one.'

'I don't need one.'

'What about work?'

'I get to the station and the basics like a desk, a chair and transport are provided. It's called an unmarked car.'

'Sarcasm now from the guy who suggests us meeting up 'cos he wants a favour?'

''Fraid so. But it's a small favour.'

'Ask away.'

Goodhew paused to put his bottle down gently on the glass table top, suddenly feeling at odds with the previous minutes' banter. Bryn hadn't queried where Goodhew had been for the last four weeks, or commented on the slightly terse voicemail he'd been left the last time he'd texted Goodhew about meeting for a drink. He just waited until Goodhew was ready to say more.

'I split up with Claire at the start of the month.'

Bryn studied Goodhew's expression for a good few seconds, then drew a breath. 'Sorry, mate.'

'I'd booked a holiday, wondered if you wanted to come.'

'Me and you in a double room?'

'It's a three-bed bungalow in the grounds of a hotel . . .'

'Sounds boring.'

'Coming or not?'

'Tell me more.'

'Like what?'

'The basics – like where, when, how much it's going to cost me, and what the hell happened to Claire.'

'Two weeks at the seaside, start of May, all already paid for.'

'And Claire?'

'Are you coming or not?'

‘Gary, you don’t really do off-hand conversations and you definitely don’t do easy-in, easy-out relationships. You and Claire went from zero to serious like that.’ Bryn snapped his fingers. ‘Not my thing, Gary but . . .’

‘Hang on,’ Goodhew began, ‘you don’t want to know the ins and outs of anyone’s relationship, so you don’t give a toss about mine, do you? Your concern is noted and appreciated, that’s it.’

Bryn thought for a moment, ‘OK, here’s the holiday deal: no conversation about Cambridge, about work, or about any women who aren’t immediately within sight.’

‘OK.’ Goodhew managed a wry smile and clinked their drinks together in agreement. For another hour, they watched the players on the badminton court and made sporadic comments about the game.

It was like practice for the holiday conversation, and their kind-of silence was good.

Gary finished off his bottle and swung it between his forefinger and thumb like a pendulum. He made a conscious effort to clear his thoughts of everything but the badminton match in front of him. Each time his mind wandered, he pushed such distraction away. He succeeded every time until his thoughts settled on Kaye Whiting.

How was he supposed to put her out of his mind in favour of watching a sport he didn’t understand and between competitors he didn’t know? Between the badminton and his beer bottle Bryn, however, seemed to have achieved total immersion. Maybe switching off thoughts of work just took more practice.

Goodhew reminded himself that his phone was switched on, and in his pocket, just in case he was suddenly needed. Doing nothing didn’t suit him.

CHAPTER 5

MONDAY, 28 MARCH 2011

Kaye Whiting stared, unblinking, into the night. A thinning patch of cloud had revealed the ghost of a half-moon, while the cold night air pricked her eyes and made them water. She watched as the moon's familiar face appeared to fly across the sky, but she knew it was only the clouds that moved, and they'd soon blot it out again.

Tearing her gaze away, she forced herself to scrutinize her alien surroundings. She strained against the rope as she tried to free her fingers, but her wrists were bound tightly behind her, and lashed to her similarly tied ankles.

Kaye lay close to a large lake; three feet in front of her the grass fell away and the bank shelved down to the water's edge. For the first time since dusk, she could see the ripples and their polished-pewter tips but, beyond that, the far bank lay swathed in shadows.

Another sharp gust of wind sliced through her jumper and grazed her skin. As she started to shiver again, she forgot the distraction of the moonlight and screwed up her eyes and clenched them shut. She tensed herself against the uncontrollable shaking that rattled through her bones.

The gag stopped her teeth from chattering, but made her dribble, leaving her mouth dry. She'd given up trying to scream, though she couldn't stop the involuntary whimpering that accompanied her spasms of shuddering.

When she opened her eyes again, the moon had disappeared behind the clouds, and all she could see now was the outline of the nearest bushes hanging over her.

Why have I been left? And why here? And for how long?

She questioned herself and at the same time blamed herself. Because of her anger, she'd chosen to make her own way home and thus ended up in an unidentified street in an unfamiliar town, with no mobile and no idea where to find any transport back to Cambridge. As her temper cooled, she'd begun to appreciate her dilemma and it was then that she'd made the crucial error.

The sight of a familiar face had made her drop her guard. Somehow it felt wiser to step into that car than invite attention from whoever else she'd imagined might be lurking nearby. The window had lowered and she'd smiled in recognition. She felt disbelief at that now, but it was true: *she'd actually smiled.* They'd both smiled. And logic had told her that she'd be safer than with a complete stranger.

But what else was someone who'd done nothing more intimate than browse the same aisle of the same shop? Even killers bought apples and yogurt and ready meals. She'd known nothing about this person, just snatched at the link to home.

It had rained heavily during the first night. The initial drops had been cold, but she noticed that a little less as her sodden clothes became plastered to her skin. In the fullness of the subsequent downpour she'd made the decision to wet herself, trusting it to continue long enough to wash away any humiliating stains.

She'd promised herself that there wouldn't be a second time, but now her bladder was aching and her distended belly pressed against the waistband of her jeans. She twisted around in the mud, just enough to inch her knees towards her chest and provide slight relief.

Eventually she dozed, and jerked awake only as the tentacles of dawn poked their way across the sky. Increasing daylight cast cold shafts of light across the lake, and Kaye prayed for warmth.

Her fingers and toes throbbed with cold and her back ached from constant shivering, but Kaye had progressed beyond the panic she'd felt when she'd first been abandoned here. And even being able to fall asleep had been an achievement, she told herself. She'd never slept outside before, and in the blackest part of the night her fear had escalated to hysteria. She'd thought she might die of fear but, of course, she hadn't.

She watched the grey morning light lift higher and turn to day. She lay on a patch of mud broken up by the odd tuft of coarse grass, and was shielded from the rest of the world by clumps of nettles and hawthorn. Between her and the water, the slope of the bank was sand and gravel, and Kaye guessed that she had been deposited beside a flooded quarry.

She'd been in the car for an hour at most, so she could still be in Suffolk. But, for all she knew, she could also be in Essex, or even back in Cambridgeshire.

She needed food and water, and most of all she needed to be found. She focused her gaze on the far bank of the lake and watched.

At noon, she saw a grubby gull dip towards the water, then buck skywards with an angry squawk.

Later she took comfort from the warmth of a trickle of urine as it seeped through her jeans and into the ground. She tilted her head in what she guessed was a westerly direction and stared at what she hoped was the night sky over Cambridge. That was her only link to home now.

CHAPTER 6

MONDAY, 28 MARCH 2011

On the edge of Cambridge city centre another girl, older than Kaye, bent her head into the wind. It gusted round her face, tugging at strands of her hair and whipping them against her fleshless cheeks. It rushed past the traffic queuing at the lights by the war memorial, snatching up a crisp packet and sending it dancing in spirals between the cars, to land eventually in the gutter below the bronze soldier on his plinth. He was clearly returning from war, helmet in hand and his belongings slung over one shoulder, striding out and portrayed as hopeful and victorious.

Unscarred by violence.

Lucky him.

The statue stood in the centre of the T-junction where Station Road met Hills Road. The three converging routes originated from the railway station, the city centre and the main commuter route from London and the M11.

A row of shops, cafés and wine bars occupied one corner while the other two were overlooked by low-rise offices. In the past she'd tried each of the eateries. All but one she immediately knew were wrong, they'd been too small, too open to the road, with tables exposed to every other customer.

The clientele of the Great Northern bothered her: they all seemed neat, corporate types and made her feel conspicuous. But the view from the window was ideal so she tried the bar in any case and then spent an uncomfortable hour with the feeling that the staff viewed her business as inadequate.

Every day since she'd gone to one of the two pubs located on the London side of the junction.

Now the only other pedestrians had their heads down and hurried on, it wasn't the day for hanging round, or eye contact. She noticed that even when people walked together nobody spoke.

'Too cold to be outside,' she mumbled, then pursed her lips and pinched them between her teeth. *Stupid, stupid thing to say.*

She pushed open the street door and hurried into the Flying Pig.

She needed to eat and studied the menu card on the bar. She already knew it by heart and on the occasions she ordered food she always chose a cheese and tomato baguette. She pretended to look at the list of sandwiches and used the time to focus on looking and sounding in control.

She stared at the words on the menu until they blurred and her cheeks puckered with queasiness.

Concentrate, she scolded herself, and scowled at the card for a few seconds more.

At the Flying Pig, Justine had spent fourteen years cultivating and maintaining an atmosphere that was a cocktail of traditional pub, bohemian hang-out and eccentric front room. She had a loyal clientele and simultaneously managed to make anyone else feel welcome, from their first visit. She still looked up when the door opened, smiled warmly as she chatted, and her enthusiasm for the business still outshone the trials of running it. As long as customers respected her pub, who they were, how they behaved and what they looked like was irrelevant.

But, of course, once in a while there had to be an exception.

Justine was sitting just outside the door that led from the bar to the stockroom. She'd been halfway through a pre-lunch break, and was using the free time to phone through to her bank. She'd been on hold now for ten minutes, and apparently her call was still 'important'. She was also 'next in line' but she hung up when she saw the woman arrive.

Justine didn't hurry to serve her but busied herself with sorting the condiment sets while the young woman picked up a menu, holding it artificially high in front of her face and looking like someone trying too hard to appear to be actually reading it.

Justine produced one of her best glowing smiles. 'Coffee or tea today?' she asked.

'Coffee, please.'

'Mug, isn't it?'

'Yes, thanks.' The woman's voice sounded dull and no hint of recognition showed in those hollow eyes. After paying, she sat down by the window, just cupping her mug of coffee as though warming her hands, not drinking it.

Justine continued to rearrange the condiments sets, hoping this made her look as if she was preparing for the lunchtime rush, but really watching and pondering on the lone woman. When she'd first started coming to the café, Justine had silently bet herself ten quid that she could make her smile. Now she couldn't even remember exactly when that was, but it had to be at least two years ago – maybe three.

Justine had since nicknamed her Greta, and the customer seldom missed a day, hardly ate and rarely spoke. But her routine was always the same. She would come in at a quarter to twelve, buy a drink – usually coffee – and sometimes a baguette, and then sit by the window.

And, in all that time, Justine had never seen her smile.

Justine positioned herself so that she could see Greta's reflection in the mirror behind the optics. Today, she decided, she looked particularly uptight.

The first time, she'd been the same, and had chosen to sit at the window table in the corner. She'd waited specially for it to be vacated, even though other tables were free and then, after just a few minutes, another couple had attempted to occupy two of its three empty seats.

'Are these taken?'

Looking them straight in the eyes, she'd replied stonily, 'I want to be alone.'

That's when Justine nicknamed her Greta – after Greta Garbo.

Justine finally turned and snatched a direct glimpse at her. *Perhaps she's ill?* she wondered.

Greta raised the mug as if to sip coffee but lowered it again immediately then turned to operate the jukebox mounted on the pillar behind her.

Justine answered her own question as Greta's current favourite track began to play. *Nope, same old same old.*

Every day Greta selected a record, sometimes playing it several times, but each day she'd choose the same one. Same one every day for weeks, until a different one caught her fancy. This was week three of her current choice.

It had been a long time since any patron had stirred Justine's curiosity the way Greta did. She would focus her attention on the new customers arriving, but continued to wonder who Greta really was and what had gone so very wrong in her life.

Greta watched the Station Road/Hills Road junction and let the warmth of the coffee and the mellow rhythm and blues soothe her. She didn't want to throw up again.

She ran her hand along the rounded edge of the dark wood table. *Relax. You can cope. Keep calm. Keep calm.* She'd been feeling better recently. Thinking about that girl's face must have caused the upset. That girl who looked like her. Greta hated seeing her own features on someone else.

At exactly noon she checked her watch, then fixed her gaze on the tide of workers leaving Dunwold Insurance. As they flowed from the building, many were wearing only lightweight jackets and so hastened past the others towards the warmth of the wine bars and coffee shops. Her elbows dug into the table as she tilted forward, her head closer to the glass.

At two minutes past twelve she caught sight of him, carrying a folded umbrella but strolling along as if it was summer. He paused for a beat as he waited for a slim girl who lagged behind him, fiddling with the catch on her handbag. So he was still with Paulette. Greta could just pick out her features: milky skin, fair hair and large almond-shaped eyes.

She didn't know the colour, but guessed blue. Like her own.

Paulette curled her arm through his and they walked in step, heading away from the window and out of sight.

Greta sagged back into her seat and frowned as she mulled things over. *Paulette resembles me – and so did the last one. What does Paulette have that I don't? He obviously wants women that look alike.* She gnawed her lip and stared into her coffee. *But not me.*

She turned her face into the cold as she left the Flying Pig, crossed over to the newsagent's, and bought the first edition of the *Cambridge News*. She glanced at the front-page photo but quickly turned her gaze away, clutching the newspaper under her arm and determined not to read it in the street.

She fell into a jog down Hills Road, dodging the shoppers, and ran across Gonville Place, weaving through a muddle of cars and cyclists before scurrying into the nearest cubicle of the female public toilets. There she slumped against the partition wall, resting heavily on one shoulder, and raised the newspaper in both hands.

She scanned the accompanying article, picking out the key phrases and searching for a sign, but her instinct told her, *they still have no idea.*

Finally she drew a small pair of scissors from her inside pocket, letting the inner pages slide to the floor, as she carefully cut Kaye's picture from page one, before she folded it neatly and slipped it inside her jacket.

She paused for a moment to stare into the polished stainless steel that served as a mirror. Her reflection stared back at her like the face of a woman she recognized but no longer knew. *Helen looked like you, Kaye looks like you.* She turned away from her reflected image and whispered, 'But you're alive.'

CHAPTER 7

MONDAY, 28 MARCH 2011

Pete Walsh called to Paulette as she again paused to fumble with the catch on her handbag. 'I know we've got an extra half hour for lunch today but can't you hurry up? It's freezing out here.'

'My bag keeps coming open.' Paulette scowled as she strained to twist the clasp shut.

'Why didn't you fix it when we were still inside?' He stopped and waited for her to catch up.

'For God's sake, Pete, be patient.' She managed to persuade it to stay in place this time. 'There we go . . . And you don't look that cold anyway.'

He turned towards the town again as she fell into step and slipped her arm through his. 'Everybody's cold. It's winter.'

'No it's spring, and *I'm* not cold,' she began, and Pete dragged in a deep breath before expelling it as a weighty sigh. 'You keep me warm,' she continued, and wrapped her fingers around his sleeve, tilting her head to rest against his shoulder.

He gave her the flash of a smile. 'Where do you want to go?'

'I don't mind.' She shrugged. 'There's a new pizza place up on the corner.'

'Really?' He sounded surprised.

'Well, no – not if you don't want to.' She shrugged again.

'I don't think it looks much, but if that's where you fancy . . .'

'No, I really don't mind. That was just the first place I thought of. We can go somewhere else.' But Paulette couldn't think of anywhere. 'You choose.'

'Prêt à Manger maybe? Then I can check out the CDs in HMV.'
'That's, like, a mile and a half.'
'No, it actually *is* a mile and a half.'
'Right.' Paulette withdrew her hand from his arm and sank it into her pocket. 'I get really bored in there.'
'Oh, come on, we'll have a brisk walk and I'll spend ten minutes maximum.' He grinned again and gave her a sudden hug. 'Is just ten minutes OK?'
Her mood evaporated. 'Charmer!'
'Great, we'll go there first, then we've got the rest of lunchtime to ourselves.'

Paulette checked her watch as Pete began flicking through the CDs. It was now 12.26 p.m. She hung close beside him for the first few minutes, waiting for him to chat to her. Eventually he paused to inspect a Corrs disc.
'They're not your type,' she joked.
He didn't even reply.
She pulled the case from his hand. 'OK, then, which one do you fancy most?'
He held out his hand for it, but she kept it out of reach. 'Oh, I don't know,' he conceded.
He turned back to carry on looking through some other CDs, and Paulette dropped it back into its slot.
Pete lifted it back out. 'The singer's attractive, very sultry.'
'Would it suit me to have my hair done that colour?'
'I don't know. I think you'd look ill. Anyway she's a celebrity.'
'And what's that supposed to mean?'
'Nothing, except she's going to look more glamorous.'
'I can look glamorous.'
'I never said you couldn't. What is your problem, anyway? She's attractive but I don't fancy her. And so what if I did – do you really feel threatened by someone's photo?'
'No, of course not.'
'You're getting jealous again.'
'No, I'm not.' Paulette checked her watch again: 12.30 p.m. 'Can we go?'

'In a minute.' He again turned his back on her and began browsing the next section.

'Well, I'll be over by the magazines,' she snapped. 'I don't need to waste my lunch hour like this.'

The magazine rack was loaded with music and fashion titles, and Paulette picked up the latest issue of *Red* and turned to the article she'd already noticed in her own copy. She held the magazine as though she were reading it, but kept it tilted so that anyone nearby could see the bold title *Single and Loving It!*

She watched him go over to pay the cashier, but then, instead of coming across to her, he waited at the door. 'Shit,' she said, and a teenager looked up at her from the rack of games. She sauntered across to the cash desk and paid for the magazine.

'Don't worry about a bag.'

She rejoined Pete, who didn't appear to notice the magazine rolled up in her hand, but began heading back towards Dunwold Insurance.

'What about lunch?' Paulette called after him, and then ran to catch up with him.

He kept on walking. 'I've had a busy morning, and I was really looking forward to seeing you, but I didn't need all of this hassle.'

Paulette tugged at his elbow. 'I'm sorry.'

'You've spoilt it.'

'Please, Pete, I'm sorry, really I am. You took it the wrong way. I never meant to turn it into a big deal.' She had to make him stop and listen to her. They had to sort this out before he got back to work. A lump had risen in her throat but, instead of fighting it, she let it turn to tears. 'Please,' she insisted.

He stopped and glared at her, and then his expression softened. 'Paulette, you're pretty and you've got a great smile, but you've also got to stop getting jealous all the time. I can't cope with it. It isn't what I want to deal with, and it's become a big problem.'

'I know.' Paulette nodded. 'I'm sorry.' She stretched up and planted a soft kiss on his cheek. 'Forgive me?'

He nodded. 'OK.'

'I'll see you later, then?'

'OK,' he repeated. She held his hand tightly until she'd walked back into reception with him.

She trudged back to her own work, trying to identify the precise moment when their lunchtime had turned sour. She wondered why she felt as though she wasn't good enough. She was more than good enough, and he just needed to realize it. She then tried to devise a plan from the furthest recesses of her mind. Something to make him put her back on a pedestal.

Any plan at all. But it was dark and hopeless, and she returned to work still churning the big question over and over: *What if he leaves me?*

For the rest of the afternoon, she counted away the minutes. Through the window she watched the traffic, and the school children swarming out of the buses.

School represented the great lie that there was more to life than talking on the phone and filling in forms. This job wasn't the reason she'd taken Economics and English A-Levels, but Pete made it all worthwhile.

At 3.55 p.m. she swung away from her desk and threw down her telephone headset. She stretched her neck back, and watched the other girls still concentrating on their phone calls and terminals.

'Drinks anyone?' she called out.

She then stood at the sink to rinse their lunchtime mugs. Placing the last one on the draining board, she plunged her hands back into the grubby water. Cupping them together, she scooped some water from the washing-up bowl and watched it trickle through her fingers. Everything seemed to be slipping away from her.

Perhaps he's tired of me. She shuddered. *No, he wouldn't have suggested a joint holiday if he planned to leave me. Or would he? Would he?*

Returning to the desk, her gaze fell on her copy of *Red*. He himself wasn't really immune to jealousy; no one was. 'I'll show him,' she muttered, and thumbed quickly through the magazine, crumpling pages as she raced through it.

When she found the Issey Miyake aftershave advertisement, she tore out the scented strip, pulled up her jumper and rubbed it on her bare stomach.

CHAPTER 8

TUESDAY, 29 MARCH 2011

Goodhew lived in a small flat up in the roof of a townhouse facing on to Parker's Piece. There were three storeys beneath his, plus a basement, and, although it had been almost a year since he'd discovered that he was the owner of the whole building, he had never felt inclined to substantially alter his living arrangements. The biggest change had been to create a study in the second-floor room that had once been his grandfather's library. The rest of the building stood empty but, as Goodhew walked down the stairs, he still glanced through each open doorway.

He'd reached the first-floor landing just as he heard the letter box rattle. As he descended the final flight, he saw that his only item of mail today was a postcard. From twenty feet away, he could see that most of the picture on it was vivid blue sky.

He read the caption as he took the short walk to Parkside police station: 'Cairns and The Great Barrier Reef'. He turned the card over and found that the note from his grandmother was typically brief. 'You and your sister are very different propositions. This will be more work than holiday, and I might not get home till Christmas!'

His sister Debbie had recently turned twenty-five. She'd departed Cambridge with the intention of working her passage around the world, but once she'd made it as far as Australia she seemed to run out of momentum – and, more recently, money. His grandmother had felt this wasn't the appropriate moment for handing over a large inheritance and, instead of doing so, had set off in an attempt to instil a degree of work ethic into Debbie.

Goodhew had guessed it would prove a challenge but wasn't sure how to interpret the comment about Christmas. His grandmother rarely used exclamation marks, so maybe it was a joke. She'd been away for less than a fortnight, but he missed her company already. And, though he saw his sister far less frequently, the simple arrival of this message had reassured him that both were obviously well.

He turned the postcard over in his hand and considered how much it would mean to Margaret Whiting to receive something like this. Right now she must be praying for just three little words from her daughter: 'I'm OK, Mum.'

But Kaye Whiting was still missing.

He'd put all the other work to one side since taking the statement from her mother. Kaye had been missing since Friday at the earliest, and Saturday at the latest. She had no boyfriend, was close to her family, and was a reliable employee. No one could suggest a plausible reason for her to decide to disappear.

Gary thought of her face in the photograph. Was she dead? There had been little response from the appeal in the *Cambridge News*, and from the nationals. Goodhew knew he needed to visit Margaret Whiting again. If Kaye had been abducted, then statistically that wasn't good, since most females abducted by strangers were dead within three hours. He liked to appear optimistic but, even so, had found himself deciding that nothing less than a smart suit would be appropriate for a second visit to her mother.

Goodhew pushed open the doors to Parkside police station. *Let her turn up safe, and soon*, he prayed silently.

He sensed Margaret Whiting's gaze already on him as he parked his car in front of her neighbour's house. As before, she opened the front door even as he opened the gate. But this time she withdrew into the house before he'd reached the doorstep. She'd only needed a glance at his expression to know that he didn't bring the news she wanted.

He stepped straight inside, closing the door and removing his coat before following her to the kitchen. 'How are you, Mrs Whiting?'

She wore the same clothes as she had when he'd last visited, but they were unpressed, and her pallid complexion had deteriorated into a poor imitation of puckered parchment.

'White tea, no sugar – that's right, isn't it?' She avoided making eye contact.

'We haven't any news for you, I'm sorry, he said.

She turned to face him and he could see the sharp flickers of distress that lit her listless eyes. 'Girls do go missing and then turn up unharmed, don't they?'

'Occasionally, yes. Can we sit down?'

Margaret Whiting led him back to the sitting room. He knew he needed to take great care with his words. He waited until they were both seated before beginning. 'We all need to stay positive, Mrs Whiting, but we also need to be realistic. Sometimes girls do turn up, but usually they've chosen to leave home in the first place because of depression or domestic difficulties. From what you've told me, Kaye had no reason to vanish.'

'That's right. And I certainly don't want you giving me false hope. But I've been going over and over it, and I keep thinking she could have been in an accident, or have been kidnapped. She could be lying somewhere dark and cold.' One corner of her mouth trembled and her voice rose as she choked out her next words. 'I can't bear to think of her afraid.'

'Is there someone who can be here with you? Your husband, or your mother maybe?'

She shook her head. 'He won't take time off work – says he wants to keep busy. And Mum? No, it just wouldn't work. It's the waiting that's so difficult; no one's going to help with that. Except you,' she added, as an afterthought, 'because you're trying to do something about it.'

Goodhew tapped his pencil on his notepad. 'Look, assuming a crime has been committed, we need to know whether anyone Kaye knows has any kind of motive for abducting her. And obviously we've been checking for similarities with other crimes.'

'And?'

'Nothing, so far. But that's not surprising when we really don't know anything at all. To be frank, Mrs Whiting, without knowing where or when she vanished, it becomes very difficult to make any progress. But I do need to go through the relationships you know about.'

'OK, well, she doesn't have a boyfriend at the moment, if that's what you mean.'

'Perhaps we can start with some background. Kaye's twenty-three and Michelle is twenty-one. How long have they lived away from home?'

'They moved out when Michelle was seventeen and Kaye was nineteen. They found a room each in a shared house, first of all, then Kaye moved into her own flat back in the autumn.'

'And they still get on well?'

'Oh yes. They go out together at least once a week, even when they're tied up with boys.'

'And Michelle's boyfriend, Carl, does he know Kaye?'

Margaret curled her nose up in distaste. 'Not that I was there of course, but apparently they both met him on the same evening. They were at De Niro's, you know in Newmarket, and Carl and a friend kept buying them drinks. He was talking to Michelle, and his friend was talking to Kaye, but I got the impression that it was really Kaye he was interested in. Not that I was there of course,' she repeated. 'But, anyway, Kaye wasn't bothered about either of them. That Carl must have known he'd struck it lucky with Michelle, and they've been together ever since. I still think he's keen on Kaye, though.'

'But it wasn't that which caused Kaye to move out of the house they shared?'

Margaret Whiting paused, uncertain for a second. 'No, Michelle is totally besotted. She's a bit like me, can't always see what's under her nose.'

'Meaning?'

Mrs Whiting shook her head. 'Nothing specific, but it's just in my nature to be a bit naïve sometimes.'

'And Carl's friend, do you know who that was?'

'No idea, sorry.'

'Steve, your son, he's nineteen and still at home. Was there any reason the girls left home at such a young age?'

'Such as?' Margaret asked with sudden wariness.

Goodhew remained expressionless. 'I don't know; that's why I asked.'

Margaret scowled. 'Teenage girls in a poky house,' she shrugged and threw up her hands, 'hormones and I don't know what. Something obviously had to give.'

'And your husband . . . ?' began Gary.

'He would never harm them,' she cut in. She was on her feet immediately, taking a step in the direction of the kitchen, but she didn't move any further.

Gary stared down at his notepad as though he hadn't noticed her reaction. 'I was going to ask you what time your husband will be home,' he finished quietly.

Margaret lowered herself into her chair again. Goodhew could imagine that the foundations of everything she took for granted in her life were crumbling. As her panic dissipated, her eyes started to fill. 'Six o'clock.'

'OK.' He decided to move on. 'When we spoke to your brother, he was vague about his reasons for missing the party. We will be speaking to everyone again, but has he since told you why he didn't attend?'

Margaret was still fighting against a tide of tears that threatened to swamp her, and she replied in a small hoarse croak. 'No. I left a message but he never rang back. He can be very quiet, though. Gets on best with Mum, so I expect he's told her.'

'Isn't it odd that he hasn't contacted you since all the publicity about Kaye's disappearance?'

'I s'pose it's funny.' She pulled a tissue from her sleeve and dabbed her eyes. 'Bad choice of words, eh? It definitely isn't funny, is it?'

Goodhew shook his head. 'Can you tell me who Kaye's closest friends were?'

Margaret twisted the tissue into a tight spiral, and she stared at it, not at Goodhew. He wondered if she had heard him. He waited patiently.

She let go of the end of it and the tissue slowly uncurled. She now crumpled it into a ball.

'Were,' she gasped. 'You said "were".'

CHAPTER 9

TUESDAY, 29 MARCH 2011

Goodhew spotted WPC Gully ahead of him in the second-floor corridor. 'Sue,' he called out and quickened his step to catch up with her. 'Hang on.'

'No problem.' She waved her notepad. 'Marks will just assume it was you that made me late. I've been taking telephone statements since yesterday.' They continued to head towards the end meeting room.

'Have I missed anything?'

'Still nothing.' She screwed up her nose. 'There are a lot of *maybe I saw her* calls, but not one of them stands out. Young and Charles are trawling through most of them, but it'll take them an absolute age.'

'I'll stay on for a couple of hours and give you a hand, if it's stacking up.'

'OK,' she gave a grateful nod, 'as long as you mean it. I know what you're like for getting distracted.'

'Unless there's an emergency,' he protested.

'Well, in that case I'll believe it when you show up.'

They entered the briefing room and he assumed they were the last to arrive but, as he turned to close the door, he saw DI Marks striding along the corridor towards them.

'Thanks,' he grunted to Goodhew, who held the door as he marched in. Goodhew clicked the door shut and would have remained standing, but Marks nodded him towards the chairs. 'Gary, sit. It's time you got out of the habit of being last in and first out.'

His colleagues Kincaide, Gully, Clark, Young and Charles were all seated, but Kincaide sat closest to the front, with his chair angled slightly away from the other five. Goodhew dropped into the chair next to Aaron Clark, who tutted a quiet reprimand.

DI Marks folded back the cover sheet of the flip chart to reveal the first page, where '25/3/11 p.m. – 26/3/11 p.m.' was inscribed in red ink. 'As far as we've ascertained, then, Kaye Whiting disappeared sometime between 8 p.m. on Friday 25 March and the evening of Saturday 26th, when she failed to turn up at a family birthday gathering.'

Kincaide already fidgeted in his chair, and started speaking as soon as Marks paused. 'That's if her sister's boyfriend Carl Watkins is telling us the truth. He's the one who supposedly saw her at 8 p.m. on Friday, sir.'

'Quite so, Kincaide. The previous sighting to that one, was by a work colleague, Doreen Kennedy, who dropped her off at her home at six-twenty. Any comments so far?' He scribbled a blue question mark above the '8 p.m.', circled it, and drew an arrow from the circle to one side – where he now wrote '6.20 p.m.'.

He looked around the group and rubbed the end of his nose a couple of times with his knuckle, before continuing.

'She was reported missing by her mother, and we have no other sightings to go on. Her entire domestic situation appears to have been in order and—'

Kincaide raised his hand this time. 'Sir?'

'Yes, Kincaide?'

'I've just interviewed her uncle, Andrew Burrows, who also missed the family get-together. Didn't feel well he says, but seems rather an antisocial type, sir.' Despite facing away from the others, his voice was louder and more demanding than Marks'.

Marks fidgeted with his nose once more. 'Michael . . .' he paused and made a conscious effort to keep the sarcasm from his voice. 'I suspect every family has a relation who's no party animal, so—'

Kincaide butted in again. 'But this was for his own mother, sir.'

Marks rattled the flip chart as he tore off the top sheet. 'I too didn't go to one of my mother's birthday bashes, but it wasn't because I was busy abducting my niece!'

Marks scowled, aware he'd made a few people smirk. 'But don't drop that thought, Kincaide. Stranger things happen.'

'Yes, sir.' Kincaide nodded.

On the second sheet, Marks now wrote three headings: 'Own Choice', 'Accident' and 'Crime'.

'While we cannot discount the possibility that she's met with an accident, we do know that she is not in any of the nearby hospitals or morgues, and we should therefore discount this avenue at the current time.' He drew a line through the word 'Accident'.

'Clark is keeping tabs on everything from her bank account and credit cards through to her store cards and even her Boots Advantage Card, and there has been absolutely no activity recorded on any of them. This, coupled with the now national publicity we've generated for this case, leads me to conclude that we are reasonable in discounting the idea that she's decided to flit off for a long weekend without telling anyone.' He drew a line through the heading 'Own Choice'.

'Which leaves us with "Crime". It may seem like an overly simplistic route to that conclusion, but I want you to be absolutely clear that it's the only option we're looking into right now. This is also a good moment to remind you all that you do not speak to the press, and when I eventually do, I will be stressing the hope that we will find her alive.' He stopped for long enough to direct a studied look at each of them in turn. 'We all know the reality of the situation, but we will keep the public interest for far longer if they believe they are helping in a race to save someone's life, rather than just a body search.'

Goodhew glanced round. There was no one in the room who hadn't been exposed to this logic in the past. Marks drew two more of his arrows, this time from the word 'Crime', and in green pen.

Marks added a title beside each arrowhead: 'By stranger' and 'By person(s) known to K.W.'. He then circled the latter. 'Until we have further information to the contrary, I want us to look more closely at her family and friends.'

Goodhew's gaze strayed outside. *We're not helping her at all by sitting in here*, he thought.

Marks glared at him. 'Goodhew!' he said with a sharp hiss.

'Sir?'

'Are you with us? Good. Please sum up for me, then.'

Goodhew nodded, taking the opportunity to close the briefing swiftly. 'So in summary: We have a missing girl and no clues. We need to pinpoint her movements after the last sighting, and pick up on any friends that may have information.

'"Was she meeting someone?"

'"Did she have a date?"

'"Where was she when she was abducted?"'

When Goodhew had almost finished, he could see that Marks was also ready to wrap it up, so he added, 'And one more thing. Can I suggest that we push to have at least one other photograph of her circulated nationally? And a televised press conference, perhaps?'

'Thank you, Goodhew. The media details are already in hand, but the alternative photograph is a good suggestion. This room will become the incident room for the course of this investigation, so I want you to move anything you may need in here straight away.'

When finally they dispersed, Goodhew was the first through the door. Marks caught up with him in the corridor. 'Do you suffer from some kind of claustrophobia, Goodhew?'

'I don't think so.' Goodhew kept walking.

'Briefings may well bore you, Goodhew, but if you have one of the vital pieces of information and a colleague holds another, it's a briefing like this that can make it all come together. I see you're going to visit Kaye's colleague, Doreen Kennedy?'

'I don't want to be late.'

Marks paused at the top of the stairs. 'Clark's already seen her.'

Goodhew stopped and jiggled the loose handrail. 'She's had time to think, so she might remember something else.' He started to back down the stairs. 'You know I wouldn't go to see her if I didn't think it could be important.'

'That's why I'm not stopping you,' Marks replied grimly, and turned back towards his office. 'Just use your time wisely, Gary, and . . .'

'Keep you informed?'

Marks nodded and entered his office, where he took a Rennie from his drawer and washed it down with the dregs of coffee from a plastic cup. 'Don't add to my stress, Gary-bloody-Goodhew.'

CHAPTER 10

TUESDAY, 29 MARCH 2011

PC Sue Gully sat alone in the incident room. As she held her pen over the page, ready to write, she could hear the caller's deep breathing, and traffic surging past faintly in the background.

Gully knew the caller might hang up if she spoke, but then she figured they might hang up if she didn't. 'My name is PC Sue Gully and you can speak to me in confidence.'

The breathing stopped and she expected to hear a voice, but the only new sound was a short sniff.

'Are you OK?' she asked, keeping her voice relaxed and even.

The caller replied, 'Yes,' in a stifled whisper.

Gully scribbled 'Female. Twenties?' on the page, and waited as the woman fell silent again.

Through her earpiece she heard a heavy bell clanging at a slow beat, and pivoted in her seat to look out from her window and across the rooftops towards the protruding tower of the Great St Mary's Church. She wrote 'Phone boxes – Market Hill?'

She imagined the woman huddled in the call box, with her back to the door, hiding her face so no one could see her crying. Gully heard the woman's breathing become steady and knew she was about to speak.

'I have some information about the disappearance of Kaye Whiting. I don't want to give my name.'

'That's fine,' Gully encouraged.

The line clicked and to Gully's surprise the woman hung up.

Gully dropped the receiver back on to its rest and circled the notes on the paper with three big rings. 'How odd,' she murmured. She tore the sheet from its pad and folded it in half. She stood it, like a greetings card, at the back of her desk.

Several calls and fifteen minutes later, Gully took another call. There were no traffic noises, clock chimes or sounds of breathing, but in an instant she knew that she was connected to the same person.

'I have information about Kaye Whiting.' The voice was now monotone and bereft of the distress that she'd heard so clearly the first time. 'You're WPC Gully, aren't you?'

'Yes, that's right.'

'It was you before, wasn't it?'

'That's right,' Gully repeated as she flattened her original sheet of paper back on to the top of her pad.

'I bet you think she's dead.'

Gully didn't reply, but lodged the receiver under her chin and held the pad still with her left hand while she wrote with her right. 'Drunk???' she jotted.

'Don't you?' demanded the woman, and Gully suspected that she was smiling as she'd said it.

Gully decided to play the official line. 'We are obviously very concerned, but we are not assuming anything at this stage.'

'That's good, because I think when you find her you'll realize that she was still alive at this point.'

The skin at the back of Gully's neck began to tingle as goosebumps rose beneath her collar. 'How do you know?'

'I don't know, not for certain. But I don't think there's long before it's too late.'

Gully bit her lower lip and made sure that the caller had finished before she responded, 'Where is she?'

Gully heard the woman laugh, in a bitter snort of derision. 'I can't tell you that. Peter Walsh, that's who you need to speak to. He works at Dunwold Insurance and lives at 26 Hanley Road. This is all I can do, phone you and tell you how it is. Do you understand that?'

'No, not exactly. Can you explain it to me?' asked Gully, as she repeatedly underlined the word 'Drunk'.

'Arrest Peter Walsh and the killings will stop. Do you know, I feel it so much I can guarantee it. One hundred per cent. And if you are really quick, you may save Kaye Whiting.'

Gully realized that she was holding her breath. She exhaled quickly as she spoke. 'How do you know?'

The caller mumbled, 'It doesn't matter. I've told you now and it's not going to be my fault any more.'

'Why are you to blame?' Gully said, just as she realized that she was talking to a dead line.

She picked up the phone again and dialled Goodhew's mobile. 'Damn,' she groaned as she found herself directed to his voicemail. 'Gary, it's me, I'm in the incident room. Can you phone back? It's urgent.'

'Sue?'

She spun round. 'Oh, hello, Michael.' Kincaide grabbed a chair and pulled it alongside hers. 'What have you got?'

Gully followed Kincaide's gaze, and saw he was looking at her monitor, probably already eyeing the *play* button.

'An interesting call, I think. Hang on, I'll play it for you.'

She scooted the mouse across the desktop and hit the red triangle, then looked up at Kincaide, keen to see whether her excitement would be reflected in his own expression.

'What's so special about this one, then?' he asked, glancing at his watch.

'Wait till you hear it,' Gully enthused. 'She's called twice now, she names a suspect, and she doesn't sound like a crank.' Gully played the message for a couple of seconds, then skipped forward to find the start. 'She might have had a couple to drink, though, because she sounded nervous the first time and not the second.'

Knowing she was talking too much, Gully felt herself redden.

'Anonymous, I suppose?' he asked, talking over the first few moments.

'Yeah, unfortunately.'

'Anonymous and drunk, then?' was all he said, as he listened. He tilted his head, resting it on one hand in the pose of Rodin's *The Thinker*.

By the time Gully clicked the *stop* button, her enthusiasm had evaporated. Kincaide made a dismissive sweep of the hand as he jumped to his feet.

'Chase it up if you want. Sounds like a loony to me. Or is there some more I haven't heard?'

'No.'

Kincaide scowled. 'Get it checked out, along with the others.' Then he shrugged and turned to go. 'Don't worry, Sue, we've all jumped to silly conclusions. It's all part of learning.'

'All part of learning,' she mimicked with contempt, once he was out of earshot. She rested her elbows on the desk and pressed her forehead on to her fists. She stared down at the blue ink stain just an inch below her nose. Out of focus, it looked a bit like Australia, or next-door's West Highland Terrier, depending how she viewed it.

She didn't hear Goodhew come in. 'Sue?'

'Hi. I thought you were seeing Mrs Kennedy?'

'I was, but she'd already gone home, too upset to stay at work, apparently. She's coming to see me first thing tomorrow.'

'Oh.'

'You said "urgent".'

She now raised her chin on to her left palm, clicked the rewind icon and pressed *play*. 'I thought this was important.'

As the recording replayed she watched a flicker of interest ignite in Gary's eyes, and then felt her own first impressions rekindled.

Intense concentration burnt between the pair of them and the recording. As it finished Goodhew leant over and clicked *rewind*. It skipped backwards by several seconds.

The woman's voice repeated: 'Arrest Peter Walsh and the killings will stop.'

Gary stretched across WPC Gully again, and clicked the *stop* button.

'We've had plenty of calls so far, but this one stands out, Gary.' She sat alert again, completely regalvanized.

'And who's heard it, so far?'

'Kincaide did, but he thinks it was a crank call – just said I should check it out along with all the others. But I wanted you to hear it, because I thought you'd say something more than that. I've got a really strong feeling about this, even after hearing it several times over.'

‘Yes, I can see why.’

Sue nodded in relief.

They both fell silent. Goodhew was gazing in her direction, but his green eyes were slightly out of focus. She watched him thinking until she wondered if she seemed to be staring, then she reddened again.

‘She talks of . . . “killings” in the plural,’ she said finally, stumbling over words.

His eyes readjusted and locked with hers. ‘Yes, I know.’ He hesitated, then straightened up, his tone suddenly becoming detached and efficient, ‘So let’s hope that wasn’t a threat.’

CHAPTER 11

TUESDAY, 29 MARCH 2011

Goodhew checked the street map in the station lobby. He found Hanley Road in Newnham, to the south-west of the city centre. It ran behind Barton Road, in a small development of starter homes built on land sold off by the local authority.

He already knew the general area and in less than ten minutes his car crawled into the low-number end of Hanley Road itself. The light brick houses sat in terraces of four or six, the general pattern occasionally punctuated by a couple of boxy detached three-beds or a two-storey block of studio flats.

Through the gaps in the newer buildings, on the even-number side, sprawled the long narrow back gardens of 1930s semis, mostly drowning in uncut weather-beaten grass and impaled by rusted washing-line posts. On the odd-number side, the houses backed on to an old allotment strewn with broken cold frames and choked with weeds.

It wasn't the prettiest road in Cambridge but, because of its close proximity to the town centre, it had become popular with the young professionals in the nine to five-thirty office regime.

Goodhew pulled up outside number 15, and opposite number 18. He counted out four houses along, to Walsh's number 26. He checked his watch: quarter to five. He then stepped from his car and clicked the door shut. He didn't bother locking it.

The sulphurous orange light from the street lamp outside number 22 spilt on to the front of Walsh's unlit home. Goodhew knocked and waited, and knocked again, then crossed back to his unmarked car.

The house was neat, and the garden consisted of a few shrubs and a small patch of lawn, indicating very low maintenance. Tidy paintwork, tidy curtains, too. Goodhew ran his eye over the adjoining houses. Lights shone, through unlined curtains, on to handkerchief gardens, most decorated with hebe and cotoneaster shrubs and the first shoots of spring daffodils. These residences were all very similar, efficient, practical investments for the future.

Headlights appeared in his rear-view mirror, and a car parked behind him. A middle-aged man stepped out, locked the door with a remote, and crossed to number 20. Goodhew relaxed again and waited.

He decided to wait until 5.30 before making some enquiries of neighbours.

At 5.20 precisely, a man walked past Goodhew's car, crossed in front of it and pulled out a door key as he approached number 26. Goodhew guessed this was Peter Walsh, and watched him open the door, then slip out of his jacket and drape it on the middle coat hook, in one practised move. As he turned to close the door, the man realized he had a visitor.

'Peter Walsh?' Goodhew asked.

Walsh was about Goodhew's height, with a crop of dark hair which sprang out over his forehead, giving him a mildly surprised look.

'Yes, what can I do for you?' But the young man seemed relaxed enough, as he undid his tie and ruffled his hair while he waited for Goodhew to respond.

Goodhew held up his police ID. 'DC Goodhew from Cambridge CID. I'd like to ask you a couple of routine questions.' Goodhew stepped briskly into the small lobby area.

'Come through.' Walsh led the way into the lounge area and dropped into one of two large armchairs. 'Take a seat,' he said, motioning towards the other.

'Thanks.' Goodhew nodded. 'Have you lived here long?'

'About six years.'

'Just before the prices shot up again?'

'That's right. I couldn't afford it now, I suppose.' Walsh drummed his fingers on one knee, and he gave a puzzled frown. 'Can I get you something to drink, tea or coffee?'

'No, no.' Goodhew shook his head. 'I'm investigating the disappearance of a local girl, Kaye Whiting. You may have heard about it?'

'In yesterday's *Cambridge News*?'

'Yes, that's right.' Goodhew dipped into his breast pocket and produced a snapshot of a blonde girl holding a tabby cat up towards the camera. She was smiling. 'Recognize her?'

'No.' Walsh smiled slightly then. 'But if she worked anywhere in town, I may have walked right past her and not noticed. No, I don't recognize her,' he gave an apologetic shrug, 'but I'll help if I can. Fire away.'

'Our incident room received an anonymous phone call suggesting that you held vital information that could point us to the present whereabouts of Kaye Whiting,' Goodhew said evenly. He let his gaze roam casually around the room, before directing it back on to Walsh.

'What sort of information?' Walsh's frown returned, the perplexed furrows on his forehead deepening.

'I have no idea,' Goodhew answered coolly. 'Perhaps they thought she was *here*?'

Walsh shook his head and rose to his feet. 'Well, we can answer that one straight away. I'll give you the guided tour.'

Goodhew followed in dutiful silence.

Walsh held open the door to the kitchen. 'As you can see this is the kitchen, not really big enough to conceal a body, but let's check under the sink just to be on the safe side.'

Goodhew opened the kitchen units one by one, then swung them closed. 'I wasn't expecting a body under the sink, Mr Walsh, but if you're happy to show me round the rest of the house, that's great.'

Walsh nodded towards the window. 'The garden's too small for a shed or a patio so I think I'm in the clear there, too.'

Goodhew pointed to a full-length cupboard. 'Vacuum cleaner?'

Peter Walsh opened it and gave Goodhew a few seconds to glance at the Dyson, blue broom, and roll of dustbin sacks. He then closed it and led Goodhew upstairs. 'First the bathroom and second bedroom.'

Goodhew looked into each room in turn. The boxroom contained no bed, just an assortment of half-unpacked boxes.

'Been sitting there since the move. I keep thinking I'll get round to them one day.' Walsh stepped back on to the landing, opening and then closing the airing cupboard door. 'Linen cupboard.' He continued further and flicked the light switch for his own bedroom. 'Last room in the house, apart from the loft.'

The main bedroom, like the rest of the house, was furnished with restraint. The double bed, flanked on one side by a low table and on the other by a bedside cabinet, faced an extensive built-in wardrobe.

One door was ajar and Goodhew peered inside.

Walsh swung the other door open. 'Be my guest.'

Clothes hung in neat rows, above four pairs of shoes, a pair of trainers and a video camera returned to its case.

'I need to get myself a new one. Can't afford it at the moment, though,' Walsh explained.

'No computer, either?' Goodhew asked.

'No, same story. Can you tell me what sort of person tries to implicate someone innocent in a crime?'

Goodhew studied Peter Walsh. 'You've been very forthcoming in letting me look around like this. It makes me feel that you're not altogether surprised I've turned up here.'

'So I can't win?' Walsh threw his hands in the air. 'It hasn't done any harm, has it? You've had a good look, and I've been easygoing about it, so now the least you can do is find out who's responsible for harassing me. That's a crime, isn't it?'

'Yes, harassment is a crime, as is wasting police time and perhaps even perverting the course of justice. We'll see how it goes.' Goodhew turned and caught sight of a framed print on the wall beside the door. A man in a suit stood alone on the beach, his trousers rolled up to his knees and the surf splashing around his calves. 'Robert Mitchum?'

Walsh followed Goodhew's gaze. 'Yes,' he nodded, 'but I'm not really a fan. I just liked the picture.' He turned back to Goodhew. 'So what can you do about these calls?'

'Well, it's obviously someone who knows where you live – and you do work at Dunwold Insurance, don't you?'

Again Walsh nodded.

'Well, the caller knows where you live and work, so it is obviously someone who knows you to some degree. Most likely someone you are on speaking terms with. Any ideas?'

Walsh focused somewhere beyond the closed curtains, and a ghost of sadness passed across his face. 'I'm twenty-eight this year, and single, and I've had a few girlfriends. An average number, I guess. And some can't deal with rejection,' he replied, sounding subdued.

'Can you suggest a name, please, Mr Walsh?'

'Just one?' Walsh gave a thin smile. 'I don't think so, no.'

'This is serious, Mr Walsh. Like I said, wasting police time constitutes an offence, and that goes for you, too. If you know anyone remotely capable of making a malicious call regarding you, you need to tell me.'

'Sorry, I realize it's serious. I suppose if I look back I could say hell hath no fury, and all that,' Walsh tapped his temple a couple of times, 'but that would be going too far. All women can be a bit mad, but I don't know one that would go this far. Can't we just leave it?'

Goodhew ignored the question. 'And what if the caller was male?'

'Then I can't think of anyone.' Walsh's good humour returned. 'I'm not even playing around with someone else's girlfriend at the moment.'

He gave an impish grin, and Goodhew relented. 'I think that will be fine for now. Ring me if you think of anything else.'

'No problem. And don't leave the country?'

Gary grinned. 'Just let us know about it first.'

CHAPTER 12

TUESDAY, 29 MARCH 2011

The rain sprayed across the lake in gusts of icy splinters. Kaye's skin smarted as dribbles of water slid inside her clothes.

She turned her face into the downpour, hoping the rain would fill her mouth and wash away the blood that had dried into her gag. But the water seemed to fall everywhere except on her swollen tongue.

She tried to open her mouth wider, but her jaw throbbed as the skin stretched and tore further around her split lips.

A small puddle expanded on the dimpled ground inches in front of her. She waited until it filled up to almost an inch, then wormed forward until her ear sank in the softened earth. She pressed her cheek against the mud, trying to coax a trickle of water into her mouth from the growing puddle.

She couldn't push her face into the water to suck it in, so she waited until it soaked into the gag and, drip by drip, ran down along the back of her lacerated throat. She tried to imagine sweet tea and the delicate china of her mother's Eternal Beau cups, as she swallowed these muddy dregs.

Suddenly something caught against the back of her tongue, small and hard and uncomfortable. She coughed but it only slipped further back in her mouth. Her arms strained against the rope, shearing another fine layer of skin from her wrists. Her tongue then convulsed and she sucked in a wheezing breath, before spluttering the beetle back into the mud.

It righted itself and scuttled off under her shoulder. Thankfully, insects were scarce in winter. The flies in summer would have made her ill by crawling all over her face to feast on her blood, and over her soiled clothes.

Stop thinking about them, she told herself, and tried to remember what she would do on an average Monday. *Is it Monday now, or Tuesday?* She tried to work it out, distracting herself enough until she drifted into a fleeting interlude of half-sleep.

People always came to save her, when she dreamt. Even in the little dreams that flashed by as she only dozed. The gnawing questions of why she'd been left here and who was behind it vanished. She lay totally exposed, but in her sleep she believed it would all be OK.

It will be OK, she repeated to herself as she came round again. She then asked herself, over and over, what she'd done to make anyone hate her so much.

The light had faded into deep dusk and this was the hardest part of the day, when huge silhouettes crept out from her surroundings and night stretched before her.

Today she had realized that her abductor wouldn't be returning. And she could be dead already, for all anyone knew.

It will be OK. The family are looking for me. She wished she could say it aloud for reassurance. *And the police will be looking. Yes, surely the police, too.*

The plummeting temperatures made her eyes ache. By mid-evening, she pressed them shut. Could they freeze over and crack, or would she be dead before then?

The creaking of the trees and plops of dripping water both fell into a steady rhythm, as Kaye dozed.

Hushed voices reached her.

'Come on, Greg, over this way.'

'Shhh.'

'It's all right, there's no one around.'

Kaye tried to make a noise but only managed to force a whimper. Nobody heard.

A torch clicked on and its beam swung in an erratic arc before settling on the water's edge.

Kaye heard them coming closer, stumbling through the shrubbery, and she knew that the first one through the gorse would tumble right over her.

Her heart began to pound and her muffled voice strained to rise above the breaking twigs.

The torch zigzagged through the undergrowth. The man carrying it spotted her too late, tripped over her legs and crashed forward, dropping the torch into the water.

Kaye awoke.

And for a moment that tantalizing sense of elation hung in the air, dancing around her before the silence of the lake swallowed it whole. It had just been another cruel dream.

But something was different. She twisted her head until facing towards the water. And there it was, a rowing boat bobbing and surging towards the centre of the lake.

Whispers carried across the water. Impossible to hear the words but she could decipher several different voices. They had a torch, and it was being flashed along the shore to Kaye's right.

They're looking for me! Thank God, thank God.

Then the flashlight whipped around, pointing into the boat itself, and Kaye saw the face of a girl about her own age, laughing and flushed with excitement.

'Hey, behave! Look out for the jetty,' shouted a man's voice.

And the flashlight moved back to the reeds and back towards Kaye. She felt its light hit her face and sway over her legs.

Utter desolation hit her as she realized that, from the boat, she was probably just a bumpy outline, nothing more than a mud-and-gravel feature of the bank.

'Is that it?' the girl asked, focusing the torch further to Kaye's right.

'Well done. I can't wait to get out.' The yellow beam of the torch moved on. They joked and laughed as they struggled to moor and step out of the little rocking boat.

They headed away from Kaye. She listened hard until the last shreds of their voices vanished. Silence returned, but worse now. The only people she'd seen in three days; she knew she couldn't bear three days more.

What kind of decaying mess would she be by then?

Tears trickled, leaving silted tracks down both her cheeks before sliding into her matted hair. *No more*, she decided and fixed her thoughts on the last face she'd seen: the face of a healthy young girl, just as she herself had been only a few days before.

A greasy layer of rainwater helped her slide and writhe towards the lip of the bank. It took half an hour to reach the edge; then she stared into the water for several seconds longer before one final twist of her legs toppled her into the deep cold lake.

CHAPTER 13

WEDNESDAY, 30 MARCH 2011

Paulette Coleman grabbed another jumper from the wardrobe and draped it over the top of her suitcase. Her mum shouted up from the hall, 'I can't believe you're still going.'

Paulette flew on to the landing and leant over the banister. 'Of course I am. This is *our* holiday,' she snapped. 'D'you think we'd have just one row and then cancel all our plans? I don't think so. We're going to have a great time, and I'll tell you what I'm looking forward to most. Getting out of this sodding house.'

Her mother glared up at her. 'You're such a stupid little girl sometimes, running round the house, stamping your feet and shouting, and then expecting me to respect you as an adult.' She shook a tea cloth at her daughter. 'You're not mature enough to be in love, and you're going to come unstuck big time. And then it'll be me picking up the pieces. You'll be glad of this *sodding* house then, I can tell you.'

Paulette stormed back into her bedroom, but carried on yelling. 'You're right, I'm stupid, because I actually believed you would be pleased I'd met someone special.' The pitch of her voice escalated. 'But, oh no, you realize I'm growing up and you can't stand it, can you? You're jealous, aren't you?'

Her mother trudged up the stairs, lowering her voice to try and diffuse Paulette's tantrum. 'For pity's sake, Paulette, I know you came home crying again last night. You're not happy, so why do you keep seeing him?'

Paulette appeared in the doorway, holding a box of Tampax in one hand and a can of deodorant in the other. 'I am *happy*, but you don't understand anything, do you? What would *you* know? We've had a few rows, but we're getting it sorted out.' Fury glinted in her eyes. 'And I'll tell you about them, they start because I get possessive, and that's your fault because that's just how you are, and that's how you've made me.'

'Don't be ridiculous. I don't like him, I never have, but I'm not *jealous*.' Mrs Coleman then goaded Paulette with the word. 'Jealous?' she repeated with venom. '*You're* jealous because it's you who's doing all the chasing. You're bound to feel insecure, because he just isn't that interested.'

'Of course he's interested,' Paulette retaliated. 'We have a fantastic sex life, if you really want to know.'

'You make it so easy for him,' Mrs Coleman snorted, 'he just clicks his fingers and you go running. And where do you get that from? I never brought you up to be that stupid.'

Paulette threw some toiletries into a shoulder bag. 'No, you brought me up to walk all over people, and that's not how I want to be. I've never been as happy as I am now. I love him.'

Mrs Coleman crossed her arms over her bosom, and clicked her tongue behind clenched teeth. 'And I suppose he loves you, too?'

'As a matter of fact, yes, he does.' Paulette snatched a black blouse from the end of the bed and barged past her mother and into the bathroom. She slammed the door shut and rammed the bolt into place.

Her mother turned her head as Paulette passed, but didn't move. 'Well, it doesn't cost him anything to say that, whatever he really thinks.'

Inside the bathroom, Paulette stood with her back pressed to the door. 'I can't hear you.'

'Of course you can't. But you'll hear *him* when he hoots his horn, won't you? You'll be trotting out there quick enough, then.'

Paulette chose not to answer. She pulled off her jumper and T-shirt to reveal a black bra trimmed with hot-pink lace. Paulette pulled it down at the sides and scooped each breast fully into its cup. She piled up her hair and held it on top of her head. She turned sideways and checked out her reflection. Satisfied, she started on her make-up. She squirted too much foundation from the tube, then applied it in a heavy swathe across her forehead, nose, cheeks and chin. As it smeared, she cursed her mother and rubbed the excess into her neck. Her fingers fumbled with the mascara and she counted out five strokes on each side, top and bottom, to ensure it was even. She chose a shade of pink lipstick called Hot Candy and began to apply it, just as she heard the familiar double-beep of Pete's car's hooter.

She paused, listening for a car door to slam. After a few seconds he hooted again, so she rushed back to her room to collect her bags.

As she passed the hall mirror, she caught a glimpse of her unblotted lipstick and single-tone skin, and paused just long enough to press her fingertips on to her lips and dab some lipstick on to her cheeks. She smeared it along each cheekbone in an improvised attempt at blusher.

She opened the front door. In full daylight, the end result almost certainly looked like a scald across each cheek. But she'd run out of time and decided to fix things in the car.

As Paulette ran down the path towards the car, her mother emerged from the kitchen and stood on the doorstep, ready to wave goodbye. Paulette ignored her.

'Stupid bitch,' she breathed as she jumped into the car. She leant over and kissed Pete, and then pulled away to check that her mum had seen. Pete waved at the house and her mother waved back, but Paulette just turned her head away.

Mrs Coleman slammed the front door.

Paulette turned to Pete. 'D'you know what – she's been having a go at me for going on holiday with you. She doesn't understand how it is between us. She's jealous, and I told her she was, too.'

'You haven't had a row with her as well?'

'I was upset when I got in last night, so she says it's because you're not making me happy. And I stuck up for you.'

'What did you say?' He pulled away from the kerb and accelerated into the flow of traffic.

'Told her it was my fault we fell out, but we'd got it sorted.' Paulette looked at him, suddenly worried. 'It is OK, isn't it?'

'I don't know.' He shrugged. 'I am getting fed up with the fights all the time.'

'I'm sorry, though. You know I am.'

'I know you're sorry but, as I've said before, it keeps happening, doesn't it?'

Paulette nodded and held her breath, trying to force tears into her eyes. She managed to make them water, and her face reddened.

Pete squeezed her hand. 'Tell you what, let's make the most of the holiday, and then see how we feel. OK?'

Paulette nodded. 'I love you lots.'

Pete indicated and pulled into the outside lane. He must have heard her but he didn't comment, and she let it go for a few minutes. Paulette felt good about this trip. She'd waited for it: it had been the light at the end of the tunnel. She'd show him how much she loved him. 'Don't you feel this is special? Really romantic?'

'Yes, I suppose so.'

'I've never been away for a holiday with a boyfriend before. This is really special.'

'Did you bring lunch?'

'No, was I supposed to?'

'You said you'd bring food for the journey, don't you remember?' When Pete glanced at her, she made a face and her nose and top lip twitched involuntarily. She reminded herself of a twitching, nervy guinea pig.

'Sorry, I forgot,' she muttered, and began rummaging in her shoulder bag. She produced a crumpled pack of chewing gum. He shook his head. She giggled and apologized again.

She beamed at him every time he looked across, but she realized that 'sorry' seemed to have become her favourite word.

CHAPTER 14

WEDNESDAY, 30 MARCH 2011

Goodhew pushed open the door of Interview Room 3 with his foot and stepped inside. He carried two coffees and placed one of the vending-machine cups in front of Doreen Kennedy, then sat down opposite her with the other.

'Thank you,' she said. 'I've been feeling ever so upset about poor Kaye, so I want to help. Really I do, but I don't know anything.'

Goodhew raised a hand, hoping to halt her rambling discourse. 'Mrs Kennedy?'

'Sorry.'

'No, it's fine. I can understand how you feel, but things that may seem like nothing to you may help us all the same.'

She gazed at him over her cup as she sipped her coffee.

'Do you work closely with Kaye?' Goodhew held his pen just an inch above his notebook, ready to catch any stray comments spraying out from her chatter.

She nodded. 'I work opposite Kaye – you know the facing desk; they're arranged in pairs – so we talk to each other more than we talk to anyone else. She would have told me if she had arranged a date or anything.' She began to swill the remains of her coffee around in the cup.

'Did you know what she had planned for Saturday?'

'Yes, it was her gran's birthday party and she was getting a lift there with her sister, I think.' Doreen still stared into the sludge at the bottom of her cup and Goodhew wished he had brought a stirrer.

'Mrs Kennedy?' He waited for her to look up before he continued. 'What about Friday night, then?'

'No, I'm sure she was staying in. I was reading the paper and she asked me what was on TV. I can't remember her saying there was anything she particularly fancied watching, though.' She looked down again into the thickening mix of coffee powder and synthetic milk. 'Is there a bin?'

'I'll take it.' He tipped the dregs from her cup into his own and stacked the two cups on the windowsill. 'OK, now how about the Saturday earlier in the day? Are you sure she wasn't planning to go anywhere?'

Doreen shook her head. 'She didn't mention anything, I'm sure.'

'Had she mentioned buying a birthday present for her grandmother?'

The woman hadn't quite finished shaking her head over the last question when she froze with a jolt. As the seed of memory germinated, she stared at Goodhew, appalled.

Goodhew recognized her bewilderment; Doreen's shock was clearly due to the fact that she hadn't remembered it earlier.

'Oh!' she whispered.

'Is it something about the birthday present, Mrs Kennedy?'

'Yes, yes.' She leant towards Goodhew excitedly. 'You see, it was Kaye's gran's eightieth birthday, and Kaye thought she'd like to prepare her a present that was a sort of hamper full of things that would have been common when her granny was young. It was a couple of weeks ago that she was talking about it, and last time we spoke she still didn't have everything. She was looking for some old grocery items, and I suggested she went to Woodbridge, because there's a museum there. Can't remember what it's called but it's full of old packaging, and there're all sorts of unusual things in the gift shop. There're a few antique shops close by, too.'

'And what makes you think she would have gone there last Saturday?'

'Well, I asked her if she had anything still to buy, and she said she would like to buy a 1920s newspaper and maybe some sweets in an old-fashioned tin. So she was going to have one last look around.'

'But what makes you think that she might have gone to Woodbridge?'

'Nothing,' Doreen conceded, 'except that I'd mentioned it to her, and she'd already tried everywhere she could think of around town. Where else would she try?'

'Wouldn't she have driven there, though?' Gary mused.

'I guess.'

'But her car was still at her flat when she was reported missing, and her family seem to think she would have taken it if she had wanted to travel further afield than Cambridge.'

But Doreen shook her head again adamantly. 'Like I say, if she wanted to buy things like that, where else could she try?'

Goodhew wrapped up the interview at that point, and escorted her to reception. He stood alongside her in the main doorway. 'Thank you very much, Mrs Kennedy. You've been very helpful.'

Of course there were plenty of other places. Most towns within a similar radius to Woodbridge had shops selling antiques and vintage bric-à-brac. But as far as he knew none of them had been suggested to Kaye.

Goodhew was listening politely to Doreen Kennedy's response, but at the same time picked out the sound of quick, regular footsteps descending the stairs and echoing along the corridor towards them. He glanced aside and saw Sue Gully.

She stopped as soon as she realized he'd spotted her, and held up a sheet of notepaper.

He turned back to Mrs Kennedy who continued chattering. 'Oh, I do hope she's found soon. She's such a lovely girl, so sensible.' She shook his hand. 'If I think of anything else, I'll call you straight away.'

'Thank you.' He took a step back from the entrance.

'I really hope you find her,' the woman called out, as the door between them began to close.

He nodded. 'So do I, Mrs Kennedy.'

'I mean I hope nothing terrible has happened.' That final sentence drifted back to him as he moved towards Gully.

But Goodhew already knew, from the agitated expression on Gully's face, that hope had just died for Kaye Whiting.

CHAPTER 15

WEDNESDAY, 30 MARCH 2011

'What's happened?' Goodhew demanded, as he reached her.

Gully shook her head. 'She's dead . . .' Her voice trailed away.

'I guessed.' He looked at the notepaper and saw she'd written *URGENT* across it in red biro. 'When did you find out?'

Gully cleared her throat. 'About ten minutes ago, Ipswich rang through with the details of a body, and it sounds like a definite match.' She produced a set of car keys from her pocket. 'Marks and Kincaide have already left. I'll tell you what I know on the way.'

Gully drove the patrol car like a dodgem, weaving it in and out of the traffic until they broke free along Newmarket Road towards the A14. She glared at the road ahead as she banged through the gears.

'So what *do* you know, then?' Gary asked, once they were clear.

'Her body was found south of Ipswich, at one of the lakes between the town and Alton Water. She was submerged, but I haven't heard much else. Marks and Kincaide went straight up there, and there's been no news yet on cause of death.'

'Who called it in?'

'A group of six people taking part in one of those management training courses. They'd been on an overnight exercise, like a treasure hunt I think. Found her this morning. They'd crossed the lake mid-evening yesterday, and moored the boat at a jetty about thirty feet along from where the body was found. They didn't see or hear anything then. But when they returned this morning, they walked around the lake and one of them spotted her in the water.'

'What time was this?'

'About nine-thirty this morning I think. They rang the local police immediately, of course, but it wasn't until a patrol from Ipswich had gone out that we were contacted, after they realized it was likely to be our girl.'

'And it's definite?'

'Too early for a formal ID, but everything's matched up so far: right age, right description, right jewellery.' Sue fell into tight-lipped silence and accelerated.

Goodhew watched the speedo nudge eighty. 'We all knew the odds weren't good, Sue.'

She didn't reply, merely shook her head, obviously not wanting to talk. She hooked a wisp of hair back over her ear, and fiddled with a hair clip for a moment or two.

'You knew this might happen, didn't you?' he persisted.

She stopped fiddling with her hair and instead raised her hand, gesturing for him to stop. 'I know, I know,' she floundered. The road split and she kept left, skirting around Ipswich while following the signs for Felixstowe. 'It caught me out,' she muttered in a hoarse whisper. 'We all knew she was probably dead, but I've been taking all those phone calls and saying positive things to the callers.'

Goodhew tugged a tissue from the box under the dashboard and passed it across to her.

'I feel so silly for crying, Gary, but I'd talked myself into believing she might still be all right.'

'Wishful thinking.' Goodhew glanced ahead, across the fields in the direction of flooded gravel quarries lying somewhere just beyond the near horizon. 'It catches everyone out sometimes.' He tried to think of a temporary change of subject, but anything not related to the case seemed inappropriate for now, so he settled for a minor diversion. 'Doreen Kennedy thinks Kaye may have gone shopping in Woodbridge last Saturday.'

'Well, this is the main route from Woodbridge to Cambridge, so she could have been abducted on the way there, or else on the way home.' They turned off the A14 at Wherstead. The first of the lakes became visible almost immediately.

'Which one?' Gary surveyed the expanses of water shimmering behind hibernating hedgerows.

'Number Thirty-Seven – pretty name for a lake, don't you think? But then it's not exactly the Lake District here, is it?' Gully grimaced. 'I'm glad I don't get the job of telling her mother.'

'I don't want it either.' Gary nodded ahead towards a cluster of parked vehicles and a handful of people wearing waxed jackets and anoraks. 'That must be it, over there. Looks like the press have arrived already.'

Two uniformed officers stood at the entrance, but Goodhew and Gully were waved through. They parked alongside the other vehicles standing halfway down the lakeside track. Goodhew got out and skirted the lake alone. He could see a few white-suited people milling around in the distance, and within a few moments he spotted DI Marks in discussion with the SOCO, while DC Kincaide stood nearby, as if in meditation, gazing down at a body bag.

Goodhew changed into a tyvek suit and joined his two male colleagues and the SOCO.

Marks nodded a greeting to Goodhew. 'Good, I'm glad you're here. No real doubt that this is the right girl. She was found nearly an hour and a half ago. We've just fished her out. All we know so far is what we can see. She's bound and gagged. No visible injuries, drowning's a possibility, but obviously we'll know more on that later.' He paused.

'When did she die?' Goodhew cut in.

'Strangely, initial thoughts are less than eighteen hours ago, and it appears that she was still alive here for quite some time.'

Gary's attention strayed as he rested his gaze on the anonymous bag shrouding her remains. The mystery caller's words stuck in his mind like dark bloodstains: *I think when you find her you'll realize that she was still alive at this point.*

Gary refocused his attention on Marks who was elaborating on the state of the body. 'She's a bit of a mess; her jeans are stained with her own urine and faeces, and there are several patches on her body that are extensively bloodstained. The initial inspection indicates chafing from the rope securing her, rather than any other injury.'

He turned and gestured just beyond the corpse, to where white-suited forensics officers were busy gathering evidence. 'There is a fairly level patch of grass just there that has been severely disturbed. Hopefully the imprints and stains we find there will provide us with some firm evidence.' Marks stopped abruptly and eyed first Goodhew and then Kincaide. 'What are your initial thoughts, Michael?'

Kincaide raised his voice to lecturing pitch. 'Well, if there has been no evidence of sexual assault, I'd definitely say that it was perpetrated by someone she knew – someone who had a motive for killing her but didn't actually have the bottle to finish her off. It certainly wasn't robbery either, she has a twenty-pound note in her pocket and a nice watch and a ring. If it started as rape, I don't know why she'd end up being abandoned. I can only think of two reasons for that. Either whoever did it thought she was going to get found or' – he paused for full effect – 'they knew she *wasn't* going to be found. That would be important, of course, if the killer was someone she knew.'

Marks' raised eyebrow twitched. 'Thanks for that, Michael. Rather a melodramatic way of putting it, but perfectly logical. Do you have anything to add, Gary?'

'Not exactly; that does make sense up to a point.'

'Good.' Kincaide nodded.

'But,' Goodhew emphasized, 'I have some leads of my own to follow up, like—'

Marks raised his hand to cut him off. 'Tell me about that later. First I want you to come with me to visit her parents.'

CHAPTER 16

WEDNESDAY, 30 MARCH 2011

It was almost 11 p.m. as Michael Kincaide twirled around and around on the black PVC office chair. He gripped one end of his pilfered Argos pen between his teeth and parted his lips like Clint Eastwood. He savoured the image of Goodhew being silenced and sent to talk to Kaye Whiting's parents.

Love it, he thought with glee.

The front door clicked shut and Kincaide stopped and frowned at his watch. He waited for his wife to speak first. Janice didn't bother though, and instead he could hear her removing her coat and shoes.

'I'm in the study,' he called out. He heard her give a tut. 'Working,' he added.

She entered the living room and scowled at him in his makeshift office crammed under their open-plan stairs. 'Good day?' she muttered with a perfunctory nod. No smile from her tonight, but so what?

'Absolutely spot on,' he said.

'So you've made progress, then?' she queried, sounding detached, and began flicking through the TV channels with the remote.

'Yep, we've got a body for a start,' he said, knowing that would draw her attention. She lowered the control and he continued, 'And that's a big step in the right direction.'

'She's dead?'

'Of course she's dead,' he replied in a *how dumb are you* tone. 'She was always going to be dead, Jan. But it's a big plus getting hold of the body.'

'How can you be so callous?' she demanded, then turned up the volume and slumped on to the sofa without waiting for a reply.

He turned his back on her and dragged and dropped a couple of text boxes on to the screen, connecting them with lines and forming the basis of an organization chart. 'I do well here and I could be headed for promotion.'

She pretended to ignore him but he knew she would be listening.

'Marks wants me to prepare stuff for the briefing tomorrow. He didn't ask Goodhew, so I'm the one in the good books this time.'

He began typing names into the Burrows family tree, waiting for curiosity to make her speak.

She flicked channels again.

'Look, Jan, I'm trying to work. I need to concentrate.'

Sudden anger flashed across her face. 'Tough. I've been working all day and I'm entitled to my evening, Michael.'

'Well, as long as your precious career is all right, that's fine, isn't it?'

'Here we go again,' she snapped and jumped to her feet. 'Fuck you, Michael.' She disappeared into the kitchen, and he followed her. She ignored him and began slamming cupboard doors.

He leant against the doorframe. 'You've got a nasty mouth on you, Jan.' He deliberately smirked, and she glared in return.

'Don't preach at me. You're the one who needs to pull his fucking socks up.' Her bag lay on its side next to the bread bin; she reached into it and withdrew a credit-card bill, then stepped towards him, thrusting it into his face. 'For example, what the fuck is this?'

'It's addressed to me,' he smiled bitterly, 'but what's that got to do with anything, right?'

'Clothes, CDs, stupid gadgets . . . anything but spend money on our home,' she spat. 'I need to see it 'cos I'll end up paying it, won't I?' He ignored the question. 'Won't I?' she repeated.

'I'm not getting into this, Jan.' He calmed his voice to an oily trickle. 'I'm working on the briefing notes for tomorrow, remember?'

'You're a wanker, Michael.'

The corners of his mouth curled downwards in distaste and he poked the Argos pen towards her. 'You don't appreciate other people's needs, that's your problem. You're not the only person on the fucking planet who's chasing promotion, you know. Staying late with the boss isn't the only way to get it.'

'Is that what you think?' She stepped across the room, closing in on him. 'Michael, what the hell is up with you?' she hissed. 'Every night you're in a stinking mood. I think you can't handle it because I earn more.'

He turned away and headed back to his PC. 'Just for once, Jan, I wish you could be a bit supportive.' He paused but couldn't resist throwing in a final snipe. 'It isn't in your nature, though, is it?' He dropped into the chair and tried to pick up his earlier train of thought.

His concentration failed, though. He knew he needed somewhere else to redirect his anger, so he chose his favourite target and mentally wandered back to an imaginary Goodhew. He pictured Goodhew looking stupid.

He hated that his colleague was Marks' golden boy. Well, fuck him.

And, as if she'd somehow read his mind, a quieter Jan then returned to the room. She still held the credit-card statement and passed it to him. 'Is this something about Gary?'

Kincaide shrugged. 'Not really.'

'He winds you up, though?'

Maybe it wouldn't hurt to tell her a little. 'He's getting extra money from somewhere. A lot of it. For a start that flat he lives in, right in the centre, he says he rents it, but it was transferred into his own name a few months back.'

'So he's bought it?'

'No mortgage and most of his salary's just accumulating in his bank account.'

'So, you've said before how he's got next to no social life.'

'Right, but he's managed to book himself and his girlfriend on to a trip to Hawaii.'

'I thought you said they'd split up?'

'That's not my point. No one ever saw them together in the first place, so maybe she didn't exist. But he has booked the trip and paid off his mortgage, and spends bugger all.'

Jan sighed. 'Inherited?'

Kincaide sighed more loudly. 'His grandfather died when he was a kid, but the rest of his family are all alive and well.'

'How do you know all of this, anyway?'

'Jan, if I delivered milk or painted walls for a living, I could understand that question.' He was starting to wonder why he'd thought he could ever get through to her but he added, 'No one starts acquiring money out of the blue like that.'

Jan crossed her arms and fixed him with her serious look. 'If he's bent, drop him in it, Michael.'

Kincaide curled his feet under his chair and slid his hands under his thighs. 'It's not that simple.' He puffed out his cheeks with a deflated sigh. 'Marks won't act.'

'Because he thinks Goodhew does no wrong?'

'No, I could live with that. Marks knows Gary's breaking the rules, and he just lets him get on with it. No one else would ever get away with it like Gary does. We all push the boundaries sometimes, but Marks is there to slap us back behind the line before we've even crossed it. But with Goodhew? No.'

'But you're saying Goodhew's done worse than that? You're saying this money's got a dodgy source.'

Kincaide shrugged, although he wanted to nod. 'Maybe, yes, but I don't know that I can prove it. And without proof . . .'

She raised her eyes towards the ceiling but in thought more than exasperation. When she spoke again her voice contained an unusually sympathetic tone. 'You're looking at this all wrong, Michael. Goodhew's money's not hurting you in any way. Until you can prove where it came from and have evidence that it's part of something illegal, forget about it. What's really getting to you is Marks and the unfairness of the situation.' She paused and Kincaide nodded. 'Marks cuts Goodhew slack because Goodhew's getting him results. So Goodhew's had a couple of *winning* performances? So what? He's been in the right place at the right time, that's all. Marks knows that Gary doesn't have your experience or skills. You just need to beat him to the prize . . .'

Kincaide sat quietly as she continued with such flattery for the next few minutes, as the sudden disappearance of the earlier tension between them had caught him off guard. He even ignored the patronizing twang that accompanied a couple of the comments, and held on to her two main points: Marks would pay attention to results, and the end would justify the means.

CHAPTER 17

WEDNESDAY, 30 MARCH 2011

The plan had been to meet Bryn for a beer and a game of pool, but by early evening Goodhew decided he was in the wrong frame of mind and he sent Bryn a text to cancel.

Goodhew retreated to the second-floor study and lit the fire. He had been lying on the floor, staring at the ceiling, for some time when the doorbell rang.

He found Bryn waiting on the doorstep, holding two packs of beer and a takeaway.

'You shouldn't cancel by text, Gary.'

'You do it all the time.'

'Yeah, but to girls not mates. Made me think you were going to vanish for another month. Can I come in or what?'

It wasn't that Goodhew consciously kept people out; more that the need for them to come in never really arose. He stepped back and let Bryn into the hallway. 'Second floor.'

Bryn walked up the stairs ahead of him and Goodhew followed, wondering whether his friend would start to ask questions about who lived in the rest of the building, and not wanting to either tell him the truth or lie.

But, in typical style, he showed no curiosity about the building or conducting any personal conversation whatsoever. For the first thirty minutes Bryn's attention was evenly split between the lager and the curry.

Eventually his interest moved away from food and found its way on to the Kaye Whiting case.

Now Bryn was perching on the edge of the armchair as he screwed up pages of scrap newspaper into balls and tossed them into the fire, aiming at the glowing orange gaps between the logs. The flames glowed through his latest bottle of Stella Artois. 'I couldn't tell someone that kind of news.'

Gary shrugged. 'Someone has to, don't they?' He drained his own bottle and slipped upstairs to the kitchen, returning with two fresh ones. 'I'll tell you what, though; it really is the worst thing.' He left Bryn's fresh bottle on the hearth and sank on to the settee.

'How did they take it?'

'Badly, of course.' Gary took a quick swig. 'Each time I've gone to visit Kaye's mother, she's been there all on her own and she's opened the front door before I've even reached it. Like she's standing behind it just waiting for me. This time I thought she was out. I went with Marks and he waited at the front while I looked round the back. Mrs Whiting opened the door just after I'd gone. She took one look at Marks and knew why we'd come.' The memory made him wince.

Bryn rolled two of the pages into a tube and nudged a stray sliver of kindling wood from the edge of the fire into its heart. 'Poor woman,' he murmured.

Gary thought about Margaret Whiting and the way she'd put her hands first over her ears and then over her face, as if trying to block everything out. Then she'd collapsed into one of her low-seated armchairs. She'd pressed herself against its big soft arm, rocking slightly and groaning, 'No, no, no,' until she'd accepted the news enough to ask them what had happened.

Bryn's newspaper ignited and he still held it like a torch as it blazed above the hearth, until the paper was burning within an inch of his fingers, then he dropped it into the grate. 'So what happens next?' he asked.

'Attempted arson charge?'

Bryn dropped back into the chair and continued to throw paper balls. 'It's addictive.'

Gary ignored him. 'Usual stuff, family and so on, plus finding this anonymous caller. Hopefully she'll ring back, now the body's been found.' Gary paused, about to take another swig, but lowered his bottle again. 'We'll see.'

'Listen to you, waiting for a girl to ring.' Bryn smirked, and carried on. 'Then again, she might be a psychopath, in which case you might as well see my sister!'

'I don't think so, Bryn, not unless you've got another one I haven't met.'

'Sorry, just Shelly.' Bryn's smile faded.

Goodhew's did too. 'Forget I talked about the case.'

'Of course. But who else have you got at the moment?'

'You really know how to cheer me up, don't you?'

They finished off another two bottles before either of them spoke again.

'Gary, are you in trouble?'

'No, why?' Gary frowned, puzzled.

'Money trouble? I mean, you can't afford this place on what you earn. I know it's none of my business but I've seen how much renting a flat round here costs. Debt creeps up on people. Is that why you don't go out much and can't buy yourself a car?'

'No, that's because I'm a boring bloke and I don't want a car.'

Bryn had been drinking at more than twice Gary's speed, but the sudden display of concern and puzzlement stood out through the inebriation. His friend's concern was touching, if misplaced.

'I inherited some money,' Gary explained. 'Enough to move in here.'

Bryn checked Goodhew's expression, looking for a sign that he was being wound up. 'That's not the sort of money problem I've ever had.'

'Exactly. That's why I haven't said anything.'

'Where did it come from, and how much are we talking about?'

'It doesn't matter.' Some old beliefs about money changing relationships began to surface, and Goodhew hoped he wasn't going to later regret telling Bryn anything.

Bryn drained his bottle. 'As my mother would say, you're a dark horse.' He checked his watch. 'I'd better go.'

Gary followed Bryn to the door and watched him sway past the rusted Volvo parked directly across the street.

'I'll pick it up tomorrow,' Bryn called back. 'Unless you want to buy it from me?' he added as an afterthought.

Gary laughed. 'Try the scrappy.'

He closed and bolted the front door and returned to the fire. The fading embers puffed and smoked, leaving shrivelled flakes of newspaper and crumbs of scorched wood in the grate. He slid the guard across the hearth, picked up eight empty bottles from around the room and took them up to drop them in the kitchen bin. He then returned to the second floor and sat on the edge of the coffee table, staring into the fire and sipping the remains of his second bottle.

He finally switched out the lamp. Small orange glows bloomed and faded in the fire's final throes. He finished his drink and closed the door on it, leaving it to die and turn to dust.

CHAPTER 18

THURSDAY, 31 MARCH 2011

Gary propped a five-by-three snapshot of Kaye Whiting up on one corner of his desk. She had been looking straight into the camera lens when it was taken, and now her eyes met his every time he glanced at the photograph. He stared back at her and wished she could communicate, but the forensic report would be the only way she'd be telling them anything now.

Sue Gully and PC Kelly Wilkes sat in the opposite corner of the room, with DC Young perched on the desk next to them. He was regaling them with an account of his house-to-house enquiries. Fragments of it reached Gary. 'And he answered the door with his flies undone . . .' Young continued, grinning broadly, 'and you won't believe the next bit . . .' He stopped abruptly as Kincaide thumped open the swing door and plonked a wedge of photocopying on to his own desk.

Kincaide brushed a couple of specks of hole-punch confetti from his suit. Gully meanwhile checked him over. The hems of his jacket and trousers were sharp, and the brogues unscuffed. 'New suit and new shoes? What's the special occasion, Michael?'

Gary smiled to himself. She was always on the ball, and Kincaide never quite rose to her chirpy banter.

Kincaide cleared his throat and straightened his protruding shirt cuff as he replied. 'As you know, we're having a briefing at oh-nine hundred hours. If you make your way along to the briefing room now, I'll be with you in a few minutes.'

They all watched the door swing shut after him, Goodhew and

Gully raised their eyebrows at one another, and Wilkes shrugged in an I-don't-know gesture. 'He's taking his new suit a bit seriously, isn't he?'

Kincaide was in fact taking the whole day very seriously and from the enquiry room ducked into the gents' toilet. He ran a dash of water into his palms and smoothed both sides of his black hair, studying himself in the mirror as he twisted his head from left to right.

Looking good.

He'd watched his wife do that whole self-motivation bit plenty of times before; it had always been easy to dismiss, but right now he was getting it. He stood straighter, shoulders back, chest puffed out.

Notes: check.

Thoughts collected: check.

Preparation: check.

Own it. He gave himself a parting nod, returned to the corridor and strode towards the briefing room.

Marks spotted him approaching and waited. 'Thanks for your notes, Michael.'

'No problem.' Kincaide beamed, and continued to smile as they made their entrance together.

Goodhew glanced at the photocopied notes in Marks' hand and the set that Kincaide held, and knew at once that they were a duplicate. He then squinted at one of the handwritten sections, and recognized Kincaide's writing.

He checked his watch and hoped they'd be finished by half-past.

Marks rapidly covered the key points. 'The priority is to trace Kaye Whiting's movements from leaving work on Friday 25th until as near to the time of her death as possible.' He nodded towards Kincaide, Gully, Clark, Charles and Young. 'I want you to re-interview most of those at the grandmother's party, plus work colleagues and the owners of the lake. Leave the victim's uncle, Andy Burrows, her brother Steve and her sister's boyfriend, Carl Watkins. Michael will be picking them up.'

Kincaide was staring at the sheet in front of him, but from where

Goodhew sat it looked as though one corner of Kincaide's mouth twitched slightly with self-satisfaction.

Marks continued, 'Gary, go and check out Doreen Kennedy's lead in Woodbridge. Uniform haven't come up with anything there yet, but it doesn't mean you won't.'

Packed off to Woodbridge.

At the end of the briefing, Goodhew slipped past the others to catch DI Marks in the corridor. He fell into step with him.

'Good morning, Gary. I thought you might want a word.'

'Really?'

'Being sent to Woodbridge, perhaps?'

'It's a beautiful place . . .'

'But hardly the hub of this investigation.' Marks wore a quizzical expression.

'I guess that was Kincaide's idea?'

Marks nodded. 'You and Kincaide need to start working in . . . *harmony*.' He paused and Goodhew wondered whether he'd had trouble not choking on the word. 'All right, that's a poetic way to phrase it, but the point is I'm busy, and not about to waste my time on any petty politics from you two.'

'No, that's fine. I mean Woodbridge is fine. It's about the phone calls actually.'

Marks held the notes in front of him and flicked through them as they walked.

Goodhew shook his head. 'There was no mention of the calls at all.'

'Yes, there is.' Marks halted and flicked through Kincaide's notes. 'Here's the list of leads that Clark and Charles are following up. I think they have it covered, don't you?'

Goodhew shook his head, again. 'No, I mean the anonymous phone calls. They're not highlighted here, and I'd like to look into them if no one else is.'

Marks shuffled Kincaide's notes again, and scanned several pages of his own. 'You saw Peter Walsh and there appeared to be nothing more to pursue. All the calls obviously need following up, but these ones already seem dead to me.'

Marks' eyes hardened and Goodhew knew how much he hated

having his time wasted. Nevertheless he had little in the way of explanation to offer his boss.

Goodhew shrugged. 'Gave Gully the creeps, sir.'

Marks narrowed his eyes and pursed his lips, as if he was sucking a lemon. 'That's pathetic, Gary.' He glanced at the final page again and then back at Goodhew. 'Go to Woodbridge first and follow up the calls when you get back.'

CHAPTER 19

THURSDAY, 31 MARCH 2011

Charcoal-scuffed clouds churned above the Woodbridge skyline, threatening to top up the puddles left by estuary storms. Goodhew skirted the heart of the town as he followed the brown tourist signs for the Station and the Tide Mill, and eventually caught sight of the railway line curling its way into a parallel path alongside the road.

Everything about the day was damp and dirty. On the far side of that single strip of track lay the boat yards. Masts poked into the sky from immobile sailboats, laid up for the winter, with their rain-stained tarpaulins and unwashed windows.

Even the station itself, with its traditional tearoom and its roof capped with a cheery white picket fringe, couldn't shake off the gloom. The centre of the building housed the tourist information office, its windows facing on to an apron of three car parks filled with commuters' cars. Goodhew found himself a parking space in the furthest corner.

He unfolded a two-page fax from the tourist office and checked the name on it. *Contact Teresa Armitage* was written in black across an indistinct picture of swans swimming beside a pleasure boat.

He locked the driver's door and skipped through an inch-deep puddle and on to the footpath. It was just a miserable day.

As Goodhew crossed the tarmac, the office door opened and a woman raised her hand in a curt salute.

'Teresa Armitage?' he called, but the wind had risen and snatched his words away. She held one hand in front of her lacquered black bob, to protect it from a rogue gust, and beckoned for him to move faster with the other. Her hand signals and indestructible hair reminded him of an eighties air hostess.

'Shut the door after you,' she called out and turned away from the entrance. She had already crossed the gift shop by the time Goodhew stepped inside. He followed her navy-blue-suited rear end into the first room beyond the open-plan tourism section, closing the door behind himself before he took the chair opposite her desk.

She ran through the usual preliminaries and introductions: it was an unstoppable and overused monologue full of theoretically promising words like *communication* and *responsiveness*. It probably took less than two minutes for her to reach the end, but long enough to make him prickle with irritation.

'Miss Armitage, as you know I'm here as part of our efforts to determine Kaye Whiting's last movements—'

'Yes, I know,' she interrupted. 'We had the police here all yesterday afternoon. I appreciate it's important, and we're quiet mid-week during term time so it doesn't matter so much, but I must stress how important it is that we don't have police visible everywhere at the weekend.'

'Well, I'm not guaranteeing that and, if we do have a positive sighting, we'll be questioning as many of the general public as we can this weekend.'

She slapped her manicured hand on to the table. 'Mr Goodhew, I'm the manager of this office. Woodbridge is a centre for tourism. I'm not trying to damage your investigation but I must try to protect the local economy. Asking you to keep a low profile is just me doing my job.' She rose to her feet and glowered down on him. 'Coffee?'

'No thanks.'

'It may be off season, Mr Goodhew, but every visitor still counts. It's vital that people know this is a safe place to visit.'

'Even if it isn't?' he asked wryly.

She glared at him then turned away to switch on the percolator in the corner of the room. Gary let her brew alongside her fresh coffee. The rich smell of freshly ground beans smothered the stale odour of Kaye's body that continued to linger in his nostrils.

'I need to speak to the staff in as many local shops and restaurants as possible, Miss Armitage. Would your CCTV pick up all the visitors passing through here?' Gary smoothed the first page of the fax on the desk and indicated the layout of the station area. 'Can you show me the position of all your cameras, internal and external?'

She stared at the sketch for a moment. 'We only have one, situated at the back of the shop, and it catches everyone from the doorway. Once inside there's a blind corner, around by the free leaflets, but that's picked up by the station CCTV, which has external cameras fixed in three locations. Between us we pick up most of the public areas.'

'What about other premises around the town?'

'Well, I do know that most of the shops in the town itself and towards the Tide Mill have their own systems. You're not planning on going through them all, surely?'

'Absolutely,' he replied.

'There'll be masses of footage,' she said.

'Yes,' he retorted, 'but that's just us doing our job.'

She stroked the patch of bare skin above her neckline and looked as though she was fighting the urge to make him come back later. She stepped up to her desk and rolled open a deep drawer designed to hold hanging files. She then reached down and pulled out a Sainsbury's carrier bag and handed it to Goodhew.

'Footage from here and from the station's cameras. The station manager had them ready, just in case. Tell me, is there any chance that she was killed here, actually in Woodbridge? I mean, it wouldn't be so bad if we could say she hadn't died here.'

Goodhew checked the contents of the bag, ignoring her. 'Is this all of them?' he asked.

He stepped back into the dank car park, and crossed the main road towards the town centre. Staggered terraces of quaint shops climbed the hill on both sides. He passed the junction with the Thoroughfare, where one narrow trading lane crossed another. On the corner of the junction stood a café, its round tables and scoop-back chairs waiting in groups inside full-length windows.

All but one were empty, and this one was occupied by a forty-something, frothy-haired woman with a cappuccino and a copy of the *Daily Mail*. She glanced up and Goodhew nodded through the window; but her gaze instantly dropped back to the front page of her newspaper.

Goodhew knew Kaye's picture appeared on page seven. He also knew that last Saturday had been cold here and he couldn't imagine that she'd lingered outside, with icy gusts slicing across the waterfront. If she'd been here in Woodbridge at all, she would have started promptly at the shops.

The Thoroughfare lay ahead of him, brimming with tourist treats: gift shops, clothes boutiques and antique-shop arcades.

The street, however, was almost deserted. Two women with pushchairs were in deep conversation outside the hair salon. Goodhew scanned the shopfronts: toys, sweets, pizza, coloured stones, and a shop called Fantasia selling gifts and cards.

He stepped in through its postcard-lined doorway, mobiles and light catchers twirling above him. He fished Kaye's photo from his pocket and introduced himself to Mrs Murley, the proprietor, who pointed out that he was the third policeman since yesterday.

Goodhew nodded patiently. 'I'm doing a follow-up.' He placed the picture on the counter. 'This is a different photo, for one thing.'

Mrs Murley lifted it by one edge and held it so it wouldn't reflect the light. She passed it back with equal patience. 'I don't think so. Lots of people come in here but, as I said earlier, I didn't serve her.'

Goodhew continued from shop to shop, noting the names of the Saturday staff and the names of all the staff that swore they hadn't served Kaye Whiting. His next stop would be the museum that Doreen Kennedy had mentioned.

He passed the coffee shop again on the way back down the hill. He turned the corner into the Thoroughfare and noticed the *Daily Mail* lying open on page five. The frothy-haired woman was at the counter, her hair now subdued by a burgundy-striped waitress hat, and she was serving the two mums and their three toddlers. He'd come back to her later.

The lady dispensing tickets at the museum smiled apologetically. 'I am very sorry, but I'm sure she wasn't here. She's the same age as my youngest granddaughter you see, and I've tried my hardest to remember. I was serving in the gift shop and I'm sure she didn't come in.' She handed the photo back. 'I'm afraid you may be on a wild-goose chase.'

Drizzle greeted Gary as he left the museum. Every building looked back at him blank and unhelpful, and only the coffee shop staff and the bag of video tapes seemed to stand between him and admitting that Kaye Whiting had never been in Woodbridge.

Of course he didn't know then that the waitress had poured herself another coffee, returned to her paper and flicked to page seven.

CHAPTER 20

THURSDAY, 31 MARCH 2011

She ripped the little hat from her head as she burst through the front door and galloped towards Goodhew with a mass of unruly curls and her ultra-small apron flapping in the wind. She seemed to know exactly who he was and bore down on him with remarkable speed.

He didn't catch what she said at first. She was definitely yelling specifically at him though and, as she reached him, she grabbed his elbow and spun him back to face the museum. 'She's the Bile Beans girl,' she repeated.

'Kaye Whiting?'

'That's right. I'm Zal, and I work in the coffee shop, and she was here last Saturday. I served her first after she'd bought the last Bile Beans advert from the museum opposite.'

Gary felt the hairs prickle across the back of his neck; he knew a good witness when he saw one. 'What are Bile Beans?' he asked.

'No idea, actually, but they're bound to be foul. She had the advert out on the table and I joked that we can't put those on the menu. Bile beans on toast? I don't think so.' She laughed then and it erupted as a dirty cackle. 'Has anyone else here recognized her so far?'

'No.'

'You poor sod, bet you've been from pillar to post. And you asked in the museum gift shop?'

Goodhew nodded. Zal propelled him through the door of the museum and slapped her broad hand on the counter to attract the attention of the woman behind the desk.

'Ruth, are you the dozy cow that just told this young man he was on a wild-goose chase?' She steamrollered on without waiting for a reply. 'Tell me this, then, if it wasn't that poor dead girl who had you shinning up a ladder for the last decent Bile Beans advert?'

Ruth blinked, bewildered for a second, but then she obviously remembered, and Goodhew knew he had found a second witness. 'Oh, God,' she breathed.

'Gawd? Is that the only bloody useful thing you can say? Is the display copy still up?'

'Yes. I'll take it down now and you can take it with you, Mr Goodhew.'

'Thanks. I'll get some details from Zal here and come back to you afterwards, is that OK?' he asked, as she whipped a tissue from her sleeve and sniffed into it.

Zal led him through the museum, past a display of soap powder and chocolate wrappers, to the gift shop. 'That's the item,' she announced, pointing to a reproduction tin advert showing a radiant blonde in a sunny-yellow, two-piece swimsuit, climbing up towards a diving board. 'Bile Beans, the medically tested laxative, that gives you health, grace and vitality,' she read. 'Charming, eh?'

Gary lifted the advert off its hook. 'Do you know whether she bought anything else in here?'

'Sure. She bought a book, *Good Housekeeping in the 1940s*, and a birthday card from the main shopping centre. You'd better check with Ruth, though, in case she can remember anything else.'

'I will, but I'd like to go back over to the café first.'

'Good idea. I left it locked up and Adolf Armitage will be on my back if I'm not careful.' Zal led the way back into the courtyard, 'You met her at the tourist centre, I suppose?'

'Teresa Armitage?' queried Goodhew.

'Goat dressed up as mutton.' Zal pulled the waitress hat out of her pocket. 'All 3-D make-up and up her own arse. Owns shares in the café, manages the tourism centre. She's not the real manager; just covering for a long-term sick leave, and now she's pissed off because he's almost better. The only way she'd have cracked a smile was if she'd had the chance to donate to his funeral flowers.' She yanked the hat over her hair and tucked up the worst of the stray strands. 'Right, what do you want to know?'

'Firstly, where did Kaye Whiting sit?'

Zal pointed over to the windows. 'She sat at the corner table, by the plants, and she kept looking out all the time.'

'OK, let's sit over there, then.' Goodhew sat down in Kaye's seat, with the windows on his right and the doorway straight ahead. 'What did she order?'

'Hot chocolate. We do it in glasses in holders, floating with fresh cream. I think she had two.'

'At the same time?' asked Goodhew sharply.

'No, one after the other. Both for her, but she was thin enough to take it. Unlike some of us.' She grabbed the excess flab on her stomach and wobbled it. 'When diet food comes out of a packet as fast as a Mars Bar, that's when I'll lose weight.'

'And how did she seem?' Goodhew asked.

Zal paused and gazed into thin air, as if remembering. 'Fine.'

'Fine? Not at all ill at ease?'

Zal shook her head; again she was quite sure. 'You don't drink hot chocolate if you're not in the mood to indulge yourself, do you? But I think she was waiting for someone.'

Gary's gaze locked into hers. 'Who?'

Zal smiled apologetically. 'I didn't see anyone, I'm afraid. I asked her if she wanted anything else, and she said she wouldn't have time, but then she sat here another twenty minutes. Well, I *think* she was waiting for someone, and that someone was bloody late picking her up.' She pointed back to the counter. 'I was over there the next time I noticed her, but I think she spotted whoever it was, because she suddenly gathered up her bags and called thanks, and said she wasn't stranded after all, or something like that, and she left.'

'And when exactly did she show you what she'd bought?' he asked.

'Between hot chocolates. She got chatting when I cleared the next table, so I stopped with her for a couple of minutes. Adolf would say that's idleness, but I think it's part of customer care, don't you?'

Gary nodded. 'And is there anything else at all that you can remember?'

The woman shook her head.

Gary was now keen to leave for Cambridge but he still had a statement to take from Ruth Collette at the museum. He fought the desire to rush and scanned his notes in case any other questions jumped out at him. Nothing did, but he needed to be thorough, so he asked, 'Do you mind if we run through it one more time?'

'No problem, as long as it's over some hot chocolate.'

CHAPTER 21

THURSDAY, 31 MARCH 2011

Gary dumped the carrier bag of videotapes on to the passenger seat and pulled a reporter's notepad from the glovebox. The front sheet was covered by a spider's web of words and phrases that he'd jotted randomly across the sheet. He'd circled some of the words and then linked some of these with lines and arrows.

Ruth Collette's statement had added nothing to Zal's but between them the two women had provided a key piece of information.

In an empty corner of the page he wrote 'Woodbridge' and ran an arrow from the heading 'Last Sighting' to point at it directly. He doubted the victim had made it back to Cambridge, because somehow, between a happy afternoon in Woodbridge and home, she'd been abducted and abandoned.

After a few minutes he paused, resting his gaze on the water. He couldn't imagine how she would have been abducted by anyone other than the person she'd been waiting for in the café. Had she unwittingly stepped into the car with the killer's plans already made, or had she fallen out with her driver – or companions – somewhere along the journey home?

If the driver or any fellow passengers weren't connected to the killer, why hadn't they come forward? Perhaps he or they were protecting someone else.

Goodhew next wrote 'Who gave Kaye a lift?' and went over the question mark several times until it made a heavy black indentation on the page. He stared alternately at the words 'caller' and 'killer'. Were they one and the same?

Gary quickly ran through some possibilities. If the person or persons who had given her a lift had killed her, then it was almost certainly someone she knew.

What if the anonymous caller had given Kaye a lift? Perhaps Kaye was seeing the mystery caller's husband or boyfriend, and perhaps the other woman had found out. But then Kaye wouldn't have gone shopping with her; she would have gone with her lover instead. And was he now protecting his spouse? No, that theory didn't quite work, but . . .

Gary tapped the paper impatiently with his fingers as if he was trying to nudge the correct answer on to the sheet.

But what if Kaye was stealing this man away from a friend?

What if Kaye thought her friend didn't know? She would be happy to take a lift from her, then.

Was the mystery caller this same friend? If so, how did Peter Walsh fit in? Was he the cheating boyfriend?

Had the caller made the abduction just to scare Kaye . . . or to scare Peter? Perhaps she hadn't intended Kaye to die.

Too many permutations. He buckled up his seatbelt and started the engine. He drew one final line leading from the heading 'Woodbridge' out to a new query: 'Where are the presents?' He then dumped his notes on the passenger seat.

He headed out of the town on the same road that he'd come in on. The breeze from his slightly open window caused the top sheet of his pad to quiver slightly, then ripple and lift to reveal the blank second page. He stopped at the next roundabout and reached across to toss it back into the glovebox. The last words he'd written suddenly jumped out at him from the page.

'Oh shit,' he groaned and swung the car back towards Woodbridge.

Zal Pearson beamed widely when she spotted him crossing the café floor. 'Didn't expect to see you back so soon. Fancy another hot chocolate already?'

Goodhew shook his head. 'I forgot to ask you. Could you show me which birthday card she bought?'

Zal wiped her hands on a tea towel and removed her apron. 'I don't know if I'd actually recognize it, but we can have a go. I think it was in a Fantasia bag.'

She locked the café for a second time, and they crossed the Thoroughfare and headed into the crammed gift shop. Zal scanned the rows of cards, then picked out a handmade one with rough-cut paper shapes mounted on a square of ribbon. She ran her fingers across it thoughtfully; something about its texture seemed familiar, but it wasn't the one. She dropped it back into its pigeonhole. 'I don't know,' she groaned. 'I only saw it for a moment.'

Gary was standing beside an upright display stand. He spun it through one hundred and eighty degrees. 'How about these?'

Zal shrugged. 'You don't want much, do you?' she began, but then her eye fell on the bottom row of cards, each adorned with slivers of paper curled into leaves and petals. 'Quilling – that's it!' She grabbed a handful of about fifteen cards and flicked through them; each was slightly different. 'They're all of them one-offs, but I'd say this is the closest.'

She passed it to Gary. He frowned as he read the message on the front. 'Except it said "Happy Birthday, Grandmother", I suppose?'

He passed it back and she held it on top of the others, concentration wrinkling her forehead. Finally she flicked through the pile again and pulled out a second card. She passed them both back to Gary. 'I remember now, she bought two. A *Happy Birthday, Grandma* card similar to that one, and definitely this one too.'

Gary bought the two cards, thanked her, and headed back towards Cambridge. He cut easily through the miles, losing them under the wheels. Once in a while he glanced at the card on the passenger seat. It was pink with a raised spray of fuchsia and cream paper flowers beneath the words *Happy Birthday, Mother*.

CHAPTER 22

THURSDAY, 31 MARCH 2011

The junction at the top of Station Road in Cambridge is almost triangular. The war memorial stands in the middle, and anyone overtaken by the desire to admire it or watch the endless stream of traffic, or even study the mundane elevations of the nearby offices, would have the choice of standing in a doorway or sitting at a café window or making the short walk to the Flying Pig and sitting at one of its pavement benches.

The girl with the scarred wrists sat between an American tourist and a traveller with his collie dog.

She gazed down between her thighs and through the slats of the wooden bench to the concrete below. The heels of her scuffed shoes shook as the balls of her feet reacted to uncontrollable nerves.

She found a penny that had landed in a bare patch between pink and taupe splodges of dried-out chewing gum. *See a penny, pick it up, and all the day you'll have good luck.*

She didn't pick it up though, just wondered whether she should.

I can't be bothered, she decided, and pushed her knee down until the shaking stopped. She gulped a few deep breaths before climbing to her feet. The lack of oxygen made her feel queasy and she panted a little as she pushed open the door and entered the bar, waiting at the counter.

The landlady glanced at her and smiled, as she finished pulling a pint for the man in front, then pulled a stubby pencil from her pocket and jotted his food order on to a small pad. And the whole time she continued to smile, almost to herself as if there was a joke in her head.

Who does she think she is? the girl wondered.

She pretended she hadn't noticed and turned away. Her gaze slipped on to the front page of a *Cambridge News* lying on the closest table. She tore her gaze away again; she didn't want to see that face any more either.

She studied the customers, and finally the landlady too. No one looked at her now. *They'd be staring at me if I really looked like her.*

She checked her watch: 11.55.

Above the heads of the customers and through the plate-glass windows she could see the main entrance of Dunwold Insurance. 'Peter,' she whispered, and her heart surged as she felt his name on her lips. He was nowhere to be seen, but he'd come out soon. She needed to be at her seat by the window, ready for what she called *her next fix*, the moment that would satisfy her addiction to him for another day.

With a start she realized that the landlady was now waiting for her. She'd already put an empty cup and saucer ready, and was killing more time in sharpening her pencil over the bin. 'Drink?'

'Coffee.' She scowled. The woman was like a bloody Cheshire Cat. She handed over the correct money and tried not to ask herself if and why she was being laughed at. Over-analysis was bad; she knew that, and had been taught to remember it.

She settled in her usual seat and waited.

Come on, Peter, where are you?

She looked down and across the square outside. She scanned the groups of pedestrians, looking for those familiar bobbing heads, but there was no sign of either Peter or Paulette.

She began an argument with herself: *I couldn't have missed him, could I?* The butterflies flew faster in her stomach and she shivered again. *Why can't I forget him and get on with my life?* she wondered.

Because you're obsessed by him, you stupid girl. Get some help. It's gone on too long.

I tried, didn't I? Anyway, who would understand? She continued to argue with herself and stared down at the table top as ugly tears threatened to screw up her face. She pinched the fleshy skin next to the knuckle on her index finger and watched it redden around the twin dents left by her nails.

You must make it stop. You can't spend the rest of your life like this.

I won't, she promised and squeezed her eyes tight shut, pressing her face into her clasped hands. A tear still escaped and ran on to her thumb. *I'll stop him. Everyone will see it was him that's mad and not me. And then he'll be gone and I'll be OK again.*

You'll never be OK again. She shook her head, and continued to shake it as she replied to herself.

Don't say that. She rocked gently in her seat until she felt calmer. *I'll phone again. I'll do it now.*

As she left the Flying Pig, she immediately noticed how busy the streets had become, the pavements in particular. She hurried towards the city centre, watching for a safe route through the crowd. She felt as though she was suffering from tunnel vision. Around the periphery a kind of nothingness, and in the middle, in over-sharp, over-bright detail, face after face. She stumbled on, watching for Peter. Looking into strangers' faces. Trying to find someone staring back into her own.

And what if someone recognizes you? she taunted herself. *You won't have the guts to grab them and demand to know what they're staring at, will you?*

They'd think I was crazy. She carried on watching, though, but nobody even glanced at her. *I'm the only one who thinks I look like Kaye Whiting, aren't I?*

Perhaps you don't at all. It could all be a terrible mistake, then you'll pay.

I know. I know. She thought of the sleeping pills she'd been taking since she'd first seen Kaye's picture in the paper.

She decided to use one of the call boxes in the row beside the newsagent's. There were eight of them, and plenty of people around, so she hoped no one would notice her.

She picked up the receiver, began to tap out the numbers and, when the call connected, she recognized the same female voice from the last time.

'I rang before with some information about Kaye Whiting's disappearance.'

'Can I have your name please, caller?' asked the police woman.

'No, listen. I rang on Tuesday. I told you she was going to die if you didn't stop Peter Walsh. Well, you didn't and now she's dead.'

'What else can you tell us?'

'Nothing.'

'Do you have any evidence?'

She knew that the officer was trying to keep her talking. 'No. I don't have anything for you. I'm sorry.' She hung up then and pushed her way out of the call box, forgetting to hold the door open for the pensioner waiting outside.

She felt no better. The emptiness she had carried for three years swelled to form a vacuum. She stumbled into a jog and ran towards her office, with one hand closed tightly around the landlady's pencil sharpener.

She would unscrew its sharp little blade, if she had to.

Anything to stop the pain.

CHAPTER 23

THURSDAY, 31 MARCH 2011

Goodhew and Gully sat facing one another across the table. Their hands, resting on the polished surface, were almost touching.

A lock of hair fell forward from behind her ear; she tucked it back again and ran a self-conscious hand across the crown of her head. He didn't look up and her cheeks flushed as she tried to hide her desire to flirt with him.

But, working or not, she couldn't overlook the fact that they were alone and she was enjoying his complete attention. Well, sort of. She waited for him to speak. 'Is there anything I can do for you, Gary?' she asked, and immediately cringed at the accidental double entendre. *Silly cow*.

His gaze met hers for a moment. 'You could get yourself into trouble with questions like that, Sue.' He smiled, but his tone was too matter-of-fact to be flirtatious and she knew he hadn't even noticed her deepening blush.

'You know what I mean,' she retorted, and banished the impulse to find out how it would feel to squeeze his hand. This was one of the only times in her life that she'd found her constant blushing to be a blessing.

Having a crush on your rescuer; Gully knew there had to be a medical name for it, just like she knew that *idiopathic craniofacial erythema* was the correct term for her involuntary blushing. She'd been searching for the phrase on every diagnose-it-yourself website she could find, and had terms like *transference*, *Inverse Stockholm Syndrome* and the worryingly titled *Erotomania* thrown up as possibles. All were incorrect.

Besides, putting a name to it wasn't the same as finding a cure, and she guessed the slightly juvenile reaction she felt every time Goodhew was somewhere within one hundred paces would eventually fade of its own accord. And the sooner the better.

Gary's hand was almost touching hers because they'd been highlighting sections of the transcription of the first and latest phone calls.

'We need to find her, Sue. This call implies that she knew Kaye was still alive on Tuesday.'

'And she was.'

'For most of the day, yes. We need to know how she knew that. I need another visit to Kaye's family, but then I'm going to see Peter Walsh again.'

'Do you think he even knows who she is?' she asked.

Gary shrugged and stared at her directly. Or possibly through her, she realized with disappointment.

'He's a bit cocky, almost like he wasn't surprised to see me turn up. That's not an indication of anything, of course, since too much indignant outrage can be just as suspicious, but I did have a feeling that he might know who the anonymous caller could be.'

'What if she's just some crank that sees him regularly at work, or in the street, and is just fixated with him? He might not actually know her, then.'

'We'll see.' Gary ran his fingers along one highlighted line in the first transcript. 'She talks of "killings", and that needs some more research. Can you start looking for similar cases while I'm with Walsh?'

Gully strummed her fingers on the desk. 'What about Marks? Is he OK with this approach?' she asked.

'Kincaide's hot on the family or friends theory, and I guess it's still the most likely,' he replied, 'but Marks was fine about us following up the phone call, and that's all we're doing, isn't it?'

'Of course it is, Gary.' She raised her eyebrows. 'But you're not talking about a mere five minutes tapping parameters into a terminal, you know. Have you any idea what you actually want me to look for?'

'Better make it quite broad to start with. Say women aged between fifteen and forty, bound and gagged . . .'

'Sexual assault?'

He shook his head. 'No.'

'Cause of death, drowning?'

'Yes.' He paused and flicked through the pages on the desk. 'Or maybe exposure or starvation,' he added.

'Why?'

'We don't know that drowning was the intended cause of death.'

'We don't even know that she was supposed to die.'

'If the killer had no plans to return and reckoned she wouldn't be found soon enough, then it's premeditated murder, isn't it?'

Gully grimaced. 'I've never considered murder by the elements before.' She realized the search could prove vast. 'What about geographical area?'

'Anywhere in the UK, I suppose.' They both reread the list. 'Over the last ten years?' he added. 'I don't know, but I'm just trying to think of something to narrow it down without losing what we most need. It's not very specific.'

'Don't worry, I'll see what I can come up with,' she said, with little enthusiasm.

'Sure?' Gary began gathering the notes. 'Grab me if it's not working.'

'No problem,' she said and blushed again.

'And if you get bored we can widen the criteria,' he added.

She shook her head in disbelief. 'I hope you're being sarcastic!'

He laughed. 'Yeah, just kidding.'

'As it is, I'll be at it all night.'

'Lucky you!'

She followed him as far as the water-cooler, where she filled a paper cup and held it against her cheek until the hotness subsided.

CHAPTER 24

FRIDAY, 1 APRIL 2011

Carl Watkins' uniform hung loose on his bony shoulders. Kincaide wondered how strong he was.

'How well did you know Kaye Whiting?' he asked him.

'Quite well, I guess.'

'She was your girlfriend's sister?'

'Yeah. I met her when I was out with a mate. She was with Michelle and we all had a laugh.'

'Who were Kaye's closest friends, do you think?'

'There's a girl, Debbie – friend from school I think. And Michelle, of course. She's had mates but no one else she was particulary close to.'

'What about boyfriends?'

'No.'

'No?'

Carl didn't look him straight in the eye as he replied, but swivelled his head to look down at his hands. He studied the rough ends of his nails for a moment. 'She wasn't easy to get close to.'

'Did you ever try, Carl?'

Carl tilted his head up to stare at Kincaide. 'I saw her only as a friend. I wasn't interested in her in any other way. Remember, I go out with her sister.'

'Ah yes. And congratulations on your engagement.'

'Yeah, thanks.'

'Was Kaye pleased?'

'She never knew. We only announced it on Saturday, at her grandmother's party. You know, before we knew about Kaye.'

'I see. And what were you doing before the party?'

Carl glared at him then. His top lip curled slightly, forming the beginning of a scowl. He'd clearly had enough by now and spat out the words defiantly. 'I worked in the morning, drove the van to Bedford and back – had sex all afternoon. With Michelle, of course.'

'And the night before?'

'Stayed in, watched TV.'

'Is that what you usually do on Friday nights?'

'Sometimes.'

Carl stood up and faced Kincaide direct. 'Nothing personal but I've got a problem with what I think you're implying.'

Kincaide stood up and held his hand out to him. 'You're right, Mr Watkins, it is nothing personal. Thank you.'

Kincaide was still smiling as he parked in front of Andy Burrows' flat. He'd given Carl Watkins something to think about. Now for Andrew Burrows.

Since the first brief, when he'd been ridiculed for picking Burrows as a suspect, he'd liked the idea of proving him guilty.

Andy Burrows was the antithesis of Carl. Middle-aged, drawn, tired, there was no fight in him as he opened the door, seeming to sag inside his crumpled clothes.

Kincaide kept all expression from his face and narrowed his eyes to disinterested slits designed to out-psych Andy Burrows from the first. Burrows tried to smile as he spoke, but the attempt was faint and watery. 'Come in. Do you want a drink?'

'No thanks.' Coffee would have been very welcome but Kincaide was now too busy. On entering the living room, Kincaide wondered whether tea or coffee had been the drink in question. Two bottles of Jack Daniel's sat beside the TV, and Burrows scooped a tumbler into his hand and drained it.

'Mr Burrows, I need to gather as much background information on your niece Kaye as possible. I know this is difficult so soon after her death, but I'd appreciate any help you can offer us.'

Burrows nodded with a small twitch of his head. The corners of his mouth flickered and, for a horrible moment, Kincaide thought he was going to cry. The thought of a forty-five-year-old man blubbering repulsed him slightly.

Burrows' reply was hushed: 'Of course I'll try to help.' He took a deep breath and the crisis passed.

Kincaide started with the easy question. 'When did you last see Kaye?' Burrows stared back with such vacancy that Kincaide wasn't sure if he'd taken it in at all. So he prodded gently, 'Can you remember the last time you saw your niece?'

Andy nodded. 'Last week, at my mother's house.'

'Did you talk to her about her plans for last weekend?'

'We all had the same plan. Mother's party.'

'Why didn't you yourself go?'

'Not my thing.' Burrows poured some more Jack Daniel's into his empty glass.

'But you just said you were planning to?'

'I might have felt like it on the night itself – but I didn't, so I stayed at home.'

'And?'

'And what?'

'And what did you do at home?'

'Drank and slept, what do you think? I've hardly got much company here, have I?'

'And Kaye, did she have company?'

'Like a boyfriend? No, I don't think so. Not recently and not anyone serious that I know of. She was a lovely girl – I thought the world of her, really I did.' For the first time Burrows placed the tumbler on the table and slid it away with his fingertips. Kincaide was sure this was a gesture that preceded an important statement and he leant forward a little, silently encouraging Burrows to speak, eager for his confidence.

Andy Burrows struggled to find his voice, gulping back the lump in his throat. Finally, he spoke. 'Did she suffer much?' he whispered and simultaneously tears ran down both cheeks. 'Did she?' he gasped.

Kincaide glowered at him in disgust. Burrows knew enough about the case to also know the answer. The only reason for asking was to make Kincaide couch the truth in white lies; to give Burrows a cosy fantasy of painless death to hang on to, and in the process burden Kincaide with guilt. Contempt made his nostrils flare and he clenched and unclenched his teeth several times before replying.

'Considerably, I'd say, Mr Burrows,' he hissed.

Kincaide had never allowed himself to become emotionally embroiled with victims, their relatives or the dismal array of mitigating circumstances that seemed to have put many wrongdoers and do-gooders on the same team. Kincaide was capable of feeling sympathy but it was a route he had chosen not to follow; he wasn't aiming for popular, just efficient, and he knew such emotional impenetrability would ultimately save him from the trials of trauma counselling.

Kincaide pulled up in front of Mike and Margaret Whiting's house. He checked his expression in the mirror, setting his features in a hard man's glare. Leaving Kaye's brother Steven until last was deliberate; he wanted to visit when he knew the man would be home alone.

He was going to make the lazy bastard squirm. Give him the treatment that would keep him awake and sweating in the night; make him get off his fat backside and do something with his pathetic life.

Kincaide was going to do him one hell of a favour.

He checked his hair and nodded at himself before pushing the rear-view mirror straight.

Kincaide hated being messed around, he hated having the truth hidden and he wasn't going to let any of them get away with it. He rang the bell and squared up to the front door, ready for the squealing little runt to open it. *Mess me around and I'll knock your fucking head off.* Verbally, of course.

Kincaide was therefore very unhappy when it was Margaret Whiting who invited him inside.

Steve sat in one armchair and Margaret seated herself in the other. Kincaide was left with the settee, a pink frilly affair. He was not going to look tough sitting on a pile of chintz padding. He let out an angry snort. It was all very wrong: Steve's chair was in front of the window so the bright daylight was shining straight into Kincaide's eyes.

What followed was forty-five minutes of 'dunno' and 's'pose so', interspersed with regular interjections from his mother.

Apparently the kid hadn't been particularly close to his sister, and apparently he'd been at home all Friday and Saturday, until he went to celebrate his grandmother's birthday with his parents.

And apparently he wasn't particularly interested in girls at present. So, very apparently, Kincaide wasn't the lucky recipient of the whole truth.

He decided to leave it. For now.

Kincaide stayed long enough to drink his coffee. He accepted his cup without a smile or a word of thanks. Margaret and Steven Whiting watched him silently, and that suited him. He wanted them to understand that the investigation was well under way, and to feel control and confidence oozing from him.

He hoped this would give Margaret genuine comfort, and provide quite the opposite for her son.

He knew it was a fact that in eight out of ten murders the victim knows the killer. He had studied books on domestic crime and had therefore selected the three most likely suspects, based on average statistics. Statistics that included age, marital status and career type.

And, now that they had been re-interviewed by him, he remained confident that one of these would emerge as the clear favourite. But which one?

Carl Watkins, sharp-featured, smart-mouthed and arrogant?

Andy Burrows, flaky, alcoholic and probably frustrated?

Or Steven Whiting, selfish and petulant and jealous?

Kincaide wasn't interested in the sensibilities of the innocent two: all three were sufficiently flawed that he was sure a brush with the law would ultimately do them good.

Bunch of shits, he decided as he thought of them.

He drained his coffee and passed the empty cup to Margaret Whiting. 'Thank you very much.' He smiled softly, then turned to Steven Whiting with only a slight modification to his expression. 'We'll be in touch,' he said.

CHAPTER 25

FRIDAY, 1 APRIL 2011

Margaret Whiting opened the door and let Goodhew make his own way in.

He settled on the chintz settee and she sank into the opposite chair.

He left a couple of seconds of silence before speaking. 'How are you today, Mrs Whiting?'

'Good, bad,' she shrugged, 'can't say. The doctor's packed me full of drugs, sedatives or antidepressants, don't know actually. And it's all passing me by. Do you know that feeling?'

'Like you're watching someone else's life?'

'Yes, that's it.' The end of a tissue protruded from her sleeve and she pulled it out, ready. 'Just in case I get a burst of reality.' She attempted to smile and her glassy eyes welled with tears that subsided. 'Someone's been around already – for Steve, actually.'

'Something's just come up and I decided to come straight here. It's a lead,' he added quickly, in case she expected an arrest so soon. 'It appears that Kaye was shopping in Woodbridge last Saturday. We have a witness who also thinks that she was waiting for a lift from there, either to head home or to somewhere else.'

Margaret gazed at him, misty-eyed. 'I don't understand.'

'What?'

'I don't understand why that's important.'

The sun streamed in through the window, so it might have been just the two of them in the whole world. 'Mrs Whiting, it's important to us that we pinpoint her last known movements.'

'I know that, but it happened on Tuesday, didn't it?'

She couldn't say 'died' – not yet, maybe never.

'She wasn't there all that time since, was she?' Her expression was open wide, as if ready to be slapped.

Goodhew wondered why no one had yet told her; why she was two steps or more behind speculation in the press. The left hand not knowing what the right was doing, most likely. 'I'm sorry, but we are working on that theory.'

Margaret stared down at her tissue and turned it over several times before she looked back up at Gary. 'It's better to know what's going on. I lie awake thinking about all the possibilities.' She shuddered, then continued, 'When on Saturday?'

'Mid-afternoon, just before three. To your knowledge has Kaye ever visited Woodbridge in the past, Mrs Whiting?'

'I'm sorry, but I wouldn't really have any idea. I don't remember hearing the place mentioned before, but you can't keep up with everything they do once they've left home.'

'And do you know who might have given her a lift from there?'

Margaret shook her head slowly. 'It feels neglectful of me to know so little, but you never expect you'll need to answer all of these questions.'

The back door clicked open and Goodhew heard voices in the kitchen. He looked questioningly at Margaret.

'Andy and my mum,' she answered.

Edna shuffled into the room, leaning heavily on her cane. Her rheumy gaze flickered beneath thin, vellum-like skin. She had aged since he'd met her, and she kept saying, 'I don't understand'.

Gary explained the Woodbridge sighting to Andy Burrows, too. 'Do you know whether she'd ever visited that area in the past, Mr Burrows?'

Andy shook his head. 'No, she never mentioned it to me, if she did.'

'We have some CCTV footage to check, but at the moment we have no idea who offered her a lift. Do either of you have any suggestions?'

Andy watched his mother shake her head, then began to shake his too.

Gary looked at the three of them, all fragile and brittle and faded. Like a plastic set of the three wise monkeys. Perhaps they're not 'all wise'. He scribbled down his mobile number on a slip of paper, and handed it to Andy before he left. 'Call me if you think of anything – or if there's anything you would like to ask me.'

Margaret took him to the door. 'Thank you, Mr Goodhew.'

'I'll be in touch, Mrs Whiting.' He shook her cold hand. 'Oh, just for our records, what's your date of birth?'

'It's 22 December 1961.'

As soon as he reached his car, he wrote the date on his notepad. He let scraps of intuition and facts guide him, and he now knew that the *Happy Birthday, Mother* card hadn't been bought for Margaret Whiting.

CHAPTER 26

FRIDAY, 1 APRIL 2011

The day was drawing to a close. A bank of grimy cloud had swamped the earlier sunshine and the light was beginning to fade amid a dull blanket of constant rain.

A man parked his car in Hanley Road and banged on Peter Walsh's door.

He didn't care about the weather. His hair and skin glistened in the wet, and when the door didn't open he scanned the street for his quarry.

From the lobby of the studio flats she watched him, and reached into her pocket to jiggle the remnants of the pub landlady's pencil sharpener with restless fingers. From her vantage point she studied him with interest, and in turn asked herself, '*Who is he?*'

He was tall and slim and, although it wasn't possible to see his features clearly, she could pick out an angularity to the line of his jaw and nose, and an intensity of demeanour.

She took her mobile from her pocket and rang Peter's number. She watched the stranger listen to the phone ringing. He then opened the letter box to hear the answerphone message.

She pressed the *end* button as soon as she heard Peter's voice start up. Funny how she could cope with hearing him on his answerphone, but then she often rang it if she needed to know where he was. Her mobile was permanently set to 'number withheld' and she'd already used it to ring Peter's office. He hadn't answered his phone, so she'd hung up.

Clearly this stranger didn't know how to find him either. Perhaps he hadn't been at work today.

She watched the young man through the pouring rain. He'd moved away from the front door and stood, straight-backed and patient, watching the entrance to the road. The weather didn't seem to affect him.

She couldn't see him clearly enough; she wanted to look at his face.

Peter's not home, she told herself as she slipped into another inner conversation.

What if he comes back? You can't just walk straight past his house. You wouldn't dare.

But she suddenly realized that she could cut through an alley situated three houses beyond Peter's, then back into the adjoining street where she had parked. She could easily walk straight towards the stranger, on past him, and disappear.

Yes, I dare.

Gary thought nothing of the woman walking towards him. At least nothing suspicious.

He noticed her rain-sodden clothes, and that she was feeling cold by the way she clutched the front of her jacket. Otherwise she was just a passer-by in a hurry. She strode towards him, staring at the pavement in front of her, avoiding the uneven paving slabs, though once or twice she glanced towards him and beyond.

He glanced towards the main road again. Still no sign of Peter Walsh. Number 28 was empty, and for sale. Gary decided to call at number 24, just in case they could shed light on Walsh's whereabouts.

He stepped away from number 26 just as the woman passed number 24. He paused before stepping from Pete's garden path, allowing her time to pass by. She glanced up at him, and her blue eyes took a moment to scan his face before she directed them back down at the pavement.

Her hair was soaked, rainwater running from her fringe and trickling down her nose and cheeks. He gave a spontaneous smile. 'Nice weather, eh?'

She gasped and her eyes widened slightly as they darted up to meet his. Her lips, red and wet from the cold rain, parted as if to speak, but she merely stared at him and walked on by.

Goodhew knocked at number 24. Instinct made him turn his head towards her, and he caught the last second of her gaze as she stared at him over her shoulder. Biting her bottom lip, she turned away quickly, breaking eye contact. She headed down a side alley and hurried out of sight.

Gary stepped back from the doorway, torn by an unexpected urge to run after her. What had just passed between them? A shiver rippled down his spine.

He hurried to the near end of the alley, but already she'd vanished. Above the sloshing of traffic in the distance and the dripping of gutterings, he thought he caught the sound of her running.

Pete's neighbour's front door suddenly opened and a blonde in a BHS uniform called across to him, 'Can I help you, mate?'

Kaye Whiting obviously had to come first. 'Do you know if Mr Walsh is away at the moment?'

'Pete next-door? No idea.'

In the end, he posted a note through Walsh's letter box and drove home after one quick trawl along the next street. Not that he expected to see her still. And if he had? He didn't know if he'd even recognize her properly again, but could only conjure up a vague image of her – wide-eyed and uneasy, like a startled deer.

He left the unmarked car in the bay opposite his house and unlocked his front door. The hallway was dark and silent; tonight the house seemed too big and too empty.

CHAPTER 27

FRIDAY, 1 APRIL 2011

Pete unlocked his front door and stepped inside, with his suitcase.

He scooped up the clutch of letters lying on the mat. A folded note lay amongst the others, but he tucked it between them. He didn't even want to see it now and dropped the pile on to the table next to the answerphone. It bleeped and flashed the number three. That was currently his favourite number. He slid the volume to *off*.

After switching on all the downstairs lights, he turned up the thermostat to dispel the chill in the air. He kicked off his shoes and filled the kettle with fresh water, then took his case upstairs and put his jacket in the wardrobe. Next he visited the bathroom and brushed his teeth. He shook out the toothbrush and dropped it into its glass.

The ghost of the answerphone's bleeping still played in his ears, encouraging him to listen. Avoiding it was pathetic; he ought to listen to it straight away. It would be better just to get it over and done with. But, as he reached the table, he picked up the post instead; bills, statements and junk mail. What else did he expect?

He tucked the loose note under the phone. 'Paulette, Paulette, Paulette,' he murmured – once for each phone message. As he scalded the coffee granules with the boiling water, he added another 'Paulette' for the note too.

He wrapped both of his hands around the mug and stared into the black coffee as he waited for it to cool. Little things gave him such satisfaction.

But Paulette, she wanted the big things: the grand gestures of love. Absolute devotion, for one.

He leant on the doorframe between the kitchen and the sitting room and contemplated the flashing red light. He then tipped his head back, closed his eyes and sighed.

Her good looks and the sex still did it for him, but nothing else. He needed to be free of the fussing, the attention-seeking and, worst of all, the jealous tantrums always followed by grovelling and begging for forgiveness. Why had he hoped their holiday would change that? There was no future in it, at all.

Enough was enough. Play her messages, but harden up. No matter what she said in a message, he needed to remember that she wouldn't change. She *couldn't* change.

He crossed to the answerphone and pressed *play*. He stood still, concentrating, waiting, determined not to be swayed.

'You have three messages.'

The first two were hang-ups. Probably Paulette, all the same.

The third was definitely Paulette. 'Pete, it's me.' Silence, interspersed with sobs, dragged on for several seconds. 'I love you, please phone me,' she whimpered. 'I can't stand this, I need you.'

She sniffed and spluttered more words at irregular volume. 'Tell me what I've done wrong. I'm sorry if it's my fault.'

Pete reached out and pressed *delete all messages* before she'd finished talking. His decision had been made. He wouldn't change his mind now. It was impossible.

He slipped the note out from under the phone and unfolded it, expecting more of the same pleading.

It was brief and to the point, and from DC Gary Goodhew. 'Please phone' was all it said, accompanied by Goodhew's name and mobile number.

Pete flicked it against the back of his hand as he considered the policeman's request.

Perhaps there had been another anonymous call. He badly wanted to know who would do that.

Pete thought it through for some time before he decided that he would contact Goodhew, and somehow then make him understand that the deaths were nothing to do with him.

CHAPTER 28

SATURDAY, 2 APRIL 2011

The little brown prescription bottle of diazepam tablets lay clasped in her curled fingers.

She'd taken extra again and had sunk into sleep, thinking of that man in the street.

In her restless dreams she continued to let their encounter replay again and again. She watched him turn and look at her and puncture her belief that she was alone. She had felt so the moment it had happened; like a hot blade skewering the emptiness she'd carried within her for so long.

She dreamt that she crept up to him and tapped him on the shoulder, wanting to see him as he turned to face her. His features blurred, however, and instead she smelt Peter's skin as his cheek brushed her lips.

The other man had then vanished, leaving only Peter.

Her heartbeat quickened and, as if he knew, Peter squeezed her left breast. His lips brushed hers and his tongue poked between them, curling its way into her mouth.

They were still outside his front door and at first she didn't move, just let him kiss her. He forced her to kiss him, too, and then she tasted his sweat as he made her lick his skin.

People started to walk by, and she waited for someone to intervene. Peter pulled open her blouse and she twisted her head towards the street, pleading for help. He bent down and bit her nipple; it throbbed and she bit back the desire to yelp. Her clothes fell away from her but she made no attempt to shy away or cover her nakedness. She knew he expected her to stand still, and that thought alone seemed to be enough to guarantee her petrification.

He straightened up and she saw blood on his lips. He turned away and she stood, unmoving, too scared to examine her injured breast, too traumatized to see who was watching, or to ask for help.

She sank to the ground and curled into a ball, ashamed of both her humiliation and that inescapable rush of unwanted arousal.

She jolted awake as the bottle of tranquillizers tumbled to the floor. Her warm and sodden undersheet told her that she'd just wet the bed.

She pulled the bedding on to the floor and rushed to the shower, turning away from her dim reflection in the cubicle door. She didn't want to look at her naked body.

She hated it.

She knew she had only been dreaming again, but she felt ugly and debased.

She tugged the showerhead from its hook and hosed herself down, avoiding her hair and spending longest in rubbing soap under her arms and between her legs.

She pushed away the dreams by returning to her thoughts of the stranger in the street.

Today she'd find out who he was.

She dressed quickly, pulling on a jersey and jeans, and dragging her hair back into a ponytail. Her make-up bag remained unopened in the bathroom cabinet and she didn't bother with breakfast either, only ducking into the kitchen for her purse and keys.

It was just after 7 a.m. as she drove to the centre of Cambridge and along Park Terrace. It didn't look as though his car had moved since she'd watched him pull up outside the endmost terraced house the night before. And it looked like her assumption that she'd followed him home had been correct. Now all she needed to do was find out who was registered at that same address. She pulled away from the kerb, but curiosity made her drive round the block so that she could crawl past for another look.

The one-way system required her to turn right at the end of Park Terrace, then follow the road around the perimeter of Parker's Piece. She watched his house as her engine idled at the pedestrian lights in front of the swimming pool, and she continued to stare across at it as the traffic edged forward, until the house finally vanished behind some other buildings.

By the time she re-entered Park Terrace, the earlier idea of a quick drive-by wasn't enough, so she swung into a parking space beside the old cricket pavilion and settled back to wait for the man to leave his house. She passed the time by staring at the terrace house's end wall and trying to picture what lay behind those regular, rectangular windows.

After about twenty minutes he appeared, closing his front door, stepping out on to the footpath and across to his car in one fluid movement. His reversing lights flashed on as he backed up by a few feet, then swung forward into the traffic, pulling into the main road twenty yards ahead. She waited until he was a good fifty yards in front, then followed him along East Road and on to the dual carriageway leading over the Elizabeth Way bridge.

The traffic thickened and for a moment she lost him behind a minibus, but caught up with him again at the next roundabout. She turned up the heater in an attempt to stop her shivering, but she knew it was due to nerves.

He eventually turned right, then left, heading into the warren of streets off Arbury Road. Kaye Whiting's neighbourhood. She followed him until he turned into Acacia Road. She stayed on the main road with two wheels on the grass verge and the other two straddling double yellow lines. She watched as he parked in front of number 16.

He knocked and waited, then knocked again.

She drove back to Cambridge centre, parked in the multi-storey and hurried up the steps of the Reference Library.

The electoral register was bound in nine black files, and kept on the bottom shelf immediately behind the librarian. She flicked through until she found Acacia Road. With her pen poised ready to write the name listed next to the address, she ran her left index finger down the list.

Number 16, Michelle Whiting.

Her stomach lurched. Michelle Whiting, Kaye's sister.

She didn't write it down; she knew that name well enough already.

She pushed the book away and dragged the next volume across the desk. She started at the front, then flicked further through until she found Park Terrace.

Only one name appeared against his house and this time she copied it down.

Gary Goodhew.

'Gary Goodhew.' She tested it out loud, then quietly spoke the name again and again slowly, varying the emphasis on its syllables.

'Gary Goodhew, Gary Goodhew.'

She doodled boxes across the page, and then scored them out again.

'Gary.' The pen gouged the paper. 'Goodhew.'

CHAPTER 29

WEDNESDAY, 27 APRIL 2011

The reception area at the head office of Dunwold Insurance Services was furnished in black and chrome, with copies of the *Financial Times* and the *Economist* neatly arranged alongside the Company's Annual Report on each of the three glass coffee tables. The two receptionists were enjoying the mid-morning lull in activity. Karen, the elder of the two, was in her mid-twenties, with no greater career aspirations than to reach the end of each day and receive a cheque at the end of the month. Donna was a huge help to have around, filling their days with chatter and jokey observations about almost every visitor and other member of staff.

Donna leant towards Karen and lowered her voice to an excited whisper. 'So he said, "We can have some privacy at my place." So I thought why not?' A smile flickered across Donna's lips. 'But we got there and he still lives with his parents, doesn't he?'

'No!'

'No, really. Twenty-seven years old and his idea of privacy is being in the TV room with his parents sitting next-door. He said, "I'd better get them a cup of tea." That took him about twenty minutes, so I didn't know what to do.'

'I'd have sneaked out.'

'No, I couldn't. He was quite sweet, really.'

'So what did you do?'

'Well, I switched on the telly and I'm sitting there watching it, and he comes back in and sits on the next chair, kind of facing me more than the TV. And he just sat there – staring.' Donna curled up her nose and waved her hands in a shooing-away motion. 'Ugh, no, it was horrid.'

'Bet you wish you'd left then?'

'Well, I decided to get out quick. But you'll never guess what he did next?'

'What?'

'Well, I went to the loo and when I came out he was sitting on the stairs, waiting for me.' She began to giggle. 'Said he'd missed me.' They both giggled then.

'No way.'

'It's true, I tell you.'

'You always pick them, don't you?'

'That's just it, I don't. He picked me and I fell for it. I might be better off if I picked my own.'

'Give it a go. There's plenty in this building.'

'Like who?'

'Marcus Bagley in Accounts? Or John Brent in Marketing?'

'No thanks.'

'Wait, I know, that guy on the third. The one you liked a while back, what's his name?'

'You mean the one with the sulky girlfriend that waits for him?'

'Yeah, but I don't think he's with her now.'

'No. I'm sure he wouldn't be interested.'

'Don't sell yourself short, Donna. Just go for it if you fancy him. So what is his name?'

'Peter Walsh.'

'What have you got to lose?'

She wasn't quite his usual type. Her hair was shorter and she looked a little bit tomboyish, and she laughed a lot.

Laughing a lot was a good thing, of course, but too much of it was as wrong as none at all. The idea of any laughter right now seemed such a pleasant change that it was a risk worth taking.

He wondered whether he was a fool for looking at another woman, when he'd only just split from the last troublesome one. But, for all his laddish bravado, he knew he really wanted to find himself that one *special* girl.

He now leant on the reception desk, casually flicking the pages of the company brochure, as he waited for her to finish on the phone.

'I think you've got a delivery down here for me?'

The girl flushed but kept her voice level. 'There must be a mistake.'

A scowl flickered across his forehead.

She frowned back at him. 'I really don't know anything that's come in. Sorry.'

'Don't worry about it.'

She lifted a folder and flicked through some loose sheets of paper in the in-tray underneath, then shook her head earnestly. 'I'll find out about your delivery and run it up to you, if it's around, but I really think there's been a mix-up.'

Pete gave her his full attention for a few seconds. 'That would be great. Thank you . . .' he looked at her name badge '. . . Donna.'

They both smiled then, and the ice was broken.

He asked her a couple of questions about her job; she asked him the corresponding questions about his. She then asked him about his girlfriend and, before he thought about it too closely, he asked her what she was doing on Friday.

She hesitated as though the question had caught her off-guard and she now needed a moment to consider it. He threw a couple of potential dates into the silence, and she tentatively suggested meeting the following week.

'I'd like that,' she added, 'but I won't hold you to it. You can ring me.'

'I'll do that.'

She levelled her gaze on him, the corners of her mouth curling into a smile as she tried to look serious. 'Now let me get back to work.'

'Thank you very much, Karen.' Donna pretended to be cross but she didn't look at all annoyed.

'So? What happened?'

'It was weird. One minute it was awkward, and the next minute we just clicked. He's really nice, and he's split up with that girl. He says he doesn't want anything serious now, and I said neither did I.'

'Liar.'

'There's no need to rush, is there?'

'Well, it doesn't sound like you're hanging around too much from what you've said so far.' Karen looked at Donna's smug expression. 'Is that it, then?' she asked, knowing for sure that it wasn't.

'I was really casual about it, but I mentioned the cinema next Friday. I said there would be a few of us going, and it'd be fine if he wanted to come along. I wasn't being pushy, which is why I said next week. I was just friendly, and he said "maybe". Then he rang down once he got back to his desk. Said he'd love to. So we're meeting for a drink first and taking it from there.'

'Well, let's hope *he* doesn't live with his mum!'

'Don't worry, I'll practise safe sex. Safely back at my place!'

CHAPTER 30

MONDAY, 2 MAY 2011

Andy Burrows liked to *see* people when he spoke to them. He used his phone to ring for a pizza, or check on his mother, but anything more crucial could only be face to face.

So Andy didn't make use of Goodhew's mobile number; instead he carried the piece of paper to the police station in his breast pocket, and plucked it out as he waited for the desk sergeant. He needed to make sure he was asking for the young detective by precisely the right name.

'Goodhew?' Sergeant Norris squinted at him over half-moon spectacles. 'I'll find out,' he said and picked up the phone to call the incident room. 'No reply. I'll try again in a few minutes. Take a seat.'

Burrows sat down on one of the six black, almost vandal-proof metal seats. Messages had been scraped into the paintwork of the one on his right. The tiny engraved letters fitted neatly between the punched-out diamond shapes.

Fucking Pigs.

He looked away. He wondered whether the diamond-shaped holes were for decoration or just to save on metal. Or perhaps it made them easier to wash down.

Sergeant Norris tried another number, and Clark answered the call. 'Is Goodhew up there?'

'Not in at present. Don't know what he's doing right now. D'you want me to find out?'

Norris pressed his glasses against the bridge of his nose. 'Well that might help, don't you think?'

Clark grunted, rested the receiver on the desk and peered over the filing cabinet to speak to Kincaide. 'I've got Doris on the phone, and he wants Goodhew.'

Kincaide frowned. 'Well, he's not here, is he? Ask him what it's about.'

Clark grunted again and picked up the receiver once more. 'Kincaide wants to know what you want Goodhew for.'

'*I* don't want him, but there's a Mr Burrows down here, and he doesn't want to talk to anyone else.'

'Hang on.' Clark covered the mouthpiece. 'That Andrew Burrows is down there. Doesn't want to talk to anyone else.'

At that, Kincaide's head popped up over the partition. 'Yes, well he'll have to. Tell Doris to tell him Goodhew's on his way, and not to let Burrows leave.' Clark removed his hand from the receiver, but Kincaide butted in. 'Forget it. Just give me the phone.' He grabbed it from Clark and barked out his instructions personally.

Sergeant Norris hesitated for a moment. What Kincaide said was reasonable enough; it was the way that he spoke that put Norris' back up.

'I said don't let him leave. Have you got it?' ordered Kincaide and he slammed the receiver down. He sprang back over to his desk, swept up his notepad, pen and mobile phone. 'If anyone wants me, take a message and I'll get back to them,' he called over his shoulder as he strode towards the door.

'Yeah, OK,' muttered Clark. 'What am I now? A sodding secretary?'

Kincaide guessed Andy Burrows had some new information. Why else would he be here? And he guessed it was something of a delicate nature, as people found it easy to confide in Goodhew.

He opened the door to the waiting room, where Andy Burrows was busy chewing his thumbnail while trying to have a sly read of the graffiti under the notice board. He turned in dismay towards Kincaide's firm greeting: 'Mr Burrows.'

Kincaide did his best approximation of a warm smile, but Andy's face fell further, then he set his jaw determinedly. 'I wanted to speak to Detective Goodhew.'

Kincaide relaxed; this was going to be easy. He held the door open. 'He'll be down in a minute. He's on the phone just now. Come on through.'

Andy's mouth relaxed into a smile and he trotted along behind Kincaide to Interview Room 3.

Kincaide left Burrows alone for the best part of an hour. Kincaide kept an eye on the time, picturing Burrows chewing his nails and generating a warm fug of BO, as the time ticked by.

By the time he returned, Burrows looked relieved to see him.

Clark slid into the room next, and into the vacant chair next to Kincaide.

Kincaide leant across the desk and addressed Andy Burrows face on, beginning with a quiet apology. 'Unfortunately Detective Goodhew decided not to join us, but we've got all night, Mr Burrows, so take your time.'

By now, Andy Burrows wondered what difference it would make anyway. They were all trained the same, weren't they?

CHAPTER 31

WEDNESDAY, 4 MAY 2011

After weeks of getting nowhere, DI Marks' news should have come as a relief.

He'd gathered them all together in the incident room. Clark and Kincaide sat closest to him, on chairs pulled side by side; the others sat in a large arc spread across the room.

Except for Goodhew.

He sat on his desk, leaning against the wall and staring at Marks; present only in body, but trying very hard to coax his reluctant brain back into the room.

Marks addressed them generally, switching his attention between each of them in turn, but never letting it settle on Goodhew, probably because he'd already spotted the mutinous look on his subordinate's face and therefore wasn't prepared to be distracted by it.

Marks continued, 'We have proof that Kaye Whiting was in her uncle's car on the afternoon she disappeared, the twenty-sixth of March 2011. Yesterday we also received two independent confirmations of him drinking heavily whilst in the Anchor at Woodbridge on that Saturday afternoon.'

Goodhew's thoughts drifted again. Perhaps he had become just too sympathetic towards Margaret Whiting and her family, and there was a small part of him that felt irritated that Michael Kincaide should have made the arrest.

Gully turned her head sideways and caught his eye. She pressed her lips into a cheerless smile and shrugged. He returned the smile and shook his head sadly. Burrows had yet to be charged and Goodhew couldn't accept the idea that the man was guilty.

He reminded himself that the evidence so far was largely circumstantial, but still compelling. The second birthday card that Kaye had purchased – the one that read *Happy Birthday, Mother* – had later been given to Edna by Burrows, and was proof that Burrows had had contact with Kaye during or after her trip to Woodbridge. Proof, therefore, that Burrows had lied. Now, by his own admission, Burrows accepted that he was to blame for Kaye's death, in a statement albeit too incomplete to be considered a proper confession. Add to that the independent witnesses who could confirm that Burrows had appeared both drunk and bad-tempered just prior to his meeting with Kaye, and it seemed as though it would only be a matter of time before charges were pressed.

Goodhew asked himself what reason he had to complain that such leads had converted into an arrest.

He stared out of the window beyond Marks. Students lazed on Parker's Piece, reading books while catching snatches of warm sunshine. They drank Coke and played their iPods, oblivious to the dirty tune of murder playing in Goodhew's ears.

Where had he himself taken any other line of investigation?

Nowhere, that was where.

The best he had come up with was one anonymous caller and a feeling that she knew something. Maybe that was just his wishful thinking, too.

He'd been enjoying working with Gully, though. He liked her sense of humour, and the way she cared about everyone's feelings. He even liked the way she ate too many Jaffa Cakes, but none of those were reason to give undue weight to the fact that she remained convinced those anonymous calls were relevant.

'Sir?' he interrupted, and everyone turned.

'What if she'd been found alive? She would have identified her uncle.'

Kincaide replied, 'If she'd been found she could have identified anyone.'

'But she knew her uncle well. And what was his motive?'

'We haven't established that fully,' Marks replied, 'but it appears that something spontaneous blew up between them while they were on the way home. Andrew Burrows has admitted responsibility, and we'll continue gathering evidence, but I wouldn't be surprised if it's just a matter of time before he tells us the rest.'

After a few more minutes, Marks shuffled his notes together and threw his plastic cup into the bin: sure signs that he was winding up the meeting.

Goodhew slipped back into his office chair and took the photo of Kaye Whiting from the top of his desk. He opened his top drawer and placed it face-up in the largest compartment of his empty pen tray. She didn't look dead, she seemed so bright and fresh. He closed the drawer again, reminding himself to visit Margaret Whiting once more.

Not that he'd forget.

'Something bothering you, Goodhew?' Marks hovered over Goodhew's desk.

Gary shook his head. 'It's not what I expected. I was just sure it wasn't Burrows.'

Marks said nothing, but then he didn't need to point out the stupidity of Goodhew's comment. There was no one who ever really knew the limits of another's behaviour, no way of determining the circumstances that could push the average person to kill.

'But I'm not the best judge of people sometimes, sir.'

'None of us are, Gary.' He smiled genially. 'I noticed that your leave was booked for this week. It doesn't need to be cancelled, now we appear to be winding this up. I know you're bang up to date with your paperwork. Just.'

'But he hasn't been charged yet.'

'Whatever happens, we can manage.'

'I don't mind staying on.'

'I do, Gary, and I expect your girlfriend minds too. Where are you taking her, anyway?'

Mention of her name conjured up a fleeting memory of her bare suntanned back and the scent of her Ghost perfume. 'Nowhere, sir. I was just going off to the coast with a mate. He's gone already.'

'Well, I'm not going to stand here arguing with you. Take your leave or I'll assign you to two weeks on Crime Prevention. All those little old ladies would love you.'

CHAPTER 32

THURSDAY, 5 MAY 2011

The laziest of Hawaiian waves lapped the shore just feet from their restaurant table, and to Bryn it seemed that the sun was only a stone's throw away as it tumbled like a giant slow-motion pompom into the Pacific.

Nadine glowed in the reflection of the incandescent sunset. Her hair was clipped back and adorned with fresh orchids, and hundreds more were woven into the lei that was draped from her bare shoulders.

Bryn reached across and squeezed her hand. 'I'm glad we met.'

'Well,' she laughed, 'you'd have been pretty lonely here if we hadn't.'

'And so would you!' he retorted. 'You've seen nothing of your friend since she met that dentist bloke.'

'But that's hardly surprising, Bryn,' she said. 'This is just about the most romantic place you could imagine, isn't it?'

He gazed deep into her eyes for what he estimated was the requisite time and tried not to notice that she vaguely resembled his sister Shelly. 'And there's nothing wrong with having a holiday romance, is there?'

'Not at all,' she beamed, and lowered her lashes. 'But don't move too fast. You've only been here a day!' She curled slender fingers around her glass. 'So how can you afford to stay here, really?'

A helicopter swooped above the bay, then swung round to land on the sand and drop a sole passenger.

'I told you, my mate booked the holiday for him and his

girlfriend. They've split up and now he's had to work.' Bryn realized how improbable it sounded, even as he said it.

She fluttered her eyelashes again. 'No, really, stop teasing. No one works instead of coming here.' She raised her glass. 'I think you're a millionaire looking for a girl who's not after his money.'

Bryn raised his glass and clinked it against hers. 'You found me out!'

The passenger waved thank-you as the helicopter's blades beat faster and it rose above him and away from the beach, levitating to palm-tree height, then swinging back towards Honolulu.

He swung a small rucksack over his shoulder and turned towards the hotel. 'Blimey!' Bryn spluttered mid-sip. 'It's my mate, Gary.'

Nadine peered towards Goodhew. 'The one who booked your holiday?'

'Yup.' Bryn grinned, waving with both arms. 'That's him.'

Gary waved back. He hopped over the low ornamental hedge and cut across the lawn.

'And what does he do for a living?' she wondered.

'Police,' he replied, and grinned at her obvious disappointment. 'He's not a millionaire either.'

'Don't be silly.' She laughed.

A waitress ran to the patio doors and slid one across for Gary. 'Aloha, Mr Goodhew, how are you?'

'Aloha! I'm very well, thank you.' He smiled and joined Bryn. 'They've arrested her uncle.'

'When?'

'Yesterday, no charges yet, but Marks told me to take my holiday.'

Bryn frowned as the waitress pointed him out to one of her colleagues. They both then waved. 'Does that waitress know you?'

'Not really.' Goodhew waved back before turning to Bryn's companion and shaking her hand.

Darkness had settled on Kauai, when Gary found Bryn leaning on the bar beside the pool. 'Where's your friend?'

'Having a bath.' Bryn slid a glass of Coke towards Gary and added more ice to his own. 'Unfortunately she's having it in her own room and I'm not invited.'

'And no alcohol for either of us?'

Bryn shook his head and moved to a quiet spot near the water's edge. He placed his glass on the bamboo table top and hovered next to his chair. 'What's going on, Gary?' he whispered, thrusting his hands into his pockets and glaring at the floor.

Gary shrugged. 'What do you mean?'

'You said that Andy Burrows got arrested yesterday, so how did you manage to get halfway round the world so quickly? I don't believe you've booked this holiday on police pay.'

Goodhew sighed and took the seat opposite. 'I saved up,' he lied.

'Right. Chartered helicopters aren't thrown in on package trips, and even the waitresses seem to know you.'

As Goodhew had spoken he realized how poor he was at even small untruths; so the only way to satisfy Bryn's curiosity would be to give the honest if incomplete story. 'I've been here a couple of times before with my grandmother. It's always been special to her, and it was to my grandad, so it's a bit of family tradition. I thought it would be a special place to bring Claire.'

Bryn's eyes widened. 'You were going to propose?'

'No, no. But I came here by myself once when I was at university.'

'When you were dating her the first time?'

'Exactly. She went home to her family at the end of our second year and I came here. I was sorry she'd missed it, so it seemed to be the right thing to do this time.'

'But obviously not meant to be?'

Goodhew latched on to Bryn's mildly sarcastic tone immediately. 'You don't do that fate and destiny stuff, Bryn, so what was that about?'

'We had a deal on this holiday: no discussing work, or any women who aren't within two hundred yards. If you're breaking the rule, at least do me the favour of boring me with the whole story. She dumped you, right?'

'No.' Goodhew sipped his drink, then shook his head. 'I ended it.'

'What did she do?'

For someone with a self-declared avoidance of all things monogamous, Bryn was extremely persistent in his quest for details, and he made several random guesses before Goodhew stopped him.

'It was going well, but I felt uncomfortable with her coming to my flat. I think she sensed it because she asked several times about spending the night there, but I always preferred to be at hers.'

Bryn shrugged. 'Fair enough.'

'Yeah, I thought so too, at first.' Goodhew let out a long slow breath and spread his hands in an expansive gesture that seemed to say it all. 'Then I booked this trip and . . .' Finally, he shrugged too.

'And what? "And . . ." doesn't explain anything. You don't like anyone going into your flat, not even your grandmother, as far as I can work out. So why are you surprised that you felt odd about having Claire there?'

'Yes, I like privacy, but this was different. In some ways it was going well between us, but there was always this thing about her coming to the flat that really bothered me. Couldn't put my finger on it until I booked this holiday. It was going to be a surprise for Claire, but when the tickets arrived I just put them on the top of the fridge and didn't even bother opening the envelope.' Goodhew didn't offer a deeper explanation, just the bare facts he'd already laid out, but Bryn no longer looked puzzled.

'I get it, Gary. My dad goes on about this: he calls it a moment of truth. Says it can happen at any point, first date, first kiss. Maybe the first lie or first bust-up. At any point really, and in your case the first time Claire came home with you. It's the moment you realize it's not going to work – not long-term.'

Goodhew stared at his friend with renewed interest. He'd expected sarcasm or lack of interest, maybe a mix of the two, but definitely not wisdom. 'I couldn't give up, not just like that.'

'Why not? Women go on about men being "commitment phobic", but that's not you. You're too hung up on the fucked-up idea that you'll find a soulmate. And she wasn't it, was she?'

He still considered Claire to be as beautiful now as when he'd asked her out that first time, during their first year at university, but she'd changed. They both had. 'It wasn't the same, I suppose,' he conceded – and, if he was honest, he knew it had never been, the second time around. His job had caused some of it; his inheritance too. She saw her progress to becoming an architect as a series of exam/experience milestones that would take her to an ordered but conventional life: modern house, new car, all safe and secure. Nothing wrong with that but, for himself, Goodhew neither saw his life nor wanted it that way.

'Who else have you spoken to? Anyone at work?'

'No, they never met her. Look, I don't need to talk to anyone about Claire.'

'So who met her, apart from me and your grandmother?'

'What does it matter? I've never met Valerie.'

'Valerie with the Volvo? That's different, I wasn't in a relationship with her. But you could've met her, whether or not I thought it was serious. What about Sue?'

'Gully?'

'Yeah. I'm sure you could've introduced her to Claire without it being awkward.'

'Then what?'

'Then you might have talked to Sue instead of keeping it all to yourself for the last few weeks. How many other mates have you got outside work?'

'What is this? Bryn O'Brien, personal counsellor?'

'No, it's Gary Goodhew, sad bloke who gets dumped as soon as his only mate gets a better offer.' Goodhew followed Bryn's gaze towards the woman now walking from the main hotel towards the pool. She wore a semi-transparent sarong over her bikini. 'Nadine's such a lovely name.'

'She's heading for the pool, not you.'

Bryn looked at him in disgust, 'No, Gary, a woman doesn't *swim* in a bikini like that.' He abandoned Goodhew at the bar and moved towards Nadine, only taking his eyes off her for long enough to throw one last piece of advice at his friend. 'I'm just saying you should take a risk or two.'

Room service provided Gary with a fresh-fruit breakfast on the balcony of their bungalow at 6.30 a.m. Bryn still hadn't returned. Goodhew leant over the low balustrade as he ate, watching the sea and allowing juice from the fresh pineapple to drip on to the rocks below.

Sometimes shoals of fish darted in bright-coloured ribbons just below the surface of the bay in the mornings here, and he'd risen early in the hope of spotting them. No luck today, he thought. He took his tray inside, wiped his hands on a napkin. He then took an apple to eat as he sauntered through the long corridors and down to the foyer.

The hotel lobby was deserted apart from the receptionist.

'Aloha, Jana.'

'Aloha, Gary.' She smiled warmly and reached under the counter, producing a Hertz keyring. 'Your car is here, and I had it brought round already. I guessed you'd be going out early.'

He nodded his thanks. 'Mahalo.'

He folded back the roof and drove along the almost deserted Kūhiō Highway and then left on to Mā'alo Road, winding up through cane fields towards Wailua Falls.

As the road climbed further above sea level, the gentle breeze swept up the sounds of gushing water and Gary caught his first glimpse of the waterfall. Recent rain had swelled the mountain streams, and three freshwater cascades leapt from the eighty-foot cliffs, diving into the deep cup below.

He pulled on to a dusty patch of verge and scrambled down to an old path, marked with knotted rope, that would eventually take him to the water's edge. The first time he had walked to the falls had taken the longest, since he'd struggled to follow the route whenever the path vanished, but now he recognized its landmarks: the muddy twists and turns, the giant swaying grasses, and finally the driftwood thrown down by the waterfall itself.

He clambered over broken branches and on to a rocky ledge some thirty feet above the edge of the pool. The sun blazed down on to his back as he removed his shirt and threw off his shoes. He inhaled deeply, drawing the perfect morning into his lungs. Cambridge seemed another world, a world he rarely left for long and missed deeply whenever he did. Even so, he was now filled with the sense of a perfect moment, as he dived in. Before he even hit the water, the perfect moment had been replaced by the guilt of forgetting, however briefly, the suffering of Margaret Whiting.

His body sliced through the dark surface, the cold cutting right through him, like flying shards of glass. The thought of Kaye came with him.

He swam underwater with his eyes open, watching the sun's rays twinkle on the surface and pick out plumes of tiny bubbles gliding up from the bottom.

It was stimulating: a different kind of cold to the lifeless gloom that she had met. He turned into the current and swam towards the base of the Wailua Falls, where it was colder and the water darkened and it rumbled like distant thunder. He stayed under until lack of oxygen made his lungs begin to strain.

But he wondered what it was like to drown, and forced himself to swim deeper. The churning torrent buffeted him and his chest ached against the pressure. He tried to swim deeper still, until the weight of water threatened to pin him down. *Stop it!* He rolled away and propelled himself upwards to the surface.

The waterfall now spilt on to the rocks to his left, shooting jets of spray upwards like ribbons dancing in the air and the sunlight refracted into tiny rainbows. Droplets showered Gary's hair and face as he paused, treading water. He was gasping as his lungs struggled to refill.

In his mind, Kaye's skin had dried slowly, repelling the water as if she were made of wax. She'd stared up at him with dead eyes that no one had bothered to close.

Spray saturated his face and he felt it trickling down his nose and over his cheeks. His pulse was still racing but he ducked under again anyway, and swam slowly towards the tranquil waters further away from the falls.

With a sudden jolt, he broke back up again through the surface and threw himself into front-crawl, panting hard as he struck out for the path to where he'd left his clothes. There he hauled himself out of the pool and up the bank.

His shorts and shirt clung to him damply and he shivered, but not from cold.

Instead, Gary shivered with excitement as he dashed back up the steep path, clutching at the undergrowth for support. Running, wherever possible, back to his car.

He could see it now: the girl in the street resembled Kaye. That was the way she looked, too; pale skin and mesmerizing blue eyes just like Kaye's.

I should've followed her right then. I'm such a stupid git.

He revved the Chevy's engine, swung it around in the roadway, and sped back towards Po'ipū.

He'd been determined not to become blind to other possibilities, and he wondered if that was why he'd been so quick to doubt his own judgement. *Follow one's instinct*: it sounded like an excuse to favour wishful thinking over facts. His grandmother disagreed, of course, arguing that instinct was the conclusion the brain reached after processing a lifetime's learning.

From now on he'd listen to his instinct more.

He grabbed his bag from the hotel and drove straight to the airport. He had to get home immediately. He had to find her and ask her why she had made those anonymous calls.

CHAPTER 33

FRIDAY, 6 MAY 2011

The wardrobe doors had been lying open for half an hour now, and each time she returned to the room she picked through another few items. A first date was always so difficult.

Her elder sister Chloe caught her holding up her Christmas party dress. 'Don't do it, Donna,' she laughed. 'Whoever he is will run a mile if you turn up for the cinema like you're going off to the Oscars.'

'Yeah, you're right, but it's that first-date problem again. I want to look good, but not too over the top, or he'll think I'm up for it.' Donna grinned mischievously '. . . Even if I am.'

Chloe studied the open wardrobe. 'Let's see what you've got, then.'

'That's s'posed to be *his* line.'

'You're a tart, Donna. You'll come unstuck, you know.'

'OK, I won't overdo it. I wasn't going to anyway. Just check out the underwear.' On the bed lay a black lacy Wonder Bra and some pink knickers with daisies printed on the front. Chloe picked them up and held them in the air. 'Oh, my God, these must have been a Christmas present, they're so bloody hideous. That will kill it all stone dead.'

'It's a safety device. The bra's a turn-on but I won't be letting him get too carried away when he could come across knickers like these.'

'Bad choice of words, Donna.' They both giggled.

'Yeah, well, thought I'd better make sure I'm gonna see him again, before I let it go that far. After all, I see him every day at work, so it could be embarrassing. But, anyhow, I thought something different from what I wear at work. Nothing too dressy, but at the same time I thought jeans might be too restrictive.'

'No, I'd wear the jeans. What about these black ones with the pink Lycra top? It shows off your cleavage, but it'll look like it's accidental.' Chloe winked. 'Trust me, he'll be hooked, and you'll have a great time. If you don't want to do it with him, you can still tease him to death!'

At five to eight that evening, Donna stepped through the door of the Regal pub. She quickly felt the back of her fair hair to check that it still lay smooth against her neck. As her hand dropped, it ran along her collarbone and lightly stroked her breast. A buzz of anticipation sent a tiny smile to her lips.

She stared straight ahead, absorbing the atmosphere of Friday-evening entertainment. Peter Walsh sat alone at a table near the bar. He looked up then, and she waved.

He smiled easily. 'You look nice, Donna. Can I get you a drink?'

'Thanks, half a lager.'

She watched him as he stood waiting to be served. She'd liked his body since she'd first noticed him at work, but dressed casually was an improvement still. She imagined herself creeping up behind him and pressing herself against his back. She imagined him thinking of her right now, and hoping that she fancied him.

He returned with the drinks, and watched as her gaze smouldered at him from beneath a little too much mascara. 'You have lovely eyes, Donna. I bet you look good with no make-up.'

Like first thing in the morning? she thought, but didn't say it. Too corny. Too forward. She just smiled.

He returned her smile briefly. 'Who else is going to the pictures, then?'

'Just a couple of mates and their boyfriends.' She watched his reaction, hoping to see him relax.

'Oh, so it's a couples thing?' He didn't seem worried by that, but she remembered his comment of 'nothing serious' and wasn't sure of the right answer.

'Just the way it worked out,' she offered brightly, 'but I don't mind if we miss it. We could just go and have a drink somewhere.'

He smiled and nodded. 'Much better idea.' A knowing look flashed between them. 'But I could do with dropping my car off at home if I'm going to have any more to drink.'

'Sure, no problem.'

Donna and Pete. She liked the sound of that, she decided, as they drove to his house. She looked forward to seeing where he lived, seeing how she might fit in.

She shivered nervously as she waited for him to unlock his front door. He held it open for her to step inside. 'I'll order us a taxi in a minute.'

'Could we have a coffee first? I'm a bit cold.'

He boiled the kettle, and she curled up catlike in the armchair opposite the kitchen door, watching him attentively until the kettle boiled.

As he turned away to rinse a cup in the sink, Donna unwound herself from the chair and quietly entered the kitchen. She placed one hand on each shoulder and ran them leisurely down his back. 'Want a hand?'

He turned slowly, so that her hands remained in contact with his waist. He leant forward and his lips parted as they met hers. She teased her tongue between them, and ran it behind his open teeth, drawing his mouth more tightly against her own. He responded instantly, sliding his hand inside her top and swiftly unclipping the catch on her bra. The suddenness aroused her further, and she was relieved that she'd taken a minute to pop into the pub's Ladies and remove her pink knickers.

His mouth moved away from hers and hungrily tasted the soft pale skin beneath her right cheek. She tilted her head back to allow him full access to her bare neck.

Her breathing quickened as his hands explored her breasts and, as the fingers on one hand reached her nipple, he pulled back slightly and withdrew the other hand from beneath her top.

His gaze locked on to hers as he pushed his two middle fingers between her lips. She sucked them eagerly, drawing them under her tongue and running her teeth lightly over the knuckles. Her unwavering gaze met his challenging stare.

She pressed her fingers flat against his chest and ran her hand down to his belt. Her fingers working deftly, flicking open the buckle and the shirt buttons.

She pushed him gently back into the corner between the sink and the fridge, and kissed the triangle of skin that now showed at the neck of his shirt.

One hand cupped each of his hips and she slid well-practised fingers down inside his clothing.

His bare flesh felt cool against her palms as she worked her hands further downwards. Her face skimmed his torso as in one fluid movement she dropped to her knees and enveloped his penis in her mouth.

She clutched the back of his thighs as she pulled deeper still. *Fuck, I want him*, she thought, as she massaged him with her tongue.

She felt his excitement suddenly increase, with an almost electric jolt that fused them together. She responded with increased frenzy. He grabbed the back of her head with both hands, holding her face hard against him. She took quick gasps of air, struggling for breath.

He pushed himself deeper towards the back of her throat. Trying not to choke, she dug her fingers into his thighs, stopping him from going deeper. And also stopping him from pulling back.

His fingers pressed hard, bruise hard, against her scalp and then he came. Gasping and shuddering.

She slid her teeth back along his penis, slowly releasing him from her mouth.

She stood up and again her eyes met his. She smirked, then smugly and deliberately she swallowed and licked her lips.

She pulled her clothes straight, and flicked the kettle on again as he refastened his trousers.

'Mine's with milk and one sugar, thanks, Pete.'

She didn't stay the night. Instead she returned home, sure now that he would want to see her again.

After all, he now knew that she wasn't the kind of girl to sleep with a man on their first date.

CHAPTER 34

FRIDAY, 6 MAY 2011

Gary flew from Lihu'e airport to Honolulu on the next available Hawaiian Airlines flight, then by American Airlines to Los Angeles, and back to Heathrow with British Airways.

He took a black cab from the airport to home, and opened his front door at 8 p.m.

The evening light illuminated the hallway just enough for him to spot the solitary item of mail lying on the doormat.

He dropped his rucksack inside and flicked on the hall light. As he bent to pick it up, his attention was drawn to the front of the envelope. It was cream Challenger stationery, face up and with no stamp. Three words in careful blue handwriting jumped out at him: 'GARY GOODHEW – URGENT.'

He jerked his hand away and flicked the door shut with his heel. He stepped over the solitary letter and hurried up the stairs, flicking on the interior lights on his way to the kitchen. There, from the second drawer beneath the sink, he produced a pair of gloves, some tweezers and two evidence bags.

He knelt beside the front-door mat, picked up the envelope by one corner and opened it carefully along the short edge. The writing paper inside matched the envelope, and Gary extracted it with the tweezers. He unfolded it and slid it into one evidence bag, then dropped the empty envelope into the other.

He returned to the kitchen and placed the unfolded letter face-up on the worktop. It read:

Please help me. I feel I'm going mad. I've tried to do the right thing, but it's all gone wrong. Kaye's uncle didn't kill her. I phoned and no one listened, and now Kaye's dead.

I feel like it's all my fault. I can't stand it on my conscience. Kaye's not first and won't be the last, so please believe me when I say I want it to stop.

I need you to help me. I'm not going to give you my name because I don't want you to hand this over to anyone else. I don't want to talk to anyone else.

Meet me on Thursday at 12.00 in Market Hill, outside the Guild Hall. I know what you look like. If you wait there, I'll find you.

The other girl was Helen Neill. She didn't drown but her death was just the same. Find her file before we meet and tell me if she's not like Kaye Whiting.

'Shit,' he spat. 'I've missed her.'

CHAPTER 35

SATURDAY, 7 MAY 2011

Margaret Whiting clasped her mug with both hands, as if to steady herself. 'Mother!' she snapped. 'Which one?'

Edna remained unruffled. 'I don't know his name, dear, but it was the nice one, the one you like.'

'Goodhew?' Margaret asked, while forcing herself to sound calm.

Edna shook her head. 'I told you I don't know.' She directed her vacant gaze into her tea as it swilled around in the bottom of the cup.

Margaret rubbed her eyes, still hot and pink from crying. She knew she mustn't vent her frustration on her mother, therefore fought to suppress the tightness in her voice. 'When was this?'

'Oh, a few days ago now – just after he was at yours, I think.'

'Oh, Mum, why didn't you tell me?'

Edna shrugged. 'I forgot, I suppose. My memory's not what it used to be, you know. I haven't forgotten it *all*, though. He asked me your date of birth. And first of all I was muddled between you and Andrew, but then I got it right. He asked me about my own birthday. He was very nice, took a real interest.' She creaked on to her feet and Margaret waited as Edna fumbled in the drawer above the video player. She returned with a small pile of birthday cards and eased herself back into her winged armchair. 'I showed him all these, and I said there wasn't one from Kaye.'

'Well, he knew that.'

'That's what he said, too. But he looked through them anyway, and you should've seen his face when he came to our Andrew's.'

Edna pulled a cotton handkerchief from her sleeve. 'Poor Andrew,' she gulped.

Margaret leant closer and placed her hand on her mother's wrist, squeezing it for her to concentrate. 'What about his face?'

'Andrew's?'

'No, Goodhew's. You said I should've seen his face.' Margaret tugged on Edna's sleeve, trying to drag the answer out of her. 'Why did you say that? How did he look? Worried, shocked . . . excited or what?'

Edna paused and closed her eyes, trying to picture his expression, and Margaret found herself holding her breath. 'Disappointed,' Edna answered finally. 'No, actually, I'd say crestfallen is a better word for it. And he took the card with him, so it must have been important.'

Margaret slipped off into the kitchen, and stood with her back resting against the door. Everyone was fallible but if Goodhew thought her brother was guilty, perhaps she needed to listen to what he had to say. Her head spun at the concept.

'I'll tidy the kitchen while I'm out here,' she called out and ran the taps and clattered the dishes, trying to block out the chant now beating incessantly through her head. 'My mother, my brother, my daughter . . . My mother, my brother, my daughter . . .'

The sitting room was warm and the homely sound of washing dishes soothed Edna Burrows so that she drifted into sleep.

She drifted away from the reality of murder and suspicion. She forgot her granddaughter had been killed. She even forgot her only son had been arrested.

Instead she dreamt that she was eight again. She was running along a path through the woods, between giant oaks with bluebells and snowdrops sprouting at their feet.

She was racing towards a five-bar gate; her leather shoes were wet with dew and the skirt of her pinafore flapped around her knees. She stretched out her hand to reach the finishing point. 'I won, I won!' she shouted with delight.

Three children chased her, as another walked behind them with a willowy lady in a navy-blue coat. Her heart soared: her mother, brothers and sisters were all here. *Silly me*, she thought, *they were here all along.*

She wondered why she'd never noticed how beautiful her mother had been. Edna now picked her a handful of flowers and ran over to present them.

She stretched her hand further round her mother's waist, knowing she must never lose any of her family again.

When Margaret finally came out of the kitchen, Edna's skin was grey and already turning cold.

CHAPTER 36

MONDAY, 9 MAY 2011

Goodhew wished he wasn't in the room. It had been just like sitting in the headmaster's office telling tales. Kincaide and Marks were directly facing one another, as if ignoring his presence.

DI Marks stood beside his desk, his hands clasped behind his back. 'Goodhew's convinced that Andy Burrows didn't do it.'

Kincaide shot a fierce glance at Goodhew, pink spots of irritation blotching in his cheeks. 'Well, he would say that, wouldn't he? Sir. He didn't make the arrest and it was my idea . . . sir.'

'Oh, for heaven's sake, this is a murder case, not a playground game of conkers. He was the one that made the link with the birthday card, Michael.'

'I realize that, sir, but I really think Goodhew's just jealous. In the same situation as me, he'd be pushing to convince us that the evidence was sufficient.'

Goodhew scowled. 'He's been charged so, yes, there does appear to be a case against him, but do you really want him on your conscience if there are any doubts?'

Marks finally turned to Goodhew. 'Gary, get out. I'll speak to you afterwards,' he barked.

Before Goodhew had reached the door, he heard Marks continue slamming Kincaide. 'If Goodhew's jealous, then I'll deal with it, but in the meantime Burrows is under arrest, and his mother's died not knowing whether or not he murdered her granddaughter. So I bloody well do hope we've got it right. Go over the evidence again . . . and what about these anonymous calls pointing to a suspect, Peter Walsh?'

'Cranks, we decided,' Kincaide said. Which was the last thing Goodhew expected to hear clearly, as he closed the door behind him.

Goodhew leant against the outer wall of the office in the hope of catching some more fragments, but such was the level of pique in DI Marks' voice that every word carried into the corridor.

'Is that the royal "we" I hear, because Goodhew and Gully don't share your opinion. Are you aware of the note that Goodhew had pushed through his front door?'

A couple of seconds passed before Kincaide answered. Goodhew filled in the gap with the familiar image of Kincaide gnawing the skin beside his thumbnail.

'I know he received a note, and I had a quick look.'

'And what exactly did that "quick look" tell you?'

Another pause, enough time for Kincaide to remove a piece of bitten-off dead skin from the tip of his tongue and flick it to the floor.

'We need evidence for the prosecution. That's what I was focusing on.'

'The last thing anyone needs, and particularly that family, is the arrest of the correct person that fails to deliver a conviction just because we've failed to do our jobs thoroughly.'

Goodhew barely caught Kincaide's next words. 'I don't see what the problem is, since we all want the right result, don't we?'

DI Marks lowered his voice to a dangerous whisper and fired his next words like darts from a blowpipe. 'Kincaide, get me everything you've got on Burrows. That includes each scrap of information I haven't yet seen. And think of a good reason why you ignored this note and "because Goodhew got it first" won't wash.' He slammed his hand down on to his desk. 'You may feel that there have been instances when I have given Goodhew too much latitude, and on those occasions I have been fully aware of your resentment, for which I apologize. It has been a failing of mine that I need to address, rather than a policy I plan to extend anywhere else within the team.'

A moment later, Kincaide flew through the door as though one of those darts had harpooned him in the buttock. Obviously a septic missile, judging by his expression.

* * *

Goodhew later returned to Marks' office, where his boss's expression had returned to its usual state: placid and impenetrable. Marks held up a photocopy of the anonymous letter. 'I've heard the phone calls, Gary, but what makes you think that this letter comes from the same woman?'

'I visited this Peter Walsh's house and a girl walked past me in the street. There was something . . .' he paused, searching for the right word '. . . I don't know, something odd about her, I suppose. I looked at her directly and she seemed startled. Afterwards, when I was away I realized she looked just a little bit like Kaye Whiting. This sounds ridiculous, doesn't it?'

'Well, it does seem rather tenuous, but go on.'

'That's it, really. I had a feeling she was the anonymous caller, but I didn't get the note until Thursday night. I was checking out Helen Neill when you called me in.'

'I know, and I had the details of that case brought in here as soon as they arrived.' Marks laid his hand flat on a half-inch pile of faxes, emails and other assorted documents. 'I'm sorry I didn't give you a bit more scope to chase up the Peter Walsh lead. Whether Andrew Burrows is the killer or not remains to be seen. Personally, I hope he is because I don't want to be in the middle of a wrongful-arrest fiasco. But, even more, I don't want a total balls-up that leaves a killer still roaming around.'

A wave of claustrophobic tension swept through Gary, he wanted to be out working. 'Are you saying I can get on with it, sir?'

'Gary, be patient, will you? You're like my wife the day before the January sales. Ready, fire and aim – you and Kincaide both.' He sighed a deliberate, long, slow and incredibly irritating sigh.

Goodhew sighed too, and waited.

'OK, Gary, here's what I want you to do. Check out Helen Neill. If, and only if, there are reasons to connect the two cases, then investigate Peter Walsh and anyone he knows who may have written this letter. Keep me informed at every step.

'Remember, there's nothing to indicate that a man abducted Kaye Whiting, so your letter writer is a suspect.' He knew he had already stretched Goodhew's attention span to its brittle limits. 'I'll make a resource available to you, if you need it.'

Gary was already lifting the Neill notes from the desk. ‘Gully would be my first choice.’

‘Mmmm, thought it might. Anything I should know about you two?’

‘Yeah, we work well together.’

And, with that comment, Goodhew made the second quickest exit in the history of DI Marks’ office.

CHAPTER 37

TUESDAY, 10 MAY 2011

The 8.57 from Paddington pulled into Gloucester at 10.38. The disjointed journey from Cambridge had consisted of two late-running trains punctuated by a shuffling Circle Line tube.

Gary stepped from the carriage on to Platform One, and jogged past the slow-speed tourists to claim the first black-and-white Cathedral cab on the rank.

'The Fosters, Gloucester Docks,' he instructed. 'How long will it take?'

''Bout five minutes, that's all,' the driver replied, in a rounded Gloucestershire burr.

Gary checked his watch, he'd be half an hour late.

'Where're you from, then?' the cabbie enquired, and spent the journey extolling the virtues of local tourist attractions. 'That's the Docks,' he announced, at last.

Goodhew saw a cluster of red-brick warehouses perched shoulder-to-shoulder beside the road. Wrought-iron entrance gates opened on to a vista of deserted car parks.

They abutted the shadowy waters of the dock basins, whose surfaces rippled with the undercurrent of poverty and child labour still reflected from the uniform dark windows of the scrubbed-up Victorian grain and timber stores.

The taxi followed the road leading into the hub of the docks and pulled up in a half-empty staff car park. It lay across a narrow inlet from the Merchants' Quay shopping centre, a huge green and glass conservatory-style building that resembled a do-it-yourself kit interpretation of the Crystal Palace.

The driver pointed to a pub. 'That's the Fosters, one of those theme pubs.'

Goodhew paid him and walked across to the front door, aware that he was being watched from inside.

Before the door closed behind him, the landlord nodded to a corner table. 'Mr Hayward's waiting for you.'

Ron Hayward, Detective Inspector retired, gave a brief nod and beckoned Gary across. They shook hands.

'I took the liberty of getting you a glass of Coke.'

'Thank you.'

Hayward held up his pint. 'Shame you couldn't join me in a pint, but you're on duty and I'm not.' He chuckled at his little joke. 'So you're interested in Helen Neill, then?' he added, rosy-faced.

Gary nodded. 'I was hoping to talk to DCI Barnes, but he's not available.'

'Dead, actually. Heart attack. But I think you'll find I'm not a bad second choice.'

Goodhew wondered whether there was an intentioned barb in the comment. He placed his pile of documents in front of him, with a fresh sheet of paper to one side, and removed the cap from his pen.

Many retired inspectors would relish the opportunity to dabble in a serving officer's investigation, and he was ready for the role of listener.

Hayward launched into his story, unconcerned at being overheard. 'I remember the Helen Neill murder very well indeed. She was found in the Forest of Dean, a couple of miles from Cinderford. She'd been lying there about a month, we reckon.' His voice rose to a merry blast. 'She was as rotten as hell.'

'Who found her?' Gary asked quietly.

Hayward leant forward and whispered, 'Well, there'd been a bit of a fire on the edge of the forest, about a hundred yards away from her. I reckon it was started by kids. Anyhow this labourer, Jimmy McCue from Pycroft Farm, is cutting through the trees. Using a shortcut down one of the paths, so he says, and he sees the smoke and heads across to investigate. And, bingo, he practically trips over the body.' Hayward raised his eyebrows and his voice. 'So he says.'

'So he says?' Goodhew queried. 'He was a suspect, then?'

Hayward drained his glass but continued talking from up at the bar. 'Well, of course, he was. He found the body. And by the time he'd finished he'd mashed the ground to porridge with his great size elevens.' He returned with two pints of Tetley. 'Don't worry, I didn't get you one. There's just no point going to and fro like a yo-yo, is there? As for McCue? I hope he still is a suspect. I interviewed him a couple of times, didn't like him at all. He's one of them Irish gippo types, call themselves labourers, but they're unreliable as far as I'm concerned. Bloody dids.'

'So you didn't manage to find any evidence against him?' Gary asked.

'No,' he snorted with disgust. 'We had to let it drop. They stick together, those people.'

'Hmm.' Goodhew sipped his Coke, exhaled slowly, then persevered. 'What about Helen – how did she disappear?'

Hayward rolled his eyes from behind his pint. 'Usual story. Been out with friends, they lost track of her during the evening, and there you go, Bob's your jolly old uncle.' He banged the glass on the table for emphasis. 'Another silly girl who should've been more careful. Not that I'm condoning it, of course, but it's not like they've never been warned, is it?'

'For God's sake,' Goodhew muttered.

'What?'

'What are the facts? You know, those little things that definitely happened,' he growled.

Hayward glared. 'Well, in my opinion I'm giving them to you. But if that's not what you want, that's up to you.'

'No, no. Sorry, carry on. What leads were there after she vanished?'

'Well, there was a car, a red Astra Estate, that was sighted around the corner from the Cathedral.'

'In Cinderford?'

'No, here in Gloucester. The registration number was picked up on city-centre CCTV. Registered to a Tony Vitale. Well, it wasn't right or it was a false number, because Mr Vitale and his car were in Birmingham all that weekend.'

'And she disappeared on a Saturday?'

'Yeah, that's it. Can't remember the dates.'

'I've got them: Saturday, twenty-fifth of April 2009 and her body turned up on Wednesday, twenty-seventh of May 2009.'

Hayward tapped his index finger on the table top. 'Now, what did seem odd was the body. Not much left, like I said, but the forensics people said there was no sign of any sexual assault. Seems funny, that. Young girl, out for the night, has a few drinks and chances her luck with some bastard who kills her. Well, he's going to rape her, isn't he? Or what's the point? But the report came back "gagged and bound, no evidence of a fight".' Goodhew already knew this but the words still made him prickle.

Hayward waggled his finger. 'But they admitted it was hard to tell. I thought then maybe it was a domestic, but not likely. Nice family, hers, completely devastated. At the end of the day,' he paused to shrug and give a you-win-some, you-lose-some smile, 'it's one we didn't solve.'

'Amazing,' muttered Goodhew drily.

'So what's new now?'

'We had an anonymous call linking this to another more recent case in Cambridge. And there are similarities.' Goodhew doodled a speech bubble. 'Did you receive any unusual anonymous tip-offs at the time?'

Hayward shrugged again. 'Can't remember now. You'd have to go over the notes.'

'Yeah, I'll do that,' replied Goodhew, standing up and simultaneously gathering his papers. 'Thanks.'

'Is that it?' Ron Hayward rose to his feet and shook hands with Goodhew. 'I can make the time if there's anything else you'd like help with.'

'No, no, I really don't want to take up any more of your retirement,' Goodhew replied. 'You were clearly looking forward to it for a long time,' he added to himself as he stepped out into the fresh air.

He used his mobile to call a taxi, and agreed to wait for it back at the entrance gates. 'I bet they had a party when he left the force. What a waste of time,' he cursed.

CHAPTER 38

TUESDAY, 10 MAY 2011

As he rinsed the red and yellow mug, Pete was reminded of his first date with Donna. A swift thrill of pleasure rushed through him as he recalled her urgency.

He dried the mug and tossed the tea towel to the back of the draining board. As he placed the mug back on its shelf he stared at it, trying to focus on that first night.

Nothing wrong with it, he decided. Definitely better than last night, when there was too little conversation and he'd taken her home straight after dinner.

Something was lacking, though. Perhaps he was feeling overtired, or maybe it was all happening just too soon after he'd been seeing Paulette.

He wiped down the draining board with the tea towel and threw it into the open washing machine. Perhaps he was on the rebound? He walked through to the living room and sat in the chair beside the window.

Bright sunshine glistened back up from the rain-soaked pavements and he guessed there was a rainbow outside somewhere. That was what Paulette had been like; sunshine and rainstorms all rolled into one.

He didn't want to keep thinking about Paulette. He'd been over it and over it in his head. No more walking on eggshells, no more emotional smothering; he'd made the right choice. Now he had to consider Donna.

He imagined two columns on a sheet of paper, one headed 'good points' and the other one headed 'bad points'.

Donna was more independent than Paulette, also pretty and cheerful. But she had no real ambitions, just saw herself getting married and maybe being well-off one day.

He stopped there: if he was totally honest with himself, he knew he wanted someone who sought more from life.

He watched a single raindrop slide down the pane, sparkling and gathering momentum as it joined up with others on its descent.

That's the girl he wanted to find: unique, pure and exciting. He wasn't sure a woman like that truly existed but, for as long as he could remember, he'd had the idea that she might. Letting go of that would feel like accepting a consolation prize.

He'd asked himself many times whether his expectations were too high, and he still didn't know the answer. Except he knew that his parents were happy, and so were his sister Selena and her husband Phil.

Perhaps he needed to try harder.

He decided to surprise Donna with flowers, hoping that the walk to the shop would refresh him and leave him in brighter spirits.

He stepped outside just as a middle-aged man and a thin blonde woman emerged from the unoccupied house next-door. Another estate agent, he guessed, looking at the man's grey suit and co-ordinated shirt and tie. *Smarmy salesman*, he thought, but then the woman looked no better; too earnest to be much fun.

Pete saw her rattle the house details against her free hand, in irritation at the man's fawning attempt at charm. 'Lovely, lovely,' the estate agent kept saying, while gazing at her hopefully.

Pete liked the idea of a single person moving in. His old neighbours, Anj and Bart, had half-killed each other night after night for six months, until Bart moved out and put in for a divorce. Anj had claimed that it was her own fault for marrying someone called Bart in the first place.

Pete grinned at the prospective buyer. She smiled back and suddenly didn't seem at all surly. He jogged towards the shop and hoped that she'd make a much nicer neighbour.

CHAPTER 39

WEDNESDAY, 11 MAY 2011

Someone had slapped a Post it note in the middle of the small clear patch on Gully's desk. It read 'Goodhew wants you all afternoon'.

Gully had smirked and muttered a wicked, 'I wish,' before duly rearranging her workload. She made sure that she was available at 12.00 and fidgeted until 1.20, when Goodhew finally arrived.

They settled at Gully's desk with two mugs of coffee and a packet of Jaffa Cakes. Goodhew first cleared Sue's desktop, unceremoniously dumping every item removed in one dodgy stack on the floor against the filing cabinet.

'How'd you get on in Gloucester?'

'Well, I saw Hayward, also the location of the body, Helen Neill's parents and I've brought back copies of most of the information collated during the murder investigation.' Goodhew paused to sip his coffee. 'Hayward was a wind-up, who certainly improved the quality of the police force by retiring. He clearly didn't give a toss that the killer's never been caught. Anyway, I think the only way we can get the OK to chase Peter Walsh and our woman caller is to show that she knew what she was talking about when she linked the two cases.'

'So,' Sue interjected, 'we need to spend this afternoon mapping the two and then see what we come up with.'

Goodhew nodded, handing her half the pile of notes. 'Go over these and see what you find. I'll do this other lot, then we can go through it all together and compile a comprehensive list.'

Goodhew moved himself to the adjoining desk, and settled down with the paperwork. He glanced across at Gully, as she concentrated with her head resting on her left hand. Her right hand held a pen that followed the notes as she read them. She was bright and very able but she now looked like a schoolgirl sitting an exam. She clearly didn't realize that he was watching her, and he smiled as he noticed that every time she moved her hand to the notepad, it returned via the Jaffa Cakes.

They worked on in companionable silence until, at 3.20, they were finally ready to compile a joint list.

'Let's start with the victims,' began Goodhew. 'There's the obvious physical similarities: both white, medium build, fair complexion, shoulder-length hair.'

'Similar ages,' added Gully, 'only Helen was two years younger.'

'But the killer was three years older by the time Kaye was abducted. That's a relative difference of only one year.'

'If it's the same killer,' warned Gully.

'Yeah, yeah. Don't worry, I'm not going to turn this into something it isn't.' He nodded at her list. 'What else?'

'Oh yes, both single and not known to have a boyfriend at the time of their disappearances. Neither had any history of going missing. But this isn't showing anything conclusive.'

'It doesn't matter. It's just a picture we're building. On the crime itself, though, the similarity is far less commonplace. Both girls were abandoned alive, and both were bound and gagged.'

'What with?'

'Nylon rope – but you know that.' He nodded to the pile of papers. 'You've got the forensic reports.'

'Yes, I know. I was just making sure you did.'

'Thanks. So were they of the same brand?' he replied, testing her in return.

'No, one was dark green, several years old, and originally stocked by Woolworths, the other was pale blue and available at almost any garden or DIY shop,' she replied with confidence.

'Tell me about the knots.' He flicked through the file, hunting for photographs.

'In each case the rope was secured by wrapping round and lashing, and then finished with a knot.'

'The same type of knot?' He slid two pictures from the folder.

'Oh,' she flustered slightly, 'I didn't read that bit.' She took the prints from him and studied the pattern of the ropes. She didn't let her eyes dwell on the dead hands they restrained.

'The knots are identical, but we can't read too much into that. It's called a Fisherman's Bend, but it isn't so obscure or clever that it couldn't be merely a coincidence. Now tell me what strikes you about the similarities in the crimes.'

'Well,' replied Gully, 'when Kaye Whiting's body was first found I assumed it would be a rape and murder investigation, so I was really surprised when there was no evidence of any sexual assault, and not even any sign of a struggle. Helen Neill's murder has the same feel to it, and I would say that's a strong similarity. Also, although the locations aren't in the same area, they were both found outdoors, in sites with easy public access, and in both cases the abductor would have required a vehicle to get them there.'

'Hmm,' Goodhew nodded, 'that seems good reasoning.'

'And, on the subject of a vehicle, there was a sighting in the Helen Neill case. What about double-checking Vitale's alibi?'

Again Goodhew nodded. 'We could check his whereabouts for Kaye's disappearance and, if that's suspicious, then double-check his original story. But we mustn't be sidetracked into Helen's case if there's no genuine connection.'

'How common is it for abductees to be abandoned alive?'

'Considering there's no sign that either case was money related, or linked to any relationship conflict that either victim was suffering, I would say very rare.'

Gully picked up the Jaffa Cakes, tipped out the last one and threw the box in the bin. She waggled it enthusiastically in Goodhew's direction, as she spoke. 'What's the motive, Gary?'

'Motive?' he began slowly, letting his thoughts brew into a logical flow of mental text before releasing them. 'Let's assume for the moment that it is the same killer. The motivation may come in the form of a trigger, or a series of triggers. But in this case we're not seeing killing committed in a frenzy. We don't even know whether the murderer was present when either girl died, and I see no reason even to assume it was a man.'

'So it could be our anonymous caller?'

'It's a possibility, since she could more easily catch these girls off guard. And, although there's no apparent sexual motive, have you heard the phrase "Eligibility Paraphiliac"?'

'No.'

'It's about repetitive desire for someone who, in some way, is taboo to have as a sexual partner. The woman I saw outside Walsh's house bore a physical resemblance to both these girls, so it could all be part of a fetish she has.'

'Or her along with someone else?' Sue added.

'I suppose anything's possible, really.' Goodhew pondered that idea for a few seconds. 'No, but this much is certain: our killer – or killers, for that matter – left virtually no clues. There are no hair samples, minimal fibres, and the strange contradiction of a murder location that is both publicly accessible whilst being isolated enough for the girls to be abandoned without risk of discovery. In both cases, careful planning was involved and there was also a risk that the girls could have been found alive.'

'That sounds sexual to me. The thrill of the planning and execution of the crime, and then the suspense of waiting for the outcome. It's like a metaphoric courtship.'

'A metaphoric courtship?' Goodhew repeated in wonder.

'Abducting the girl is meeting her. Tying her up is captivating her and getting her attention. Then there's the wait to see if the courtship is paying off, and then *bing*, the body turns up and it's a big sexual kick. That's how it usually is when you start seeing someone, isn't it? Getting your hands on their body is one of the highlights.'

Goodhew raised his eyebrows and just blinked at her for a long moment. 'Could you write that bit down for me, so I can digest it properly? And if there's no sexual motive, and it's murder for murder's sake, then the killer's rituals will help us build a picture.'

'There will be more deaths if that's the case, won't there?'

'Maybe even some already that we don't know about. That's why, as soon as we've finished with this list, we need Marks to agree to release Andy Burrows and let us concentrate on finding our anonymous caller.'

CHAPTER 40

WEDNESDAY, 11 MAY 2011

Fiona Robinson stepped from the shower and bent over to dry her face on the warm bath sheet draped over the radiator. She wiped an arc through the steam on the mirror, enough to see her hair. She combed it until it fell in a sleek curtain of straight strands trickling tepid water down her bare back.

She then separated it into three even sections and wove a plait, securing it at the end with a hair band. Still naked, she applied her make-up, wiped down the shower cubicle, brushed her teeth and washed her hands. And, in accordance with her usual routine, she checked her hair again in her bedroom mirror before dressing herself in the clothes lying ready on the bed.

She couldn't remember when she'd first learnt to plait, but guessed she must have been five or six years old at the time. Since then it had become a habit she turned to whenever her hair hung loose. Her fingers would reach for it automatically and intertwine long thin fair strands of it until five or six braids hung beside her left cheek. Then she'd disentangle them and start again.

Fiona made herself a coffee and set it down on the edge of the low table next to her armchair. She switched on the TV for the news and, without thinking, pulled the band from the end of her damp hair, then subdivided one of the existing sections – blissfully unaware of the irony that her fate was already interwoven with two other lives.

Fiona Robinson, Marlowe Gates and Stephanie Palmer had never met, but they now tumbled towards each other on a fatal collision course.

They'd started far apart: one in Cambridge, one in Crewe and one in Auckland – until, with broken hearts fanning the desire for change, Australia was exchanged for London, and Fiona left the Derby Dales for the flatlands of the Fens.

They all three always visited the cinema alone, watched late-night television, read books, and each kept a diary. No close friends, no boyfriends, minimal family contact and no pets.

They all tried to keep it simple, and lived by their own rules of distrust and isolation.

Stephanie's alter ego was the ultimate party girl. First to the bar and last out the door. Loud and brash in public, laughing loudly at jokes, drinking pints with the lads but never getting involved with them. Not emotionally anyway.

Just physically – but she could handle that.

And if they ever wanted to see her again, they'd just have to go on wanting, wouldn't they?

Fiona and Marlowe played it safer. They just avoided men altogether.

Fiona reached the end of making her braid. She curled the end of it around until it hovered a few inches from her face. She studied the end, then began to unpick it.

'Why does it do that?' she wondered.

And it never failed to annoy her. Every time she plaited her hair, she started with three almost identical strands. There would be nothing to choose between them and she was always careful, but whenever she reached the end she found that one of them had mysteriously run out.

CHAPTER 41

WEDNESDAY, 11 MAY 2011

The single-decker wove its way along a twisting route from Cambridge centre, via the industrial units in Newmarket Road, to the post-war housing estates of Fen Ditton, which lay three miles to the east. Marlowe sat at the back until the stop before her own, then made her way to the front, ready to alight as soon as the bus came to a standstill.

She stepped out on to the pavement, opposite a small shopping parade and ducked under the steel railing next to a row of lock-ups. A patch of surplus concrete led on to a strip of waste ground, providing a shortcut to the alley on the far side. She was careful to miss the dog mess and discarded condoms, and climbed through the hole in the mesh fence opposite, without incident.

The footpath, a privet-lined alley, brought her into Laburnum Gardens where she turned right and hurried towards number 17. She eyed the house's windows; a mishmash of unmatched net curtains prevented her from seeing inside, but she saw a silhouette move behind one of them.

The gate's metal hinges squealed as she pushed it open; it swung back against a straggling pansy. The first tingle of nerves began as she pressed the bell. She didn't hear it ringing inside so she rapped the chrome knocker.

Marlowe made fists in her pockets as she waited, and the cuffs of her coat covered the fresh bruises on her wrists and forearms. The delicately speckled, criss-crossed scabs itched, and her knotted stomach sent out frustrated messages that made her scratch at them through the beige raincoat.

She waited almost two minutes, then knocked again, this time banging eight times.

She shifted her weight from foot to foot. 'Come on!' she growled, and checked the street in each direction. It was still deserted.

She turned back to the door and clouted it several more times with the flat of her hand, then snapped open the letter box. The stairs and hall stared at her impassively through the oblong slot.

'Open the door. I know you're in there,' she called. 'I only want to talk.'

She continued to peer inside, hoping to spot a movement or perhaps a shadow. After another long minute, Marlowe straightened up and eased the letter box shut.

She stepped back and scrutinized each window in turn. Without warning, her frustration boiled to the surface and she leapt forward to the letter box again. 'Open the fucking door,' she screamed and kicked it hard enough to make it move slightly in its frame.

She strode back to the gate and threw it wide, back into the unfortunate pansy. 'I know you're in there,' she bellowed, her voice rising to a screech. 'You stupid bitch!'

She then turned and darted back along the empty street towards the alleyway.

Behind her, a face pressed the net curtains closer to the glass. The woman watched until Marlowe had vanished from sight. She then tore down the stairs and across to the telephone housed in a corner beside the front door. With her gaze still riveted on the letter box, she raised the receiver and dialled the six familiar digits.

The answerphone clicked on and she waited for the tone. Then, in a small voice, she whispered, 'Pete, it's me. Phone me. There's something you need to know.'

CHAPTER 42

WEDNESDAY, 11 MAY 2011

'Julie, please open the door,' Marlowe called from the landing of the block of flats.

'Who is it?' Julie Wilson called back.

'My name's Marlowe. You don't know me.'

The door cracked open. 'What do you want?'

'I need to talk to you about Peter Walsh.'

Julie hesitated, but then allowed the door to swing wider and she took a few seconds to assess Marlowe.

Julie wore a towelling robe and her hair was still damp; she clearly hadn't expected a visitor. There was a strange look in her eyes: contemptuous maybe, or cynical or embittered, or perhaps she'd just been caught off-guard – Marlowe couldn't tell.

'Go through.' She waved Marlowe inside, and through to the lounge. Julie herself didn't follow. Marlowe sat down beside the window and looked across to the car park, trying to guess whether Julie owned a car and, if so, which one. Only an Escort, a large Citroën and a small Fiat occupied the parking area. Knowing which car someone drove was a small piece of very public information, but it made her realize how very little she knew about Julie Wilson. She turned her gaze back to the sitting room and something about the bookshelves caught her eye. Without thinking, she was on her feet and across the room. She squatted suddenly to inspect the lower shelves.

Her concentration was broken by a loud cough. Marlowe turned sharply, like a startled rabbit. Julie stood close behind her, now dressed in a purple jumper and an ankle-length black jersey skirt, with coffee mug in hand. She had clearly watched as Marlowe began poking through her bookshelves.

'Sorry,' Marlowe muttered.

'Don't worry about it.' Julie's voice had chilled from cool to icy. 'He said you weren't all there, so it's nice to see you can at least read.'

Marlowe scrambled to her feet. 'And write and add, if you're really interested.' A cheap clock ticked loudly from the wall above the television. 'I'm not thick, if that's what he told you. I know, for example, that he gave us both a bad time and . . .' She let her sentence trail into nothing.

'And?' Julie demanded.

That single word instantly filled Marlowe with huge disdain for the other woman. 'And?' she echoed, her tone suddenly oozing with heavy sarcasm. 'Oh yes, and you're not that thick either, are you, so I thought you might be the one to give me the answers to some questions that are bugging me.'

'About him?'

Marlowe felt a familiar anger beginning to fill her, and heard her words becoming angrier, driven from within. 'Yes "him". It's wicked even allowing his name to pass your lips, isn't it? Even after so long.'

'What's the point of this?' Julie turned away, placing her mug on the table to avoid looking at her visitor. 'Life goes on, you know.'

'Maybe for you.' Marlowe hesitated, picked a paperback from the lower shelf, and continued. 'I have this book too, and most of these in fact, and that picture, and at least half of your videos . . .'

'And so does Pete.'

'But I had them first. And I've watched him with you, and with your replacement, and now with the latest one. And he's taken us all to the same places and tried to make us the same.'

'So what?' Julie answered, turning back to Marlowe, her face now a mask, the eyes hard and ungiving.

Perhaps Julie doesn't care. Marlowe dismissed the thought. 'Julie, have you ever heard of a girl called Helen Neill?'

'No, who is she?'

'A murder victim. Her body turned up about a year before you met Peter. In the Forest of Dean.'

'Did she look like you?' Julie asked.

'Yes, like both of us, I suppose.' Marlowe stepped towards her. 'You know who I mean, don't you?'

Julie shrugged but didn't move. 'Pete showed me her picture in the paper one day. Said it was a bit like you.'

'If I said I think Peter's connected to her death, would you help me trap him?' Marlowe reached forward to touch her arm.

'No,' Julie jerked away, 'that's crap.'

Marlowe pressed on. 'He needs to be stopped.'

'Stopped from what? Going out with other girls?' Julie kept backing away until they reached the narrow passage approaching the front door.

'No, from killing them,' Marlowe pleaded, unaware of her left fist thumping the wall beside her.

'You're obsessed.' Julie felt behind her for the door. 'You and him are two of a kind. But he's out of my life now, and you should stop trying to vilify him and just come to terms with being dumped.'

'You're wrong,' Marlowe breathed.

'No, no, *you're* wrong! Wrong coming here and trying to drag me into your therapy.' Julie unclipped the latch. 'So what if Pete likes girls that look alike? And it's all our own fault if we stick around for his abuse. But that's what you haven't come to terms with, isn't it? He treated you badly because you let him. Get your head around that. Deal with it. Put him in the past.' She stepped to one side. 'Now I want you to leave.'

Marlowe dropped the book at Julie's feet and drew herself closer until they stood eye to eye, and Julie's shoulder blades were pressed against the passage wall. Marlowe's voice went quiet. 'You may be right about some of it, Julie, but I'll tell you this. The next time another girl is murdered, it will be on your conscience as much as it's on mine.'

Julie pushed herself away from the wall and shoved Marlowe back against the opposite one. 'My life's going well and he can't touch me now,' she hissed. She then clamped her fingers around Marlowe's upper arm, digging her nails into the underside, and thrust her out of the flat.

CHAPTER 43

MONDAY, 16 MAY 2011

Fiona Robinson loved entering other people's homes. It was the best part of being an estate agent, and it kept her competitive. She could always judge her own progress by comparing her home with the ones she was viewing, to decide whether she was achieving enough.

And, given her age, she knew she was doing better than at least ninety per cent of the clients she saw. *Including this one*, she thought, as she waited on the doorstep of the old terrace house in Glisson Road. The aluminium door opened a crack and Mrs Reynolds squinted at her from behind the chain.

'Hello, I'm Fiona Robinson,' she beamed, 'from Sampson's, the estate agents.'

'Right-ho, dear. Hold on and I'll let you in.' The arthritic fingers trembled as she struggled with the chain.

Fiona wondered why such security gadgets weren't designed to be easier for the elderly to use quickly.

Eventually the door opened and Fiona entered a small hallway bedecked in large-print, dark-brown leafed wallpaper.

She knew instantly this would be a 'plenty of original features' property, but 'in need of updating'.

'How are you, Mrs Reynolds?'

'Oh, not so bad, my dear. Can I get you a cup of tea?'

'No time, I'm afraid. I'm really busy today.'

Mrs Reynolds was a widow about to move into a development of flats for the retired. She talked constantly. 'I lost my Eric four years ago this September, you know.'

Fiona smiled sympathetically, for a second.

'He had cancer – was ill for two years before he went. We've got one daughter, a bit older than you, but I don't see her much. She's very busy. Well, you all are, aren't you, you young people.'

'Uh-huh' Fiona noted down the dimensions of the dining room and proceeded to the kitchen.

'Like you, I expect – busy getting ahead. So I've decided to buy a flat and spend any money left over so it never gets wasted on nursing fees when I'm really old.'

'Good idea,' Fiona replied, as she checked the under-stairs cupboard.

'That's what my daughter said. I said, "What about you?" and she said "Don't worry, I'm doing fine." I must admit that I thought, then, if you don't need all the money you're earning, perhaps you could come round more often. But I didn't say so, of course.'

'No.' Fiona made her way upstairs, still pursued by the lonely Mrs Reynolds.

'Do you have family nearby, then?'

'No, they're in Bradford.' Fiona wrote some brief notes and hurried on to the last bedroom.

'Not married either?'

'No, no, quite happy single, actually.' Fiona reached the head of the stairs and closed her notebook. 'All done, thank you, Mrs Reynolds,' she said, smiling brightly.

They made their way back down, and Mrs Reynolds carried on chatting. 'A nice young lady like you should be courting at least.' Fiona opened the front door, keen to move on to her next appointment but, before she could speak, Mrs Reynolds continued, 'Unless you're one of these modern women married to their careers. I've been out with one or two men from the social club.' She wrinkled up her nose. 'I'd love to have a young man – or at least one with his own teeth and all his marbles.'

Fiona laughed then, caught off guard.

Her 3.30 appointment was in Queen Edith's Way, viewing another property about to go on the market. The owner, Anita Marshall, hadn't yet signed a contract and wanted to meet first to discuss details.

Fiona pulled into the cobbled drive and parked behind a new black BMW cabriolet.

This house, she decided, belonged to a client in the other ten per cent.

A dark-haired woman answered the door and motioned Fiona inside, whilst she continued chatting on her phone. Fiona hovered in the hallway, already making mental notes for the sale literature. Finally the woman finished her call. Her hand shot out and gave Fiona's a swift shake. 'Anita Marshall.'

'Fiona Robinson, pleased to meet you,' she said to the back of Anita's head, as she followed her towards the kitchen. And then into each successive room, as she was marched swiftly on a tour of the house.

A brief fifteen minutes later, she was back in her car, her ears ringing from Anita Marshall's self-satisfied tributes to her own success. 'I worked for all of this.' And, 'I love living alone.' And, 'What could a man give me that I haven't got here?' And even, 'I'd never have succeeded like this if I'd had children.'

Fiona realized how she herself probably sounded the same. Unconvincing. Unfulfilled. Lonely.

For the first time in her career, Fiona's determination had wavered just a fraction. Oh, yes, she was galloping forwards all right. But she suddenly realized that she wasn't sure where her final goal lay.

Her original motivation to succeed had been twofold: firstly to prove she could, and secondly to assure herself of an independent future. Even last Christmas, when everyone else was enjoying festive flings, she had been glad that she'd been too occupied to have time to meet anyone.

But now?

Now, she suddenly decided, she didn't want to turn into poor, isolated Anita Marshall.

CHAPTER 44

THURSDAY, 19 MAY 2011

Fiona was waiting in Hanley Road. She stayed in her car and flicked through her diary, as six o'clock came and went.

Mr Kimber was late, but viewers often were.

Fiona doodled little boxes around the day's appointments, then shaded them with light pen strokes. Yesterday she had written 'Busy today, had lunch at Brown's – very good. Sold Easter Cottage.'

Her diary entries were rarely more than one or two brief comments on the day's events. And, so far today, she had nothing she wished to write down.

She looked up just as Peter Walsh crossed the road on to her side. He had spotted her already, and nodded to her as he approached. *The neighbour? It wouldn't hurt to say hello*, she thought, and stepped out of her MX-5 to meet him.

They smiled politely at one another.

'Have you been waiting long?' he asked.

'No, just a few minutes. I guess it's just one of those afternoons,' she said.

'Estate agents are a nightmare.'

She smiled. 'Aren't they just!'

'Yup, they should all be shot.'

'You're going to kill me, then,' she laughed, reaching into her pocket and pulling out a set of keys clearly marked '28 Hanley Road'. She waved them in front of him. 'I'm the estate agent, actually.'

He laughed, too, and then shook his head. 'I've put my foot in now it, haven't I?'

'Depends on whether you were being sexist when you mistook me for the buyer.'

He pursed his lips, screwing up his nose, as he gave her a sheepish smile. 'I think I probably was. That's unforgivable, isn't it?'

'At least you're honest,' she admitted, and quite spontaneously she touched his arm.

Her diary entry for the day was to be typically short. She doodled a little bunch of flowers tied with a bow and wrote: 'Client d.n.a. at Hanley Road, but neighbour interesting.'

CHAPTER 45

FRIDAY, 27 MAY 2011

The custody sergeant rang Goodhew as soon as Andy Burrows' paperwork was in order, and he was thus free to leave.

Burrows waited for Goodhew in the lobby. 'They said you'd offered to give me a lift home. I'd appreciate it – if it's still OK, that is.'

'Of course,' Goodhew said, then walked him through to the car park.

As soon as Burrows fastened his seatbelt, he started to talk. 'You heard about my mother, I suppose? I wish she'd lived to see me get let out. Since I found out I was going home, I've been saying to myself that she knows, though. She's looking down on me, that's what I think.'

'Did you miss her funeral?'

'No, it was on the Monday before last, and I had an escort, of course. I saw Margaret then. I felt so sorry for her, I couldn't look her in the eye. You heard what I did, I suppose?'

'Bits and pieces,' Goodhew fibbed.

'Well, I've made a proper statement now, but I don't mind telling you again that it was you I wanted to talk to when I came in, in the first place.' He paused and the silence jarred him into talking more quickly, chattering simply to avoid another lull. 'She was keen to visit Woodbridge, and she'd mentioned it several times in the past, but with Mum's birthday coming up it now seemed ideal. I don't know what she found so interesting for so long, and the first hour was fine, but then she kept going round and round all the antiquey shops, peering at every little display case. D'you know what I mean?'

Goodhew nodded. 'Not my cup of tea, either.' He eased his foot from the accelerator simply to prolong the journey.

'Well, I decided to wander off on my own for a bit, and in the end I popped into a pub for a pint. By the time I met up with her again, I'd had three but I was fine to drive. It had been a couple of hours since, and it's supposed to wear off at a pint an hour. And it's OK to drive on two, isn't it?'

'So I've heard.' Goodhew made a deliberately non-committal response, keen to avoid being sidetracked into a debate on drinking. 'Is that what you and Kaye argued about?'

'How do you know we argued?' Andy frowned.

'Something made her get out of your car.'

'How do you know she was ever in it?'

'We found her purchases, remember?' Goodhew glanced at Burrows, realizing that he'd now broken the flow of the story. 'Where did she get out?'

'We'd travelled five or six miles and we were approaching the centre of Ipswich – you know, near the hospital, by the roundabout? I'm not even sure that's the best way back to Cambridge from Woodbridge, but that's just where we ended up.'

Burrows' voice trailed off and he turned his head away from Goodhew to stare through his window. Goodhew kept quiet, and when Andy spoke again the pace of his words had quickened. 'She said I was irresponsible. She jumped out, yelling, said I had no right to put her at risk by drinking and driving. She marched off towards the city centre. I was sure she'd get the train or the bus. And I thought serve her right for being stroppy, although I expected her to tell on me, just to make sure I'd get a hard time. So I didn't go to Mum's party.'

He began rubbing the knuckles of his left hand up and down in a curve on the inside of the door, making a deliberate distraction for himself, and his voice dropped to one notch above a whisper. 'I didn't even know she didn't get back.' His voice wavered, then choked with tears. 'I feel so guilty . . . But I tell myself I wasn't to know. Was I?' Gulping, he rambled on, 'Kaye made time for people. She was nice. And Mum's died not knowing if it was me . . . I don't understand why anyone would do this to us all.'

At last, Goodhew pulled up at Burrows' flat.

A pane of glass in the front door had become the thoroughfare for half a brick. The jagged edges of the wound poked inwards, as the remaining glass fragments held each other in a wobbly grip.

Andy's mounting anguish vanished, as if cut to size by those shards of glass. 'I'm not popular, am I?' he observed, and turned back to look Goodhew straight in the face. 'Look, I know I've ballsed up from start to end, and I'm so, so sorry, but all I can say to help you is that I can't imagine Kaye taking a lift from anyone she didn't know. Even from a woman.'

Goodhew left Burrows standing on the pavement, glad to be free but not glad to be home.

He immediately rang Gully. 'Sue, it's me. I've just dropped Andy Burrows home. Can you find out who's following up his statement? I'm sure they're already checking the security cameras at the train and bus stations in Ipswich, but could you suggest they include the hospital? Just in case.'

'Which one?'

'Don't know, but it's a big one near the centre, at a roundabout, I think.'

'OK, I'll find it. Are you on your way to see Peter Walsh now?'

'Yeah, I'm dropping in on him at work. See you later.'

Goodhew waited for Peter Walsh in the foyer of Dunwold Insurance. The lone receptionist directed him towards a suite of low black leather settees, which he decided had been designed solely for the purpose of intimidating job candidates by placing the seats a mere six inches from floor level.

A few minutes later the receptionist approached him. 'I'm sorry but apparently he's in a meeting until ten.'

Goodhew studied her expression, sure he'd caught a definite note of contempt in the word 'apparently', but there was no clue as to whether it was for visitors, team meetings, her job or Peter Walsh?

'That's OK. I'll wait. I've always wondered what this place is like inside.'

'Stuck in the eighties, that's what,' she snorted. 'With nineteen eighties furniture and eighteen eighties attitudes.'

'Have you worked here long?' he asked.

'Too long,' she replied, as she excused herself to answer the phone.

After fifteen minutes, Peter Walsh himself stepped from the lift. In direct contrast to Andy Burrows, he seemed quiet and relaxed, nodding to the occasional passing colleague.

'How are you, Mr Walsh?' Goodhew asked.

'Fine, thank you. I was considering ringing to see whether you'd found the person trying to drop me in it, but I thought it must have blown over.'

'I'm afraid not. That's why I wanted to see you.'

'You've received more phone calls?'

'A note this time, actually. I really need to find the woman who's been contacting us, and I believe she's someone who knows you. An ex-girlfriend or perhaps even a colleague?'

'I could listen to the tape, and maybe I'd recognize the voice.'

Beyond Walsh, the receptionist watched them, partially obscured by her raised workstation.

Goodhew shook his head. 'I'm afraid that's not possible at the moment. Instead, I'd like a list of your ex-girlfriends and also colleagues and acquaintances that may bear you a grudge for any reason.'

Walsh strummed his fingers against his cheek, thinking, deciding. 'Look . . .' He lowered his voice. 'Look, I don't want to cause any trouble, but I only have one recent ex-girlfriend – you know, aside from girls I've been out with only once or twice. We split up about the time I saw you last.'

'I thought you were a bit of a ladies' man?' Goodhew commented, querying this apparent contradiction.

'Yeah, I did act like that, didn't I? But I didn't want to get into it, not then. But if it hasn't stopped, then I can only think it's Paulette.'

'Your ex?'

'Yes. She didn't take it very well when we split up,' Walsh replied.

Goodhew handed him some paper and a pen. 'Could you write her full name and address here for me, please?'

Walsh printed the words, and muttered, 'We tried to work it out, but she has a really short fuse. I'd basically had enough of her temper.' He looked up and smiled as he passed the page back.

'And before that, who did you see?'

'God, you're going back years. There was a girl called Julie for a few months.' His tone was dismissive. 'No, there's nothing malicious about her. And that's it.'

'No one else?'

'Not since my teens. And as for colleagues and acquaintances, well, I keep pretty much to myself.'

Goodhew stood up, Walsh following his lead.

'I'll check out Paulette first, but we two will almost certainly need to speak again.'

'No problem. But it's wasting your time and definitely wasting mine.'

Goodhew nodded. 'Thanks for your help.'

Walsh walked with him back to the reception desk.

'Have you always lived in Cambridge?' Goodhew enquired.

'Since I was a toddler. My parents moved here from Leicester.'

The receptionist pushed the visitors' book towards Goodhew and tapped the 'time out' column.

'It's ten twenty-two,' she instructed.

'Thanks.'

She picked up some newly arrived post and turned away.

'I'll be in touch,' Goodhew reminded Walsh.

'And if I think of anything, can I contact you directly?'

'Just ring the station and ask for me. If I'm not available, ask for PC Sue Gully.'

Goodhew knew that the receptionist's hearing was fully functional, even though her smile wasn't, and he guessed the rumour mill would soon begin to turn. And as he passed through the heavy chrome doors into the dirty rain outside, he would not have been surprised to learn that, behind him, a scrap of paper had just been slipped inside the credit-card section of a well-organized purse. It read 'G. Goodhew or PC Sue Gully'.

CHAPTER 46

FRIDAY, 27 MAY 2011

Paulette Coleman's home was in her parents' place, a grey post-war terrace house in the dormitory village of Fen Ditton. The adjoining properties had been repainted cream and the dark-green door of drab number 17, against its drab elevations, made Goodhew's subconscious expect equally dull occupants.

It was on his third knock that Mrs Coleman opened the door.

'Mrs Coleman? I'm DC Goodhew from Cambridge CID.'

Eye-shadow and mascara flickered in astonishment.

'I've come to see Paulette regarding some police enquiries we're making. Is she at home?'

'Oh.' She surveyed him, her serious green eyes rapidly reading and reasoning. 'Is she in trouble?'

'Not that I'm aware of, Mrs Coleman.'

'Well, she'll be back from work in about twenty minutes. I'll make you some tea while you wait.' She led the way through to the kitchen. 'My husband's upstairs, as he works nights. He said someone had been banging on the door earlier. Was that you?'

Goodhew shook his head. 'Sorry, no.'

'Milk? Sugar?'

'White, one sugar, thanks.'

Mrs Coleman made the tea with her back turned to him. Her hair, a dark chestnut at the front and sides, was a more mellow brown at the back, suggesting clearly she was her own hairdresser. As she passed him his mug, he noticed the only-nearish match of her lipstick and nails, and adjusted his observation to hairdresser *and* beautician.

'You don't look like a policeman.'

'That's the point of being in plain clothes,' Goodhew replied helpfully.

'No, I mean you haven't got a policeman's face. Oh, well,' she patted his arm, 'just goes to show looks can be deceptive.'

'They certainly can, Mrs Coleman.' Goodhew then continued, 'Where does your daughter work?'

'At Boots in Cambridge. She's on the make-up counter. She's had the same job for about three years – really likes it there.'

'Does she catch the bus to work? Or drive?'

'Oh, the bus. She has a car, though. Bought herself a lovely little one as a treat to herself. Before that she had another car, of course, but older.'

Gary swigged thirstily. 'Excellent tea, Mrs Coleman.'

'Another cup?' She stood up.

'Thank you.' Goodhew leant back into the corner of the chair and slouched slightly, with his elbow on the table. He'd observed Mrs Coleman's pose and was now mimicking it. As she sat down again, she returned to the same relaxed pose and continued chatting.

'What was I saying?'

'You'd just finished telling me about her new car.'

'Yes, she's had that car for about six weeks. New car, new haircut, new boyfriend. Out with the old, in with the new; she gets that from me.' She wiped a hand across that table top, then looked up at Goodhew with new interest. 'And what case are you working on?'

'Murder.' He kept his tone smooth and level. 'I've been told that Paulette may be trying to falsely implicate someone. Does that sound like your daughter?'

'Of course not.' The ever lively Mrs Coleman froze and stared at him, a tide of colour seeping across her face. 'It can't be true. Everything's been OK again.'

Without warning, the back door opened and a thin mousy-haired girl entered the kitchen.

'Hello,' she muttered.

'Paulette, this is Mr Goodhew from the police. He wants a word with you.' She put the mugs in the sink. 'I'll leave you to it,' she added for Goodhew's benefit.

Paulette's blue eyes hadn't left Goodhew since they'd been introduced. 'Will this take long, because I'm supposed to be going out tonight?'

'Hopefully not.' He poised his pen over the notepad. 'Does the name Kaye Whiting mean anything to you?'

No visible reaction. 'No.'

'How about Helen Neill?'

Nothing but a small shake of the head.

'Peter Walsh?'

Paulette drew her breath sharply. 'What's happened?' she gasped, sinking into the chair opposite.

'I'm investigating the murder of Kaye Whiting, and someone has been making anonymous calls suggesting that Peter Walsh should be arrested.'

'No, that's not right.'

'What's not?'

'It's not right that anyone would cause him trouble.' Her voice was small and thin, and nothing like the voice on the tape. But, of course, Paulette didn't know that.

'I've spoken to Walsh, and he says you were very upset when he ended your relationship. Is that correct?'

'I, um . . .' she stumbled over her words. 'Yes, I, I . . .' It took her several awkward seconds before she could continue. Any make-up she wore did nothing to hide the faded magnolia tinge of her skin and the dark shadows beneath her eyes. 'I wouldn't do that.'

'You're seeing someone else now, aren't you?'

'Not really. He's just a friend at the moment. I hoped Pete and I would get back together.' Tears suddenly welled in her eyes. 'Why would he think I'd do that? I mean the phone calls.'

'He says your temper was always a problem.'

'Not temper, no. When I started going out with him, I felt so lucky. I wanted it to work so much that I became obsessed with trying to avoid anything going wrong.'

'Obsessed is a strong word, Miss Coleman.'

'I was determined to make him happier than he'd been with anyone else before. I wish I could do it over again, but differently.'

'Had he been unhappy before?'

'He'd had a couple of girlfriends, I think. He only ever mentioned the last one, called Julie. He was gutted when they split up, but he said she'd met someone else.'

Paulette rubbed her tired eyes. 'I think she may have come to this house about two weeks ago. I was here alone when I heard the doorbell go. I looked out the window and there was a woman standing at the front door. I recognized her from a photo I saw at Pete's place.'

'He showed it to you?'

'No, I found it in a drawer. I didn't want to talk to her, but she must have seen me because she started yelling through the letter box.'

'Yelling what, exactly?'

'She was shouting my name. And she kept pacing up and down. Really agitated. She yelled, "I need to talk to you about Peter. I know you're in there. Open the door."'

'And did you?'

'No way . . . And then she left.'

'And did you tell Peter Walsh?'

'I left him a message, asked him to ring – but he never did.'

'Did he know you'd found the photo at his place?'

'No.' Paulette dropped her gaze to her lap, which was a common response from someone about to confess. 'No, I only looked because I was jealous, and I wouldn't admit to that, would I? But I memorized her address too, if you want it.'

CHAPTER 47

FRIDAY, 27 MAY 2011

The clouds had burst open and heavy raindrops pelted Goodhew's car. The passing traffic had swelled to a swishing flood that gushed past him as he opened the door and ducked inside.

He dropped his notepad into the passenger seat, and it fell open where he'd wedged his pen between a couple of pages.

'Julie Wilson, 125 Gilmerton Court' his note said.

He rang the station to check his messages. Condensation was quick to mist the windscreen, and he turned the fan on full as he waited for a reply.

No messages.

He dropped his phone in his pocket and pulled away, flowing into the main stream of traffic. He decided to call on Julie Wilson unannounced, since he preferred visits that way.

He opened his window a few inches, allowing stray spots of rain to dart through the gap. Occasionally one misjudged the space and crash-landed on the top rim of the window glass, before teetering and tumbling down the inside surface.

Gary wiped away these drops with the outer heel of his hand, recalling the raindrops running down the cheeks of that girl in Hanley Road. She wasn't Paulette Coleman, he now knew. And neither was Paulette Coleman the anonymous caller, for the timbre of her voice had been all wrong. Besides, he had convinced himself that the girl in the street was owner of the voice recorded on the tape.

The rush-hour traffic thickened but, despite the congestion, the quickest route to Gilmerton Court was around the airport and through the slow-moving streets of Cherry Hinton and past Addenbrooke's Hospital. He inched forward, nose to tail with all the commuters who accepted this crawl homewards as part of their daily routine.

Paulette caught the bus each day, while Pete walked. So what? He wondered whether she watched out for Pete, or whether her self-confessed obsession manifested itself in other, more obscure ways. She'd looked different from what he imagined to be Pete Walsh's type. He'd expected someone more colourful, and bolder by nature too.

The rain slowed to a frustrated drizzle. Goodhew sincerely hoped Julie Wilson would be the girl from Hanley Road.

Number 125, Gilmerton Court was a two-bedroom flat on the second floor of a three-storey residential block. Julie Wilson wasn't at home, so Gary waited in the stairwell, on the second step of the flight leading up to the third floor.

After ten minutes he heard the lobby door open, and wet footsteps slapped the stone steps on their way towards him.

Gary stood and watched the handrails of the flights lower down. A female left hand appeared and curled around the rail as she ascended. He could just make out the damp pinkness of her skin against the black cuff of her jacket. As she reached the half landing ten steps below him, she drew a sudden breath and froze, her gaze flashing upwards to the floor above. Goodhew instantly recognized her pallor: he'd seen it twice before, and more times if he counted the dead ones. But this was the first time he'd set eyes on Julie Wilson.

Goodhew leant over and held out his badge. 'Sorry, I didn't mean to make you jump. I'm from Cambridge CID. I'd like to ask you a few questions in connection with a current investigation.'

'Is this house-to-house? I mean, are you seeing everyone who lives here?'

'No, just you.'

Julie didn't move. 'Throw me your ID.'

Gary complied. 'I'm sorry I didn't phone first.'

'Don't you usually make visits in pairs?'

'Not always, no.' He pulled out his mobile phone. 'Do you want to call the police station and check on me?'

Julie shook her head and headed up the last few steps. She opened the door of her flat and gestured Goodhew through in front of her. The hallway opened out into a lounge and Goodhew took a seat on the blue settee at the far end, nearest the only armchair.

Julie Wilson stood with her hands in her jacket pockets and glared at him.

'Some anonymous calls have recently been made to us regarding a current murder investigation. These may be offering us genuine information or they may simply be malicious. I'm here because I've been told that you may be able to point me in the right direction.'

Julie shrugged. 'So?'

'I believe you once went out with a Peter Walsh, of Hanley Road?'

Julie's lips, suddenly compressed, seemed to struggle with more than one syllable. 'Yup.'

'Do you have any grievance against him?'

She shook her head. 'Nope.'

'So your split was amicable?' he prodded, keen to prise an involuntary second syllable from her.

'Well, I don't want him back and I'm sure he's not interested in asking me out again. Up to you if you want to describe that as amicable.'

'So you wouldn't be the caller who's accusing him of being somehow involved in a murder, then?'

'You're barking completely up the wrong tree.'

'So you think it's a ridiculous accusation that's being made against Mr Walsh?'

'Look, some women are bitches, and some blokes are bastards. It doesn't make them killers, though. I don't know what you want me to say, but it's got nothing to do with me.'

Gary nodded in sympathy. 'I really do understand your point of view. I don't want to rake up anything distressing, but this is important.'

The redness steadily creeping up Julie's neck became less angry in shade. She removed her anorak and dropped it on to the armchair beside him. 'I shouldn't get so wound up, I suppose.'

'No, it's fine.'

'No, it's not. I should keep it under control.'

'But you're still upset about him?'

'I'm only upset that it still bothers me after so long.'

'What exactly?'

'Oh,' she threw her hands in the air, 'I don't know.' She stared at Gary, maybe hoping he'd move on. He didn't speak. 'Everything, nothing – you know the usual relationship stuff.'

'So if you didn't call us, can you think of anyone who might bear him some kind of serious grudge?'

She shook her head. 'I can't imagine him doing anything to make himself particularly unpopular at work. But I don't really know for sure – especially after this long.'

'When did you see him last?'

'Last summer, I suppose: probably around July 2010.'

Gary opened his notebook and flicked through a couple of pages. 'What about his ex-girlfriend, er . . .'

'Marlowe?' offered Julie.

'Thank you. Is that a first name or a last name?'

'First,' Julie muttered.

'And what's her last name?'

'I don't know.'

'Where can I find her?'

Julie surveyed him for several long seconds, the redness gathering around her throat again. Her jaws clenched and unclenched before she spoke. 'How much do *you* know about your ex-girlfriends' ex-boyfriends? I don't really care about Marlowe, Pete or anyone else who might be giving you the run-around. I don't stick my nose where it doesn't belong. I made a resolution to put him in the past and, as far as I'm concerned, that's the end of it.'

The rain was again beating hard on the roof of his car as Gary pulled out of the parking bays situated outside Gilmerton Court. Murky figures hurried home in the dirty gloom. His wipers swooshed back and forth accompanying the voice in his head which kept repeating, 'Mar-lowe-Mar-lowe-Mar-lowe.'

CHAPTER 48

FRIDAY, 3 JUNE 2011

The offices at Dunwold Insurance were deserted; even the cleaners had finished for the weekend. Fridays usually saw all but the keenest leave by 5.30, and the last stragglers out by 6 p.m.

And, bar one person, this evening was no exception.

At 7 p.m. Peter Walsh still occupied his desk, but only a fraction of his thoughts were on his work. He didn't realize that a full ten minutes had passed since his last touch of the keyboard, until his screensaver flashed on.

He knew that his biggest mistake had been to pick someone from work but, as ever, it was easy to be wise after the event. He'd compounded the error by dating a receptionist, which meant there was now no privacy for him. Every time he passed through the foyer, to go in or out of the building, she knew about it.

Even if she wasn't there, she'd be informed by her nosy-parker colleague. Even Marcus 'bean-counter' Bagley from Accounts had given him a knowing smile. *And he never smiles*, Pete thought glumly. It seemed that everybody knew about him and Donna, and he now felt under constant scrutiny.

He nudged his mouse to clear the screensaver and continued working. Almost immediately his PC bleeped at him. 'Shit,' he muttered. Three times he'd made mistakes in entering straightforward details on a new car-insurance policy. Silly mistakes that confirmed how much his mind was elsewhere.

But he knew that already.

He pushed back from the desk and snatched up his mug. At least everyone else had gone, as the last thing he needed was more conversation about Donna. He'd never meant it to be serious. He'd made that very clear, dammit. But now it seemed that half of his colleagues were waiting for an engagement announcement, whilst the other half hovered in the 'said it wouldn't last' camp for it to end.

He slung his fresh coffee into the sink, after barely tasting it.

He needed space to think – away from work and away from Donna. Perhaps she wouldn't be too put out if he cancelled tomorrow. He could spend the day getting his thoughts straight, and see her on Sunday instead. He could explain the situation then.

Pete turned from the kitchen, back towards his desk. He'd phone her straight away. He almost walked past the first bay of workstations without noticing the figure waiting in the last swivel chair. But, as he realized that he wasn't alone, he also realized that Donna's unexpected appearances were becoming repetitive.

'Donna, hi,' he muttered and forced a smile. 'What are you doing here?'

'I came to see you,' she purred, smoothing her hair with one hand whilst leaving the other draped along the armrest. 'I thought you might like company.'

'I need to catch up.'

She pouted a little, 'But, Pete, you've worked hard all week.' She uncurled herself from the chair and smoothed her short silky skirt over her bare tanned thighs. She slunk towards him, but Pete turned and continued back to his desk.

'Donna, I really must catch up.' He took in a breath and released it in a slow huff. *Sunday* he reminded himself, as he dropped into his chair. When he spoke again, his voice had softened slightly. 'I was going to ring you. I need to work tomorrow, too. Can we make it Sunday instead?'

She stopped following him and stood with her arms folded across her low-cut top, and with her mouth set in a less than seductive pout. 'Why?' she challenged.

'Because,' he began, keeping his tone at its most even, 'for the third time, I'm really busy.'

'So, am I supposed to go home now, or what?' A deep angry frown creased her forehead and petulance poisoned her voice.

She was so tense that it appealed to him for a moment. He smirked at her and winked. 'What did you have in mind?'

'Have you ever done it in the office?'

Pete studied her. The temptation palled in an instant, evaporating like spit in a bonfire. It was so contrived, so predictable. He knew that she'd left work early. Gone to wash and change and manicure her nails, no doubt. Yes, she'd gone to town on it: long, pink false nails and just enough make-up to act the part of a seductress.

'No.' He didn't bother to add, *Have you?* because he couldn't see the point.

She crossed the office towards him and stood in front of his chair, leant forward and whispered in his ear. 'All day I think about you being up here, and I think how I'd love to work upstairs with you, and screw you in the kitchen while everyone else's working out here.' She ran her tongue along his cheek until it brushed his ear. 'But, as we're alone now, I'd like to get on my hands and knees for you, so you can fuck me from behind.'

Pete remained silent. She assumed his primary motivation was sex; that he was as easy as she was.

His right knuckle was being manoeuvred up her inner thigh. She wanted sex on the office floor. How many times had she done this kind of thing in the past? Anger surged through his bloodstream as he considered it.

She'd probably been planning this all day, telling that tart that she worked with – Karen or Sharon or whatever she was called. And what if they did it now? Would everyone know about it on Monday?

He stood up abruptly, so she tottered backwards on her high heels as she struggled to maintain her balance. 'I'm sorry, Donna. I'm not in the mood.'

CHAPTER 49

WEDNESDAY, 8 JUNE 2011

Constable Pearse received the call to Brookfield Farm as he returned from his weekly trip to investigate the Brinkley Close dustbin arsonist. As ever, there were no clues, no witnesses and no damage apart from Mrs Cameron's galvanized dustbin, which grew blacker on each visit.

The dustbin and its week's worth of cremated newspapers vanished from Pearse's thoughts as the controller advised him to attend the farm where a newly discovered body waited.

Pearse's adrenalin accelerated, along with his squad car, as he swung sharply left and raced the last half mile to Mr Anderson's farm. He could hear the ambulance approaching too, probably followed by another patrol car.

Mr Anderson and his wife were both waiting outside their stone farmhouse. Mr Anderson paced back and forth beside a parked VW Estate, whilst Mrs Anderson leant inside the open car door, near the body slouching in the driver's seat.

Pearse parked on the opposite side of the farmyard and burst from the car, spurred on by a rising panic that warned him to stop Mrs Anderson disturbing the body. 'Come away from the car, please, Mrs Anderson,' he called out.

She stepped back. 'Oh, I'm so glad you're here. It seems ages since we phoned.'

Now centre stage, Pearse knew he had to secure the scene but, just as he began to usher the Andersons back indoors, a husky voice muttered, 'She's in the field.'

He turned back to the VW to find his 'body' was an ashen-faced male.

Just then an ambulance pulled into the gap behind the VW.

Pearse dismissed the desire to announce that this was also his first time with a fresh corpse. Instead he said with forced authority, 'Right, did you find the body?'

The man nodded.

'What's your name?'

'Mr Rodgers, Marlon Rodgers.'

Pearse made a note. 'OK then, Mr Rodgers, I'll take some more details in a moment. Now, please show me where.' He turned to the paramedics. 'Follow me, but wait as we get nearer to the body, and I'll call you if you're needed.'

And so Pearse led the way along the perimeter of the first two crop fields and, through a gap in the hedge, into the third. Marlon Rodgers followed, directing him in a wavering voice. 'She's just along there,' he pointed straight up along the furrow they currently followed, 'but to the right when you reach that clump of hawthorn jutting out.'

'OK, wait here.' Pearse walked on alone. He felt the urge to run, in case the victim wasn't dead, but was desperately in need of help. So he maintained the same pace, careful to disturb as little of the ground as possible.

The rape-seed crop rose to waist height from deep furrows of soil. Its yellow flowers unleashed a dirty odour that attracted plenty of insects, but Pearse knew he was approaching the right spot, for his nostrils braced as a new smell began to greet them. The crop ahead was buzzing with an even more intense population of bluebottles.

He felt he needed a deep breath of fresh air but, as he parted the stems and spotted her body, the sharp inhalation filled his lungs with the stench of rotting flesh.

He hurriedly retreated. *Don't be sick, don't be sick*, he pleaded with himself. And by the time he rejoined the others, he knew he could safely speak without the likelihood of vomiting. 'You won't be needed,' he informed the paramedics, and quickly turned his attention to his radio. 'Confirm dead body, white, female, aged twenty to thirty.'

Pearse and Marlon Rodgers rejoined the Andersons at their front door. They watched the departing ambulance in silence.

Pearse wondered if the others also felt the creeping presence of the corpse looming over their shoulders. He wanted to go back to look at her again. He tried to recall her injuries. Her hair sprouted from bloated raw flesh which seethed with busy insects. He closed his eyes briefly, hoping to see the corpse as a photograph projected on the back of his eyelids.

Nothing.

But he was sure his memory served him well, and in that brief glance, he'd seen no dried black blood, no ligature marks around the neck and no ripped garments. Just as he'd read in the station copy of the *Police Gazette*, it appeared that she had been bound and gagged but otherwise unharmed.

Except that she was dead.

CHAPTER 50

WEDNESDAY, 8 JUNE 2011

'Where are we going, Gary?'

'I'll fill you in in a minute, Sue. Let's just get in the car and I'll explain on the way.'

Gully gathered up the folder and a pile of loose notes from her in-tray and slipped her digital camera into her bag. Goodhew had already put all he needed in the car, and Gully hurried to catch him up.

Only as they reached the M11 did Goodhew finally begin to explain. 'The article in the *Gazette* may have paid off. I had a call this morning from a PC in Essex who'd read it, and he was waiting alongside a newly discovered body even as I spoke to him. It sounds like a matching MO, but we won't know until we get there.'

'So who is she this time?' Sue asked.

'There's no ID as yet, and the PC that rang me didn't think he'd be thanked for tipping us off, so we'll just have to wade in once we get there.'

Gully smiled as the implications of this tip-off hit her. 'Oh, I see, now you want me to ring Marks, explaining that we're well on the way there, and can he smooth the politics for us so we get a bit of cooperation at the scene once we arrive?'

'Spot on, Sue.'

She pulled her mobile phone from her pocket and threw it into Goodhew's lap. 'I think you should do it. I just can't ask.'

'Oh yes, you can. Say I insisted, and you can't get hold of me now, and I'm sure he'll rise to the challenge.'

'He'll guess I'm in the car with you.'

'Hang on then.' Goodhew pulled off the motorway, on to a slip road, and switched off the engine, then passed the phone back to her. 'Just think about it – he can't demand that I come back if I'm not here, can he? Tell him you're passing Stansted, and I'm ahead of you somewhere in a separate car. Say it's the last thing I said to you before my phone battery went flat.'

'You're a devious git sometimes.' She tapped out the number, and turned her usual shade of embarrassed pink as she made her call to Marks. 'He said he knows you're sitting next to me, and he doesn't want you wasting your time in Essex.'

Goodhew grinned. 'We won't waste any time. If there's no obvious connection, we'll head back straight away.'

'He said that, too – and that he'll ring ahead and square it with their murder squad.'

The area around the body site was sealed off, and the concrete courtyard in front of the Andersons' farm was milling with official murder business. Goodhew parked behind a police patrol car and straight away they found themselves approached by a uniformed officer with his arms spread wide, like he was rounding up geese.

Goodhew showed his badge, and was directed towards the entrance to the first field, now cordoned off with phosphorescent tape. Beyond the tape, a series of figures in sterile overalls and matching gloves, hoods and shoes could be seen moving with meticulous care through the field itself, and the next one, and probably also the one beyond. One of these detectives now approached the gateway.

'You must be the two from Cambridge. I'm DC Janice McNamara. Get yourselves suited up and I'll take you on through.' McNamara carried on talking to them while they dressed. 'The police surgeon's been down there for some time, and I haven't yet heard when he reckons she died. You know how it is: we don't know anything definite yet.'

'Have you actually seen the body?' Goodhew enquired.

'No, she's in the third field, and I've been posted in this one the whole time.'

Gully felt the simultaneous lurch of trepidation and adrenalin. Her head buzzed from the atmosphere of intense concentration that enveloped the entire farm and even permeated her lungs. McNamara was now addressing her, but she'd missed the question and stared back blankly.

'For the preservation of evidence, I was saying that it would be better if only one of you approached the site of the body.'

Gully's face flushed with disappointment. 'Yes, of course.'

'There's plenty else you can do here to keep yourself busy,' McNamara told Gully. She turned and smiled at Goodhew. 'Ready?'

'Actually,' he lied, 'it's Gully here who's the crime-scene expert.'

'Oh,' McNamara looked uncertain, 'I just assumed . . .'

'Bad habit for a detective,' he commented and turned to Gully with a wink. 'Do you think you should handle this one?'

'No, Gary, I think you'll do OK. I have a lot of background stuff to be getting on with.' As Goodhew set off after McNamara, she added, 'Just ask me if there's anything you're not sure about.' She then followed them as far as the nearest field, where she'd start doing a bit of investigating of her own.

By this stage, only one item of significance had been found on the body. Constable Pearse passed the evidence bag containing some form of security badge to Goodhew, who held it up to study more closely through the clear plastic.

'Stephanie Palmer, Network Rail Staff,' he read out. 'Has it been confirmed yet that she's missing?'

Pearse shook his head. 'Last I heard was about fifteen minutes ago, when McNamara had a call from Network Rail's HQ, saying that she's not been in today. But apparently that's not unusual, as she's erratic with her attendance. They're going to ring back once they've found out more. I think it looks like her, though, don't you?'

Goodhew held the ID card between himself and the corpse, and compared the two faces. 'Looks very likely,' he agreed. He passed the evidence bag back to Pearse.

'It was found inside a little money pocket tucked into her waistband. Obviously the killer missed it.' Pearse waited until Goodhew turned back to him, before continuing. 'Can I ask you something?'

Goodhew nodded. 'What's that?'

'Is this likely linked to the others?'

Again Goodhew nodded, but more reservedly. 'It appears that way.'

Goodhew caught sight of Gully now standing just beyond the police tape. She had soon changed back out of her overalls, and appeared detached from the main thrust of the search as she scribbled notes on whatever she had observed.

'It's a really good place to hide a body,' she muttered as Goodhew later joined her, doubtless hoping to provoke him into comment.

But he didn't speak or even move, and for several minutes they stood side by side on a grassy knoll, surveying the same patch of ground in the neighbouring yellow field.

Eventually he muttered an irritable, 'Why?'

And Gully, whose thoughts had moved on, replied, 'Why what?'

He scowled. 'Why is it such a good place to hide a body?'

'Well, it already stinks, for a start. Smells as bad as a men's toilet. It's rape-seed, you know.'

'Yeah, so?'

'Well, even the name's hardly romantic, is it? No couples likely to go strolling around here hand in hand, are they?' She turned towards him. 'And stop being so ratty.'

'I'm not.'

'You bloody well are, Gary, and you know it. How could you have found her? How could anyone, when no one even knew she was missing? We don't even know it's the same killer, so don't start getting pissed off because we wasted valuable time keeping Andy Burrows locked up.'

Goodhew reached out and gently turned Gully back to face the rape field. 'It *is* the same killer. The rope's the same, tied the same, and she was gagged the same way, too. And you're right, it's a brilliant place to hide a body. That sign down there says "KEEP OUT – Pesticides in use", and the place is muddy and crawling with bugs. No fun for kids playing or dog walks or secluded sex. And if you were abandoned out there, trussed up like that,' his hand swept an arc in front of them, 'just in the fields we can see, how long do you think it would take me to find you?'

She wasn't sure how big the field actually was, but guessed that the yellow swathe of rape-seed crop, which descended from the distant hills into the level ground at her feet, must run into hundreds of acres. And, besides, the crop stood at least three feet high. 'I doubt if you could even find me there unless you waded through it row by row.'

'Exactly – and this is just one location. There are places like this all over the country. Even the smell of a decomposing body would be masked by the stench of this yellow stuff.'

'So how was she discovered?' she wondered.

'Some guy called Marlon Rodgers had been taking aerial shots of farmland from a microlight aircraft. When he had the pictures developed, there she appeared as a bright blue blob. But over twenty-four hours intervened between yesterday morning, when he took the photos, and when he came back to have a look today.'

'She wasn't still alive in the photos, was she?' Gully asked in horror.

'Can't tell for sure till we get the pathology report. I suppose it's possible since, after all, she probably only disappeared on Saturday.'

'Three and a half days ago, hmm.' She thought of Kaye Whiting and Helen Neill and she shuddered. 'Kaye lasted a lot longer than that.'

Goodhew nodded. 'Yeah, and in much colder weather, too. This Marlon guy's beside himself, of course. He's desperate to know whether he could have saved her. I told him I thought she must have been already dead by then.'

'You got a close look at the body?'

'Yeah.' Goodhew grimaced. 'It's really rotten already, so I reckon she must have died on Sunday or maybe Monday. There's discoloration around the face, spreading down on to her chest, and she's started to balloon.'

'Beetles eating the skin yet?' she asked.

'Yup,' he replied.

'More like Sunday, then.'

CHAPTER 51

WEDNESDAY, 8 JUNE 2011

Andrew Hansen arrived at Colchester police station at exactly 7.15 p.m. He wore a blue suit and carried an iPad as well as his mobile phone. He was escorted straight through to DC Pugh and DC Goodhew, who were both waiting for him in the identification lounge.

A group of armless, mustard-coloured chairs were positioned in a semicircle around a low table. A water-dispenser stood in a far corner, and to one side of the group of chairs a large television set was bolted on to a chest of drawers.

That was all there was in the room, apart from three boxes of Kleenex tissues, one at each end of the table and one on top of the water-cooler.

DC Pugh introduced both himself and Goodhew. 'Thank you for volunteering, Mr Hansen.'

'That's OK. I guess it gets difficult when a victim hasn't got any relatives in the country.' He put his laptop on the nearest seat, and rested the phone on top of it. 'She's from Australia, you realize?'

'Uh-huh,' nodded Pugh. 'First I need to take some of your details. Like your full name and date of birth.'

'Andrew John Hansen, eighth of April 1969.'

'And your relationship to Miss Palmer?'

'She's one of my staff, an administrator.'

'And your job?'

'I'm a senior projects manager based at the Network Rail office in Euston Station.'

'And how long has Miss Palmer worked for you?'

'Last week was only her seventh.'

'Would you say you knew her relatively well?'

'Fairly well. As well as anyone else in this country, I suppose.'

'OK, that's great. I'll be requesting some more details if the identification is positive. A close-up of the victim's face will now appear on the screen, so take as long as you like. It is vital you only give us a positive identification if you are one hundred per cent sure. Do you understand?'

'Yes. I'm ready when you are.'

DC Pugh paused while pointing the remote control at the TV set. 'I must warn you first that, whilst we've done what we can to make the face presentable, it isn't a pleasant sight.' He pressed *play*.

Andrew Hansen's naturally jovial face was fixed on the screen as a mottled image took shape. The man waited for the true horror to hit home. 'Yes, that's her,' he mumbled. He kept staring, but he couldn't quite grasp it. The blisters and fissures of decomposition, the bloating of a once pretty face. No, it didn't seem real. 'Yes, that's her,' he repeated again, but louder.

CHAPTER 52

THURSDAY, 9 JUNE 2011

A pile of dirty clothing slouched in a hungover heap in the corner, as if infused with too much alcohol and tobacco smoke to be able to party any more.

'Halfway between a whorehouse and a squat,' announced DC Pugh cheerfully, as he introduced Goodhew to Stephanie Palmer's eight-foot-square bedroom. 'Fingerprints haven't been collected yet, so don't touch anything. But I don't need to tell you that, do I?'

Goodhew shook his head silently and stepped into the room.

Pugh meanwhile chatted on. 'The forensic guys will be up to their ears in these dirty knickers for weeks.'

The bin brimmed with grease-spotted takeaway cartons and swigged-out cans of Tennant's Extra, all of them decorated with several brands of cigarette ash and dog-ends.

'Sex wasn't the only thing she had an appetite for, by the look of things.'

Goodhew glanced up. 'Did she?'

'Did she what?'

'Did she have an appetite for sex, or is that just based on observation of this lot?'

'The flatmates said it was one after another, two at once on at least one occasion. She was no nun, that's for sure. And if she was killed by your guy, would she have been raped too?'

A duvet and pillow hunched together on the sagging single bed, providing the only two items in the room that belonged together.

'No, not unless he's changed his pattern. Might not even be a he, as it happens, but I expect it is.'

Three unopened letters lay on the bedside table, two of them the inevitable junk mail and one from Barclays. A statement, Gary guessed. He'd know for sure later, once the forensics were done.

Pugh still waited by the door. 'Do you think the killer was here?'

'Unlikely.' Goodhew pivoted slowly, absorbing the room into his consciousness, trying to forge a link between its recent past and the present. He lodged its smell and silence in its own little memory compartment, and watched as glittering dust particles floated in a shaft of bright sunlight above the bed.

That's when he saw it, hidden under the mattress – like a schoolgirl might do.

Stephanie's diary.

Her self-portrait, and Goodhew's introduction to another girl too late to be saved.

Thursday

Had letter in the post from Mum today, wants to know why I'm still in London and not seeing more of England. Still picking holes. If she knew how expensive it is here, she'd get it. It's easy for her to sit at home thinking I've got it easy.

Out of the hostel now, thank God. Moved yesterday but got too pissed to write it down. Sharing flat in Lewisham with three others, Cherie, Jody and Grant. Going out with Jody at weekend (another piss-up).

Friday

Temping work due to finish today but they want to keep me for another month, so won't be seeing the 'glorious' English countryside in June either. Just as well, with my asthma, I've been wheezing non-stop. Sucked on my inhaler more than I've sucked on anything else this week. I guess that makes a change!

Don't see how I'll ever travel round anyway, it's too expensive here. Can't afford to keep my flat while I travel and bought too much stuff to take with me.

Tuesday

God it's Tuesday. Didn't write anything at the weekend. Guess why! Me & Jody stayed out all night on Saturday with two lads we met at the Walkabout. Nothing happened; just a good laugh. We're doing it again next weekend (drinking, that is). Will write in my diary at the time, however rat-arsed I am.

Wednesday

Work was shit today, too much to do, nobody helped out. Didn't even get time for lunch. If people think it's glamorous working in these London offices, they don't know what they're talking about. Spent hours doing the same thing, and it just gets filed away at the end of it. What's the bloody point? That's what all the girls said, so we went down the Euston Flyer, the nearest pub apart from that shitty one at the station with all the winos. Guess what? Pissed again! I'll put that as a skill on my CV, can still write drunk. Ha!

Friday

What's so clever about walking round with FCUK splashed across your chest? If I want to say 'fuck', I'll just come right out with it.

And if I want to do it, I just do.

These girls walk around with innocent expressions plastered across their faces, flirting around some worthless guy, inviting him to enjoy the advertising slapped across their cleavage, and then complaining when he wants more.

Complaining that they're not like that! Hypocritical bitches base their whole purpose in life around their ability to get a bloke and hang on to him. And for what? They're all the same.

Users. Foul-mouthed, dirty-minded liars.

I love it when I use them for sex, when all the time they think they're using me. Half the time, I lie there bored out of my mind. It's like going to the cinema, the chance of catching a classic film keeps you going back, but usually it's all pretty forgettable.

Like that bloke last night, Alex or something. He looked all right and kissed pretty good too, but the sex was boring, boring, boring. While he was at it, I kept chanting it in my head, 'boring, boring, boring.' I don't think I said it out loud, though. He would have mentioned it, I think. Lol.

He was one of those small-minded types, assumed when it was over for him, it was over for me too, like all I wanted out of it was to make him come! What a fucking honour!

And then it's always the same, they say they'll ring, and they know they are saying it because it's what they think you want to hear. Or maybe because they don't want to face the fact that they're addicted to performing such a basic bodily function, but are too tight to pay for it.

Told him I didn't want to see him. Ha! I should have taken a photo of his face, that would have been a top souvenir!

He didn't know what to say. Hope he's not there tomorrow! Don't think he will be!!

CHAPTER 53

THURSDAY, 9 JUNE 2011

Diving into the water cleared his head and purged that dirty feeling that had increasingly infected him during the previous twenty-four hours. Goodhew thought as he swam, but it was not focused thinking. Disconnected thoughts followed their own drifting course around his consciousness.

The woods, the lake, the rape-seed.

What was the motive?

The case had changed gears, accelerating from missing persons through abduction and ending in murder. With each new scenario, the stakes had been raised, and now the race appeared to be on with a serial killer.

But, however distorted the motive had become, there had to be a reason and a trigger.

Goodhew executed a swift turn in the water, propelling himself back towards the deep end. *Why would I kill?* he asked himself. He swam the length with his head down and his eyes open, watching the little mosaic tiles on the bottom of the pool flash by in a liquid blur.

Love and greed were the commonest motivators. *Love, greed and madness*, he corrected himself. *Maybe I'd kill for revenge, if someone I loved was hurt. Do I have anyone I love that much?* he mused. *And I wouldn't murder for passion or money*, he was sure. *I'd have to be mad.* He surfaced and took long steady breaths of chlorine-filled air that he slowly exhaled through several determined strokes. But then he spotted Shelly watching from the viewing gallery. *Now, there's someone I could kill*, he thought, *and I could definitely plead insanity.* He immediately scolded himself. It was a bad joke.

But she didn't let it rest.

So he pretended he hadn't seen her.

Shelly was leaning over the railing in a short skirt and a stretchy blue crop-top. The same shade of blue that Stephanie Palmer had worn. The colour took on the shape of that rotting torso, and his irritation at Shelly swelled into anger.

He swam several more lengths, pounding the water with ruthless efficiency. His anger spurred him on.

Where are the clues?

The bodies, the locations, the dates, the anonymous caller.

Find the pattern, find the killer.

He left the pool quickly, glanced at the spectators' stand to find Shelly had gone.

Home, he hoped.

His car was parked in the last bay on the third floor of the adjoining multi-storey; unfortunately so was Shelly. She'd positioned herself with her dainty bottom, in its daintier skirt, perching on the edge of his bonnet. One bare leg extended to the tarmac, while the other was curled barefoot around it. Her missing shoe dangled from her crooked right index finger by its thin ankle strap. The moment he saw her, Goodhew rushed towards his car.

'Surprise.' She beamed.

'Yes, I can see that.' Goodhew scowled.

'Do you want to give me a . . .' she flicked her tongue out from behind straight white teeth '. . . lift?'

'No, but I will.' He pressed the remote to release the central locking and left a safety zone of several feet between them as he strode past her to yank open the passenger door. 'Get in and stop flirting.'

'I'm not,' she cooed indignantly, and slid from the bonnet to the ground. 'Why can't you be more fun, Gary?'

Goodhew held the passenger door open until the second she'd folded her legs inside. He slammed it shut and marched around to his side of the car, swung himself inside and slammed that one too.

Shelly stared at him, astonished and bewildered. 'What's your problem, Gary?'

'You have a dangerous combination of assets, Shelly. Good looks and stupidity.' He poked an angry finger at her. 'What do you think you look like?'

'Shit, you sound like my fucking mother, Gary.' Shelly unclipped her seatbelt and reached for the door. He thumped the central-locking control switch and she slouched back into her seat. '"You can't go out looking like that!"' she mimicked her parent.

'No, I sound like a fucking policeman who's just spent the last two fucking days picking over the remains of a girl who didn't have enough sense to care about who she was screwing. Seatbelt.'

'Fuck off, Gary.'

Shelly glared in defiance from her position leaning against the side window. He reached across and tugged the seatbelt back round her, started the car and pulled forward, towards the exit.

'What do you actually know about me, Shelly?' he demanded, but she didn't reply. 'Well, I'll tell you then,' he shouted. 'Nothing, that's what. And at what point do you stop and ask yourself who you're really with?'

'Stop it!' Shelly spat. She grabbed the door handle and released her seatbelt again. 'Let me out. I'm going to walk.'

Goodhew ignored her.

'At what point, Shelly? Before sex, after sex, or when you suddenly realize you're staring a killer in the face?'

Goodhew slowed as he approached a junction. Shelly tugged at the door release. 'Let me out now, Gary,' she screamed.

Goodhew slapped his foot down hard on the brake and they lurched to a halt. He released the central locking.

'Why are you such a bastard?' she yelled, spluttering back tears, before she slammed the door behind her and strode away.

Goodhew lowered the electric window. 'Don't trust anyone, Shelly,' he shouted after her.

CHAPTER 54

THURSDAY, 9 JUNE 2011

A splinter of guilt tumbled over and over inside Goodhew's stomach. Every few minutes it gave him a little prod until he picked up the phone and left a message on Bryn's answering machine.

Bryn responded soon after by appearing on Goodhew's doorstep. He followed Goodhew up to his flat.

'Coffee or tea?' Goodhew shouted from the kitchen.

'Tea, cheers,' Bryn replied as he poked his head around the door. 'What's up?'

'Shelly again, but my fault this time.'

Bryn rolled his eyes towards the ceiling. 'You haven't!'

Goodhew tossed a teabag into each mug. 'Be serious, Bryn. Of course I haven't.'

Bryn opened the food cupboard and grabbed a packet of custard creams. 'Shame really. I bet everyone else has.'

'I bet they haven't, actually, and that's no way to talk about your own sister.' Goodhew handed a mug of strong tea to Bryn. 'You're supposed to stand up for her.'

'You can say that, because you don't share a house with her. She's a pain in the backside.' Bryn took a sip, then put his mug back on the worktop. 'Go on, then, what have you done?'

'Well, I've had a go at her for flirting, for a start. And then I made her cry.' Goodhew dunked a biscuit in his tea. 'I'm sorry, Bryn. I know I should've handled it better, but I'm not going to apologize – except to you. She needed to be put straight.'

'Don't apologize. She'll just think you like her after all.' Bryn smiled and took Goodhew's mug from him and poured both drinks down the sink. 'Come on, let's have a pint and a game of pool.'

They walked to the Anchor pub and sat on the balcony with their first round of drinks. Goodhew rested his elbows on the railing and gazed down at the rows of punts tethered in the Mill Pond for the night. Further down the Cam, two students struggled with their craft, as the flow forced them back upriver towards Silver Street Bridge.

Punting had been seen on the Cam for the last hundred years. The colleges had been there for the last eight hundred, and Cambridge itself for two thousand. And, amidst it all, people lived and died trying to make their mark.

Or in this case, lived and killed.

Bryn bought them a second round and placed the two bottles next to the pool table while he racked the balls. Goodhew stepped back in through the French windows to watch Bryn potting a run of three yellows. His thoughts wandered back to Shelly.

'Girls like Shelly think they're smart, and that makes them really vulnerable. Every time I'm investigating an assault case, I notice how many girls wander around alone.'

The fourth yellow stopped short of the pocket, and settled against a cushion. Bryn straightened up. 'Shelly would insist she's got the right to walk around on her own.' He rubbed more chalk on the cue. 'I had two shots, didn't I?'

'Yes, and in theory she's right, of course, but that's not going to keep her safe, is it?'

Bryn hit the same yellow again with a relaxed shot that rolled it parallel to the cushion and left it hanging across the lip of the pocket. He returned to his bottle of lager. 'This case is really getting to you, isn't it?'

Goodhew chalked his cue. 'Not getting anywhere with it is getting to me.' He potted his last red and rolled the white smoothly into the black, toppling it into the middle pocket. 'My round. Same again?'

'Get two bottles each, if it suits you. I'll set them up again.'

Bryn pushed another coin into the slot and waited until the balls had made their rumbling journey to the front of the table. He rattled them into the triangle and gave the black a spin before replacing the triangle on the lip of the light shade.

Goodhew's mobile rang as he waited at the bar to be served.

Bryn noticed that a commuter had left an *Evening Standard* lying on an empty chair. He took it over to the pool table and opened it out on the empty end, flicking over each page after a cursory glance.

On page eight he came face to face with Stephanie Palmer, under the headline 'Police probe connection with earlier deaths'. Two smaller photos – of Helen Neill and Kaye Whiting – accompanied the article.

As Goodhew returned with the fresh bottles, Bryn folded the newspaper and dropped it back on its chair.

'Cheers. Your break.'

Goodhew nodded and cracked open the pack.

Bryn wondered if Goodhew would still be able to concentrate if he knew his investigative work was slapped across the pages of a major newspaper. Bryn potted two reds and looked up just as Goodhew welcomed Sue Gully by passing her his second bottle of beer.

She grinned at Bryn and he raised his cue in greeting. She had turned her attention back to Goodhew before Bryn could line up his next shot. 'It's in the paper again,' he heard her say.

'I know. I saw it,' Goodhew replied. 'I wonder who else has.'

'Yeah, me too. I just hope it stabs someone's conscience.' Sue pulled the cue away from Goodhew. 'I'll take your go this time. I shouldn't have brought the subject up.'

Sue potted one yellow and left the cue ball safely behind another. 'The problem is,' she confided to Bryn, 'we won't get any conversation out of him at all now. He'll be incapable of thinking about anything else.'

Gary Goodhew wasn't the only one whose thoughts were focused on three dead girls.

Just over a mile away, in a silent unlit room, the BBC News Channel was currently displaying their photographs. Julie Wilson's hand reached for the remote control and increased the volume enough to catch the newscaster's broadcast. In her photo, Stephanie

Palmer wore a white T-shirt with turquoise sleeves and the slogan 'I'm No Angel' across the front.

'Well, you are now,' she sniffed and pressed the *off* button. The picture vanished but the screen continued to glow in the dark. In the end she turned it on again, fed up with seeing the ghost of Stephanie's photograph in her head. She flicked between the five channels; avoiding the news on BBC1, then sport on both BBC2 and ITV, and a documentary about American crime on Channel Five. She settled therefore for a 'made for TV' potboiler on Channel Four.

After another twenty minutes, she wished she owned a gun. She could then be like Elvis and shoot a hole in the TV set.

Julie fell asleep in her chair and awoke to the late news. Again the three images flashed across the screen.

'Not my problem,' she told herself.

But it was then that a cold, hard sabre of guilt unsheathed itself and sliced its steel blade into her conscience.

CHAPTER 55

MONDAY, 13 JUNE 2011

Pete Walsh eyed the time display in the bottom right-hand corner of his PC monitor; it was two minutes past twelve noon and he was counting the minutes until five past, when he knew that Donna would have already left Reception for lunch. Then he would be running only the Karen gauntlet.

It was still raining outside, and from his desk he could just see the grey sheen of the sky reflected in the beige pavements below. Only a week ago it had seemed like the middle of summer, but now the day couldn't look more dismal if it were relayed back to him in black and white. Things had to brighten up soon, he assured himself.

He unhooked his jacket from the coat-stand and slipped it on as he waited for the lift. As the doors opened, he was pleased to find it full of other employees heading out to lunch. *Safety in numbers*, he thought wryly. As he headed towards the main doors, he noted Karen sitting alone at the main desk. He busied himself with his jacket zip, hoping she wouldn't notice him – and, if she did, that she wouldn't bother him.

'Pete!' her voice hissed at him.

He nodded, and gave a brief half-smile in her direction, but carried on walking.

'Pete, where's Donna?'

Pete's glance flicked swiftly around. Two women waiting at the lifts were talking quietly. One watched him over her colleague's shoulder, but the man waiting on the sofa continued to gaze rigidly out through the smoked glass.

Pete walked back over to Karen. 'I don't know.'

'Is she still off sick? She hasn't phoned in or anything.'

He shrugged. 'No idea.'

'I'm worried about her. She was off all last week, too.' Karen's gaze scanned his face.

'We both were,' he sighed.

'And is she OK?'

God, she's persistent, he thought irritably. 'Look, Karen, I don't know, because we split up.'

Karen flushed. 'Sorry, I had no idea.'

'And I'd appreciate it if you didn't announce the fact to everyone else in the building. I'm getting fed up with all the speculation that goes on about our private lives.'

'I don't know what—' she began.

'You *do* know. It wasn't my decision for us to split up, but the sooner it's all forgotten about the better, as far as I'm concerned.'

Karen watched him hurry across the pavement outside, bowing his head under the beating rain. She was glad that Donna had dumped him. She'd hadn't been able to decide whether she liked him or not, until today, but he'd always been moody and she didn't like people who were shitty with her. Still, she decided, turning back to answer the ringing phone, it would be a good bit of gossip to brighten the afternoon.

Once outside, Pete relaxed a little. He'd never warmed to Karen and wished their last conversation hadn't happened. He needed time with his own thoughts.

He didn't notice the few quickening footsteps that splashed behind him, but slowed as they approached him.

'Hi!' called a woman's voice.

He scowled as he looked up, but regretted it at once as he recognized Fiona and saw her smile fade into a look of uncertainty.

'How are you?' she continued, with less enthusiasm now.

'Sorry, I was miles away. I bet I looked really ratty just then.' He laughed.

She wrinkled her nose. 'A little bit.'

'Now, I feel like I've been rude to you.'

'No, really, not at all,' she answered.

'Monday at work and this weather, it's a miserable combination, you know.'

'It's fine, really. Everyone's rude to estate agents, anyway. I need to go inside, I'm getting soaked through.'

'I know. Let's get a coffee, then.' And, before she could argue, he took her arm and they were dashing across the road and up the steps into the Flying Pig.

From her table by the window, Marlowe had observed their entire exchange. A new girl with Pete? He'd been taking lunch breaks on his own for weeks now, since his last outing with Paulette. And, as far as she knew, there had been no one since. Until today. From her viewpoint she could just make out his expressions through the rain. He was flirting.

Suddenly they turned and started to run towards her.

He'd never come in here flashed through her mind, before her frantic reflexes sent her hurtling in an involuntary reeling motion towards the ladies' toilet.

In her wake, her coffee cup teetered for a moment before crashing to the floor.

She slammed the cubicle door and snagged her nail as she fought with the lock.

She sat, balanced on the edge of the toilet bowl, and concentrated on taking slow, deep breaths. The thudding of her blood pulsated through her head, and she wondered how she had ever ended up in such a mess.

CHAPTER 56

MONDAY, 13 JUNE 2011

Marlowe wondered why she couldn't will her heart to stop. It was hers after all, and it would have seemed right that it should obey her commands.

She could hear it beating out its strange slow-quick, fluttering rhythm. It never supplied enough oxygen, always leaving her yawning or drawing in quick, short gasps. And her limbs floated, drugged with lethargy.

Why couldn't she just tell it to stop?

But Marlowe knew there was no such easy release from her nightmare.

She returned to her desk, late again. She had made-up excuses ready but, as with most times she turned up late, nothing was said and the excuses went unused.

Mr Butler emerged from his office with a clutch of notepaper and passed it to his PA. They spoke a few syllables each, but nothing audible to Marlowe above the slowly creaking hands of the wall clock. He tilted his head as he spoke, but in a neat way, and Marlowe could see he wasn't prepared to ruffle his meticulous appearance even to deliver a sacking.

He turned to her and smiled, with the smallest flicker at the furthest corners of his mouth. 'Marlowe, can I see you for a few minutes, please?'

It wasn't a question, more a demand, and she followed him into his office.

'Your timekeeping and lack of concentration are becoming a

serious problem. You do realize that, don't you? As the senior partner in this firm . . .'

Marlowe tried to stop her eyes wandering into mid-nowhere.

'. . . it is important that all our employees are treated fairly, and the law states . . .'

Is he sacking me or not? she wondered, not quite able to pin down his words and assemble them in the correct order.

'. . . You've been here for several years and you're clearly a very able young woman . . .'

Perhaps he's not, she mused and tried to make better eye contact, but his mouth ran on and on and still she couldn't focus on his words. There was only one downside to losing her job: she'd be left with too much thinking time, and that was one hell of a downside. Agree and be humble, she decided.

She stared down at her lap and tried to appear remorseful.

'The last time I spoke to you, we both agreed that issuing you with a final written warning would be the appropriate course of action.'

Marlowe nodded.

He strummed the tips of his fingers on the desk blotter. 'You do remember, don't you?'

She nodded again and looked up, trying to read his placid features. 'Yes, of course.'

'So I would be within my rights to dismiss you right now. But what I really want . . .' he stalled, following the line of Marlowe's gaze to the front page of the *Cambridge News* which lay on his side table, at an angle of one hundred and eighty degrees.

She leant forward and, with an involuntary thrust of her hand, snatched it up from the table. She rose to her feet and staggered backwards to collapse into his guest chair, tearing her gaze from the picture and trying to read too much of the text too quickly.

'No, no,' Marlowe whispered. She held it in her lap, with her head bent over and her hair falling in a curtain around the half-folded newspaper. Her finger ran across the grainy photograph and she struggled to breathe under the weight of emotion that clenched her lungs tight. 'I knew her,' she gasped in a jagged whisper.

'It was in the daily papers this morning.'

She shook her head. 'I didn't read one today. I just saw her picture now.' She read through the article, commenting out loud. 'She took her car through the car wash as she was leaving Cambridge, and paid for their top programme, with wax and wheel wash and everything. Why would she do that?'

She looked up briefly and saw Mr Butler eyeing her oddly. She knew she'd just divorced herself from him and their conversation. He stared at her with a mix of revulsion and morbid fascination.

She continued to talk. 'It says they've interviewed a guy at the garage, who remembers her. And so does the teenager in Wells that served her lunch. He thought she seemed "pleasant", and she had a pot of tea and sandwiches.'

She saw a tear drop on to the paper, but it hardly felt like one of her own.

'This is a shock to you, isn't it, Marlowe?' he asked quietly.

She blurted out a few garbled words between sobs, then drew a deep breath and tried again. 'She ate lunch and had her car polished, and probably made her hair and make-up look nice too. Do you know why?'

'No,' he replied, with a quick sideways glance at the clock.

'Do you know Cromer?' she asked, changing tack.

'It's on the Norfolk coast, about twenty-five miles north of Norwich. I think Veronica and I once walked along a coastal path near there.'

'What's it like? Is it pretty?'

'Striking I'd say. I don't remember much. You can't walk on the beach, because the cliffs are falling away. At the bottom, which is probably a hundred feet down, there're just rocks and mud and sand.' He coughed and clasped his hands together, the way she knew he always did when he was closing a meeting. 'But that was a while ago, Marlowe.' He'd already slipped too far from his own agenda. 'Marlowe, about the job . . .' he began.

'Forget it.' She cut him short. 'It won't work out. I'll go and clear my desk.' She passed him the paper. 'She made everything nice because she needed to feel she'd got something right.'

Marlowe clicked his door shut, and then he read the article about Julie Wilson in its entirety for the first time. The most graphic statement came from a couple out with their dogs.

We were walking back from Happy Valley and saw a car parked at the top of Light House Hill. We walked past it and I noticed the stereo was playing and a woman was sitting in the driver's seat. She was facing the sea and her side window was open. I didn't think anything was odd but then, as I walked on, I heard the engine revving loudly, and I turned back and saw her drive off the cliff. There was a huge crunching sound. A load of dust flew up and we could still hear her stereo playing, but by the time we reached the edge it had stopped. There was nothing we could do.

CHAPTER 57

TUESDAY, 21 JUNE 2011

Pete Walsh had framed Fiona Robinson's photo and placed it on the low table beside the television, where it would be easy for him to see. By that point she had become the only girl to adorn his sitting room.

The sunlight lit up her hair, and her eyes were bright as they twinkled at him through the camera lens. He picked up the picture and touched his index finger to her cheek. As he stared straight into her face, the estate agent stared directly back and he could almost hear the whisper of her voice. His heartbeat quickened a fraction as the words escaped from his lips: 'I love you, Fiona.'

He glanced at his watch yet again, and found that only moments had passed since he last looked at her. She had done that, changed time for him.

But she had done so much to change him.

Since meeting her, he had become uplifted and filled with a giddy spirit that bubbled up inside him and carried him along through the monotony of his work. She'd pulled away the blanket of melancholy that had smothered him now for . . . He paused. For how long?

He wiped over the television screen as he considered this question. He didn't know the answer, but he guessed it was longer than he'd like to admit.

The dust vanished from the glass; he hadn't realized that it had built up so much.

He studied the room more closely then, trying to view it with a fresh eye. He felt that the simplicity of the two large armchairs combined with the plain walls and wooden floor gave the room a sense of tranquillity, but to ensure this didn't translate into sterility to the female eye, he had added a large vase of flaming-orange and yellow chrysanthemums.

He had also placed a dozen tiny tea-light candles at varying heights around the room, and set a single thick church candle beside Fiona's photograph.

His watch read 7.20. Only ten more minutes. Again he experienced that tingle of anticipation, knowing he'd planned the perfect evening for his perfect woman. And now he had to just let it unfold. Savour it for the wonderful memory that it would become.

He did not even consider the possibility that anything would go wrong.

Fiona parked her car outside at two minutes before half-past. Pete turned from the window, letting the curtains fall shut behind him. He smiled contentedly as he began to light the candles dotted around the room. She was always on time, but he knew that, before leaving her car, she would check her hair and make-up, and then glance at his house to check if he had seen her.

The small flame of each tea light wavered before settling to a steady glow. He lit a joss stick, then shook it until the flame died and its exotic aromatic smoke drifted upwards in a wave of sweet musk.

Finally, as Fiona knocked at the door, he lit the church candle and glanced again at her photograph. He was ready.

As he opened the door, he knew that he would find her studying his face, looking for his approval. 'How are you? You look lovely,' he began, then stopped and instead cupped her cheek in his hand and drew closer to her. 'What am I saying, Fiona?' He drew his breath in gently as he relished her light scent. 'I've been waiting to see you all day. You look wonderful.'

Fiona's confidence surged back, and she put her arms around his neck and pressed herself against him. 'I've missed you.'

'I've missed you, too. I can't believe it's only been a day since I last saw you.'

'Me neither. I think of you all the time,' she giggled. 'It's so distracting! I didn't ever think I was the romantic type!'

Pete took her hand and led her into the sitting room. 'I didn't think I was the romantic type, either. Look what you've made me do.'

Fiona stood at the door, as if actually entering the room would break the spell. She was really here, she told herself; she really was looking at a romantic idyll that had been created just for her, Fiona Robinson.

Pete took her jacket and hung it beside the front door, then ushered her further into the room and closed the hall door, finally sealing them off from any unwanted distractions.

Fiona constantly watched him, and he hoped she longed for him the same way that he ached for her. He placed a hand around her waist and another around her back as he pulled her close and they began to kiss.

He could feel a faint tremble ripple through her as his hold tightened. Perhaps she was excited, or perhaps she was scared and would pull away. Her trepidation excited him. He let himself sink gradually back into one of the armchairs, and she moved with him, still kissing him as she slid into his lap.

The fabric of her dress moved fluidly in his hands and he explored the curves of her body through the soft cotton. His fingers traced the contour of her spine, up and down, until diverting along the line of the rolled edge of her silk camisole. He moved his index and middle fingers steadily across her back and, following the thin strap, over her shoulder and further down towards her nipple.

They stopped kissing then and he paused for a moment. Just long enough to feel her quiver again. He needed to know she wanted him to go further, and to let her wonder whether he would.

And then, with a firmer grasp, he began to tug at her dress. He heard her breath quicken as he caressed the bare skin of her neck and forced her dress aside to reach for her breasts.

Together they tipped on to the carpet. The candlelight danced on the walls and ceiling above them. Fiona's hesitancy fled and she freed herself from her clothes as quickly as he could release the buttons and catches.

As if intoxicated, Fiona relished her nakedness, and Pete knew that she was now entrusting herself to him totally. This wouldn't be just simple sex to either of them, but the consummation of a far deeper tie. She lay still and watched him as he undressed.

He watched her too, as her hair, her eyes, in fact everything about her seemed to shine in the half-light. Like an incandescent angel guiding him to a happiness, he thought.

And, when he was ready, he knelt between her legs and, lifting her hips to meet him, he resolutely thrust himself inside her. She gasped but their eyes remained fixed upon each other. Serious. Intent.

There would be other times devoted to pleasure alone. This time was about belonging and bonding.

She would own him and he would own her.

CHAPTER 58

THURSDAY, 30 JUNE 2011

Determined rays of sunlight finally poked through the overcast early-evening sky and gently began to evaporate the day's rain. The setting sun bathed the room in a warm, golden glow and illuminated the aqua and indigo checked duvet.

Fiona dozed with her cheek nestling into Pete's chest and her arm wrapped across his stomach, until the warmth of the sunshine stirred her. She wound one leg over both his legs and rolled closer, pressing her damp thighs around him. Her fingers stroked the skin along his left side, feeling his ribs and shoulder blade.

He kissed her hair, enjoying the mingled scents of shampoo and perfume. 'I love being close to you like this, Fiona,' he whispered. 'I never believed being with someone could feel this good.'

'Almost too good to be true. I don't want anything to spoil it,' she purred. 'And nothing will, I hope.'

He spoke with his face still buried in her soft hair. 'We're meant to be together.' He squeezed her hand and lifted it to his lips and kissed her fingers. 'You're my perfect woman.'

Fiona tilted her head to look up at him. 'I bet you say that to all the girls.'

'Rubbish,' he murmured and kissed her fingers again, then held the tips between his teeth and sucked them.

She pushed her fingers in deeper and ran her middle finger along his tongue. 'Come on, you've had a few serious girlfriends, so you must have said something charming to them. What's your catch-phrase, then?' She withdrew her wet fingers and traced a path from his mouth into her own, and sucked them clean.

'You're feeling randy again, you naughty girl!' He rolled her on to her back and kissed the soft skin on her neck just below the ear. 'I'll tell you something, Fiona. I've stuck it out sometimes just hoping it would get half as good as this, but it never did. And now if I think of anyone in my past, it doesn't even seem real.'

She pulled his face towards hers, slid her tongue between his lips and wrapped her legs around him again, curling them up with her ankles by his hips to make it easier for him.

'In fact,' he continued, 'it's more like an old video I've seen, but not like I was ever really there. You've eclipsed them all.'

She pretended to look concerned. 'Not some old dirty videos, I hope?' she enquired coyly.

He grabbed her ankles and pushed them back towards her shoulders. 'I wouldn't mind making a dirty video with you.'

'You pervert!' she gasped.

'No, I'm not. I just can't get enough, at the moment.'

'Well, I'm not depriving you.' She laughed and they rolled over together. She pulled herself up into a sitting position, with her legs straddling his hips. 'Which bit do you want to video, then?'

'I'd like to watch you strip, and then force me to give in to your demands!' He ran a finger down between her breasts and gave her nipple a quick tweak.

'Force you?' she giggled. 'That'll be the day; we're as bad as each other.'

'God, no, you're worse. It wasn't just fingers you wanted to suck, was it?'

'It still isn't,' she said, 'but I'm not doing that on film. I look bad enough topless in photos.'

'Oh, well, I s'pose I'll get over the rejection,' he joked and nudged her hand towards his erection.

'Uh-huh,' she murmured in agreement, as she began to nuzzle his neck and simultaneously massage his body with her own. She ran the tip of her tongue down his body, then traced circles with it on his hip. She sucked suddenly at the skin, leaving a small round love bite, before licking a thin trail along his groin.

Suddenly his hand shot between her face and his naked flesh. 'What topless photos?' he demanded.

She propped herself up on one elbow. 'When I went on holiday with Rob, he took a couple of topless photos of me.' She smiled in self-deprecation. 'I decided then that I didn't have a future as a lingerie model!'

Pete frowned. 'But what did *he* think?'

'Who cares? But he didn't let me have them back.' She ran her fingers through her hair and lowered her lashes at him, keen to restore the previous moment. 'Anyway, the less said about him the better.'

'Do you think he's still got them?' he pressed her.

'Pete, forget it. It's over four years ago.' She stroked a fingernail along the top of his thigh. 'Now, where was I?'

Pete pushed her upright, and a sudden tension in his voice sharpened his words. 'So why tell me that, Fi?'

'I don't know.' She shrugged, uncertain as she felt the stab of his discomfort prick at the back of her neck.

'Are you trying to make me jealous, or something?' he accused her.

'No, of course not,' she replied, bewildered.

'Then what? Don't start playing games with me, Fiona. I've had enough of it.'

'It wasn't meant to hurt, Pete. I thought . . .' Fiona's voice trembled for a second. 'I thought we weren't going to have secrets from each other.'

Pete looked away and shook his head. 'You're right, I'm the touchy one. I'm sorry.'

She sat for a moment in the middle of the bed, with her arms folded across her naked breasts, then reached out and squeezed his hand. 'Let's just forget it, eh?' Next she climbed over his legs, back on to her own side of the bed, pulled the duvet over them both and waited for Pete to speak next.

There was silence for a few minutes. She hoped he wouldn't get dressed before they'd made things up.

As though he sensed what she wanted, he slid on top of her and they made love again. He didn't speak, or kiss her. He just looked deep into her eyes, and she gazed back into his.

He found it hard to shake Rob from his thoughts, though, and wondered what had made Fiona talk of another man while she was lying in his bed. It was unsettling simply because everybody knew that first love was the hardest to forget.

CHAPTER 59

FRIDAY, 1 JULY 2011

The hard edge of a white morning hung over the little lake. Its grip choked the colours of summer from the trees, leaving the beech and horse chestnuts like faded sentinels huddled around the far bank.

The surface of the lake rippled, but 6 a.m. was still too early and too cold for any substantial activity.

A blackbird tried a burst of song, which died away to be replaced by the hum of a car on the Spine Road.

A maroon taxi cruised from lake to lake, slowing each time it approached a gateway and then spurting forward to reach the next. Marlowe sat directly behind the driver, hunched in the corner with her right hand stroking the armrest. 'This is definitely the one,' she assured him.

He swung in through the gateway, before parking alongside the fence.

'Here's fine,' she said.

'Are you sure? It seems very deserted.'

'Bird watching,' she muttered in explanation. Her fingers fumbled with the once familiar catch on her purse. 'How much do I owe you?'

'Fifty-six quid, I'm afraid.' He watched her through the corner of his rear-view mirror. She pushed her dishevelled hair back from her face as she fiddled with the change.

He heard her tut to herself. She clicked her purse shut and opened another compartment instead. She then reached between the front seats and passed him three twenty-pound notes. 'That's fine, thanks,' she exclaimed, and hurried to open the door.

He glanced at her in his mirror as he drove away. She loitered, playing with her bag and pretending to be busy. But it was none of his business.

Marlowe waited until the taxi had curved away out of sight before she moved. Then, sure she was alone, she turned to face the lake.

Her gaze flickered dimly over the water; she'd expected to feel something. She'd thought her heart would race and her hands would tremble, at the very least. *But what do I know?* she reasoned.

She leant on the gate. Its wood sweated cold dew, coming alive in the morning air. A shred of blue and white police tape caught her eye.

It crackled and fluttered, in contrast to everything else around it, calling for attention as it writhed from its impaled position on the fence, despite the lack of breeze.

Marlowe reached towards it and clutched it for a moment between her thumb and forefinger. It felt sacred to her, like a marker to take her to the Holy Grail. It was the only sign that this was Kaye's lake. She let it go, and it hung limply from its tack.

How was it for Kaye, she wondered, and tried to imagine her lying there in the cold, night after night. *If it had been me, would I have lasted as long?*

She shuddered as though last season's intense cold had caught up with her. *And if Kaye had been me, would it have all gone this far?*

It didn't help to wonder; thinking too much had only driven her mad. Why did she ever think anyone would believe her? Julie did, she reminded herself.

The gate was padlocked; she tugged at it but it stood fast. However, she needed to be on the other side. She moved to the end nearest the hinges and stepped on to the second bar. She swung her leg over the top and, as she straddled it, she noticed that the fence next to it was broken, fractured long ago under some impossible burden, no doubt. She knew there was irony there somewhere.

She dropped to the ground on the other side.

Enough, she told herself. *No more Julie or Helen, Stephanie or Kaye, bloody wrists and nightmares*. She trudged across to the edge of the dew-damp grass, where it gave way to a gritty slope descending to the water.

Peace had eluded her for far too long, but now it stood, cold and elegant, in front of her.

Just for a moment the sun tried hard to prise its fingers between the layers of early-morning mist. Even its rays felt icy as they retreated.

Marlowe shivered as the cold reached down inside the back of her jacket. She headed towards the water's edge, with the gravel grinding beneath her walking boots, which left only indistinct scuffmarks.

She faced the lake directly. It spread before her like a pool of mercury, cool and deadly and fascinating. She had hoped it would be like this, deserted and silent.

Marlowe stepped forward and the shallow water lapped at her ankles, spilling inside her boots and seeping up the hem of her jeans. She waded in fully clothed, focusing only on the shingle bank in the distance.

She didn't flinch as the cold water lapped ever higher against her bare flesh, soaking her knickers as it reached her thighs.

She tipped forward as it oozed over her waistband, and she began to swim a slow breaststroke towards the centre of the lake.

Her fingers soon tingled, and turned as purple as her scars. Her breath furled out from her damson-painted lips, clipping the surface only inches from her aching eyes.

She closed them and kept going.

The lake had always been too wide for her to swim right across. As she neared the middle, her heartbeat slowed and the only sound she could hear was the blood pulsing against her eardrums.

Marlowe felt at one with the water lapping against her face. At one, too, with the world. She trod water until hypothermia embraced her and she slipped into unconsciousness.

The water of Kaye's lake closed over her and she drifted beneath the surface.

CHAPTER 60

SATURDAY, 2 JULY 2011

There is no fast road from Cambridge to Sheringham, just a ninety-mile chain of battered A-roads that become swamped with tourist traffic during the summer months.

Before the morning rush hour, it is possible to enjoy the spurts along sections of dual carriageway and the inevitable crawl along the smaller winding roads, with little interference from other travellers. Pete Walsh had left at 3.30 and had skirted around the edge of Fakenham by 4.45, snagging nothing more than a single set of lights that made him wait for two minutes at a deserted junction.

He kept to a steady fifty from there to Sheringham, and pulled up eventually at the dead end of the Drift Way, where the assortment of cottages stop and the coast path starts. He checked his watch and it read ten past five. Pete switched off the engine, unclipped his seat-belt and stretched. He felt good for someone who'd missed his night's sleep. Good as in alert, that is, but not any happier.

He ached: 'in his heart and in his soul' sounded too dramatic, but that was how it felt.

He couldn't put his finger on the cause.

No, that wasn't true. He just hadn't been able to admit that whenever he found himself awash with this gnawing emptiness, his thoughts always gravitated back to Marlowe.

He pressed the *on* button of the radio and tried to think of something else. Anything would do; after all he had vowed to fight it this time. But the DJ had selected a bad choice of love song, and Elvis merely crooned salt into the wounds.

Pete turned the volume up. Here he was, watching the sunrise over Sheringham. Didn't that mean he'd fought it and lost? Couldn't he just admit that she'd meant more to him than he'd realized at the time. Perhaps he'd feel better by admitting to everything he missed.

Early morning reminded him of Marlowe: the beauty of the new day. Everything so pale, shrouded in the veil of morning mist, tinted with subtle shades picked out by the early light.

In the distance, grey clouds hung over the hills. He thought of Marlowe then, too, so pretty and bright up close but always hinting at a gathering storm.

Two gulls flew overhead, circling and swooping. They looked as though they were flirting with each other, but he guessed they were more likely competing for carrion. Nothing was ever the way it seemed.

A scrappy patch of hedgerow decorated with an occasional flower marked the start of the footpath. A clump of long-stemmed dandelions sprang from its base and swayed gently, with beads of dew clinging to their leaves.

Clinging: an invention of Nature.

For a moment Pete could have believed himself to be all alone in the world; insulated from everyone outside. He didn't mind that, because solitude brought him comfort, but he also knew that there were few places where it was possible to be totally alone, and he watched as a murky silhouette on the coast path gradually materialized into a human form.

For his own amusement, he imagined that he was watching Marlowe coming towards him through the mist. Amusement – he winced at such a poor choice of word. Amusement, yes, but not as in pleasure or entertainment, just as in passing time.

As in filling the void.

The figure solidified into a girl.

Pete became aware of another distraction as the light, rapid clicking of a bicycle freewheeling along the road disturbed the morning quiet.

A paper boy.

He stopped his bike at the head of the footpath, and waved to the girl.

Pete had never himself done a paper round: too much hard work before school, for his liking.

The boy ditched his bike and darted back towards the third and fourth houses from the end of the row, and posted copies of the *Daily Express* and the *Sun* through the first and the *Guardian* through the second. He'd probably be finished in time to do a second round, if he didn't dally too long with the girl.

She reached the bike first, and the pedal rasped the ground as she dragged it upright; the only sound to intrude on Pete and his car radio. He watched intently. A joke, a smile, the brushing of lips. Romeo and Juliet?

Another giggle passed between the pair and the girl tugged on his sleeve. The boy pulled her in tight and they nuzzled each other, exchanging private words.

Pete sighed and sank back in his seat. He dropped his gaze as his thoughts returned to Marlowe.

Marlowe with those deep, grey-blue eyes and such fragile pale skin. He had told her it was over and she'd vanished like vapour. He'd seen her once since, a chance encounter in the street. She'd recoiled like a frightened deer bolting from the hunt, and he realized then how much he'd hurt her.

But, as he'd told himself so many times, some things are over for ever. You can't go back.

She would have been with someone else by then. Wouldn't she?

He closed his eyes completely, rested his head back against the door, and imagined his lips pressed against hers.

The memory of their kisses made him tingle, as it always did during one of these spells. But today his senses were heightened, and his nerves jangled with the sensation that she was there.

He flexed his fingers, reaching for her skin, for its velvet texture and gentle warmth. His nostrils succumbed to a memory of apple shampoo and rose soap, and for a fraction of a second he *felt* her again.

That shook him and he jolted upright; he must have been dozing.

He glanced around. Had he been spotted while lost in his wishful thinking? No, no one had witnessed his foolish puppy-dog expression.

The only people in view were the boy and girl – Romeo and Juliet – now going their separate ways for the day, their backs towards him and their thoughts only on each other.

He inhaled a deep breath, but the car smelt of pine air-freshener and dewy morning instead of Marlowe.

He managed to conjure up an image of her china-blue eyes, but this time they reminded him that it had all been spoilt.

Spoilt by her weakness, by the dark side of her personality that had drained him, had sapped his own energy.

He had had to break from her before she broke him.

The final bars of the Elvis song rolled from the speakers like the last ribbons of honey pouring from an empty pot, and Pete clicked it off before the DJ spoke again.

He knew he'd hurt her, but she had hurt him too. And he still missed her.

And that was why he'd never been able to settle with anyone since. He found himself continually making unfavourable comparisons. And, as a result, he always found himself feeling let down, and returning to the same inevitable feeling of empty desolation.

By 6.15 the morning gloom had cleared, and a flotilla of fluffy storybook clouds skimmed across the pale blue sky. Pete drove back through Thetford Forest, picking small B-roads flanked by a disarray of new growth and bare dead wood. He opened his window, so the fresh smell of the woodland enlivened his senses. This was the proper England: twisting roads and medieval scenery.

The smaller roads were darker and the daylight barely flickered through the branches. A wild deer grazed in a clearing; a muddy bay colour and hard to spot in its native home. The sky didn't seem so endless now, but the forest did; a long way from Sheringham in so many ways.

Pete parked in a gravel lay-by and sat there with the door ajar. For ten minutes he soaked up the silence, then he stepped from the car, to be met by the light rustle of trees.

His head had cleared, as he slammed the boot. A faint path cut through the undergrowth, no more than a scrape through the soil traced by a giant fingernail. He breathed gently with the evenness of a man content with the world.

A man on top of the world. He smiled. *Something along those lines, anyway.*

With the whole world at his feet? *Better.*

A dizzy, giddy buzz tingled in his head as he enjoyed his own good humour.

The whole world in his hands. *That was it.* Not his whole world of course, but someone's.

He didn't know her name, no doubt he'd see it in a newspaper soon enough, but to him she was just Juliet. Beautiful and ill-fated.

He placed *Juliet* in a grassless patch at the foot of a tree. Not a pretty tree. A deformed tree buckled by old age and slow growth. It hung at a precarious angle from a forty-five degree slope, its roots digging like cats' claws into the ground, holding it in place. Its stunted limbs stretched upwards, trying to overtake the taller trees, trying to find some sunlight.

At the bottom of the bank, a ditch lay deep with fetid water, motionless except for the flies.

She looked up at him, doe-eyed, shuddering, whimpering. They did that sometimes.

So what?

He felt a familiar surge of excitement; it fed his omnipotent high.

He looked back down at her. His fingers twitched again. Her skirt was hitched up by the rope binding her wrists and ankles.

He could see her smooth thighs and wondered about her underwear. Wondered about removing it.

And then what?

No, that wasn't his game. Not at all. He straightened and moved away.

He never looked back, but he thought about her on his way to his car. He paused to wipe his mouth. He had to, it was now watering so much.

CHAPTER 61

MONDAY, 4 JULY 2011

Goodhew drove towards Julie Wilson's flat, to meet her sister. Every detail of his only previous meeting with her had stayed fresh in his memory.

He ran over it again and again. Had there been any signs that Julie had been so desperate? Or, God forbid, had he pushed her too hard somehow?

He remembered her fear when she'd encountered him waiting outside her door. But that hadn't been fear of him; he knew that much at least.

Of who, then? Peter Walsh? She'd implied that he'd been a bastard, but clearly didn't put him down as a killer. But would she have actually known?

He remembered her sarcasm. She'd been so uptight that asking her about Pete had felt like tapping dangerously hard on a sheet of glass.

Uptight but not depressed. Something must have happened after his visit to trigger this.

He turned into her road and an involuntary shudder rattled through him. It was the waste that bothered him most about suicides. The universal response from family and friends: 'If only we'd known, we could have helped.' And the truth being that the suicide always caused more distress than the secret that triggered it.

Goodhew knew he was being watched as he headed from his car across the footpath to Julie's flat. The cul-de-sac bristled with twitching net curtains and with the hush that sweeps down and steals the usual day-to-day sounds when a tragedy occurs.

The door of Julie's flat stood wide open, so Goodhew knocked on the door frame. Beyond, a sandy-haired woman of about twenty-five knelt in the kitchen doorway, filling a small removal crate. 'Nicole Wilson?'

She was packing china and had already wrapped all but one piece of a Ports of Call dinner service in sheets of newspaper. She glanced up. 'Come in.' She picked up the final saucer and stood to shake Goodhew's hand. 'The cup's missing,' she remarked.

Her hand trembled and the end of her thumb was pressed white as she gripped the china.

'I'm sorry,' he replied.

She nodded, averting her gaze to stare at the saucer. It was chipped. 'I can't bear to throw it out, but it's no good, is it?'

'What are you going to do with the rest of it?'

She shrugged and shook her head. She then covered her face with her right hand, pressing her fingers to the bridge of her nose. Tears trickled across her palm and flowed down her wrist.

Goodhew picked up a fresh sheet of newspaper and took the saucer from her. 'Why not keep it all together for now?' He carefully folded the paper around it and handed it back.

She knelt again to tuck it in with the rest of the set, before pulling a tatty tissue from her sleeve. 'Sorry.' She looked up at him. 'Go through and I'll fetch drinks.'

A pile of empty boxes stood next to the settee. Only two had been filled so far, and Goodhew flipped back their lids. One crate held the stereo; Nicole had pulled out the speaker leads and wrapped the cables in neat rolls. She'd laid the speakers flat on their backs and covered them with a tea towel to keep out the dust.

The other box held some of Julie's clothes, smoothed out and folded, item by item, so they could be unpacked ready to wear. Not that they would.

Nicole came back with two cans of Coke. 'This is all I've got.' She nodded to the boxes. 'I decided to pack up straight away. Mum and Dad were on holiday, and they're being flown back right now, so I thought I'd get on with it.'

'To save them the pain?' A photo of Julie, Nicole and their parents lay flat but face-up on the top of the bookcase. Goodhew picked it up.

She nodded. 'They won't understand why she did it.'

'Do you?' he asked, glancing at her sharply.

'No.' She held out her hand and he passed her the picture. 'We all thought everything was OK, so this is out of the blue. What could be so bad as to make her do this? We just keep asking why.' She wasn't guarded in her thoughts, like her sister. 'Why are the police involved, anyway? We've already been assured that there were no suspicious circumstances. Isn't that true?'

'Yes, it is, but I'd spoken to Julie shortly before her death about another matter, and I need to ensure that there is no connection between our conversation and her suicide.'

He knew he had just made an unfortunate choice of words and, with a flash of hostility, she suddenly looked a whole lot more like her sister. 'You mean you're scared in case you said something to upset her? Were you heavy-handed with her?'

'Of course not.' He raised his hands in protest, and some Coke slopped into the rim of the can. He used his handkerchief to wipe its top and sides, then set it down on the carpet. 'I'm sorry, but I don't think I've explained myself very well. I'm actually investigating the death of Kaye Whiting.' He paused but Nicole clearly hadn't recognized the name. 'You may remember the case: she was found in the water at a flooded quarry just south of Ipswich.'

'I remember.' She placed her can alongside Goodhew's, and by the time she straightened again the colour had drained from her cheeks. 'Julie showed me her picture in the paper,' Nicole whispered.

'What did she say about it?'

Nicole thought for a second. '"Awful, isn't it" is what she said, I think. Why do you ask?'

'We've had a variety of leads to follow, one of which was an anonymous caller giving us a name to investigate. We don't know, at this stage, if it's merely a hoax, so we're keen to find the caller.'

'It wouldn't be Julie,' she answered quickly, as if it was a reflex.

'Why not? Something clearly upset her.'

'I know. Saying it wasn't her was my gut reaction, but I'm sure it's right. But she wouldn't have called and dropped someone in it. She was loyal. Always loyal.'

'Even to people who didn't deserve it?' He didn't wait for her answer. 'We know Julie wasn't the caller, but we thought she might know who was. I must also stress that it's just one line of enquiry.'

'Who are you investigating?' she asked. When he did not respond, she insisted, 'Who?'

'It's an ex-boyfriend, Peter Walsh.'

Nicole sighed. 'Oh.'

'As far as I can gather, she went out with him for just about a year and was very upset when they split up. But that was some time back now, maybe a year ago. Would that be about right?'

'They split up last summer, and she was more than upset. Destroyed, I'd call it.' Nicole faced Goodhew unflinchingly, anger holding her rigid. 'He treated her like dirt, and shattered her confidence. So do you know what she did?'

Goodhew shook his head.

'She just waited for him to come back. She hoped he'd come back and still want her. She said she couldn't understand what she'd done wrong.' Nicole clenched and unclenched her jaws. 'I couldn't get through to her that it wasn't just her: he'd be the same with anyone.'

'And do you know of anyone else he's been out with?'

'What, since?'

'Or before,' he asked.

'Before Julie there was a girlfriend with a funny name. Marlon or something . . . ? No, Marlowe, that was it.' She grabbed Goodhew's arm and pulled him towards the long sideboard. 'I think there's a photo of her somewhere.'

Nicole opened and closed the first two of the six wide drawers. She opened the third and, as soon as she saw it brimming with an assortment of papers and greetings cards, she pulled it off its runners and scattered the contents directly on to the carpet.

Goodhew picked up a small square Paddington Bear gift tag. 'All my love, Pete.' He dropped it back next to the pile.

Nicole spread the pile of stuff more thinly with a sweep of her hand. 'Let's get stuck in.'

Goodhew sat on the floor next to her and they sifted through the heap. Brown-edged petals of a dried red rose crumbled amongst the greetings cards. He found a birthday card, a Valentine's card, a bracelet, some photos, a book called *The Cross and the Switchblade*, and several more gift tags. 'Are these all from Peter Walsh?'

'Souvenirs of a dead romance – except it wasn't dead for Julie. Unrequited love, that's what I think it's called.'

Goodhew spotted a print half hidden in the pile. It was an old black and white movie still: Robert Mitchum paddling in the sea with his suit trousers rolled up to his knees.

'What about this?'

'He bought it for her.' She smiled. 'I always liked it, even though it came from him.' She pointed to a spare picture hook on the wall. 'Julie used to hang it up there, above the video shelf, until quite recently. It was the last thing of his on display. I asked her where it had gone, and she said it reminded her too much of Pete. Said she'd been so stupid and naïve, but that was all she said.'

'When was that?'

'About a week before she died. I just thought she'd finally come to her senses.' Then she spotted the corner of a photograph jutting from inside the book. 'Ah, look, here it is.'

She handed Goodhew a six-by-four snapshot of two people standing at a bar, both smiling and holding their drinks up towards the camera.

'She pinched it from Pete's house, because he always told her how she didn't match up to Marlowe.'

Pete was standing with his right arm around Marlowe's waist. He looked happy and younger, and she looked younger too.

Younger and happier than the moment when Goodhew had come face to face with her in the rain in Hanley Road.

CHAPTER 62

MONDAY, 4 JULY 2011

Goodhew placed the cardboard box on the end of the desk standing in the far corner of the incident room. He shovelled everything else from the desktop on to the adjacent printer table. He unrolled a new pad of flip chart and ruled five columns on the first sheet with a chunky black marker. He needed to concentrate on nothing else.

He was alone in the room, but WPC Wilkes and Sue Gully were chatting out in the corridor.

'I think he was an actor,' Gully said.

Wilkes disagreed. 'No, I reckon he was a character.'

Goodhew crossed the room, pushed the door shut and was able to stop listening. He filled in a name at the head of the second, third and fourth columns: Marlowe, Julie, and then Paulette. It was the order in which Pete Walsh had gone out with them. The fifth column he left blank.

Nicole Wilson had packed the contents of that drawer into one of her boxes for him, and he reached into it now and pulled out two photographs. He placed them side by side on the desktop.

Marlowe and Pete. Julie and Pete. He'd fill in what he could about Paulette from memory.

There was a quote that went 'Know the victim, know the killer'. He wondered why it had suddenly sprung to mind. Were they all victims, and if so what was the crime?

In the first column he wrote 'date of birth' and beneath that 'occupation', 'appearance', 'address', 'education' and thus continued writing other headings, till he finished with 'hobbies' near the bottom of the sheet.

He began to fill in spaces on the grid he had devised. He knew most about Julie Wilson; just as well because he wouldn't be getting a chance of questioning her again.

As he wrote, he realized how little he knew about any of them. He could question Paulette again but not Julie, and he wondered when he would locate the mysterious Marlowe. At least he now had a name to go on.

Clarke nipped into the room to pick up his car keys, and left without shutting the door; Wilkes' and Gully's voices intruded again.

'I think that's where the name's from. But it doesn't help, does it?' Gully was saying.

'We could ask her, I suppose,' Wilkes replied.

'Yeah, or her family – if they turn up.' That was Gully talking again.

Goodhew crossed the room and pushed the door shut again, before returning to his chair.

He was going about this the wrong way. He threw the elaborate page in the bin and redrew the columns on a fresh sheet.

OK, he thought. *They are all linked by Pete Walsh. Let's start there.* He knew that they shared physical characteristics: height, colouring, similar ages. He knew too that these were all characteristics shared with Helen Neill, Kaye Whiting and Stephanie Palmer.

'*Previous relationships?*' he entered a question mark under each name.

'*Behaviour similarities*'. This time he had something to write. Assuming Marlowe and the anonymous caller were one and the same, she was clearly still also preoccupied by Pete. Julie had taken and kept a photo of Marlowe and Pete, while Paulette had taken down Julie's address. Paulette had considered her own behaviour as resulting from jealousy, whilst Nicole had described her sister as being 'unable to move on'.

And as for Marlowe, beyond the phone calls, he had yet to find out anything at all.

The door bumped open yet again. This time it was Kincaide, who held it open long enough to finish a conversation with Gully and Wilkes. 'That's the sort of question you should ask Goodhew. He's the one that's interested in shitty old films.' He looked across at Goodhew and feigned surprise. 'Oh, hello, Gary. I didn't see you there!' He smirked and dropped into his own chair.

Goodhew folded his newly annotated paper and placed it in the top of the box, covering Julie's personal effects. He'd come back to it later.

Gully poked her head around the door and called across to him. 'So, was Philip Marlowe an actor or a character?'

'Character,' Goodhew replied automatically. He carried the box over to his own rather noisier desk. Suddenly he realized the implication of what she had asked. 'Why?' he called out.

Gully was already back in the corridor. 'You're right,' he heard her say.

He dumped the box in the footwell of his desk and followed her. By the time he reached the door, WPC Wilkes had gone. 'Well, that solves that,' Gully beamed.

Goodhew's tone was tense. 'What, exactly?' he demanded.

'That girl from the lake is called Marlowe.'

Goodhew frowned. 'What girl?'

'Oh blimey, Gary, keep up,' she scolded him. 'You know, the one the taxi driver fished out of the same lake where they found Kaye's body.'

Goodhew shook his head. 'I don't know, Sue. I've been out places.'

Her eyes widened. 'Sorry, I just assumed you'd heard. She was dropped off by a taxi and the driver thought her behaviour seemed odd, so he went back to make sure she was OK.'

'And?' Goodhew grabbed her arm.

'And, she'd tried to drown herself. She was already unconscious when he pulled her out. She's now at Fulbourn Hospital Mental Illness Unit.'

Goodhew grinned. 'She's our anonymous caller, Gully, I'm sure. Can you take me up there?'

'Of course, but she's sedated and refusing to speak to anyone. Wilkes has been dealing with it, and only mentioned it because of the connection to Kaye.' They were walking towards the exit even as they spoke. 'Wilkes has just found out her full name and managed to contact her parents. Apparently she's had some emotional problems before and we've now managed to locate her counsellor, called Elizabeth Martin. Wilkes has made an appointment for two p.m.'

'We'll visit her on the way to the hospital.'

'OK, I'll let Wilkes know, and then meet you at the car.'

CHAPTER 63

MONDAY, 4 JULY 2011

Goodhew parked the car outside Braeside, a three-storey Cambridge brick terrace house in Maid's Causeway. It stood between two tidier family homes. 'Is this it?'

Gully checked the address on Wilkes' note. 'It must be.'

The front door had been left ajar and Goodhew led the way into a red-tiled hallway. A leaded panel of coloured glass on each side of the door provided the only light which fell directly on to a dark oak table. A pile of information leaflets stood propped against the wall and the only other item, a laminated A4 sheet, informed them that Elizabeth Martin's treatment room could be found on the first floor, above the premises of a chiropractor and below the offices of the Cambridge Women's Resource Centre.

'It's not what I expected,' he whispered.

'And what exactly did you expect, white coats and a posh waiting room?' Gully shrugged. 'Perhaps she's an amateur – you know, one of those dabblers.'

They both looked up towards the landing, and Goodhew shook his head. 'No, I called our Occupational Health Department while I was waiting for you outside in the car. Just on the off-chance.' He gestured for her to go up first. 'No hesitation there, they knew her name straight away. She's very well thought of, and has been called as an expert witness several times in the past.'

Gully waited for Goodhew to catch up with her at the head of the stairs. Several panelled doors faced on to the landing. A square of paper was sticky-taped above the Bakelite handle of one. It read: 'Please knock and wait.'

They knocked but didn't wait, because a husky voice called them straight in.

Elizabeth Martin's treatment room was informal. More like an aunt's sitting room furnished with a rounded collection of mis-matches. Mismatched chairs, uneven bookshelves and a display of prints across the walls with no commonality of either theme or frame. A crocheted blanket lay folded into the shape of a cushion on the window seat, its colours bleached by daylight.

Elizabeth sat in a chair in the far corner, facing the door but near enough to the window to see the road where they'd parked, one floor below. Goodhew and Gully chose the two chairs closest to her, and sat side by side.

'You look like an old married couple,' she quipped.

Gully shot a startled glance at Goodhew, then fiddled with her notepad, leaving him to speak.

'Marlowe Gates was pulled out of a lake after what we think was a suicide attempt,' he began. 'We're about to visit her, but so far she has refused to speak to anyone. When we heard that she's been receiving counselling, we hoped you'd be able to shed some light on her state of mind.'

Elizabeth Martin leant over one side of her chair to fish around inside a buff document wallet. She sat up straight again, holding a clutch of papers in her hand. 'What I don't understand is this.' She levelled her impassive gaze on Goodhew. 'If she's now in hospital, and in the care of the correct health services, why does it need to involve you?'

She was obviously used to questioning everyone's motives, and Goodhew had no doubt that she'd also hesitate to dish out any confidential patient information. 'I'll be straight with you now. We are investigating a murder, and I believe that Marlowe Gates may be a key witness. I need to understand her mental state and therefore know how far I can press her for vital information. The last thing I want to do is push her into another suicide attempt.'

Elizabeth Martin repositioned herself in her easy chair. She now sat straighter and looked sterner than before. She pressed her hand flat on the sheaf of notes in a gesture that both Goodhew and Gully interpreted as rejection. 'These notes are personal, and I am sure you're both aware of the importance of client confidentiality.' She raised her palm by a couple of inches and slapped it down again. 'I do however retain the right to discuss a client's situation in special circumstances, particularly if further life is at risk. And it is fair to say that this may be one of those.'

'Thank you,' Gully said. 'Why and when did she first come to see you?'

'She was referred to me by her doctor. That was about two years ago, and she then had several appointments over the next few months.'

'And was she suicidal then?' Goodhew asked.

'No, not at all.' Elizabeth Martin flicked through the first few pages. 'Not in my opinion anyway. But she had started harming herself, cutting herself. Her wrists mainly.'

'But not attempting suicide?' Gully frowned. 'Is she an attention-seeker?'

'That's the general misconception about self-harmers. No, they usually do it as a form of release for an overload of internal pain which they believe they cannot dissipate in any other way. In fact self-harm often provides a means to help sufferers get on with their lives. It is rare for them to become suicidal.'

'Tell me specifically about Marlowe, then. Can you build a picture of her for us?'

'Sure, just give me a minute.' Elizabeth Martin delved further through her wodge of papers. Goodhew and Gully waited patiently, and the air hung quiet and heavy. A dazzling stream of sunlight suddenly broke in through the corner of the window and a confetti of dust rose to meet it. The counsellor reached across and tugged the velvet curtain across the window a few inches further. 'It can become unbearable here in the afternoons,' she muttered. She closed her notes and looked up again. 'The sun that is, not the job.' She smiled, then began to speak rapidly. 'I'll keep it simple and quick, but stop me if I don't make sense. Please take notes. You can't have mine, and yours will be strictly only for use in your investigation. Agreed?'

'Absolutely,' Goodhew concurred.

'Marlowe's first appointment was when she was twenty-one, and her last was this year when she was twenty-three. As I said, the initial contact was because she had started to self-harm, usually cutting her wrists, but on occasion also her abdomen and breasts. Self-harm can start at any age, but when it commences in adulthood, it is most commonly the result of a trauma such as rape or physical assault.'

'And what had happened?' Goodhew asked.

'She wouldn't tell me.'

'Even after several sessions?' he pressed.

'No,' she gave him a stern look, 'I'm not holding anything back here. She just wasn't preoccupied by whatever had happened to her. But I'll return to that in a minute. As well as the self-harm, she was experiencing anxiety attacks. These manifest themselves in a series of symptoms stemming from the flight-or-fight instinct – which I assume you've heard of?'

Goodhew nodded. 'If people sense danger, they get a rush of adrenalin which makes them ready to either stand and fight or flee from the situation.'

'And the body can do either most effectively when it is at its lightest, and directing maximum oxygen towards the muscles and the brain. The body tries to lose weight by sweating and going to the toilet, and increases its oxygen supply by over-breathing and inducing a state of hyperventilation.'

Gully suppressed a yawn and squirmed in her chair. Elizabeth Martin pointed to her. 'An extreme version of what you're doing now, in fact. You're feeling restless, maybe a few butterflies, unable to relax, and feeling that something awful will happen if you don't get on with things. Am I right?'

Gully nodded. 'Sorry, I didn't mean to appear rude.'

'Don't worry about it,' the woman continued. 'That, magnified a hundredfold, is how Marlowe was feeling every day during the period I saw her. Each time it became too intense, she'd cut herself.'

'But what was the trigger?' Goodhew said. 'What exactly was preying on her mind?'

'Are you familiar with the expression post-traumatic stress?'

'Like shell-shock?' Gully queried.

'Originally,' Goodhew intervened, 'but now applied to one's reaction to a wide range of life-threatening events. Is that right?'

The counsellor nodded. 'Broadly speaking, yes. There are five specific criteria that need to be met for a proper diagnosis. Marlowe met all five of them.'

'What sort of criteria?' Goodhew asked, now intrigued.

'Re-experiencing the event in some way. Recollections and bad dreams and distress at physical reminders. Avoiding stimuli associated with the trauma, problems in concentrating, difficulty in sleeping, and so on. The first criterion is that the client has witnessed or experienced a serious threat to his or her life or physical well-being.'

'But you don't know what that was, in Marlowe's case?' he asked.

'As I said, Marlowe flatly refused to tell me any specific details. I guessed she'd suffered some abuse from her boyfriend, either sexual or physical, or both. She insisted that what had happened wasn't the point. She repeatedly told me, though, that she was concerned for the safety of her ex-boyfriend's new girlfriend. Each time I saw her, she kept repeating that he'd do the same thing again. To be honest, the pair of us weren't moving forward.' Elizabeth Martin leant back over the side of her chair and replaced the notes in their folder. 'She said she couldn't stand the guilt if he "did it again". I spent time trying to make her realize that she couldn't take responsibility for his actions.'

She paused there, perhaps for breath.

Goodhew nodded slowly. 'And she stopped coming to see you about then, didn't she? About February or March this year?'

The woman's eyes widened. 'Exactly. How in the world . . . ?'

'Did she say anything in particular? Can you remember?' he asked.

'She said that what he'd done was evil and she was going to the police,' came the answer.

'So, you're saying that she knew something that she felt she needed to involve the police with?' Gully gasped.

'No, I'm merely saying she *thought* she did. She genuinely believed that what he'd done was sufficiently bad to warrant police involvement. I talked with her, but in the end she herself had to decide whether to act upon it.'.

'And you expected that accusation to involve domestic violence?' Goodhew said.

'Something of that sort, yes.'

'Not murder?'

Elizabeth Martin paled. 'Good God, no!'

'Is she a liar?' he asked.

'No, I don't think so,' she said slowly. 'But I assume you mean how much credence can be given to her statements. Marlowe is unusually intuitive.'

'For example?'

The woman thought for a second. 'My father died, so I had to cancel some of my sessions. I didn't say why, just left a message at her work place. She then put an "In Sympathy" card through my door. The problem is she treats her intuition like a fully developed sense – and that, in itself, is a danger. It's too easy to put two and two together and make anything except four.'

CHAPTER 64

MONDAY, 4 JULY 2011

Small whisked-up clouds drifted high in the expanse of blue above Marlowe's window. The horizon had slipped towards the bottom of her view, and the line it cut through the picture was the first thing she saw as she emerged from her sedation. Heaven looked huge, and earth so tiny, and here she was still stuck on it.

A telephone tinkled at the nurses' station. Marlowe could just hear a nurse's even tones. 'She's still asleep. She woke up earlier when the police were here, but she wouldn't speak. No one else has arrived yet, but I think that her parents are on their way and the police are coming back again shortly.'

Marlowe watched the cars barely visible on the distant dual carriageway. They were just little coloured dots, like tiny coloured ball-bearings, some of them running from left to right and some from right to left. Were they really cars with drivers and passengers, when seen up close, or did her whole world end at the glass?

She knew it all existed, but it was just too much to think about. Her eyes slid shut and her mind wandered into that limbo land between consciousness and sleep.

The nurse directed someone towards her. 'She's over in the corner bed. She should be waking soon.'

'Thank you, I'll wait, if that's OK.'

And she heard his footfalls as he walked around the bed and drew a chair closer.

He sat down and she could hear his breathing, and the gentle tapping of his toe on the tiled floor. Seconds pulsed by and he dragged his chair closer, its feet squealing as his weight ground it downwards.

Something jabbed her hand sharply. Her eyes snapped open and she recoiled, before staring at the blue centre of a red dent in her palm.

His pen, she thought, feeling relieved as she watched him click it shut and drop it back in his breast pocket.

'Sorry about that. I'm DC Kincaide from Cambridge CID. I needed you awake. How are you feeling?'

'Oh no,' she groaned silently and turned her head to stare at the mint-sorbet emulsion on the wall in front of her bed. She didn't want to speak to him. Not now. Not ever. He kept talking, though. He told her her name, her personal details, where she'd been found. She tried not to listen.

'Don't ignore me,' he whispered and leant closer still. His hot breath assaulted her ear, sending shivery cold trails down the side of her neck. 'I need to know how you're involved in these killings. I need to know what you've done. You'd better start talking.'

Marlowe decided not to move and her inner voice began to count. 'One, two, three, don't listen to him, four, five, six, don't reply, seven, eight, nine . . .'

Other voices came along the corridor.

'Go on through. One of your colleagues is with her now.'

The visitor's chair squeaked its retreat but Kincaide breathed closer still. This time his face brushed against hers and she had no choice but to meet his stare.

'Talk to me, Marlowe. I want to help you out. Screwing some guy and getting pissed off when he dumps you isn't the real reason behind those phone calls. I'll see you again soon, and then you can tell me.'

Kincaide brushed his way past Goodhew at the door.

'She's still sedated. I'd come back later, Gary,' he said without turning.

'Why are you here, Michael?' called Goodhew.

'Following a lead, you know. The same one that you got from Gully earlier.'

Goodhew didn't even register Kincaide's parting barb. As he pushed open the door, his senses were overcome by a vision of cascading bright white sunlight that flooded over the patient and her white bedding. The light reflected off the polished floor so the whole room dazzled him. She was still, eyes open, but somewhere else in every way. She stared at the ceiling.

He stood beside her and studied her face, then turned towards the window and perched on the very edge of her bed, her hand resting on the top sheet only a few inches from his own.

'Hello you,' murmured Gary. 'I've been trying to find you.' He too watched the cars in the distance. 'I remember you in Hanley Road and I've regretted not speaking to you ever since.' He turned his gaze towards her. 'I feel like I've let you down because I didn't meet you afterwards. But I didn't get your letter in time. I wasn't home.'

Marlowe's eyes flickered and her gaze fell on to his.

'Marlowe, I feel guilty because I didn't help. Do you know how that feels?'

The corner of her mouth quivered and her eyes glistened as they pulled away from his gaze.

Goodhew moved towards the window and stared down at the pavement below. Thank God, she hadn't died.

Behind him the ward door swung open to admit her parents. He turned to study Mr and Mrs Gates.

'Marlowe, darling, we rushed here as soon as we heard,' her mother gushed.

Her father held back somewhat. 'Are you OK?' He was sweating on to the tight collar of his polyester shirt, the skin around his throat puckered like beetroot-stained turkey flesh. He shifted his weight nervously from dented brogue to dented brogue.

Goodhew's grandmother always said you could tell a lot from people's shoes.

Mrs Gates wore sensible shoes, and monopolized the situation with her reasonable voice. 'What a silly thing to do. Nothing can be that bad, darling. The hospital has only just been in touch, haven't they, Ron? And I just don't understand.'

Like a flower at dusk, Marlowe closed in on herself, and stared down at her fingers as they occupied one another by making weaves and spires and other interlocking patterns.

'It's no good giving us that silent treatment again.' Mrs Gates stepped back and propelled her husband closer. 'You try, Ron.'

He cleared his throat. 'Your mother and I are very concerned, Marlowe. I'm not one for interfering, but you can always talk to us.' He shuffled his feet again. 'Whatever you've done, you're still our daughter.'

Her parents were reflected as midgets in Marlowe's bedside jug. Goodhew meanwhile seemed invisible to them all. Marlowe concentrated on her fingers as they made junior-school shapes, ignoring her parents as they continued to prod and probe her conscience.

'You were such a happy child . . .' Mrs Gates continued.

Marlowe made the little church shape. '*Here's the church . . .*'

'Marlowe, how do you think this is making us feel?'

Marlowe pointed her fingers to make the spire. *Here's the steeple.* She turned her hands over, palms up. *Silly rhyme*. She jerked them apart. He's still here.

Goodhew's gaze never left her and when she looked up he mouthed the words, 'Trust me'.

She drew a deep breath. The ward smelt of fresh-cut grass and the head gardener's mower hummed somewhere in the sunshine. Tears rose and teetered as she mouthed her reply, 'Trust *me*.'

He nodded and for the first time he saw the trace of a smile touch her face, and then the tears toppled on to her cheeks.

CHAPTER 65

MONDAY, 4 JULY 2011

Goodhew locked the car and tramped across the muddy strip of grass to join Marlowe. The sun was burning low and picked out occasional strands of auburn in her hair. She leant on the gate, hands tucked inside the sleeves of her baggy cotton shirt, her hair gently blowing in rhythm with the ripples of the water behind her.

They'd returned to the lake where she'd nearly drowned. Gary had sensed she'd need to come back.

He also knew how she'd watched him closely since the meeting in hospital. He'd *felt* her concentration, silent and unwavering. And she watched him now, her face glowing in the late sun and her eyes shining, as if drawing him towards her. 'We need to be straight with each other, Gary,' she announced.

Goodhew opened the gate and motioned her through. 'Isn't that what trust is?'

'Yeah, exactly. So I'll just talk, and you can judge me how you like.'

'Don't worry, I won't think anything bad about you.'

'Listen, you don't have to tread too carefully with me,' she insisted. 'I'm not going to try again. That was a turning point.'

'It wouldn't prevent any more murders, for a start,' Goodhew pointed out.

They walked side by side along the welt of muddy footpath running around the edge of the lake. Marlowe proceeded with her hands digging deep in her pockets, and Gary kept nearer the water, plucking at random leaves as he brushed past the straggling undergrowth.

Marlowe waited for him to speak.

'I visited Julie after you did,' he began. Just the mention of Julie's name made her visibly shiver, but he continued in the same even tone. 'She could have told me that you'd been to see her. She could have told me about your suspicions, or about her own fears, but she never said anything. She chose her own way of dealing with it.' Marlowe picked up a flat stone, threw it in the air and caught it. Instead of skimming it across the water, or plopping it in at the edge, she left it on the top of a fence post. Marlowe chose her own way of doing things, too. 'But Julie got it wrong,' he concluded, 'because you're here and she's not.'

'That sounds harsh, Gary.'

He picked up her stone and put it in his pocket. 'I'm just pointing out that you need to stop being so hard on yourself.'

She shrugged. 'I really believe that if you know something is wrong and you stand by and do nothing, then you have to accept some of the responsibility.'

'So *you* are guilty because you couldn't stop him?'

'Of course.' She looked surprised, as if there was no other way of interpreting things.

'And how do you know it's him?'

'I *know*.' She studied his face, while seeking an explanation he'd understand. 'Like you know when someone doesn't love you any more, but won't admit it. You tell yourself exactly what you want to hear for a while, and keep rejecting any little sign that says you're wrong. But at the end of the day you know.'

'No evidence?'

'Nothing. And who's going to believe *me*?' Marlowe paused abruptly. 'I bet you've seen my medical notes, haven't you?'

'I know some of it.'

'Very diplomatic.' She smiled and walked on again. 'I've been totally out of control.'

He hurried a few strides, to catch up with her. 'That's how Julie described herself, too.'

Whenever Marlowe relaxed, even a little, her expressions were easier to read, and this time it was surprise that made her smile. 'Did she?' she said. 'That's funny. When I saw her, I envied how much she seemed to have her life together.' Marlowe looked up at the sky. The bottom half of the sun had now sunk below the horizon, and the amber top half cast a huge reflection that swam up the lake towards her. 'Today's the first time I've felt OK. So what can I tell you?'

'Well, Helen died around the time you were seeing Pete, so I think you could go right back to when you first met him.'

'I know the date, it was the seventh of January 2008, a Monday. I was working for a week at Dunwold Insurance, just as a temp. I'd dropped out of college and decided to temp while I was job hunting. I had to collate reports, and sat at a spare desk near Peter's. He'd bring me cups of tea and coffee from the drinks machine. By the end of the week, we'd just hit it off.' She wrinkled up her nose. 'I'd never had a serious boyfriend, and before I knew it we were inseparable.'

'And for how long did you see him?'

'Seventeen months? I'm sure it was but I'll double-check. It turned sour long before that, though. My parents are very old-fashioned. You met them. It's all about keeping up appearances: least said soonest mended and no sex before marriage – all of those values. I'd love to find out that my mother did it before their wedding; perhaps she'd come off her moral soapbox and then be a bit more human. Well, anyway, my mum had always been preaching to me about the evils of sex and, sure enough, as soon as we'd been to bed together everything changed.'

'How?'

'Oh, he seemed less affectionate, less loving I suppose. But at the same time he became possessive. He started telling me how to act and dress, and even what friends I could have. He kept telling me that I didn't meet up to his expectations.'

'But you didn't leave him?'

'No,' Marlowe shot him a rueful smile, 'that was my own stupidity. I should have left him in a flash, but instead I kept trying to be good enough, doing things just to please him. Working at it all the time. Even when things weren't my fault, I'd apologize anyway. I've been so angry with myself since for being so stupid.'

They continued walking in step. In profile she reminded him of a less worldly Lauren Bacall. 'You know, there are similarities between what you've just said and Paulette's and Julie's experiences,' Goodhew observed. 'Paulette admitted that she'd become obsessed with trying to make him happy, and Julie's sister explained how Pete told Julie that she didn't match up to *you*.'

Marlowe shook her head. 'So we've all been screwing ourselves up over him, and he acts just the same with whoever he goes out with?'

'Perhaps somehow he always picks girlfriends he knows he can manipulate. Also, you all have a physical resemblance to one another.'

'And to Helen, Kaye and Stephanie,' Marlowe concurred.

'Is that how you knew to link them?' Goodhew asked.

'Even now I look at the papers every day. It's become part of my routine. I study all the photos of missing girls. A couple of times I've been mistaken, but once a body's found, it's obvious.'

'You were telling me how you came to suspect Pete in the first place?'

'Well, we went away together for a few days – this would be right at the end, just before we split up. I'll check the date for you . . .'

'You talked about checking the date earlier?' he remarked.

'Oh, I've got all the dates written down, but I'll tell you about that in a minute. Anyway, I know it was a Saturday, and Peter had rented us a cottage in Ross-on-Wye. He said that he knew he'd been hard to get along with, and I remember having this sudden rush of hope – euphoria, I suppose – at the idea that he would start becoming affectionate again. I also remember Helen Neill disappearing while we were there. Her picture was shown on TV, and Peter asked me if I thought I looked like her.'

Gary noticed how she called him Peter, never Pete, as though she didn't want to sound too familiar.

'Did you think you did look like her?' Goodhew asked.

'Not at the time, and I said so to Peter. He insisted we looked like sisters, and that just stuck in my mind. Afterwards I could see a likeness, but only from seeing other photos, not the one on TV.'

'And did he behave at all suspiciously?'

Marlowe cast her eyes down to the mud below. 'He changed again,' she murmured.

Gary sensed her sudden unease. As he turned her stone over and over in his pocket, he let her change tack.

She sidestepped a muddy puddle, looked up again and continued. 'He behaved like that until he finished with me a couple of weeks later. Then, just as calmly as anything, he said that it wasn't going to work out and we needed to split up. Then, later on that week, Helen's body was discovered.' Marlowe shivered and glanced back towards the car. 'Can we go now? It's getting cold.'

The final strands of sunlight reached skywards. 'Where did Kaye drown?' she suddenly asked.

Gary pointed across to a stretch of shingle lining the opposite bank. 'She was found in the water just left of that tree.'

Marlowe nodded slowly. 'She must have suffered so much. I wish . . .' her voice trailed away. 'I hope . . .' she continued. 'I hope we can somehow stop it happening again.'

Goodhew unlocked the car and held the passenger door open. 'Where to?'

'Home, please.' She touched his shoulder and leant towards him. 'You've been very kind,' she whispered, and then ducked into her seat. She waited until he'd started the engine before continuing. 'I got distracted just then, didn't I? I was supposed to be explaining to you how I knew. Well, it was a few weeks since I'd seen Peter, and I came out of Marks & Spencer's and almost walked straight into him. I was terrified – because of the way that he'd behaved, I suppose. He stared straight at me and I froze. I felt completely panic-stricken and became determined never to be caught out like that again. So I started watching him.' Marlowe paused again, allowing Gary space to comment.

'And?' He smiled easily.

'OK. I started watching him, and every day I followed the same routine. I can make sure he won't surprise me again, by always knowing exactly where he is. I watched him with Paulette, and I could see it going wrong for her too. And then, right at the end, Kaye Whiting disappeared. It was just the same, a carbon copy.'

'What about Julie?'

'I watched him with her, too, but it was only after I saw Paulette in the same state as I'd been in, and learnt that Kaye had died like Helen, that I knew for sure.'

'One new girlfriend, one simultaneous murder? That's what you're saying, isn't it?'

Marlowe nodded. 'Apart from Julie – because there's no murder to tie in with her.'

'Unless we've missed one,' he replied. 'But, then, he wasn't going out with anyone when Stephanie died, so that doesn't add up either.'

She shrugged. 'Well, I can't explain it. I'm just sure that's how it is.'

Gary lifted his foot from the accelerator and allowed the car to coast as he gazed across at Marlowe. She stared back at him, ready to argue if he dismissed her theory. There were gaps in her logic, all right, but equally he realized there was no doubt in her mind. 'You're right, Marlowe, no one would have believed you.'

CHAPTER 66

MONDAY, 4 JULY 2011

It was after 8 p.m. when Pete Walsh returned home. He took the carrier bag straight into his bedroom and slid the Sony box out of it and on to the bed.

The drag round the shops looking for the right one had taken far longer than expected; but he'd got it and that was the important thing.

He scratched up a corner of the parcel tape and pulled it back until there was enough space for him to slip his fingers under the cardboard flaps and pop the box open.

The manual entitled *Digital Video Camera Recorder – Operating Instructions* lay on top. He flicked through it for a moment, then tossed it to one side. All 198 pages of it, for God's sake. Just because the last one had packed up didn't mean he had time to wade through such a pile of techno-jargon.

However, he did need to turn off that little red light that glowed while the camera was recording. The salesman had said that was easy enough to do.

He next removed the camera from its polystyrene packaging. It fitted on to the palm of one hand. Pete unclipped the side of the camera's casing, opening out the LCD display screen to access the panel of buttons behind it.

Damn, no power.

He unwrapped one of the new batteries and clipped it into its slot. It didn't take a lengthy instruction book to work that one out.

He next removed the lens cap and switched the power from *off* to *camera.* Nothing happened. There must be another control here somewhere. How many *on/off* switches do these things need?

He turned the camera over quickly, and in his impatience almost dropped it. It was the tension, of course – it always emerged at this point. He put the device to one side and glared instead at the instruction manual. Leaning across the bed, he retrieved it, then flicked through the first few pages. Page eight started with the heading 'Installing and charging the battery pack'.

For fuck's sake. He felt the flare of anger and an accompanying restlessness. He threw the manual across the room, where it hit the radiator, then tumbled on to the carpet. He repeated the thought first, then yelled it. 'For fuck's sake.' He recognized the loss of control in his own voice.

He needed to charge the battery first. He plugged it into the mains and turned his back on it, making each movement sharp and precise, assuring himself that he retained the power of self-discipline.

Self-discipline and he were old friends. It meant the strength to abstain from or even turn away from a desire. It was the opposite of decadence.

It was the rejection of short-term gratification, and the commitment to turning a vision into reality. It was the determination to see beyond the lies some women told, and to eradicate every ounce of their misplaced self-respect as punishment for the contempt they'd shown to his own ideals.

He undressed and crossed the landing to the bathroom, naked except for his watch. He showered with the door wide open. It was good to be able to do that without being pestered.

Afterwards he walked, wet and naked, back to his bedroom and flopped on to the bed. He lay on his back, staring at the ceiling, his head resting on one hand and the other hand massaging his erection. He had Fiona to look forward to. Tomorrow she'd be wet and naked, too.

After forty minutes the battery indictor showed a full charge. Now he needed to make sure that red light didn't come on.

He flicked open the manual and checked the function of each of the buttons. It related to none of them, so it must be in the on-screen menu system somewhere. Start at page thirty-four. The manual fell open at page forty-two, and the word 'lamp' jumped out at him.

He'd found it just like that.

But, then, it was funny how simple things could become when you just left them for a while.

Inside the wardrobe he'd stacked some shoeboxes up to the right height. He placed the new camera on top – where the old one had been. His shirts hung down on each side, and he arranged them so only the lens protruded.

He left the door ajar, knowing from experience that she wouldn't let him down.

CHAPTER 67

MONDAY, 4 JULY 2011

Marlowe Gates' flat was tiny: a studio apartment erected at the height of the eighties property boom, when developers could build smaller and sell faster than at any other time.

The bed settee was folded out flat and made up with a dark-blue duvet set. Marlowe tipped it back into the sofa position and pulled away the bedding, before stowing it in the airing cupboard.

She motioned for Goodhew to take a seat and left the room to fill the kettle.

The dark-blue carpet looked no thicker than flock wallpaper, while the paintwork carried the tired veneer of age. Marlowe was surviving here, not living.

To his right, an unlit eight-by-four hallway ran between the living area and the shower room. Estate agents would call it a 'dressing room', no doubt. A few blouses hung from a free-standing tubular-steel clothes rail. In the bad light he could spot the picture frame on the wall above, but not the print inside it.

He crept over to the hallway and flicked on the light. It was the same picture he'd already seen at Pete's and Julie's: Robert Mitchum paddling in the sea. This was a better version, the largest of the three prints and framed in chunky wood.

'What about it?' she asked.

And he turned to find her close to his shoulder.

'Pete Walsh has this, too,' he said.

'I know. I bought it for him.' She paused, waiting for Goodhew to comment. He said nothing. 'I had this first, and he liked it, so I bought him a copy for his birthday.'

'Doesn't it remind you too much of him, then?'

'Oh, yes, but I can't allow him to deprive me of everything, can I?' She reached past Goodhew and touched the sleeve of a blue shirt. 'Like these clothes that remind me of places we went together. Or TV programmes that we watched together.' She kicked at a cardboard box on the floor. 'Or even books we both read.'

Goodhew looked down and found a paperback copy of *The Cross and the Switchblade* staring up at him. 'I don't believe it. Pete has this, too.'

She nodded slowly. 'And Julie. And probably Paulette. Not just this book, either. Julie had the picture, too, and other books and CDs just the same as mine. I saw them when I went round there. And I've seen her wearing the same clothes, even.'

'I don't get it,' he frowned. 'Is he trying to make them all like you?'

'Oh, no, I think he is building up an ideal, and trying to mould each girlfriend to fit it. Each thing he likes, he carries forward to the next relationship and—'

'And he throws away what's left?' Goodhew cringed as he said it.

'You have an excellent way with words, don't you?'

'Sorry.'

'Forget it.' She smiled. 'I'll finish making the drinks.'

Goodhew bent and picked up *The Cross and the Switchblade*, and turned it over to read the back cover: the true account of a preacher's mission to save teenagers from a life of crime. 'What's the particular appeal of this book?' he called to her.

'It's supposed to be inspirational; shows how people can rise above their situation. Apparently,' she replied. 'Borrow it, if you like.'

He tucked it into his jacket pocket.

'While I'm out here, I'd say this is your best opportunity to snoop around.' The cutlery rattled as she raked around for a clean spoon. 'You might like to start in the middle drawer to your left.'

Goodhew pulled it open, and found it contained about eight books all the same size. Diaries. The top one was current, and each was marked on the front with a separate year. Each was A5 in size, with a page for each day except Saturday and Sunday, both of which occupied half a page each.

'I've always kept diaries.' She reappeared in the kitchen doorway. 'All my "sightings" of him are noted in there, as well as any days when I didn't know where he was.' She leant on the door frame and stared ahead for several seconds. 'It's usually only weekdays when I watch, though, because I'm working in the town centre, and so is he. At the weekends I avoid the town altogether, just in case. But I always thought there was little chance of seeing him around here, so this is where I spend most of my time. Sometimes I've driven past his road, though, or even his house.' She shrugged and picked up the mugs of tea. 'Well, it's all in there.'

She passed him one mug and sat down with her own on the floor in front of the television.

Goodhew opened the most recent diary first, and jumped to Saturday, 26 March, the day of Kaye Whiting's disappearance. No mention of Pete, so he turned back one page. Friday lunchtime, he'd left work at noon and returned by 12.30. He'd left at 4.30 and walked towards Mitcham's Corner.

'What time's his usual lunch break?' he asked.

'Twelve, why?'

'You've made a specific note here that he went out from twelve to twelve-thirty?'

'He usually has a full hour. He's meticulous about starting on time and not working later than he needs to.'

'Not a high-flyer, then?'

'No, not at all. Did he finish early that day?' she asked.

'Four-thirty, it says, and then off down Mitcham's Corner,' he said.

'OK, well, he normally leaves at five and heads to the bus stops opposite the train station. The only thing I know Mitcham's Corner for is . . .'

'I know, but I think it's been cleaned up now. Besides, is that his style?'

'Prostitutes?' she smiled. 'No, that's just my catty little joke, but I can't think what else.'

Goodhew read on for several minutes. Marlowe located a fluorescent pen and dropped it on the sofa beside him.

'You can highlight anything that you'll need to find again, if it helps,' she said.

Goodhew marked occasional entries, mainly dates that coincided with key dates in the investigation. Each abduction, the discovery of each body, and each time Goodhew himself had seen Pete Walsh. Marlowe stayed cross-legged on the floor, watching him with one eyebrow slightly raised. She still reminded him of Lauren Bacall.

He turned to Friday, 1 April 2011, the day he'd first encountered Marlowe. The entry read: *Peter didn't come out to lunch. Rang his office and he didn't pick up his phone. Wonder if he's ill. Went to his house and no sign of his car. Followed a man there to Acacia Road and Park Terrace.*

Michelle's home and then his own.

Goodhew hadn't even noticed he'd been followed. He stared at her again. She was an enigma: a teeming mass of contradictions, chaotic but organized, timid and yet undoubtedly brave. She blushed and hurried to her feet. She took his empty mug and retreated to the kitchen.

He flicked backwards, checking more dates, and discovered she'd been very thorough. 'Incredible,' he murmured; there didn't seem to be a flaw in her theory that Walsh could be the killer. Whenever he'd needed to be out of town, she hadn't spotted him. Goodhew mapped Walsh's movements against everything he knew to be true, and found they tallied accurately. Walsh clearly had no idea he was being constantly watched.

Goodhew's gaze drifted across to the next entry: *Had another bad dream.*

Finally he pulled the entire pile of diaries from the drawer and selected the one marked 2009 on the front with black marker pen.

Goodhew turned to 29 May, the Wednesday on which Helen Neill's body had been found. There was no entry there, just frantic hatching scored deeply in black with a biro, as though neat shading had given way to impatient scribbling. He held it up to the light, looking for words that had been destroyed, and noticed at once that the previous page was disfigured the same way, and the one before that, too. In fact going all the way back until Saturday, 25 April, the day Helen had vanished.

A cupboard door slammed and Marlowe exclaimed, 'Goodhew!' She came darting into the room. 'I completely forgot to tell you, but

I think he might be seeing someone new. It's in there, too.' She picked up her current diary and flicked through page after page. 'It's here somewhere.' Finally she found it. 'Here!' She held out the page: *Monday, 13 June 2011. Peter bumped into a girl in the square and they ran into the Flying Pig to get out of the rain.*

'Marlowe, could you meet me again tomorrow and show me exactly how you've been watching him? And I'll take these diaries with me, meanwhile.'

Marlowe nodded. 'Will I get them back?'

'I'll do my best, but I don't know. I'm sorry if that makes you feel uncomfortable.'

'It's OK.' Marlowe ducked back into the kitchen and soon returned with two fresh mugs of tea. 'What happens now?'

'Well, I'm going to go through these some more to find out whether you know more than you realize. I know you've made one mistake, though.'

'What?' asked Marlowe.

Goodhew held up the last of the scored-out pages. 'This is the day he finished with you, isn't it?'

Her skin flushed and she bit her lip. 'So?' She studied her mug intently.

'You thought Helen Neill's body turned up several days after Pete finished with you, but it didn't,' he said. She'd stopped even looking at him, and he could see sweat glistening in the little 'V' of her neckline. He had to know. 'Marlowe, what do all these blank pages mean?'

She glowered at Goodhew. 'I told you, he changed.' Her hands shook and the scars on her wrists seemed suddenly brighter. 'He was vicious and spiteful.' She grabbed the diary and stabbed it with her finger just in front of him. 'On all these days. Every single one of them.'

Goodhew grabbed her hand as it still held the diary. 'The first of those is the day Helen was abducted; the last of them is when her body was found.'

CHAPTER 68

MONDAY, 4 JULY 2011

Goodhew's grandfather's old library smelt of fresh emulsion and new carpeting. It smelt like a show home, but no show home has photos of dead people scattered across the Axminster.

Goodhew sat on the floor in the middle of the room. He had spread out all his copies of the crime-scene photos to his left; and the photos of Pete Walsh, Julie Wilson and Marlowe Gates to his right.

A bare bulb hung from the ceiling, casting large, unhelpful shadows across the carpet. He couldn't work like that, so he rummaged through a cupboard, and returned with his old reading lamp. He plugged it in and extended the cable to the centre of the floor, where it cast a smaller pool of brighter light directly on to the photographs.

He decided to return to his grid idea, but redrew it with pairs of names: girlfriends and victims, instead of just girlfriends.

Down one side he listed:

'Marlowe and Helen',
'Julie and Extra Victim',
'Paulette and Kaye',
'Extra Girlfriend and Stephanie',
'Girl in the rain and Planned Victim'.

If Pete finished with his girlfriends on or just after the day the bodies had been discovered, then their investigation had missed one murder: the one that tied in with his breaking up with Julie.

The last sighting of Julie and Pete in Marlowe's diaries was 26 July 2010.

And there would also have been a girlfriend to coincide with Stephanie's death, someone Pete had dumped on or just after Wednesday, 8 June 2011.

And if Pete had now met another woman, how long before the next abduction?

Goodhew phoned Gully. 'Sue, are you busy?'

'Just lying around, doing sod all,' she replied sleepily.

'I need you to check for another murder. We're looking for a body discovered on the twenty-sixth of July 2010, or in the week running up to it. Make that two weeks, so the twelfth of July to the twenty-sixth of July 2010.'

Lisa Fairbanks needed most of all to ignore the stench of her own urine and excrement. She couldn't afford to be sick, as the gag would make her choke.

She looked up. The Thetford Forest sky hung bright with pinprick stars and a moon with an opaque face like a weather-beaten gargoyle. She could glimpse it in patches through tiny gaps in the foliage of the taller trees surrounding her.

The trunk of her own tree sloped away from her, giving her no shelter and looking like it too had turned its back on her. She lay face-up, with her feet pressed flat against the bark. A few inches above the toes of her shoes, she could still make out the shadow of a sharp outcrop of broken branch protruding from the gnarled trunk.

She just couldn't reach it, though. The ends of the rope binding her wrists had been tied to the rope around her ankles, securing her hands and feet so they were less than twelve inches apart. She shuffled her feet up towards it. The rope tugged hard, digging into her wrist bone. She arched her back and thus managed to move her hands a fraction closer to her feet.

One hand was clenched over the other, and the base of her spine pressed down on them both. Both hands now started feeling numb.

She shuffled her feet forward again, but they were still at least two inches from the branch.

But too close to give up.

Lisa took a deep breath, then another – ignoring the taste of blood where the gag cut into the corners of her mouth. *Concentrate*, she told herself. *Concentrate*.

Marlowe tossed her duvet out of the airing cupboard. She had decided to sleep on the sofa as it was, instead of folding it out to make a bed.

She brushed her teeth in front of Robert Mitchum, wondering which film he had been making when it was taken.

She felt sure the picture meant nothing significant.

She returned to the living area, switched out the light and lay down on top of the duvet, staring up at the sulphur glow that the street lamp cast on her ceiling.

She tried to remember *The Cross and the Switchblade* in detail. Who'd written the book? Was it David something? She couldn't even remember the author's name.

What would Peter enjoy in a book about love and salvation? And she now doubted whether it would affect her in the same way it had when she'd first read it. She was altogether too cynical now.

She pictured the words on the back cover: 'The face of a killer started him on his lonely crusade.'

Marlowe closed her eyes and fell asleep.

Goodhew's notes had expanded to six pages scattered across the floor, overlapping with each other to cover the assembled photos.

He scanned his notes and questions. They'd have to wait for tomorrow before he could start filling in the answers.

His jacket hung on the door handle, and the edge of the paperback jutted from one pocket.

He pulled it out and leant against the wall, as he started to read the first chapter. Read it for a few minutes, then go back to the notes fresh; that was his plan.

Lisa writhed and wriggled, still trying to hook the rope binding her ankles over that sharp stump of bough. The more she fought, the more it bit into her flesh.

She ignored the pain. Another inch and she'd be there. Her neck twisted as she tried to allow her hands another inch of movement towards her feet.

She lunged out with her feet and her right toe caught the tip of the cracked bough.

Nearly there.

She thrashed around, struggling for just another inch. She grunted, fighting for breath and twisting her torso against the restraint of the rope. She felt the broken bough bump against her ankle bone. The rope was hooked.

She'd done it!

She lay there panting, her weight now resting on her shoulder blades; her hips suspended just above the ground. The flesh on her wrists was dragged taut towards her ankles. A searing pain shot through her neck, across her shoulders and down her spine. Even if she'd torn every muscle in her body, it was still worth it.

A draft of cool breeze swept through the forest, rattling the leaves and brushing against her face. It passed on, but a different rustling remained. A more determined sound.

She held herself still.

It stopped, then scurried closer.

A film of sweat erupted across her cheeks. A rat!

She dragged the rope from side to side across the sharp stump of the bough. Pulling it tight, disregarding her chafed skin; just begging for the rope to fray.

The rat scampered to the edge of the bank, paused, then scurried closer still.

She let out a strangled squeal and the rat retreated. Lisa squirmed to free her legs, but it was the stump which gave way, sending her legs skimming back down the trunk to the ground. Her ankle bone banged against the serrated bark of the tree. The wood flew apart, dry and brittle, and the largest fragment catapulted into her eyebrow. Blood oozed into her eye.

Gully slipped into the police station at 1 a.m. She turned on the second-floor lights, glad to be alone in the office. The last thing she wanted was company, especially when there was only a sweatshirt between her Dumbo nightie and the rest of the world. This wasn't how she had wanted Goodhew to wake her up in the middle of the night.

She copied the dates, 12 July 2010 to 26 July 2010, from the back of her hand on to a Post-it note, which she affixed to the bottom front edge of her monitor.

As she left her PC to boot up, she pulled some files from a box under her desk. These were the notes she'd already hunted through the last time Goodhew had asked her to search for an extra case.

Why did he think she would find one now?

She first checked the dates on all the files, in case she'd missed one. No women found bound and gagged and dead from drowning, exposure or starvation had been discovered between those two dates.

She returned to her PC and fired up her database. She'd been sent an extract of Scotland Yard's central information database, covering murders and suspicious deaths of women aged between fifteen and forty. She searched it for the specified dates and it threw up twenty-seven matches. These would be twenty-seven deaths that did not match their original search criteria in some way.

She glanced at the time display in the corner of her monitor, and sighed. The only way to check them would be record by record.

The database held basic information like 'sexual assault – yes, no, or not known'. The next field: 'if yes, type of assault'. She printed the records out as a summary sheet, and started by putting a cross through all those which included anal, oral and vaginal rape. Their killer had never raped, and therefore she decided to discount rape from the MO. That eliminated eight straight away.

She ran her finger down the nineteen remaining cases; there were bound to be others she could immediately discount.

'Body location.' Home, work, pub, car. None of those fitted either. Case by case she reduced the list.

At 2.20, she switched off the PC, leant back in her chair and stretched. She then extinguished the lights and hurried towards home and bed.

Her eyes stung with tiredness, and for what?

There was no point in phoning Goodhew, because every case on the list now had a line drawn through it. Somewhere along the way, he had made a mistake.

Her swollen right eye, reduced to a blood-caked slit, refused to see anything. Through her open left eye, Lisa fixed her gaze on the moon as it flickered at her through a gap in the trees.

Something moved, rustling the tangled grass behind her. Her heart began to thump. 'Keep watching the moon,' she told herself.

It was the same moon that lit the sky over everyone she loved. She stared at it, imagining her dad staring at it too; imagining that they were sharing moonbeams.

Another rustle, closer this time. Her heart thumped louder. Goosebumps rippled across her bare arms.

'Keep watching the moon,' she repeated. She narrowed her eye and squinted at it till it slipped out of focus. She told herself it was a huge paper lantern hanging over her bed.

She felt whiskers as something sniffed the clotting blood on her ankle. It then scampered across her shins.

Sweat trickled across her forehead, running into her hair, but she never stopped watching the sky.

She wouldn't give up. People were searching for her, people she'd never met.

And one of them would find her. She wouldn't die like this.

CHAPTER 69

TUESDAY, 5 JULY 2011

Justine had never seen Greta in the Flying Pig at any time of the day other than lunchtime. She'd never seen her meet anyone or speak to anyone either. Justine reached for her customer's usual coffee mug before she even ordered. And she saw her nod to the guy sitting at Greta's usual table.

Otherwise the pub was empty: just the three of them. Neither Greta nor the man smiled. In fact, everything about them seemed serious and Justine suddenly felt out of place.

Marlowe held out a pound coin, but Justine shook her head. 'Don't worry about it,' she mumbled and retreated to just beyond the doorway leading to the cellar. Suddenly she was the one that wanted to be alone, at least until the place started to fill up.

Marlowe slipped into the seat opposite Goodhew. 'You're early.'

'So are you,' he replied, watching her sip her coffee. 'I didn't sleep well, so I read *The Cross and the Switchblade*.' Goodhew pulled it from his jacket pocket and flicked through the pages as he spoke.

'I thought about it, too, but I don't think it means anything,' Marlowe said.

'I don't understand why he would want a copy of this. Is he religious in any way?'

'No, not at all. Goes to church for weddings, christenings and funerals, but nothing else.'

Goodhew tapped the book. 'And why did this appeal to you?'

Marlowe shrugged. 'Partly because it's true, I suppose. But apart from that it isn't particularly well written, and it isn't gripping and it doesn't stretch the imagination. It's simply a story of someone trying to improve things, and possessing this unshakable belief that there's good in everyone. It's supposed to be inspiring, I guess.'

Goodhew stood the small paperback upright on the table. 'That's not how I felt about it at all. This guy, David Wilkerson, he's a preacher, and yet he keeps asking God for signs to tell him what to do next. If he's really read the Bible and believes in God, why doesn't he know for himself what's right and wrong?'

'But he does do the right thing, so I don't think the bit about him needing signs matters at the end of the day.' She slipped the paperback into her bag. 'Well, anyway, I don't think Peter is running round killing people because God told him to.'

'Me neither,' Goodhew replied. 'I thought of something else to ask you, though. You once went to the West Country with Pete. How did you get there?'

'We drove.'

'In your car or his?' Goodhew felt something stir in the back of his mind. It drifted just beyond him, and he couldn't quite latch on to it.

'Peter hired one because he said he didn't trust his own on the journey.'

'Can you remember where it came from, or what make it was?'

Marlowe shook her head. 'I don't know where he hired it, but I know it was a Vauxhall. An Astra, I think.' She closed her eyes, trying to remember. 'Yes, it was an Astra. It was red.'

'A saloon?' With a jolt, Gary's elusive thought snapped into the fore of his consciousness, and he knew her reply even as she spoke.

'No, an estate.'

Goodhew grinned at Marlowe. 'You're a gem.'

He pulled his mobile from another pocket and had connected to Gully within seconds. 'Sue, I've got a lead. Do you remember when Helen Neill disappeared, how a red Astra estate was sighted?'

'Yeah, belonging to an Antonio Vitale,' she said.

'Yes, that's the one,' he replied. 'Well, Peter Walsh hired a red Astra estate that same week. Check the local car-hire companies for any business he's done with them. Start with the dates that correspond with the girls disappearing, and then check for any other rentals. I'll be back at the station in about an hour.'

Goodhew dropped the mobile phone back into his pocket, and turned to Marlowe again. 'I want you to tell me about Walsh's typical day,' he nodded towards Dunwold Insurance, 'and then I'm going to speak to the receptionist there, to see who he's currently taking out to lunch.'

CHAPTER 70

TUESDAY, 5 JULY 2011

Goodhew pushed open the heavy plate-glass door and crossed the black-tiled floor towards the lone receptionist. The rest of the foyer was deserted. She looked up at him and smiled brightly.

He leant over the counter and spoke quietly. 'I don't know whether you remember me?'

'Of course I do,' she replied. 'DC Goodhew, isn't it? From the . . .' she lowered her voice a notch '. . . police.'

'That's right. I'd like a quiet word, but it is vital that it stays just that, OK?'

Karen nodded, rosy spots of anticipation reddening her cheeks. 'Is it about Peter Walsh?'

'Yes, that's right. I need to trace the girlfriend he was seeing around June this year, and also find out whether he's been seeing anyone more recently. I thought perhaps you'd know if he regularly met anyone down here.'

Her eyes widened. 'Is this serious?'

Gary nodded.

'Well, I can help you with both questions. He used to see Donna, who worked here too.'

'For Dunwold Insurance?'

'Yeah, but I mean here in reception. He then said she'd dumped him.' Karen leant closer. 'But Donna says it was the other way around, and I believe her, because she was so upset after they broke up that she never came back.'

Perhaps she was just gossiping, but Goodhew sensed more than mere sensationalism. 'But you've seen her since, I hope?' he said.

'Oh, yes, but she's very withdrawn now. She won't talk about him and just didn't want to know when I told her he's been seeing someone else.' She pulled a face as though a dirty smell had drifted into the room.

'And when did that start?'

'Well, that's why I told her. It seemed to me that he met the new one very soon after dumping Donna. I even wondered if he'd been seeing them both at once. But, if not, he definitely started with her the following week. I saw them together out there.' She pointed through the slats of the blinds.

'Do you know who the new woman is?'

'Not really, but she works for Sampson's, the estate agents. I got talking to her one day when he was late coming down to meet her. I don't know her name, though.' She smiled apologetically. 'Sorry.'

'That's OK.' Gary was sure he didn't really need to ask the next question. 'What does she look like?'

'The estate agent?'

Gary nodded.

'Average height, I s'pose. Fair hair, skinny, a bit pasty-looking.'

'And what about Donna?'

'Blonde, slim and tallish.'

'Similar in a way?'

Karen shrugged. 'Maybe to a bloke.'

'Thanks for your help. Do you know how I can get hold of Donna?'

'Sure.' From memory, Karen wrote out an address in blue biro on a Post-it note.

'What's her last name?'

'King – and you'd better go now if you don't want him to see you. He'll be coming down for lunch at noon.'

'I know. Thanks.'

Gary left and Karen was alone. From memory again, she tapped out a phone number and spoke softly into the receiver, lowering her voice still further as Pete Walsh headed past her. 'Just promise you'll meet me.'

CHAPTER 71

TUESDAY, 5 JULY 2011

Marlowe sat watching Gary cross the square towards Dunwold Insurance. Her recent brush with death had left her feeling less detached from everyone else – but so had meeting Goodhew.

He disappeared from sight and she turned back to sip from her coffee mug. The Flying Pig was beginning to hum with the usual lunchtime bustle and she wondered why she didn't recognize any of the regulars that Justine clearly knew well and often greeted by name.

Till now they'd been no more than a blanket of other people encroaching on her space, threatening to speak to her or sit down at her table. Today she didn't mind their chatter and the chink of cutlery; didn't need to drown them out by playing the jukebox.

She glanced towards it as it stood silent, with just a couple of buttons flashing, as if waiting for her to select a track. Deliberately she turned her back on it.

She then recognized the first strains of 'American Pie' as the song drifted through the pub. Justine slapped her table softly as she walked past. Marlowe glanced up and the woman grinned. 'Thought you might be short of change today, or something.'

Marlowe silently looked away. Don McLean sang about how February made him shiver with every newspaper he delivered.

How could Justine know that this was the very song Marlowe had selected when Kaye Whiting's body had turned up? She probably just assumed that Marlowe specially liked it.

At least it cheered up when the chorus broke in.

She noticed a foot moving under the next table, tapping along with the beat. It belonged to an elderly man in a brown suit and a pork-pie hat, miming the words through a mouthful of sandwich.

Surprised, Marlowe glanced across to the table in front of her, where a teenage mum was scanning a glossy mag while her baby dozed. She sang it under her breath, too, as she read.

Marlowe then looked over at Justine and they both smiled at each other. Maybe she wasn't so isolated after all.

The song finished just as Goodhew emerged from Dunwold Insurance. He strode towards her, and was halfway across the square when she noticed Peter Walsh trailing behind him.

Isolated, no. Stupid, yes?

A rush of anger surged through her, hard on the heels of the fear she normally felt on seeing him. Oh, yes, she'd been stupid, all right.

Who did Peter think he was, pushing her to the brink of suicide? If she'd died, he would simply have carried on. But now she would stop him, and if he killed her in the process, so what? She'd be no worse off than she would have been had she died in the lake.

Her fingers tightened around her mug before she slammed it down on to the pub table. She pushed her chair back and barged through the other customers towards the door. She wanted to confront Peter, show him she didn't need to hide any more. Goodhew was only yards from the pub door, and Pete was following close behind.

Her heart began to pound. She stopped in her tracks and grabbed the back of the nearest chair for support, weak-legged with jittering nerves.

The man sitting at the table dropped his newspaper. 'Are you all right?'

She nodded, and steadied herself.

'Do you need to sit down?' he enquired and motioned to the empty seat. Her gaze followed his hand and she found herself looking down at Lisa Fairbanks' photo in the open pages of the *Cambridge News*.

'Sorry,' she gasped, and snatched up the paper then thrust it into Goodhew's hands just as he stepped through the door. 'Look at her,' she cried as she bundled him back out into the square.

By now Peter Walsh had gone.

Goodhew stared at the photo. 'I need to get back to the station.' A sick look transformed his expression. 'When did she disappear?'

'I don't know. I just grabbed it.' Marlowe walked alongside him. 'He was following you just then.'

'I know. I saw him.'

'What happens now?'

'He's got a new girlfriend. Her name's Fiona and she's an estate agent for Sampson's. I'll get someone on to it straight away; I need to know how you think she fits in.'

CHAPTER 72

TUESDAY, 5 JULY 2011

Marlowe hurried from the Flying Pig, headed straight past the war memorial, and continued down Hills Road towards the town. The red Sampson's sign hung over the pavement about three hundred yards along on the opposite side of the road.

The traffic surged past her in waves, as it stopped and started at each set of pelican lights. Marlowe strode along the edge of the pavement waiting for the next convenient gap. She then darted between two groups of cars and carried on running, slowing down when only two doors away from the estate agent's window.

She adopted a casual approach, glancing at the display of properties for sale, then drawing closer as if one of them had caught her eye. The advertisements hung in vertical strips, and through the gaps between them she spotted four figures working inside: two men and two women.

She slowly moved along, as if checking each column of property in turn. Neither woman was likely to be Fiona, however; one was too old and the other had short dark hair.

Four people but five desks. Fiona's would be the empty one.

As Marlowe pushed open the door and stepped inside, the younger of the two men replaced the handset of his phone and rose to greet her. He reminded her of an eighteen-year-old politician; all sincerity and false charm.

She smiled. 'Is Fiona in?'

'No, but can I help?'

She shook her head. 'I've already been speaking to her. I'd prefer to deal with only one person.'

'I understand,' he simpered. 'Unfortunately she's away on a course until Wednesday.'

'That's OK. I'll call back then,' she said.

'I can give her a message.'

'No, really, it's fine.' Marlowe stepped over towards his desk. 'I'll tell you what, though, I could do with a business card or something containing her contact details. I don't think I've got them properly written down.'

'No problem,' he beamed and rolled his chair across to the vacant desk. He extracted a card from the top drawer and handed it to Marlowe.

She glanced at it long enough to register the name 'Fiona Robinson', then tucked it into the pocket of her jeans. Not exactly a rare surname, but at least it wasn't Smith or Jones.

Marlowe stepped out of Sampson's and hurried towards a row of public phone boxes closer to the city centre. There she rang Directory Enquiries, expecting to be given a variety of F. Robinsons, but found there was only one. She jotted the number on to the back of Fiona's business card, and dialled it straight away.

An answerphone clicked on, just the standard automated BT message service. Unfortunately, no clues there.

Marlowe stepped out of the phone box and surveyed the nearby row of shops. An optician, a hairdresser, a bakery, jeweller and a travel agent. She decided to try the hairdresser's first. A brunette with copper-streaked, spiky hair sat behind the appointments desk staring at the centre pages of a beauty magazine. She reluctantly dragged her gaze up to meet Marlowe's.

'How can I help?'

'Could I just check a number in your phone book, please?' Marlowe pointed to it, as it sat at the end of the desk.

The girl shrugged and plonked it on to the counter. Marlowe flicked through to 'R', and wrote the address corresponding to the phone number on the business card also.

F. Robinson. 206 Wollaston Avenue.

CHAPTER 73

TUESDAY, 5 JULY 2011

Marks pushed the last corner of the chicken tikka sandwich into his mouth and reached to answer the phone. Suddenly his door burst open and he withdrew his hand, letting the phone continue to ring.

Goodhew waved a newspaper, with his arm outstretched.

'There's been another one, sir.' He spread the paper open on the table and pointed to the photograph. Marks scanned the text: 'Fears grow for missing teenager, Lisa Fairbanks, last seen on Saturday morning in Sheringham. She disappeared before 9 a.m. and was last seen by her boyfriend in the course of his paper round.'

'We've already had it flagged up, but there's nothing to indicate a connection. What are you thinking, then?' Marks scowled.

'Marlowe Gates noticed it first, but just study the girl's face. She's got that same look again.'

'Oh, for goodness sake, so have lots of girls.' Marks began to close the newspaper. 'If there's been any foul play at all, I bet her boyfriend did it.'

'I bet he didn't.' Goodhew laid the newspaper out flat again. 'We may have a lead, here. It seems Walsh hired a car the weekend Helen Neill disappeared. If he's hired cars each time, then he would have hired one in the course of the last week to snatch this latest girl. It's an ideal way of distancing himself from forensic evidence. But if we find the car quickly enough, then we may still find enough forensics there to link it to Lisa.'

Marks twitched his nostrils in reluctant agreement. 'Well, that sounds more reasonable,' he conceded. 'And if this really is another linked crime, there's a chance that she's still alive.'

'Yes, that's possible, but tonight will be the fourth night for her. Even if she is alive, we won't necessarily have much longer. Gully is checking out car rentals, Clark and Charles are visiting his ex-girlfriends, Paulette and Donna, to see if they remember him hiring a car at any time. Gully is also searching the crime database for yet another murder.'

'Another one? This is because of your one murder per girlfriend theory?'

'Yes, that's it. I just wanted to keep you informed.'

'I thought you'd already checked, though?'

'We have, but only regarding the original profile. We know the approximate dates of Walsh's relationship with Julie Wilson, so the last time Gully checked she was looking for the discovery of a body within two weeks of him splitting up with her. We've also been looking at victims within a particular age range and subjected to the same MO as all the others.'

'So?' Marks wondered.

'Well, as it would only have been the second murder in the sequence, he may have still been refining his methods. This time we'll widen the search for other causes of death, as well as ages and locations.'

'OK,' Marks raised his hand, 'that seems fair enough. And what about Kincaide?' Marks noted a look of stubbornness appear in Goodhew's eyes.

'Well, he believes that Marlowe Gates is in on it together with Peter Walsh, and merely leading me in totally the wrong direction,' Goodhew replied with unmasked irritation. 'He's now off doing his own thing.'

'Leave him to it.' Marks sighed. 'We don't want to burn all our bridges, do we?' He waggled a finger at Goodhew. 'But if you're following the wrong line of investigation, we'll have wasted one hell of a lot of time.' He really hoped Goodhew's faith in this Marlowe girl wouldn't prove misguided. 'And if you are right, then it's a bonus that he's out of your hair.'

'I'm sure I'm right,' Goodhew replied, but the remark only intensified his boss's scowl.

'"I'm sure I'm right" will not cut it in court, Gary.' Marks started strumming his fingers on the desk. 'You need evidence, above all, and what do you have so far? No forensics, no sightings, no connections – nothing to even put him in the right place at the right time.'

'That's not—' Goodhew began, but Marks raised a hand to silence him.

'I don't care what it's not,' he growled. 'I want to know *why* he did it. *How* he did it. And carved-in-stone proof that he *did* do it. Only then will I agree to an arrest, so if your next question was can you make one, no you can't.' He jabbed the desktop with his index finger. 'He is not likely to crack and tell us where this Lisa victim is, especially if she's dead or nearly dead already.'

Goodhew hadn't expected Marks to be so obstinate. Lisa's photo was another of those where the eyes followed you around, and she watched him now as if waiting for rescue. 'I want to search his house,' he persisted, 'look for fibre matches against other victims, prove it's him and make him tell us where she is.'

Marks closed the newspaper and handed it back to Goodhew. 'Look, Gary, this is my call, and I do not believe that someone this organized will crack in time to save the girl, and maybe he never will at all. You'll just have to find some other way.'

'OK,' muttered Goodhew and headed towards the door. He paused as Marks spoke again, but didn't turn around.

'My advice to you,' Marks continued, 'would be to study his motivation. How exactly is he benefiting from each death?'

Goodhew returned to the incident room to find Gully sitting at his desk. 'You look pissed off,' she began. 'What's up?'

'Marks won't let us arrest him.'

'Why should he? We don't have any evidence.'

Goodhew opened out the newspaper again, but Gully interrupted. 'Even so, we're getting there.' She slapped a hand flat on the newspaper, just to make Goodhew listen to her. 'It seems Tony Vitale insures his car with Dunwold Insurance, and Peter Walsh has hired cars at least five times. Always rented from Budget, because Dunwold Insurance has a discount deal for its staff. The first time corresponds with Helen Neill's disappearance, the third and fourth times with Kaye Whiting and Stephanie Palmer, I'm currently running a match for any disappearances that coincide with the second rental, which just leaves the fifth one which he hired—'

'Last Friday,' Goodhew finished for her, and lifted Gully's hand from the page. 'Lisa Fairbanks disappeared first thing on Saturday.

Lisa stared up at them both from the photograph.

'Phone them at Budget and get hold of the car. Don't let anyone touch it and, if it's been cleaned already, get the vacuum cleaner too. I'll get down there with Forensics. Oh, and speak to the police at Sheringham. We'll need her hairbrush or the like, for DNA.'

CHAPTER 74

TUESDAY, 5 JULY 2011

Fiona's voice murmured from the receiver, 'I miss you, Pete.'

'I miss you, too,' he replied. 'Are you sure you can't get back tonight?'

She laughed. 'Don't be silly. It doesn't finish until tomorrow lunchtime. But I don't have to go back to the office in the afternoon.'

'OK, come round as soon as you're back,' he said.

'You can get the time off?'

'Don't worry, I'll sort it. But I still don't see the point of them keeping you there for another half day. Just leave tonight.'

'I can't. Don't be ridiculous!'

Pete prodded the cushion at the far end of the settee with his outstretched foot. He held the phone in his right hand while the remote control rested in his left. 'So what are you doing?'

'I'm just going out to dinner with some of the other delegates, then off to bed, I guess. And you?'

'Oh, I don't know – maybe watch a video, take a shower and then bed. Nothing exciting.'

'Hmm,' she purred, 'sounds exciting to me.'

'Flirt!'

'Are you complaining?' she breathed.

'No, not at all so long as you're good and naughty for me tomorrow.'

'Good or naughty? Or both?'

'Good at being naughty will do. Can you do that for me?'

'Of course.'

'Practise now?'

'Don't be silly.' She gave a nervous giggle.

'Come on, Fiona, you're in the mood, aren't you?'

'I might be.' The worm of uncertainty had begun to wriggle in the pit of her stomach.

'Whisper to me, Fiona. Tell me what you want me to do to you tomorrow.'

Fiona hesitated. She'd started this teasing, hadn't she? She pressed her fingers against her cheek, as if to push aside the blush on it.

'Come on, Fiona, tell me.'

It was just the two of them. It was crude, but did it really matter? 'I want you to fuck me, Pete.'

A few minutes later, Pete replaced the handset. He turned the sound up on the video, as it was coming up to one of his favourite scenes. A bottle smashed against the wardrobe door. The picture wobbled, because the impact had shaken the camera. The picture settled again as the auto-focus adjusted to Julie's skin. She wiped away her tears.

Pete liked hearing his own voice. He'd achieved a satisfactorily calm and encouraging tone, considering the stress he'd then been under. 'Come on, Julie, you're being silly, aren't you?'

Julie pursed her lips and nodded. She knelt on the bed, resting her naked buttocks on her heels, then arched her back, pushing her small breasts out towards the camera. She shuffled her knees further apart and slid her right hand between her bare thighs.

Pete took a slow blissful breath as a tremor of her tears shook her voice. 'I want you to fuck me, Pete.'

The film flickered where he'd edited it. He was pleased that he'd spent time cutting out the less entertaining parts.

And he liked the next scene best of all.

CHAPTER 75

WEDNESDAY, 6 JULY 2011

The blood from Lisa's eyebrow had congealed and dried, leaving her right eye sealed shut.

Overnight her eyelid had puffed out like a bullfrog's throat, and she'd woken with a pain like a knitting needle twisting in the back of her eye socket. The entire right side of her face pulsated with fever.

Her other eye functioned normally, but at first she'd closed it against the streaks of daylight shafting between the branches. Even this meagre light made her head pound.

Lisa had fallen asleep on her back, and now her arms felt dead. Slowly she curled herself at the knees and, twisting at the waist, she rolled on to her side. As the feeling rushed back into them, it sent her muscles into a painful seizure. Spasm after spasm shot through each gradually reviving limb and finally, as that faded, she felt a new pain: the throbbing in her ankle.

She forced her left eye open, and raised her head just enough to squint towards her feet. Blood from her injured leg caked the rope like too much coating on a toffee apple, and it hung in thick, dried ripples from the knots. Her ankle had swollen till the rope was embedded in its own furrow of engorged flesh.

Fever burnt the same way in her leg as on the side of her face.

And what was that white stuff?

Her single eye widened.

Sprouting like new growth were countless little white dots. They were clustered like miniature grapes.

Eggs? She was encrusted with flies' eggs.

Both on her leg and in her eye; incubating maggots.

CHAPTER 76

WEDNESDAY, 6 JULY 2011

The smell in the interview room reminded Donna of school: cheap disinfectant amid a hint of BO. She rubbed the tip of her finger across the gouged table top and wondered whether some chewing gum would coat the underside.

She also wondered whether she could slip outside without being noticed. But she'd given them her name and address already, and she certainly didn't need them visiting her home on top of everything else.

DC Siobhan O'Callaghan returned and seated herself opposite. 'Donna King?' she began.

'Yes, that's right.' Donna's voice croaked with nerves, so she coughed to clear her throat. Siobhan O'Callaghan's hair was short and greying, and added no softness or warmth to her angular features. God, with a name like that she was going to be a staunch Catholic, too. Donna checked Siobhan's fingers. No wedding ring . . . no rings at all, in fact. A virgin Catholic spinster? Frigid O'Callaghan. *I'm going to deserve to rot in hell as far as she's concerned.*

'Take your time and just tell me what happened, in your own words,' Siobhan encouraged her.

Donna picked the last but one Silk Cut from the current pack, before she offered the final one across the table. Siobhan shook her head. 'You can't, not in here.'

Donna said nothing for a moment, just turned the forbidden item over in her fingers. 'I don't know where to start.'

'Start anywhere. It doesn't matter. We'll go over anything that doesn't make sense. And don't worry about shocking me. I'm not a beginner at this, you know.' They both then smiled.

'Shit.' Donna still fiddled with the unlit cigarette, holding it between her fingers, then tipping her head back as if she imagined blowing smoke towards the bare bulb overhead. 'I met him at work and then we started seeing each other. I saw him before he ever noticed me and I fancied him, and I suppose I chased him. We were going out together for almost five weeks.'

'How serious did your relationship become?'

'Sex, you mean? Yes, there was plenty of that, at first. But he wasn't like I thought he'd be.' Donna shook her head. 'I can't explain, but there were subtle things. I felt uneasy with him . . .'

'Unsafe?'

'No, no, like there was someone else for him, maybe. And so I sneaked into work when he was there all alone. It was a Friday, third of June, and I thought I'd do something flirty – take the lead.' Donna rolled the cigarette between her fingers. 'You know, I really thought that he'd find me . . .' she shrugged '. . . irresistible? Something like that. What a stupid cow I was.' She dropped the unlit cigarette back into the box before slouching back in the chair.

Siobhan looked up from her statement pad. 'And is that when the attack occurred?'

Donna shook her head again. 'No, he just didn't want to know. I felt so humiliated. There I was, dressed to kill and going off home on my own. Next day I sat at home all day, and then on Sunday he called me. I was so relieved.' She snorted. 'So relieved, what a fool. I met him later that evening and that's when it started.'

Donna's forefinger returned to the damaged table top, and she studied it for what seemed an eternity. One corner of her mouth twitched and, as she struggled to stop it, the tears of frustration welled in her eyes. With a jagged gasp she inhaled. 'I wouldn't have come here except you're now looking for him. After you sent someone to Dunwold Insurance, asking questions, my friend rang me and promised you'd take me seriously.' She gulped in another lungful of air. 'I'd blamed myself, but she says it's all about him. That's why I came.'

Siobhan frowned. 'Do you know who was asking these questions?'

'DC Goodhew, I think.'

'And your ex-boyfriend's name?'

Goosebumps rose on Siobhan's arms as Donna replied, 'Peter Walsh.'

Siobhan leant closer and pinned Donna to her seat with a grave stare. 'You can say no to my next suggestion, Donna, and that will be absolutely fine, but in the circumstances I would like to invite DC Goodhew to sit in with us.'

CHAPTER 77

WEDNESDAY, 6 JULY 2011

There was a break while they waited for Goodhew, and Siobhan had taken Donna outside so she could smoke.

Three butts now lay doubled up and dead in the ashtray, and the fourth smoked gently between Donna's thin fingers. A newly opened packet held the remaining eighteen. Donna held the cigarette in her right hand, but instead of drawing on it she chewed the skin on one side of her thumb. Smoke rose in a tired column past her left eye, and she seemed reluctant to return to the interview room, and barely acknowledged Goodhew as he introduced himself.

Siobhan knew that she'd now broken the flow of Donna's statement, and that introducing another person into the interview risked destroying the earlier intimacy.

Donna had reverted to giving them mere drips of detail.

Sitting to one side of Siobhan, Gary noticed the dark circles under Donna's blue eyes. They stared in fitful bursts at him and Siobhan and then the rest of the room. She glanced at him several times before he finally spoke. 'I don't have to stay, Donna,' he told her.

She shook her head. 'No, it's fine.'

'It can be easier talking to just one person.'

'Really, it's fine.'

But clearly it wasn't. Goodhew could see her struggling and floundering on her rocky recollections. He was careful to keep his own voice even. 'Did he start treating you differently, Donna? My guess is that he suddenly changed, is that right?'

Donna nodded. 'I don't know why. But he said I provoked him.'

This time Siobhan spoke. 'In what way?'

'He said I led him on, made myself out to be something I wasn't. But honestly I never did.'

'What do you think he meant?' Siobhan asked.

'First of all he said he didn't want anything serious, and that's what I said, too.' Donna shrugged. 'But that's what everyone says, isn't it? It leaves the door open.' She fiddled with the cuff on her shirt, picking at a loose thread at the hem. 'I liked him and I let him know it, but after a few weeks he told me to get stuffed, or as good as.' She glanced at the other woman. 'I was gutted but I thought, well, that's blokes for you.' Siobhan nodded sympathetically and Donna continued, her tone thick with irony. 'Then he rang me a couple of days later, said he missed me. Said we should talk.'

'Do you remember when this was, exactly?' Siobhan coaxed.

'It was the Sunday after the last Friday I worked at Dunwold Insurance.' She counted back some dates, using the fingers of her free hand. 'That Friday was the third, so Sunday was the fifth.'

Gary jotted that down and drew a box around it, as she continued to talk. 'We were both round his house, and ended up in bed together.'

'And you consented to sex at this point?'

'Yes. Oh, yes, that was fine. Better than fine, I remember thinking.' She snorted with a humourless laugh. 'Then afterwards, as we were talking, he started playing a game, talking dirty – and I joined in. He was suggesting things he'd like to do to me, getting me to say I'd enjoy it too.'

'And how did you feel at this point?' Siobhan asked.

Gary glanced at her, wondering if her questions seemed too clinical. But when he looked back at Donna, he noticed a film of perspiration forming on her neck. Her pallid features grew animated as she succumbed to her memories; totally gripped with reliving them.

Her words emerged in short, intense bursts. 'To be honest, it was a bit of a turn-on. He then asked me if I wanted to make it up properly. I asked, "How?" He said, "Stay here for a few days."' Her speech quickened and her eyes flickered as in REM sleep. 'Well, I was over the moon. I'd felt like shit all weekend, dreading seeing him on Monday, and suddenly it had completely turned around. I went home, collected some clothes and rushed back to him. We went back into the bedroom and he started asking me if I'd do things.' Donna stared blankly into the space between Goodhew and Siobhan. 'All sorts of things.'

'Such as?' Siobhan queried.

'It started with him asking if I'd like to give him a blow job. I said of course I would, and he said "No, what you need to say is please let me give you a blow job."' Donna glanced at the other woman, then looked away again. 'This all sounds like I'm a slag, doesn't it?'

'Don't worry,' encouraged Siobhan, despite the feeling of apprehension seeping through her.

Donna cleared her throat. 'So I said it and he said "No, not yet." And he got me to ask him other things. "Please fuck me, Pete" was his favourite. He said "Where?" and I had to say "My mouth, my cunt, my arse". He brought out a gift box and it contained slutty underwear. Next he said "What am I allowed to do to you?" And I said "Whatever you want". He asked me to put it on, and I did, and he said "I'd like to watch someone else fuck you. Would you let me?" And I said "Yes".'

Her voice rose a notch and her breathing quickened. 'Of course, I didn't mean it. It was just a game we were playing. He said "You're a whore, aren't you?" And I said "Yes" and he said "Whose whore?" and I said "I'm your whore". Because that was the game. That's really what I thought it was, just a daring dirty game.'

Siobhan wiped sweating fingers against her trousers to prevent the pen from slipping.

Donna slouched back in her chair and tapped the next cigarette from the pack. 'And he said "So tell me exactly what you want" and I said "I want you to fuck me till I can't take any more" and he said "But you'll want me to keep screwing you even when you've had enough, won't you?" and I said "Yes".'

One of Donna's legs began to shake as a nerve quivered in the ball of her foot, and the tension in her spine made her shiver as if with cold.

An image of Julie's car crashing on to the rocks flashed in and out of Goodhew's mind, and a razor-sharp chill shot up the back of his neck.

'And that's what happened,' Donna gasped. 'As soon as we started having sex, I realized that it was all wrong. He was rough and held my arms down too tightly, and when I asked him to stop, he put his hand over my mouth. I began to panic then. He said "This is what you wanted". He pulled me up and threw me on to my front. And he forced me to . . .' she shot another quick glance at Goodhew, as she flicked her ash into the ashtray '. . . to do it that way round.'

'Vaginally?' Siobhan prompted.

Donna shook her head. 'No,' she whispered, then she gave a weary sigh. 'Some people like it that way, don't they? I've never really wanted to, but then I didn't want him to do lots of things after that.'

Siobhan's pen paused on the statement sheet as she waited for Donna to continue. Maybe women didn't all hang around in circumstances like this, but too few left the man either, of that she was sure. When Siobhan next spoke, she couldn't suppress the fatigue in her voice. 'So, after this assault, you stayed with him?'

'He acted like nothing had happened. I said I wanted to go home then, and he drove me. He decided to come in for a cup of tea. He'd decided he wanted to meet my parents, and I just sat there nodding and smiling. I suppose I could have said "Mum, Dad, this is Pete. He just raped me". Then he starts saying what a great girl I am and, before I know it, my mum's nudging me and saying how nice he is.' She dropped the latest unlit cigarette on to the table. 'You know what makes me angry? I never thought I'd be one of those women who find themselves abused and keep going back for more. But I saw him the next day, and the next, and each time he was as bad, or worse. The last day, he made me strip and screw a bottle while I knelt in front of him, sucking him off.' She leant forward, clutching either side of the table. 'Is that clear enough for you? He watched a porn film while I was doing that – dressed like a slag and still hoping that he was going to come to his senses. And afterwards he watched the news while I sat on the floor and cried. Then he said "Sorry, Donna, I don't want to see you again." Just like that. And he kicked me out, only half-dressed.'

Goodhew reached out and squeezed her arm. 'One last question. Which day was that?'

Donna caught her breath as she worked out the date. 'The following Wednesday, the eighth.' And, as she said it, she glanced at his pad and saw it already written there, enclosed in a heavy box. For the first time, Donna's eyes locked with his. 'How did you know?'

'A guess,' he replied.

'Am I the first?' she asked.

'I don't know yet.' Gary lied, and thought of all those days greyed out in Marlowe's diary. Marks surely would agree they now had enough to bring Walsh in for questioning.

CHAPTER 78

WEDNESDAY, 6 JULY 2011

Gully returned to her PC. For once something smelt better than Goodhew's aftershave, and she was sure it was the whiff of progress.

She opened her database. Things were different now, as she too believed there had been another murder – and perhaps all Goodhew had guessed wrong was the date.

She placed two pens and an A4 pad alongside her usual block of Post-it notes. She pulled off a clutch of the little yellow sheets and on the top one she wrote 'car hire 26 to 29 May 2010'. She affixed the sheet to the top right-hand corner of her monitor, and spread the rest out beside her right hand.

Her phone rang. 'Go away,' she muttered, and answered it with a grunt, 'Gully.'

'This is Harry Kabir. I'm the crime analyst assigned to your request for female disappearances between the twenty-sixth and twenty-ninth of May 2010.'

'Oh, yes?' Gully replied. She crossed her fingers for luck.

'Well, I've looked at twenty-four hours either side. There're missing teenagers who've turned up since, also domestics and accidents, but for what you want there's nothing doing.'

She uncrossed her fingers. 'Are you sure?'

'Absolutely.'

She couldn't believe it. 'Nothing at all?'

'Well . . .' Harry Kabir sighed. 'Only thing that might fit is an unreported disappearance, but we don't know about those unless . . .' He broke off and tutted to himself.

'Unless what?' she pushed.

'Imagine a murder victim who was living away from home for a period of time,' Harry Kabir replied. 'It's more than possible for her to turn up dead before she's been reported missing.' He paused. 'Do you want me to see if I can come up with anything on that basis?'

Gully replaced the receiver and scribbled on the next Post-it note. She stuck it directly below the first. It read 'No coinciding disappearance.'

'As yet,' she added invisibly, and turned back to her own notes.

Assuming Peter Walsh had abducted the second victim in the same way as all the others, then it would be reasonable to discount all deaths on or before 26 May 2010.

She next checked the fields in the database. There was a date field for the discovery of each death as well as a reference for the approximate date and time of death.

How long could anyone survive without food and water? She slid open her drawer and shook a couple of Jaffa Cakes from the most recently opened box.

Three or four days at the most, or longer with water. But none of the others had stayed alive for more than a week.

So discount all the deaths which had occurred after 5 June 2010, one week after he'd returned the hire car.

At every step, Gully rechecked her logic and noted her assumptions on a new Post-it note. At the rate she was going, her monitor would end up looking like a big square sunflower.

She wondered how many matches she'd find if she ran a query on deaths *estimated* to have fallen within that week.

She tapped the parameters into her PC and pressed the return key. The next pair of Jaffa Cakes had barely left the box by the time a list of just four records flashed on to the screen.

She scrolled down to the causes of death: one suspected suicide, one strangulation, and two unknown. She jotted down the dates on which each of the last two bodies had been discovered. On 11 July 2010 and 25 August 2010; one of them two weeks before Walsh finished his relationship with Julie, and the other four weeks afterwards.

She crossed a line through the second. Down to one.

She stabbed the page-up key and her cursor hopped up the screen to the first record.

'Shit,' she muttered, as she saw the dead woman's name. 'Suki Chen.' She checked the ethnicity field: Chinese. Gully sagged back in her chair. No fair hair or washed-out complexion. *Shit, shit, shit.*

She pressed her face into cupped hands and stared in dismay at the monitor.

Her phone trilled again and she lifted it to her ear, expecting to hear Goodhew at the other end.

'Harry Kabir here again. I've good news!'

'What?'

'Well, I *think* it's good news,' he chirped.

'Just tell me, quick,' she hissed.

'Well, I've found a match on it all: bound, gagged, abandoned – the whole shooting match except for two things.' Harry Kabir paused. 'Firstly, this girl was discovered inside a caravan, not in the open. And, secondly, the date reported is too late.'

Gully swapped the phone to her other ear and banged a couple of keys.

'She's listed in that database extract we sent over.'

'Jeanette Freidheim?' Gully asked, as the second record popped up on the screen.

Harry Kabir laughed. 'I'll get a copy of the case file straight over to you.'

Gully slammed down the receiver. 'Bingo!' she shouted to the empty office.

CHAPTER 79

WEDNESDAY, 6 JULY 2011

Pete's consciousness jangled in anticipation; the waiting was almost over.

He looked out of his bedroom window, down on to his small square patch of newly mown lawn.

He hated the moment when he realized another relationship was floundering, but he knew also that merely denying the issue would not make it go away.

He hated gardening, too, and it was another of those jobs that just had to be done. Now, though, with the grass freshly cut and the mower hanging from its hook inside the shed, he knew he'd sorted it out for the time being, at least.

Cutting out the girlfriend was like mowing the grass; he was sorry that it needed doing, but glad once he'd done it.

He checked the time. She'd be here in an hour.

He stripped the bed, scooping up the bedding. He pushed the duvet into the linen cupboard on the landing; the sheets and pillowcases he dropped over the banister on to the stairs.

Not that it was his fault, of course. They'd all deceived him. They'd pretended to be clean-living and honest. But when he tested them they were all the same.

He grabbed the handles on one side of the mattress and dragged it into an upright position, and then let it fall on to its back.

Dust sprayed into the air. The once cream mattress lay belly-up, discoloured by dried-out, rust-brown streaks and pools.

'Marlowe, Julie, Paulette, Donna and Fiona,' he recited, just to ensure he could still put them in order.

His voice sounded croaky in the silence, so he coughed and repeated their names more loudly: 'Marlowe, Julie, Paulette, Donna and Fiona.' He caught sight of himself in the mirror and moved closer, imagining he was looking at them all. *Sluts, all of you.* 'Behaving like harlots. Pretending to be innocent. Trying to indulge yourselves at my expense.'

He pulled some fresh sheets from his overhead cupboard; the special ones he saved for days like this. 'But I know better than that, don't I?'

He smoothed them out, and looked forward to Fiona sweating on to them.

Pete glanced at the bedside drawer and checked off the mental list of its contents. He'd added a porno mag. He'd get her to choose who she wanted to do it with; that would prove it. Perhaps all women were like that underneath, even the virgins. He suddenly wondered: maybe it was there lurking obscenely inside all of them.

That same thought had hit him at other times, but he rejected it quickly. There were good women, too, and he was destined to find one. There'd be someone special who wouldn't desecrate his dreams.

But first he had to divorce himself from Fiona and the way she made him feel; and through trial and error he had found the panacea for a bad relationship. It had become a well-honed routine of using her to lacerate each of his senses, and thus bleeding her out of his system through every pore.

Tonight he'd begin in the bedroom. And it was almost ready: the bed, the video and . . .

'Shit.' He checked his watch; it was half-past already. He hurried into the spare bedroom and returned with a rectangular, flat gold box and a paper bag. He eased open the lid and spread the contents on the bed. Knickers and a short negligee stitched out of translucent black organza. From the paper bag he took a ball of ribbon, then unfolded some fresh tissue paper and laid it in the box. He wanted the gift box to look like new. He sniffed it, but found it didn't smell of anything. He sniffed again, convinced that Donna and Paulette would have left behind a residue of sex that clung to them. And Julie . . . No that had been different; he'd had to replace Julie's items. He folded the underwear into the tissue, replaced the lid and wrapped some ribbon around the box.

With the box now positioned at a decorative angle on *her* side of the bed, he knew that he'd completed his preparations. Soon it would be confirmed that everything he'd done was right, and then he'd start the process of getting over Fiona.

He jumped when the doorbell rang. It was only quarter to, and not at all like her to be early.

He paused again at the mirror and saw no sign of either nervousness or anticipation.

It was only as he saw the distorted silhouette behind the frosted glass that he realized it wasn't Fiona who had rung the doorbell. For two people, not one, were waiting for him on the doorstep.

Wondering what could be wrong, he opened the door and greeted the waiting police officers with an accommodating smile.

CHAPTER 80

WEDNESDAY, 6 JULY 2011

Gully had joined Goodhew in Interview Room 2. As ever, the room was bare apart from four chairs and the long tatty table. Goodhew was standing with one elbow resting on the windowsill, holding a plastic cup of coffee in his other hand.

'They're bringing her through now,' she said. 'Are you sure about this, Gary?'

Goodhew nodded. 'Don't worry. It'll be fine.'

Gully settled into one of the chairs and placed a buff folder and Marlowe's diaries on the desk in front of her. 'Not as regards regulations – I mean will *she* be fine? What if this tips her over the edge?'

'It won't,' he replied. The door swung open and Marlowe Gates appeared.

Goodhew gestured her towards a seat, and joined Gully on the opposite side of the table. 'This is Sue Gully, who spoke to you when you first called in.'

Marlowe gave Gully a nod of acknowledgement, then turned back to Goodhew. 'He's under arrest, isn't he?' she asked sharply.

'Yes. We've received a separate complaint against him, so we've brought him in for questioning,' he replied.

'What's he done now?'

Gully butted in, without allowing Goodhew time to answer. 'I'm sorry, but we can't discuss that at the moment.' The conversation wouldn't be allowed to stray too far off course, if she was having any say in it. 'But how did you know?'

'I was watching his house and I saw him leave in a police car. Then, about ten minutes later, his girlfriend arrived.' She turned to Goodhew 'You know who I mean – the estate agent, Fiona. She went home after that.'

'You're going to have to stop following everyone,' he suggested.

She nodded. 'As soon as he's safely under lock and key.'

'Well, that's the main reason you're here,' Gully intervened, trying to steer the conversation.

'Lisa hasn't turned up yet, has she?'

In unison Goodhew and Gully shook their heads. And it was Goodhew who spoke first.

'We've started searches in the entire area this side of Sheringham. In all other cases the victims were abandoned outdoors, but within forty miles of wherever they went missing on the way back towards Cambridge . . .'

'Except one,' Gully interrupted.

Marlowe ran through the list of victims in her head. Goodhew had said earlier that they'd all been found within a forty-mile radius. She shook her head, slightly puzzled.

Gully unfolded the flap of the file and slid out a sheaf of papers. 'We think we may have found another victim, but the circumstances don't quite fit the pattern . . .'

'And we'd like your help,' added Goodhew.

Marlowe couldn't imagine anything that she'd be able to help them with, in connection with a new murder. 'OK,' she said, anyway.

Goodhew pulled a biro from his top pocket. 'Each of the other disappearances occurred while Walsh had rented a hire car. And each time a body has been discovered, he then finished with his current girlfriend immediately afterwards. Well, that's the gist of it, but there is one exception. We didn't have a case which coincided with him dating Julie Wilson, but then we discovered that he had also hired a car at the time, so DC Gully here searched for any cases of abduction that might coincide with that. And what she found is this.' Goodhew twiddled the pen round his fingers. 'It's news to you, isn't it?'

Marlowe nodded.

Goodhew tapped Gully's folder with his fingertips. 'Can you run through it, please?' he asked her.

Gully turned over the top sheet to reveal some of her own handwritten notes on the back. 'Firstly, we know from your own diary and from Julie's family that Pete Walsh dumped her at least a month before the body was discovered – which is one of the reasons this case may not be connected, so just keep that thought at the back of your mind.' She noticed that Marlowe's gaze had drifted towards the window. 'If this isn't a match, we mustn't let it cloud our thinking,' she added reassuringly.

Marlowe looked miserable. 'What about that new girl, Lisa?'

'Everybody on this case and in Sheringham is working flat-out on it. But it's only the three of us here doing it this way. Every angle is being looked at, Marlowe, and no one's given up on her.'

Gully dropped a photo in front of Marlowe. 'This is Jeanette Freidheim, who was a German student taking time out to see the country. As she was away travelling, she wasn't reported missing. It was only after her body was identified that anyone realized she had encountered trouble. The last trace of her was a cash withdrawal and her spending a night at a B&B in Wells on the twenty-seventh of May 2010.

'Walsh then hired a car on the twenty-sixth of May, so that fits, too,' Gully continued. 'Her body was discovered on the twenty-fifth of August 2010, by a certain Brendan Turner, on his farm.'

She flicked through several photocopied pages, then pushed two of them also in front of Marlowe. 'This is the farmer's statement, and I'll let you read it for yourself.'

Marlowe pulled the pages closer, and began picking out the words of a poorly copied statement.

I spotted three youngsters aged about twelve or thirteen. They were hanging around a disused tractor shed at the far end of the farm. Up to the usual summer-holiday mischief, I assumed. There was nothing they could take or damage, really, but I thought I should check, just in case.

They cleared off as soon as they saw me.

First I poked my head into the shed and that was fine. I then walked round the back, and there's an old touring caravan about fifty yards beyond. It's been left down there for years, since the floor started rotting. I could see something black at the windows.

At first I thought it was just mould on the net curtains. But it seemed too dark, so I headed towards it. And, as I got closer, I could see it sort of shimmering, then I realized it was moving.

Every window was the same. Well, I knew straight away, it was flies trapped inside there, and that meant there was most likely something dead. I assumed it would be an animal which had got in through the floor, so I looked through the window. All I could see were the flies.

I thought the door would be locked, but when I tried it, it swung open. Dead flies fell on to the ground and live ones streamed out all around me, and the smell poured out with them. I didn't go in. I just stood on the step, held on to the door frame, and leant forward a few inches.

I could clearly see the remains of a woman. Her face had completely gone so I think she'd been there for quite some time. Now, I've seen plenty of maggots on the farm in the past, but this lot was stomach-churning.

I only knew it was a woman because of her ankle boots, nothing else. They were closest to me and I stared at them after I looked away from her face. They looked weird, still intact but covered in flies.

Marlowe shuddered and tried to concentrate on the rest, but she couldn't help picturing bones sticking out of boots, with only flies on them for flesh. 'All the other bodies were found out in the open, though, weren't they?'

'That's right,' Goodhew replied, 'but there are plenty of other reasons to assume this is a related incident.'

Gully passed another page across to Marlowe. 'These are some notes made by the investigating officer, which sum up the crime scene pretty well. Then these ones here were made by the Scene of Crime Officer. Take a close look at the highlighted section.'

Marlowe placed the new sheet in front of her and rested her elbows on the table. She read it, staring straight down at it, with her head resting in her hands.

Evidence that the victim had been alive at the scene for some time.

Excrement samples have been removed from her clothing and there was extensive staining on the floor consistent with repeated urination. A dried substance, possibly consistent with vomit was also present.

The victim was bound hand and foot. A knotted cloth hung around her neck, which appeared to be a gag which she had worked off sometime before death.

'Is this similar to the other cases?' Marlowe muttered, without looking up.

'Pretty much, apart from the gag coming loose,' Gully replied.

Marlowe rubbed one eye and looked up at Goodhew. 'Why did you want me to see all this?'

'Because I have a gut feeling that there's something vital you can tell us,' he replied gently. 'And I need you to see everything because I don't know which particular clue is the one that might solve this.'

'Well, I hope you're right,' Marlowe answered.

Gully sighed. 'So do I,' she said wearily. 'Now, there's one big difference between this case and all the others. It appears that Walsh had finished with Julie before this body was found, but we only know the date when he split up with her from your diary. Are you sure, therefore, it's accurate?'

Marlowe looked offended. 'Of course.'

'I mean, could you have written down the entry in the wrong week by mistake? Or misinterpreted what you saw?' Gully pressed her. 'If he didn't end his relationship with her until later, it would make a big difference.'

'The date would definitely be correct.' Marlowe frowned. 'But what did I write?'

Goodhew picked up the diary, flicked it open to the relevant entry, and read out: '*Pete was on his own, then Julie turned up. He pushed her away and stormed off. Think they've had a fight.*'

'No, I remember that. I'm sure they split up then. If they hadn't. then I would have seen them together later on, I'm sure, but I never did.'

Goodhew thought Marlowe sounded pretty definite.

Gully thought so too. 'Can you think of anything that was different between Walsh's relationship with Julie and his relationship with you or any of the others?' she asked.

Marlowe suddenly looked obstinate. 'Tell me why he's been arrested.'

'No, I'm afraid—' Gully began.

But Goodhew interrupted her. 'One of his other exes is now claiming that he subjected her to a series of sexual assaults.' Gully scowled but he ignored her. 'These appear to have occurred between one victim's abduction and the discovery of the next body.'

He saw her sifting her thoughts, separating the grain from the chaff. 'Well, I doubt he treated Julie any different from the rest of us,' she said at last. 'And if that's the case, then he didn't wait for the next body to be discovered, did he? He finished with her first.'

Goodhew's eyes widened, and he snatched up Jeanette's file and the rest of the papers strewn across the desk. What if Walsh knew that she'd died because he himself had gone to look? Goodhew flicked through the notes again. Her body had been there for weeks, but what if Walsh was in the caravan a second time before she was eventually found? Where was that SOCO's report? He pulled it out from between the other pages.

Goodhew leapt to his feet and dashed towards the door. 'I'll be ten minutes.'

CHAPTER 81

WEDNESDAY, 6 JULY 2011

Gully and Marlowe watched Goodhew leave. Gully wanted to talk to Marlowe, but the young woman rested her elbows back on the table, bent her head and clasped her hands behind her neck. As she studied the table top, she effectively closed herself off from Gully.

'Marlowe, d'you want something to drink?' Gully asked.

'Tea, please,' she replied, without looking up. 'White no sugar, thanks.'

She'll have to look up to drink it, Sue reasoned, *and I'll have a chat with her then.*

Marlowe barely noticed her leave. She was replaying the last hour over in her head. She thought of Jeanette Freidheim all alone in the caravan, with the gag hanging loose around her neck. All the while, shouting for help. Was it worse to be gagged, or worse to continue screaming out and not be heard?

She thought of Gary's words, 'There's something you can tell us.' What if there really was? And what if she remembered too late? Then what?

If and *then*, that's what it is all about.

If we know enough, then we catch Pete.

If we know enough, then we save Lisa.

If and then . . . *if* and *then*.

A bolt of realization struck Marlowe. *If* and *then* was exactly it.

As Marlowe pulled the door wide, Gully arrived, carrying one plastic cup in each hand, and trying to push the door with her shoulder. Scalding tea slopped on to the policewoman's hand, and she swore.

Marlowe grabbed her arm. 'I think I know why.' She started towards the exit. 'I'm allowed to leave, aren't I?'

'Yes, of course, but . . .' Gully began.

'I'm going to fetch *The Cross and the Switchblade*. It's a book.'

'Yes, I know.'

'Well, I think that contains the answer.' Marlowe started towards the main entrance. 'I'll be straight back, but if you see Gary first, tell him it's near the front. It's the bit about "the fleece".'

CHAPTER 82

WEDNESDAY, 6 JULY 2011

Fiona paced into the kitchen, set the kettle to re-boil, then headed back towards the front door. It wasn't his lateness that bothered her yet; it was the wave of expectation she was finding tough to ride. She'd gone on like this for so long that she wondered why just a few more minutes now felt so intolerable.

She checked her mobile phone again, just in case she'd missed a text, then left it on the table so she would more easily hear it ring. He hadn't been at home when she'd called there, but the house lights were on, suggesting he was somewhere nearby.

She could have waited there, but he was equally capable of making his way to her house. She was sure there'd be an explanation; he just needed to turn up and be apologetic. As she headed towards the kitchen again, the doorbell rang.

Fiona swept the door open, ready to welcome Pete. Instead she found a woman waiting outside, huddled in a thin jacket, and damp and shivering from the rain.

'Oh,' she looked uncertain, 'I was expecting someone else.'

'Peter Walsh?' queried the stranger.

'That's right.' Fiona nodded. 'Is everything all right?'

'I'm sorry, no it isn't.' The woman paused and the silence hung frozen in the air between them. Fiona saw fear or shock or something else in the woman's drawn face. 'Can I come in?'

An icy shudder rippled its way down Fiona's spine. 'Of course.'

The woman stepped inside and Fiona followed her through to the lounge, a thousand scenarios already racing through her mind. *Not dead. Not dead?*

The woman stopped in front of the mantelpiece. She made a point of letting Fiona see her staring at Peter's photo. What if this was his long-term girlfriend or, worse, his wife. *She'd wish he was dead, then*, Fiona thought, then immediately crushed the sentiment.

The woman turned to face Fiona. 'My name is Marlowe Gates, and I used to go out with Peter Walsh.'

Fiona shifted uneasily. 'What do you want?'

'I want to help you, but you must listen.' Marlowe watched the colour drain from Fiona's already pale face. 'He's under arrest, and the police are gathering evidence to charge him with rape and murder.'

'I don't believe you.'

'I need your help.' Marlowe stepped closer.

Fiona stood her ground. 'Just a minute ago you said you wanted to help me, but you've marched into my home with some tale about Pete being arrested. I really don't understand. I suppose you're about to tell me that you're helping him, too?'

'Don't be ridiculous,' Marlowe snapped. 'If they can't press charges tonight they might have to release him. Then you'll be in real danger.'

'How?'

'From him. He'll meet you and rape you, and for all I know he'll kill you too.' Marlowe ran her fingers through her hair.

'Now you're being stupid.' Fiona caught sight of Marlowe's scars and lowered her voice. 'He's not a rapist,' she whispered. 'And he's certainly not a killer.'

'So far, Fiona, he has killed or raped at least eight women.' As Marlowe spoke her voice became harder and louder. 'Currently there's one missing girl, dead or half-dead . . . and you're next. As I said before, I need your help.'

Fiona scratched the back of her head and tilted it so she could see clearly towards the door. She had started to shake violently, and she wondered whether she should make a dash for it.

Marlowe was shaking too, and Fiona looked into her face and realized that its whiteness was not due to fear or shock. It was caused by absolute determination, a cold clear single-mindedness fuelled with adrenalin. Fiona knew now that she couldn't run. Instead she'd have to wait it out. 'OK, what do you think I can do?'

'I will dictate a letter to Peter. Then I want you to post it through his door, so that he will find it if ever he is released. Then I want you to leave Cambridge, just go somewhere else until you read the news that he's been arrested. Will you do that for me?'

Fiona nodded slowly. 'That's all?'

'Yes, that's it.' Marlowe pointed towards the dining table. 'Now sit over there.' Marlowe stood over her and placed a pad of cream writing paper on the table, she handed Fiona a blue biro. 'Make it neat.'

Marlowe seemed to know exactly what she wanted written, and she spoke without hesitation.

Dear Pete,

Fiona began to write.

I was thinking about you while I was away.

Marlowe tapped the paper. 'New line.' Fiona's hand moved down.

Thinking how much I missed you.

Again Marlowe tapped the page. 'Another new line.' And thus she continued to give Fiona instructions, as she dictated.

Thinking how much I loved you. Fiona's pen wobbled.

'You've written "love". Put the "d" on it, Fiona. It's meant to be in the past.'

And thinking about how you feel about me.

Marlowe leant close to Fiona and hissed into her ear.

Then I realized, you think I'm not good enough, don't you? You have standards and I don't meet them. And I've been making excuses, feeling like I don't deserve better. But I now know that it's you who is not good enough for me.

Fiona's hand began to ache. *You make me feel dirty.* Marlowe tapped the page. 'Write it.'

You make my skin crawl with your dirty games.

Fiona continued more slowly. 'What dirty games?' she asked quietly and tried not to look at Marlowe's wrists.

'He knows what I mean. Just write.'

But I'm better than you, and I'm not giving you the chance to mess with my life any more. I'm not even prepared to discuss this with you.

What would you do anyway? Finish with me first? I don't think so, because you wouldn't be capable of making a decision like that, would you?

So I'm making it for you.

You like me saying 'Fuck me', don't you? Fiona heard herself gasp, but said nothing. *Well, fuck you, then. How does that sound? Don't try to find me either, because I've moved up in the world.*

Marlowe straightened and stared down at Fiona.

Fiona stared down at the page.

'Well, sign it, then,' Marlowe snapped. 'Obviously "with love and kisses" isn't required.'

Fiona wrote her name at the bottom. She tried to make it less like her own handwriting but doubted Pete would know the difference, anyway. Marlowe moved around further and watched over Fiona's shoulder. 'Fine. But how do I know you'll deliver it?'

'I promise I will.' Fiona felt the fingernails of fear scraping across her scalp.

She turned in her seat, wanting to see Marlowe's face. She needed to judge how much danger she was in. 'Honestly, Marlowe . . .'

Marlowe grabbed hold of Fiona's hair. Fiona's hands shot up and, as they did so, she felt something tighten around her waist. She braced herself to resist, but knew in that instant that she was already secured to her chair.

Marlowe's warm breath brushed close to Fiona's ear. 'Do exactly as I say and I won't hurt you,' she whispered. She tied a second length of rope to the arm of the chair. 'Give me your hand,' Marlowe said softly.

Maybe Fiona could have kicked out or fought against her with her free hand, but instead made only token resistance. She could sense a strength in Marlowe that she just couldn't match. 'You don't need to do this.'

'I really do.' Marlowe looked up from the knot. 'You'll be OK. Yes, you will.'

Marlowe tied her second wrist to the other arm of the chair. She made the knots tight but this time, when she'd finished, she neither looked at Fiona nor spoke another word.

Marlowe straightened up, folded the letter and slipped it into her pocket. She pulled the phone from the wall, and then Fiona heard her also disconnecting the main handset in the hall.

Marlowe moved quietly towards the front door and opened it.

Fiona willed Marlowe to leave, and caught her breath as she heard her pause, and then mutter 'Shit.' Marlowe slammed the door shut and ran back inside and up the stairs. Fiona heard her moving from room to room, then she came back down again.

When she came back into the room, Marlowe was carrying the belt from Fiona's dressing gown. Fiona started to speak, but Marlowe was fast to apply the gag. Fiona tried making eye contact but Marlowe looked away. There was no further interaction until the last second before Marlowe left the room. She paused, with her back to Fiona, her voice only just audible. 'I've dropped your mobile phone down the toilet, sorry.'

Then the front door clicked shut. Fiona kept still, listening for Marlowe's return. When she was sure she was alone, she began to strain increasingly against her ties. She laboured, grunting with her efforts, but nothing gave. Finally, she stopped trying and began to cry.

CHAPTER 83

WEDNESDAY, 6 JULY 2011

Dr Strickland placed the phial of blood inside its plastic pouch and printed slow, deliberate letters on to the label. He clearly couldn't write and talk at the same time, so Goodhew wanted to take the pen and finish it off himself.

'I don't want to make a mistake. It's the little things that count, you know, Gary,' Strickland burbled. He clicked the lid back on to his pen. 'You were asking me about vomit?'

'Yes.' Goodhew sighed.

Strickland pushed his glasses up on to the bridge of his nose before speaking. 'Usually, in the process of being sick, saliva and cells from the inside of the mouth are dislodged en route and can then be found in the vomit. As long as we can isolate either some of those from the other debris, we should be able to determine the DNA.'

'So that's a yes, then. And how long will such a comparison take?'

'Well, that depends. This evidence is only about a year old, and the forensics team at the time may have thoroughly tested for DNA. But whether they managed a result is something else. We can do much more now, so even if they didn't . . .'

Goodhew noticed a shadow looming, through the frosted glass in the door. 'I'm sorry, I need to go now but it is urgent. If it matches the blood, we can make an arrest.'

Gully was waiting in the corridor, unsure whether she should knock. 'She's gone,' she told him, as soon as he appeared. 'Said she was off to get *The Cross and the Switchblade*. I wasn't worried at first, but she still hasn't come back and she's not at home. You were only going to be away ten minutes.'

'I know, but Strychnine's on duty tonight, so that screwed things up. Did she say anything else?' They entered the incident room, where Goodhew grabbed his jacket from the back of the chair.

'She said something about the *fleece*. Said it's near the start of the book.'

'Grab your coat, and get the number for that all-night locksmith. We'll go over right away.' A minute later, Goodhew strode out towards the car, with Gully almost jogging to keep up.

'You can't just break in, Gary,' she protested.

'She'll get over it.'

'Marks will go spare.'

Goodhew dropped himself into the driver's seat and slammed the door in one fluid movement. He'd started the engine by the time Gully was properly in her seat, and she only pulled her door shut as he accelerated out of the car park.

'Sue, I'm not messing around with search warrants for Marlowe's flat. I'll just go in, make sure she's not in there, grab the book and take off.' He passed her his mobile phone. 'Call that locksmith and ask him to meet us.'

'What if he gets there first?'

'Don't be stupid. We'll probably be waiting for him for hours yet.'

Sue emitted a loud 'tut' but phoned anyway. They made the rest of their short journey in silence. The roads were empty apart from a milk float starting deliveries and a cyclist heading home from the night shift.

Marlowe's road was asleep. Parked cars and darkened windows greeted them as they drove towards her block of flats at the far end.

Despite everything, Sue smiled as she caught sight of Vic Brown's locksmith's van parked outside. 'Well, that's just typical, isn't it?'

She jumped out to greet him, as Gary headed on inside the block.

'I thought you'd given me the wrong address,' Vic Brown complained.

'No. I didn't expect you to get here so fast.'

'I was just round the corner. It's number 58, then?'

'Yes,' she nodded.

A loud crack echoed down the stairs, and Vic frowned. 'Has he just broken in?'

'No, of course not. I'd better see if he's OK, though.' Sue led him upstairs to find number 58. The front door hung open, torn from its frame and with a single shoe print clearly evident just beneath the lock.

Gary emerged from the living room, book in hand. 'Can I leave you with this, please?' he asked Gully.

'No problem.' She winked at him from behind the locksmith.

'Help yourselves to tea and coffee,' Goodhew said.

The lighter moment vanished as soon as Goodhew hit the cold night air. He was worried about Marlowe. She hadn't been home, or why else would the book still be there? He sat for a while in the car, and studied the book by the orange light of a street lamp, as it slanted through the passenger window.

He scanned each page for the word 'fleece', and at the bottom of the third one he found it.

> There in the dark outside that little church I made an experiment in a special kind of prayer which seeks to find God's will through a sign. *'Putting a fleece before the Lord' it is called, because Gideon, when he was trying to find God's will for his life, asked that a sign be made with a fleece. He placed a lamb's fleece on the ground and asked Him to send down dew everywhere but there. In the morning, the ground was soaked with dew, but Gideon's fleece was dry: God had granted him a sign.*

'So that was it,' Goodhew murmured, and gasped just as his mobile rang. 'Goodhew,' he announced.

'Gary, it's me.' Marlowe sounded tense.

'Where are you?'

'In town. I think I can get Peter to lead us to Lisa. But I need you to release him and keep watch on his house,' she said.

'How is that going to help?'

'Please, Gary, trust me. And you mustn't come near me until Lisa's safe. Promise me. It's the only way.'

'Explain to me, Marlowe.'

'Will you do it?'

Gary closed his eyes and tried to listen to his instincts. The response was silence. He looked down at *The Cross and the Switchblade*. No clues there.

Release the main suspect when they had a rape witness, and possible scene-of-crime forensic evidence? The same evidence which Marks demanded for the arrest Goodhew had sought. He knew about the fleece, and the car hire and all the other cases. He should go back and shock Walsh with the facts – *make him tell us where Lisa Fairbanks is.*

'Gary, will you do it?' she repeated.

'Yes,' he replied, finally.

CHAPTER 84

THURSDAY, 7 JULY 2011

Early-morning traffic was already trickling on to the roads as Peter Walsh travelled home in the back of the unmarked police car.

He didn't know whether to go to work or stay at home for the day. His life had been thrown out of kilter, but at the same time he was experiencing an all-new sense of excitement. He looked grey with exhaustion and felt sweaty after that stuffy interview room, but altogether it was nothing that a shower and a couple of coffees wouldn't fix.

Walsh felt confident. He had admitted nothing, although he didn't like submitting to the blood test.

But of all the women to make a complaint. Donna? She was the biggest slag of the lot. He'd always known she wasn't his type, but when she couldn't even properly remember how many men she'd had sex with . . .

He took a breath. *Forget it*. She'd get torn apart in court, anyway. Nine out of ten women in her situation lost their cases.

And it wasn't quite the same with her: all over and done with much quicker than for the others. It had been a shame that the biggest slut should have received the least punishment.

The driver turned his head. 'Number 26?'

'Yeah, that's right.'

As the car stopped, Pete automatically pulled on the internal handle to let himself out.

The other policemen stepped out to open the rear door. 'It doesn't work from the inside.'

Pete walked confidently to his front door, key in hand. As he unlocked it, he saw the folded sheet of cream writing paper lying on the mat. He looked outside and waited for the tail lights of the police car to disappear out of Hanley Road before he bent to pick it up.

He nudged the door shut with his foot even as he unfolded it.

He began to read, then he took a few steps into the sitting room. He must have misunderstood. He read it back from the start. 'What in God's name . . . ?'

Any thought of going to work evaporated.

He snatched up the handset and angrily stabbed out Fiona's number.

No reply.

'No, no . . . *no*.' He fumed, his wrath taking hold of him and burning at his insides. He slammed the handset against the wall and left it to tumble on to the floor.

He ran upstairs to his bedroom and pulled open the wardrobe door. The video camera waited on its tripod, and he picked it up and dumped it on to the bed.

He reached towards the back, beyond the shoes on the shoe shelf, and retrieved a black sports bag. He unzipped it rapidly and held the jaws of its mouth wide. It was all still in there: the videos, a new ball of rope, a new set of clothes still wrapped in cellophane.

He removed his driver's licence from his inside pocket. No time to hire a car this time, so no number plates either.

He'd find Fiona and show her how he made his decisions. She could experience it first hand, and he could leave her there and say *Fuck you*.

He started to remove the camera from the tripod. 'Damn!' He couldn't screw her either, or they'd catch him then. He'd just make her masturbate on camera; he needed that keepsake, at least.

His finger caught in a leg of the tripod as he folded it, so he threw it against the wardrobe door. *Fucking whore.* She wouldn't last long outside in this weather, but she really deserved to suffer.

Or he could leave her inside like that gullible German girl, or better still in some derelict building. Appropriate for a stuck-up bitch estate agent.

The inferno of Pete's rage swept through him, devouring even the carnal cravings that helped him plan each abduction like an illicit tryst.

'Where do I leave her?' he shouted. 'Where, where?' His voice was loud but at the same time seemed distant, disembodied and unrecognizable. No, he didn't have a new location ready, but he needed somewhere quiet. He needed a place where he could arrive and dump her without being seen. 'Where?'

The answer suddenly came like an echo replying to his outpouring. One of the old places, somewhere he already knew? That was it. Not the caravan, though, because that had been removed. Not with Lisa either. Except why not?

Walsh paused, stock-still, gazing at the tripod, his thoughts on Fiona.

That would make her pay. Lisa would be already dead or nearly dead. And Fiona could watch her rot.

CHAPTER 85

THURSDAY, 7 JULY 2011

Goodhew had witnessed Pete return home. He'd seen Pete watch the police car leaving his road. And then he'd seen Pete's front door close.

He saw no sign of Marlowe.

The sky had lightened to grey. It would not be a warm day.

His mobile rang once, before he answered it. 'Goodhew.'

'What the hell is going on?' Marks barked at him.

'I'm watching Peter Walsh's house at the moment, sir.'

'Why, for God's sake? He isn't the one!' Marks yelled.

Goodhew scowled. 'He isn't which one, sir?'

'The killer – it's her. You know, your little victim friend Marlowe Gates.'

Goodhew's stomach lurched.

'Kincaide was right,' Marks continued. 'If Walsh is involved at all, it's only with her. She's more than just in on it.'

'No . . .' Goodhew protested.

'The incident room received an anonymous call twenty minutes ago. Does that maybe ring a bell? The caller, female of course, told us to investigate the property of a Fiona Robinson.'

'Pete's girlfriend?'

'Very good,' chirped Marks. 'And they found her bound and gagged, tied to a chair with all the phones ripped out. Guess what she then said?'

'Marlowe did it,' answered Goodhew weakly.

'We have her here. And we're not letting her contact him.'

'Who, Marlowe?' asked Goodhew, as he continued to watch Hanley Road.

'No, Fiona Robinson,' Marks roared. 'Don't play me as stupid, Gary. If you've developed a soft spot for this girl, you'd better forget it. She's a killer and he's a rapist. Think about it, there are plenty of well-known examples. Couples that commit rape. Couples that commit murder.'

Gary leant forward to study a figure walking towards him from the far end of the road. Marlowe.

'Gary? Do you know where she is?'

'No, I have no idea.' She crossed between the cars parked in front of number 18, and stepped up to number 26.

Marks paused for a moment. Goodhew knew Marks would be biting on the edge of his bottom lip; as he always did when he was trying to calm down.

'Stay there until Kincaide arrives. He's still with Miss Robinson for now, but then he can watch Walsh's and I'll see you back here. And if you see any sign of Marlowe Gates in the meantime, arrest her.'

Goodhew watched as Marlowe tapped on the front door. And he watched the door open.

His hand rose and pressed his mouth shut, as if to smother an involuntary gasp.

She smiled at Pete and stepped inside.

Goodhew stared at the centre of the steering wheel. What if Marks was right? Marks was no fool.

But what if Marks was wrong?

He looked up at number 26 again. Did he still believe Marlowe?

She'd smiled at Walsh and stepped inside.

Goodhew picked up his phone and dialled. When his call was answered, he said, 'Bryn, it's me.'

CHAPTER 86

THURSDAY, 7 JULY 2011

Marlowe had been here earlier to deliver Fiona's note; pushing it through the letter box with a hesitant prod, like a Dobermann lurked on the other side.

Now she had waited on Pete's doorstep long enough to notice all the little details she'd since forgotten. A smear of paint on the brickwork. The disconnected doorbell. And the Chubb lock that she'd opened so many times when she still had her own key.

Since the front door stood five inches above the path, she'd stood on tiptoe, like a little kid, as she tried to see through one of the small panes of obscured glass.

She'd spotted a ripple of movement and shivered.

He'd known she was there.

'I'm not alone, I'm not alone,' she'd whispered to herself.

The lock had rattled, and she'd looked up just as the door had opened. Pete had let the door swing wide. He'd seemed to fill the doorway, still and expressionless.

She'd drawn a breath and held it, forcing a grin, hoping to look smug, and trying to speak. No words had come. The corner of her mouth had twitched. The moment had dragged on, making her dizzy.

Speak to him.

She'd propped up her smile, and exhaled. 'Can I come in?' she'd finally blurted.

He'd stood back to let her through, and she had stepped back into her own nightmare.

* * *

The door snapped shut behind her and Pete nudged her through to the sitting room. She stopped in the centre of the room and turned around. Her arm brushed against him and she recoiled, stepping quickly back against the coffee table.

She took a deep breath and sucked in a lungful of his smell: that forgotten cocktail of soap, fresh sweat and Aramis. Now she had to face him.

'What do you want?' he growled. His pupils had dilated, big matt pools threatening to swallow his entire eyes. Dark and soulless.

She knew she was now out of her depth. Way, way out, at that.

She nodded towards the phone still lying on the floor. 'Did you have some bad news, Peter?' she prompted. Her voice trembled; sounding too timorous, too reedy.

She tried again. 'It still looks just the same in here. And there was me thinking you had big plans for the future.'

'What do you want, Marlowe?' he repeated, glowering at her.

'I just thought I'd let you know that I told Fiona all about you.'

'What . . . ?' Pete began, then faltered. He grabbed her upper arm, digging his thumb into the bones. 'You're the bitch who phoned the police, aren't you?' He lunged at her. She staggered sideways. He held her tight and propelled her on to the settee. She squealed, landing flat on her back. She had no time to sit up before he pounced again. He now held her arms flat and pressed his body heavily against hers, crushing the breath from her lungs. 'You are, aren't you?' he repeated.

Marlowe's eyes never left his, and she forced a defiant sneer to her lips. 'Yes,' she gasped. 'You must have known that.'

He lifted his torso enough to let her breathe easier. His voice quietened to an insistent hiss. 'What did you tell Fiona?'

Marlowe had forgotten the precise feel of his menace slipping into her, the dangerous tone of his voice. And now his mouth was less than a tongue's length from her own; invasive like poison. 'I told her all of it.'

'Why do you do it, Marlowe? Why do you play these games?' He slid the fingers of one hand through the hair above her ear and wove them in and out. He twisted them roughly till her hair tightened at the roots, pulling against her scalp. He held her head still, and brought his face closer. 'Tell me exactly what you told her.'

'Well, for a start I told her how you are a rapist and a murderer.' She felt a drip of sweat run down the inside of her shirt. 'She seemed a bit upset at that.'

The muscles in his jaw began flexing, as he clenched his teeth. Marlowe lay motionless beneath him. 'There have been times when I've almost regretted leaving you,' he said, after a long pause. 'Now here you are up close. You smell the same and feel the same but, my God, you've become very spiteful.'

'Because of you,' she whispered.

'Because of me? You should have pulled yourself together. You should've tried to get over it, Marlowe.'

'I *am* over you,' she snarled.

'Tell me about your sex life, then. Tell me who's ever fucked you.' Pete released her hair and ran his middle finger across her cheek. He stroked her bottom lip. She felt him harden against her groin, and his other hand began pulling at her shirt.

'Only you,' she answered quietly.

He pushed himself away, to arms' length. 'Only me what?'

She impaled him with her eyes. 'There has only ever been you, Peter. No one before and no one since. I follow you and watch you. I know who you've screwed. I also know you made a mistake when you left me, because none of the others were any better.'

Disbelief clouded his face. 'You're a liar.'

'Oh no, you told me so many times that women shouldn't sleep around, and therefore I never did. *Never.*' She wriggled out from under and stood in front of him. He sat up straight, glowering, as she continued. 'Whatever happened to your ideals that a man should always honour a faithful woman? That he should never walk out on a commitment?'

'I never did.'

'You know you did. Sex in itself is a commitment to you, isn't it?'

He stared at her. 'You're obsessed.'

She bent over, pausing with her face only inches from his. 'Isn't it?' she demanded.

'Yes, you know it is. So what?'

'You forget, Peter, that I know your family. You've been brought up in just the same airless, suffocating way as me. Full of inhibitions, and no sex outside marriage for a start. So you can't ever leave a girlfriend; not unless it's not actually your decision.' They glared at each other. Marlowe's heart thumped loudly in her ears, and she turned away first. She moved back a couple of paces and leant against the kitchen door frame. 'I know about the fleece,' she told him, and let her words hang in the air just long enough to relish his panic.

The mention of the word jolted him and he sprang to his feet, and across the gap between them. She didn't see the blow coming, but she heard it crack across her cheekbone. She saw it reverberate through her eyes like a firework display. Then she crashed on to the kitchen floor.

Pete followed her through the doorway. Unlike her, still on his feet, he kicked out at her. The hard edge of his shoe cracked into her ribs. 'Oh shit,' she gasped, clutching her stomach.

'Tell me about it,' he screamed.

'You get tired of a girlfriend . . .' she panted. 'Or maybe you decide she's not good enough . . . But you can't just end it.'

She watched him cross the kitchen, away from her. 'Keep talking,' he demanded.

She dragged herself up on to one elbow, choking. 'Otherwise you'd be the slag, then. Of course, you would.'

Pete pulled a bottle of Budweiser from the fridge.

Marlowe grabbed the edge of the work surface. But she kept talking. 'You would then have broken your commitment, wouldn't you?' She hauled herself to her knees. 'So you abduct a girl who resembles your girlfriend and you say to yourself, "If she dies it is a sign that I am right to leave, but if she lives I am wrong and deserve to be caught."' She managed to rise to her feet, but had to lean heavily on the worktop. 'That's about right, isn't it, Peter?'

He shrugged. 'Near enough.' He placed the bottle in front of her, but just out of reach.

She knew she couldn't outrun him. She closed her eyes instead. 'And, whatever the outcome, your relationship is legitimately over, so you do what the hell you like with your girlfriend until the body is found.'

'No.' He tutted. 'They all wanted it, even you.' She felt his breath as he brought his cheek up close to hers. His fingers started to rub at her belt buckle.

'Do you think I'm rising to that bait?' Marlowe snorted. 'I don't give a fuck. I'd just go to the police and tell them you raped me. At least I'd have the evidence this time.'

Pete spun her round to face him, to open her eyes. 'Is that why you're here?'

Marlowe shook her head. 'I'm the only one who can stop you, Peter. No one believes me. They think I'm mad. So this is what I want.' Marlowe brought her lips close to his. 'It's my fleece.' Her voice trembled. 'Leave me tied up just like the others. If I die, you get away with it. If I'm found, I'll be vindicated. Simple isn't it? One wins, one loses.'

CHAPTER 87

THURSDAY, 7 JULY 2011

Kincaide screeched from the police station car park, into East Road and towards Pete Walsh's house.

Thank Christ he'd taken that phone call; at any other time he'd have left it to ring. Good thing he'd been having a nose through Gully's desk at the time. That was fate, of course.

He'd recognized Marlowe's voice straight away. He'd heard it on the tapes often enough.

He slowed for the traffic lights. They stayed green and he sped past the end of Mill Road, all terraced houses and corner shops.

A whole lot different from Wollaston Avenue with its front lawns and company cars. 'Go to number 206,' she'd said.

He hadn't realized what was up when that weeping hysterical estate agent starting blubbering on to his jacket.

Then it had dawned on him. Marlowe had tied her up, just like she'd tied up the others, but then she'd clearly bottled it.

Fiona Robinson should have been laughing, instead, at the lucky escape she'd just had.

Kincaide swung left into Trumpington Road and turned right at the roundabout into the Fen Causeway. The roads were clear, it being still too early for rush-hour traffic. Just as well, since the sooner he reached Goodhew the better.

Jan had been right, it was results that turned Marks' head. Kincaide had overheard Marks tearing into Goodhew on the phone, so the opportunity to deliver a result was now with him.

Excellent.

He sped towards the next roundabout.

And now he was about to relieve Goodhew of his duty, send him back to the station with his tail between his legs, and make the arrest himself.

He turned right into Queen's Road. Nearly there.

Better than excellent!

He was still smiling as a tatty Volvo tanked out of the side road and slammed into his passenger door. His car skidded to a halt against a 'keep left' bollard.

Kincaide unbuckled his seatbelt and flew from the car in a single movement.

The Volvo door started to open. 'Are you OK, mate? I'm so sorry,' the driver began.

Kincaide grabbed the opening door and yanked it wide, bundling the driver on to the tarmac. 'Why weren't you watching the road?' he yelled.

'I'm sorry, I just didn't see you.'

Kincaide grabbed the man by the lapels and dragged him back to his feet. 'You stupid git, I'm a police officer and you have no idea what you've done.'

CHAPTER 88

THURSDAY, 7 JULY 2011

Goodhew still watched Pete Walsh's front door. The minutes dragged by. He wanted to know Marlowe was all right, but he'd promised to stay back.

So he prayed for her safety instead.

His mobile beeped with a new text message from Bryn. He opened it and read 'Done'. Then 'Volvo a write-off'.

He felt he knew who he could trust. He remembered the first time he'd seen Marlowe. He'd wanted her to trust him. With a leap of faith, she had. And, in return, he trusted her.

He knew that now. Whatever the evidence to the contrary.

Walsh's door opened nearly twenty minutes later and he and Marlowe stepped out into the street. She waited for him to lock up and they walked together to his car. He carried a black holdall and opened the boot. He put it under the parcel shelf, unzipped it and reached inside.

She sat quietly in the passenger seat.

Walsh removed a ball of rope and slammed the tailgate.

Goodhew strained to see more clearly.

Pete got in alongside Marlowe, and passed something towards her. Goodhew saw her bend over towards the footwell. After a few seconds, he saw Pete lean across to her side of the car, and Goodhew realized she was being tied up.

He followed them out of Cambridge, and on to the A14 towards Newmarket. All the while, he kept several cars between himself and Pete's VW Golf. The A14 split, and Walsh took the A11 fork towards Mildenhall. He settled at a steady sixty-five miles per hour along the dual carriageway.

Goodhew called Marks back on his mobile.

'What's going on?' yelled Marks above the static.

'I'm following Pete Walsh and Marlowe Gates. They are travelling north-east along the A11 between Newmarket and Mildenhall.'

'We can intercept them at Mildenhall, if we're quick.'

'No, they'll be going to the spot where Lisa Fairbanks has been left. I need aerial surveillance, in case I lose them.'

'What's he driving?'

'It's a royal-blue VW Golf.' Goodhew added the registration.

'I'll call back as soon as the helicopter's ready.'

Pete had passed Marlowe the rope, she'd tied her own ankles, then he'd tied her hands together against the small of her back. He'd helped her sit upright again, and pulled the seatbelt across her body, deliberately skimming her breasts.

He'd then leant over to check the binding on her ankles, and his face had nestled against her thighs. A flutter of excitement had stirred him. Maybe it was the circumstances, just the two of them with their secret, but she was turning him on.

Now, Pete cut through Mildenhall and headed on towards Thetford.

He hadn't carefully planned this through, like the others, and he suddenly wondered if it was a mistake to leave her together with Lisa.

'There's another girl already tied up,' he explained. 'She's probably dead by now, but maybe not, and I was planning to leave you there, too. Thought I'd leave you both side by side.' He rested a hand on her thigh. 'But I've changed my mind.'

'I knew you'd take me to somewhere you'd used before,' she sniffed and turned her head away, 'but that's obscene.'

'Why?'

'Why what?' she snapped.

He pinched her arm to make her look at him. 'Why do you assume I would take you somewhere I've used before?'

She glared at him. 'You work it out. I'm not going to help you kill me.'

He drove towards Thetford in silence. If Marlowe's and Lisa's bodies were found together, he'd be implicated for sure. Unless Marlowe had killed herself?

There was the answer.

She had a history of mental illness, including an attempt at suicide. She'd already made failed attempts to frame him.

It wasn't such a stretch of the imagination to think that she'd killed those girls and, overcome with remorse, killed herself.

Marlowe's arms and back ached from being bound, and her ribs still ached from the kicking he'd given her. She concentrated on the cars in front. She couldn't afford a single glance in the wing mirror, in case he saw her looking.

His hand still rested gently on her thigh, stroking it from time to time. She'd loved that sensation once. But now those long fingers and bitten nails reminded her of his every victim. Five girlfriends, and four, possibly five, others.

She knew he planned to kill her. He wanted to rape her again; she knew that, too. If it happened, she didn't want to live.

It won't happen. I'm not alone, I'm not alone.

They took a B-road through the woods: a long and winding road that dipped through dried fords and passed around dense clumps of trees.

Marlowe realized there was no car following behind them now.

Pete checked his rear-view mirror yet again. 'I'm going to have sex with you, Marlowe.' He smiled easily, like he'd just suggested tea and toast.

'No you're not,' she replied.

The woodland grew more dense till the road narrowed through a tunnel of trees.

'Every one I abduct turns me on, but sex has its place, and that's why I've always been faithful. But with you it's different. You're the abductee and the girlfriend, both rolled into one.'

'Then if I die, they'll have something for forensics.'

Pete braked abruptly, and they pulled to a halt. The forest encroached, looming still and dark on either side.

'You'll have rotted to nothing by then.' Pete slipped his hand between her thighs. 'You know the game, Marlowe. You have to ask me.'

'Just drive on. I'm not doing it,' she retorted. The road was silent and she was alone.

'You're not going anywhere. This is it.'

The gloom of the forest stretched away from her, almost black in places from the lack of any light.

Pete walked round to her side of the car and scooped her into his arms. He trod a careful path through the muddy forest floor, using clumps of grass like stepping stones. 'When I do this for real, I buy shoes that are too small for men then throw them away.'

'This *is* for real,' she pointed out.

'No, you don't fit the pattern.' He stopped and glanced around before cutting off to his right. A few yards further, and the trees opened out into a strip of muddy clearing. About twenty feet away, Lisa Fairbanks' body lay at the foot of a tree. It was huddled, in a rancid question mark, at the brink of the muddy ditch.

Leaves rustled in the breeze, and Marlowe caught the faint sound of rotor blades slicing the air.

The helicopter's thermal-imaging camera had picked out Pete and Marlowe as he carried her through the trees.

Goodhew hung back, waiting for the order. His radio suddenly burst into life. 'They're on foot, in the forest and now stationary. Go, go, go.'

Goodhew gunned the engine and pulled off, headlights blazing on full. He changed into third and skidded round bend after bend. The engine screamed as he hammered down the final stretch leading to Walsh's car, where he slammed on the brakes, then leapt out.

He grabbed his walkie-talkie and darted off into the trees. He trampled down the undergrowth, chasing after Walsh and Marlowe under the direction of the chopper crew.

'Straight on, straight on,' came the directions from his walkie-talkie.

He jumped a culvert, sliding through the mulch on the far side.

'Two o'clock,' rattled the command.

He spotted a flash of colour. Denim?

Walsh looked up at the sky. Then he threw Marlowe into the mud. 'You set me up,' he growled, and lashed out, with a heavy kick to her stomach. And again.

'No!' Goodhew yelled.

Walsh bolted away through the trees. Goodhew raced after him, closing quickly. Within eighty yards, he was running within an arm's length of his quarry. He grabbed Walsh's elbow and spun him round straight into a tree. Goodhew's radio tumbled to the ground.

Walsh lunged at Goodhew, aiming a punch at his head.

Marlowe tried to reach the knots with her fingers. Her head was spinning, but she could still hear the helicopter and the sound of Walsh and Goodhew fighting.

Then she heard a moan. Lisa Fairbanks' fingers were moving, too. The latest victim was still alive. She was alive.

Marlowe rolled over, slipping and squirming through the rain-soaked mud, until she lay just behind the other girl. Lisa's head moved, and her tired frame attempted to roll over so she could look directly at Marlowe.

'Don't try to move,' Marlowe whispered. 'You're right by the ditch. Keep still and you'll be OK.'

Lisa twisted her head and shoulders again, desperate to see another face.

'Keep still,' Marlowe urged.

Too late. Lisa slid away from Marlowe and into the stagnant ditchwater.

Marlowe slithered across to the edge of the ditch. Lisa now lay face-down in a few inches of water, clearly too weak to lift her head.

'Help,' Marlowe yelled, and tipped herself into the water.

Walsh's punch went wide.

Sirens wailed from the road.

The walkie-talkie crackled another message from its resting place in the grass. 'Three people, plus you, on the ground. Lisa's alive. She's alive.'

Walsh and Goodhew locked eyes and again charged towards one another. Goodhew caught Walsh full in the face with his right fist, sending him crashing to the ground. Goodhew whipped his cuffs from his pocket and snapped one of them on to Walsh's left wrist.

He rolled the man on to his front and dragged him face-down through the mire to the nearest suitable tree. Goodhew wrapped Walsh's arms around its trunk, and clipped the handcuffs to Walsh's right wrist.

He left him lolling in the mud and raced back to find Marlowe.

Her face was submerged in four inches of ditch water. She thrashed her head from side to side, fighting for air, then she struggled on to her back. She pushed up with her hands, until her mouth cleared the water.

Nearby, Lisa Fairbanks lay face-down and still.

The undergrowth crackled and Marlowe heard shouts as police and paramedics came rushing through the trees.

'Help,' she screamed, just as Goodhew leapt into the trench beside her.

First of all, he pulled Lisa's face clear of the water and then tore off her gag.

'Is she dead?' Marlowe cried, and tried to struggle through the water to reach them. Losing her balance, she dug her fingers into the silt and rolled on to her side. She propped her shoulder against the bank and began to sob.

Goodhew held his palm close to Lisa's mouth and felt a faint breath slip from between her swollen lips. 'She's alive,' he announced.

Goodhew lifted the girl into his arms and stood up, hauling her head and shoulders above the ditch. 'Over here!' he shouted, to the stream of helpers hurrying towards them through the woods.

CHAPTER 89

THURSDAY, 7 JULY 2011

Marlowe was still shivering long after the ambulance had gone, and after Pete had been whisked away by uniformed officers. She huddled in Goodhew's car, wrapped in a thermal blanket, as he searched Walsh's vehicle and communicated with the SOCO and with Thetford CID.

A paramedic checked her over, found cuts and abrasions, possibly broken ribs. He said he'd feel happier if she went to hospital.

She shook her head firmly. This was the healthiest she'd felt in years.

Someone brought her tea poured from a thermos. It tasted stewed and was full of powdered milk. She watched Goodhew picking through the bag that the SOCO had removed from the boot of Pete's car. He glanced over at her and, as if he'd suddenly had enough, he walked away.

He slipped into the driver's seat but didn't turn to her. Instead he stared at Pete's car. 'What did the paramedic say?'

'I'm OK.'

'That's really what he said, or that's what you're telling me?'

'I'm telling you I feel OK.' She reached over and touched his arm. 'I'm OK.'

He turned towards her. 'What did you think you were doing, Marlowe? What if I hadn't done what you asked?'

'I trusted you, that's all. Why's that such a crime?'

'You could be dead now. How could you leave it to chance, like that?' he said.

'Oh, for God's sake, stop underestimating yourself, Gary. There's no way you weren't coming for me.' She gave an involuntary shudder. 'Was there?'

Gary gave her a rueful smile. 'You're probably right.'

He slid a hand inside his shirt and retrieved a video cassette. He handed it to Marlowe.

She turned the spine towards her. The label was in Pete's writing, and it read: 'Marlowe Gates, 25 April to 27 May 2009.' She stared at it. 'This is evidence now, isn't it?'

Gary nodded. 'There's one for each of you, except for Fiona. She had a lucky escape.'

She held out the cassette to him. 'You'll get in trouble if it's destroyed.'

He shook his head. 'There are some things we don't have the right to know.' He started the car and turned back towards Cambridge. She'd fallen asleep by Newmarket, and sagged against his shoulder, looking bruised and sore.

He parked outside her flat and waited there until she stirred.

He then squeezed her hand. 'We'll keep in touch, won't we?'

'I hope so,' she replied.

EPILOGUE

SATURDAY, 10 SEPTEMBER 2011

Autumn had chosen to arrive on the first of the month and now, after a week or so, Goodhew had accepted that the mostly warm July and August had given way to a colder, drier season. The trees around Parker's Piece had lost the energy of summer and the leaves drooped, their green fading daily.

Goodhew didn't feel ready for winter. There had been far too many distractions, and spring had rolled into summer and somehow he'd missed them both.

A parcel van had arrived at just before nine, with a delivery of fifteen boxes. Goodhew helped the driver move them just inside his front door, then he spent the next half hour ferrying them up to his grandfather's former library on the second floor. He stopped to finalize the layout of his new furniture, before starting to unpack all the newly acquired books and computer equipment.

By noon he was done, and he returned to his front steps to wait for the other two deliveries that would be arriving by one.

It was 12.50 when the first box arrived, then at 12.55 a taxi drew up at the kerb and he hurried down the steps to greet his grandmother.

She beamed when she saw him. 'I hope the pizza's here,' were her first words and he jerked his head in the direction of the front step. 'Al fresco?' she observed. 'You could have chosen a warmer day for that.'

'You should've come back sooner, then.' He carried her case up the steps and deposited it in the hall. 'Would you rather be inside?'

She shook her head, and he saw that there was the start of a smile on her lips.

'What?'

'Nothing, let's eat.'

They sat side by side, his grandmother unconcerned with the dust and dirt that was undoubtedly now clinging to her immaculate coat, and he equally unconcerned that the underside of the pizza box was sweating grease on to his jeans.

'Glad you got here before Christmas. I couldn't work out if you were joking.'

'Neither could I. Your sister—'

'What's she doing now?'

'Working at a travel agency, and dreaming of being somewhere else. Of course, that's how she ended up in Australia in the first place. She's not going to find the answers in a tourist brochure, is she?'

Goodhew shook his head. 'Guess not, but maybe she's not ready to.'

'That's deep.' She finished her second slice before she spoke again. 'You aren't very good at keeping in touch, you know.'

'I thought I did OK. You already know about Claire, about the investigation, about Hawaii. That's about everything.'

'Not so much about you, though. We haven't eaten on the front step like this for years. It was always a change of season thing, though, wasn't it?' She looked out, across Parker's Piece in the direction of the main road with the swimming pool on the other side, and, almost inaudibly, added, 'Metaphorically at least.'

Goodhew stared that way, too, guessing where her focus had been drawn. He noticed several lone figures all heading in different directions at various speeds. 'I was out here for a while before you arrived. D'you know what I was thinking?'

She didn't respond, but he knew she was listening.

'About the dangers of too much isolation,' he supplied.

'And that's why you're sitting by yourself?' she turned her head to look at him, and it struck him that her gaze seemed to have gained an additional shrewdness while she'd been away.

He'd also spent some time pondering the best way to broach a tricky topic. Now the moment had arrived, he decided it was best to just say it. 'I don't want to upset you, but I'm redecorating Granddad's library.'

She said something in reply, but he'd already begun to speak again. 'The thing is, I like my privacy, but the library's big and I thought if I put the jukebox and some furniture down there, along with my office equipment, then I could start to invite people round without . . .' He then ran out of words.

'Without overdoing it?'

He gave a rueful smile. 'Something like that. But that was Granddad's special room and I feel awkward.'

She extended an arm around his shoulders and hugged him. 'Don't, then. I was trying to tell you I'm glad. This is your house now, so you must put your own stamp on it. It can't stay just as it was, Gary.'

He offered her the last piece of pizza. 'You can have this if you wash up the dishes.'

She nodded. 'We'll go halves and you can wash up your own pizza box.' That was more like his grandmother.

'Deal.' He grinned.

She pulled off the crust and left him with the rest of the slice, making the manoeuvre seem clean, elegant and totally disconnected from the lump of cheese and tomato that now threatened to land in his lap. He swallowed it quickly.

'Why this sudden change, Gary?'

He shrugged, as he didn't feel sure that there had to be a reason. But, then again, it was always events that changed his point of view, and the previous weeks had been full of them.

'Have you had any further contact with the Whiting family?' she asked.

He swallowed before speaking. 'I've been over to see Kaye's mum a couple of times. Courtesy calls mainly: odds and ends in the run-up to the trial.'

'How is she?'

'Crap.'

He would have left it at the one word but his grandmother waited for more. He thought for a moment or two. This was a fork in the conversation, the choice to say nothing or to share the one thing that had been preying on his mind. Option A appealed more but, in the light of his recent resolution regarding self-induced isolation, he drove himself to pick the alternative. 'I had some paperwork to go through with her, and we were both in her sitting room. I was reading over a document to her, and when I looked up she had her eyes shut. I asked her if she was OK. She then said she'd been listening to me breathing – just wanted to hear the sound of someone who wasn't grieving. Or trying too hard. Or angry.

'We talked along those lines for a while. She said their family is trying to stick together, but they were in – her words – a blinding storm, and she feared how it would all look when they came out the other side.'

'But it's good she thinks they will emerge from it all.'

'I know, I know. And I now realize she's one of those people who will find an inner strength when everything seems hopeless. Marlowe, too. It made me wonder if I myself could be like that.'

'I'm sure you would—'

'I don't know. You see, after a murder it's the people left behind that stay with me. I still dwell on them all, from the first case right up to this one.'

'How exactly?'

'It's never going to be over for them, so it feels wrong to just put them out of my thoughts.'

'So you're just getting an ever-increasing list of the bereaved growing inside your head?'

'No, not exactly. Look, I've been having a recurring dream of a dead body.'

Her expression darkened as she studied his face for several seconds. 'The same person?'

'Don't know, I can't tell, but it's always the same dream, so maybe. Sometimes I hear crying, too. I wake up thinking of those people. I can still hear them cry.'

'You can't afford to carry scars that aren't yours to heal, Gary.' She rose to her feet and waited for him to follow suit. 'Let's go inside,' she said then, and gave her coat a swift brushing down before opening the front door. 'We need to talk.'

Goodhew followed her into the hall and up the stairs to his grandfather's library.

She stood in the doorway, studying the new layout.

'What are you thinking?' he asked gently.

'That the room looks lovely.'

'You wanted to talk.'

'I thought I did but, no, not today. Sometimes the change of season makes me a little sad, that's all. Do you *want* to?'

'Talk? No, not today,' he echoed.

It would wait. For now.

ACKNOWLEDGEMENTS

I have a special affection for this book. The original story idea meant so much to me and I pursued it until it grew from an outline of a plot to a full-length novel. This was ultimately the catalyst for me to leave a career in IT for the far more gripping world of crime writing. By the time I finished this book it had become clear to me that Gary Goodhew would appear in more than one novel and, with that in mind, I decided to make this the third in the series.

The Calling is, for me, finally fulfilling that moment when I said *I have an idea, I think I'll write a book.* And with that in mind I would like to thank the following: my husband, Jacen, who has been a fan of this book from the outset and has given me the greatest encouragement to write; friends and former colleagues, particularly Kimberly Jackson, Alison Hilborne and those that worked with me at Railtrack in Swindon and Waterloo. They offered enthusiasm even before the first draft was complete; David Yates, who directed me towards writing a novel in the first place; my agent Broo Doherty for agreeing to represent me and whose advice I trust and value so very much; my editor Krystyna Green who gave me my first book deal and continues to champion Goodhew; Justine at the *Flying Pig* for her cameo role and Andy Burrows at BBC Radio Cambridgeshire for his Oscar-worthy one; to Don and Jana Holden, Dawn Casey, Larry Rivera and Tom Moffatt for their Hawaiian hospitality.

I'm lucky enough to be able to call upon great expert advice from a variety of sources, and for this I'd like to thank Dr T. V. Liew, Dr

William Holstein, Richard Reynolds, Neil Constable and Chris
Bartram.

To Liz Meads and Genevieve Pease, thank you, girls.

And, finally, thank you to copy-editor Peter Lavery, and all at Constable & Robinson and Soho Press, with a special mention to Jamie-Lee Nardone who always brings a smile to my face.

THE SOUNDTRACK FOR *THE CALLING*

When I write a book I find there are songs that 'keep me company' at various points. By the time I finish I have a playlist that belongs to that book alone. Maybe the concept of a book having a soundtrack seems a little odd, but that's how it works for me.

American Pie – Don McLean
Anything That's Part of You – Elvis Presley
Blue Angel – Roy Orbison
Bring Me Back Home – Jacen Bruce
Desperado Love – Hot Boogie Chillun
Develline – Carlos and the Bandidos
Falling – Julee Cruise
I'll Remember You – Don Ho
Life Goes On – LeAnn Rimes
Since I Don't Have You – The Skyliners
Sleepwalk – Santo and Johnny
Stranger on the Shore – Acker Bilk

For more information visit www.alisonbruce.com.